Third Haven

Third Haven

A NOVEL OF DECEIT

B. B. Shamp

Tidewater Books, Delaware

Tidewater Books can bring this author to your live event. For more information
contact Tidewater@gmail.com

ISBN: 1534758968
ISBN 13: 9781534758964

The author wishes to acknowledge the generous support and
encouragement of:

Doug Shamp, Mary Pauer, Ida Crist, Jean Janssens, The Escapees,
Rabbit Gnaw, Hal Wilson,
Phyllis Theroux, Howard Norman, Rick Rath, Diversity Books, Jane
Wykes, and most particularly, Tom Shamp

For Tom

A lie can travel half way around the world
while the truth is just putting on its shoes.
—MARK TWAIN

He who is not sure of his memory should
not undertake the trade of lying.
—MONTAIGNE

Foreword

*I*n another life a few years ago I fell off a ladder. I vaguely remember the EMT asking me what hurt the most and I insisted that it was my back. "Are you sure it's not your head?" he asked. (Funny guy... drumroll—and so begins the "have you lost-your-mind" joke.) There is nothing like the pain of a broken back so how was I to know my head had crashed through the wall and landed on a metal heating register? Five days later, while still in the hospital, I blew multiple pulmonary embolisms that resulted in immediate cardiac arrest, respiratory arrest, and kidney failure. Hospital staff induced coma to save my brain while the rest of my body was in organ failure. The short story is, I lived. The long story was the comeback.

This novel has been my therapy. I want to thank all those professionals who helped me learn to walk again and speak coherently (or without a filter) over the next nine months. The other battle was my biggest loss: my memory. For five years I searched for the person I used to be but discovered that person was forever gone. In the process, I began writing a suspense novel. Salting the pages with clues that built one upon the other but never gave away too much became my own private obsession. I had to persevere to find who I was to become. This is a fictional account of perseverance in the face of deceit—and evil.

B. B. Shamp

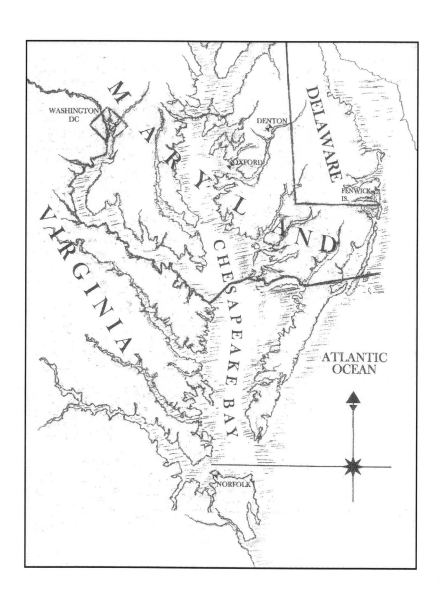

Part One

CHAPTER 1

Stepping Lightly with a Heavy Foot

Claire McIntosh stole a precious half hour of morning reverie, luxuriating in the quiet, free from the helter-skelter demands of her eight-year-old son. I will not rush, she thought. This is my time. The winter sun blazed through the picture window as she stood sipping a second cup of coffee in front of the television. Accidents littered the map of the Washington, D.C traffic report. Absently, she gathered toys, an action figure, and a can of Silly String.

Her cell phone buzzed. Seeing the name, she stopped mid-curse. A raw peace had been struck between she and her ex-husband and she had allowed herself to wallow in it. As Vance spoke, demanding and insistent, that inner peace evaporated and Claire realized she was still at his beck and call. She gazed out the apartment window at the jagged edges of the holly tree. It occurred to her that it wasn't too late to take revenge.

"You have to pick up Sam," he said.

She clenched her teeth. He never prefaced a demand with, 'Sorry to be calling you at the last minute.' Prick, she thought, not even a simple 'Hello'...just an order.

"I have to be at work in forty-five. You know I can't pick him up," she said.

"Well, then he's not going to school. I got a call from the office."

"So you'll be late. It's your Monday."

"Okay, Sam will stay here with Rebekah since you won't let him ride in the car with her."

This last taunt repeated her words on the custody agreement and they waltzed innocently enough over the phone. It had seemed bossy and well-deserved at the time but now felt like a sucker punch to the solar plexus. What choice did she have? Either Sam would miss school or she would be late for work. Vance would say to call a cab, but Sam was too young. Vance had won.

"All right. The Exxon in fifteen," she said.

In disgust she stalked to Sam's room and tossed the Iron Man and Silly String in the storage bench. She paused, staring at the blue can thinking…. stains on walls, concrete—car finishes. Claire plucked the small can from the bench and shook it angrily before she tucked it in her purse.

The weekend had been lonely, even boring, and as she passed the hall mirror, she caught a glimpse of herself. Lips pursed, eyebrows drawn, she glared at herself then cast her gaze regretfully at the picture of Sam that rested atop the hall table. She didn't contemplate on their lives because it inevitably led to guilty feelings but in that second she thought he deserved better parents. The mountain of words in depositions and accusations, inventories and appraisals, the subpoenas and postponed dates summed up their eight years together. But none of it revealed the truth of the secret between them.

Claire had seen hints reflected in the judge's eyes. Did he guess they were self-styled professionals, building separate futures not knowing how their son fit in their dreams? Claire had felt that animal possessiveness for Sam and fought hard for sole custody but eventually agreed to give him up to his dad every other weekend. She reveled in her tight case and the family money behind her. She was *the mother*, after all. In the weeks since her divorce became final she had become sick to death of the drama even though she couldn't help but contribute her share.

Claire pulled the car onto Connecticut Avenue heading to their OK Corral in Chevy Chase, the opposite direction from work. The gas station was Sam's drop off point on Friday nights, but in the bright sunlight of Monday morning too many could witness their hostility. She'd pick up Sam, take him to school, and head to her job.

Small miracles intervened instead. The first was running late for work. In hindsight, she wished that she and Vance had argued or that she was caught in a fender bender. She wished there had been no human relations meeting scheduled for nine with the junior lobbyists huddled around a conference table. As she weaved from one lane to the next, she glanced at her watch. Being late for work wasn't nearly as important as pissing off Vance one more time.

Cars crowded the Exxon station. She parked between the dumpster and a melting pile of dirty snow. Toting her purse on her shoulder, Claire stepped purposefully to the street side and tiptoed carefully around greasy puddles. She wished she had worn boots. Her suede shoes would be ruined.

She saw Vance's precious BMW nose its way to the other side of the lot and girded herself for a fight. Trotting through the maze of cars, anxious to grab Sam and get going, she waved and smoothed the frown from her face. She drew near and searched the back seat for him when abruptly the front passenger door opened. He hopped out dragging an overstuffed backpack that bumped along the dirty pavement. She swooped in, picked it up, and grabbed the boy's hand to pull him out of a car's path.

"Hey my little man, nice surprise. We get to ride into school together." She tapped on Vance's window. It opened partway.

"Claire, you are a godsend, let me tell you." False concern built ridges between his eyebrows. "I had no idea the police chief was going to call this meeting. New evidence."

"So you said." She couldn't help herself. "I don't care, Vance. I care about Sam riding in the back, belted." She leaned in closer to the window so Sam couldn't hear. 'Where's the goddamned booster seat? What kind of a father are you?"

"Right. Get over yourself." He uttered each word with emphasis like the final line in a prosecutorial summary. "Miss High and Mighty and your miserable motherhood." He turned his cheek away, looking over his shoulder and jerked into the confusion of cars trying to exit.

She stepped forward, blustering, wanting to frame her thoughts into something more than an emoji, when her foot plunged into an icy puddle and she blurted, "Yeah, well I still make more than…." His car stopped only feet away. She reached in her purse for the can, aiming low across the trunk. Blue Silly String shot out in curlicues across the glossy silver paint. Bake, baby, bake. Let the sun shine all day, she thought, right on that bumper. Smug with satisfaction, she stuffed the can into her purse and watched as he steered into traffic.

Belatedly, she remembered why she was there: Sam. She turned around. Disinterested faces glanced her way, all except one. A black man in a trim gray overcoat watched her dispassionately. "Going to make him pay one way or the other?"

"Whatever, mind your own business," she said.

"What goes around comes around," he said amused and walked to his car.

"Mom?" Sam's cheeks were pinched and pink with cold. Coat unzipped, no hat, his dark red hair ruffled in the breeze. Crumpled shirttails hung out under the green uniform sweater. What a mess. Did his father even look at him? She hugged him brusquely. "Tuck your shirt in, Coppertop. We gotta go."

The worry in his blue eyes stunned and embarrassed her. She hated for him to see her being so childish. Hated that he just assumed this would be his life forever; stuck with parents who resembled playground bullies. He was *their* adult: a neglected adult with his own needs.

She forced a smile, shook her suede shoe and felt the wetness creep up her instep. They climbed into the car, Sam buckled in back in the booster and she blasted the heat at their feet. The Mercedes crept south. It would be a drive of fits and starts through tight commercial blocks, parked cars, and Metro buses running gears as lights changed from red to green. She sighed when they could see the spires of the National Cathedral. They were close.

"Good weekend?" she asked.

"Yeah. We went to the Wizards game. Sorry I didn't call."

"That's okay. I figured you were doing something special." It wasn't okay. Calling at 8:00 every night was part of the agreement but she wouldn't quibble with Sam. "Did Dad pack you an after-school snack?"

"It's okay. I can get some chips from Nathan." And there he was again, ignoring his father's negligence to keep the peace. She knew he didn't want her baited into anger but felt increasingly unable to break the dance they all stumbled through like drunken sots. And then her moment of clarity was gone. Every other Monday when Sam returned, she could not resist digging for information that added to Vance's transgressions. Now was her chance to bring up the real blister between them.

"Did the realtor show the house over the weekend?"

"I don't know."

She sensed worry in his voice so she stopped. After the staffing meeting she would call the attorney, then the realtor. It was eight-thirty. She rounded the school's entrance circle and stopped in the shadow of the lower school. Light snow carpeted the grass and ice sleeves melted over the delicate branches of the cherry tree. She shivered despite the steady flow of warm air on her feet. Sam unbuckled and leaned over the front seat for a kiss.

"Take the activity bus tonight. I have to stay so Carlotta will meet you at the apartment. Get started on your homework, okay?" She always said the same things, as if her instructions were new, or he might forget but he never did. If a world war started before the end of the day their routine would carry on. "What do you want for dinner? Thai noodles, okay?"

"I ate Chinese last night. Can we do Italian?"

"Yeah. Go, Guido. I'm late."

"Love you."

"Love you back." She patted his backpack and watched as her boy ran up to the stone portico where a few stragglers streamed inside. He was so well adjusted. Miraculously, he had emerged from the past year unscathed by his bitter parents. For a brief moment, another splinter of guilt pierced her but there was nothing to be done about the past. She hung over the steering wheel lingering with a last glimpse and a cramped heart as he disappeared.

Fifteen minutes with no traffic. On a bad day it could stretch to forty-five. The sun had disappeared, the skies changed to steel gray, and a low cloud ceiling hung over the buildings opening to Dupont Circle. Claire sat hunched and watched as figures in black hurried along the streets, bags and briefcases in hand. Sidewalk edges were piled with three-day-old snow.

Claire turned to WTOP. "In financial news, Janet Yellen stated the U.S economy is at, if not beyond, the brink of recession. Yellen, president of the San Francisco Fed….," Claire traced her thumbnail back and forth on the steering wheel. She snorted. Somebody's head is going to roll, she thought. She straightened her back and switched to XM radio.

The tires click-clicked across the metal plate of the garage entrance and the car descended into darkness. She winced as it squealed around the first curve and her mind volleyed back to Vance. Wondering if Rebekah had moved into their home she realized that thought would lead to more self-flagellation and she quickly pushed it away. It ate at her like a silkworm on a leaf. She longed to ask Sam outright, but the mediator's words came back to her, "Your child is not to be used to feed your paranoia."

It was time to concentrate on the things that mattered: Sam and a new job, a new house—a D.C. bungalow or Tudor with a fenced yard where they could have a dog. As soon as Vance sold their home and her half of the equity was deposited in her account, she would show him her white-hot independence. She glanced at the time: 8:52.

Claire backed into the nearest empty space, a Tow-Away Zone next to the garage elevator that saved her from circling three levels below for her assigned space. Her parking habits had become a joke among her male coworkers, the ones who had tried unsuccessfully to get in her pants since news of her separation hit the office gossip mill. Their come-ons and winks –winks stopped short in her icy stare.

They knew it was her habit to grease the building super's palm weekly so he would move her car. Watching her side mirror, the red glare of her car's brake lights reflected on the white tiled wall. Behind a concrete stanchion she glimpsed a grocery cart filled with cardboard, black plastic and coats. On the floor was a familiar pile of rags. A head raised and a fist emerged, rubbing an eye. She rushed out of her car.

"Stokes, you gotta get up. It's almost nine."

The pile of rags moaned and Stokes took shape, reaching up to scratch his scalp under his knitted hat. "That you Miss Claire? Jackson ain't found me this morning."

"Well, he's going to. Come on, give me your arm."

Stokes raised his arms like a toddler waiting to be picked up by a parent. He was surprisingly light and Claire threw her weight into it, balancing on her heels as he gained his feet. He grunted and coughed, his sour breath in her face. She brushed his hair out of his face and tucked it under his hat, leaning him against the concrete pole. Gathering his blankets from the floor, she threw them into the grocery cart. "You okay? Got your balance now? Okay let's get you pointed in the right direction. Jackson will be by here in no time and you know he'll call the police." She directed his hands to the cart and gave him a little push. Stokes stumbled slowly toward the exit light, pushing his worldly belongings in the cart. Claire reached in her purse and pulled out a couple hundred. "Take this and go spend the night at the Y, will you?"

He mumbled his thanks and tottered off. Claire slammed her car door shut, thumbed the lock on her key fob and turned, smacking right into Calvin Jackson, the building super.

"Oh, Mr. Jackson," she said delightedly trying to block his view of the retreating Stokes. "I'm late. Can you do me a favor and just move my car?"

"You know, you're the whole reason I got to deal with that sorry piece of shit. If you'd stop giving him money, he'd stop spending the night in my garage."

"Mr. Jackson, I know you aren't that hard hearted. It's so cold outside and he's not causing any problem. Listen, I have a meeting upstairs. Just bring me my keys later after you've moved it, okay?"

Sorry, Ms. McIntosh. You got to keep this space clear this morning. We movin' stuff today."

"Okay." With a fixed smile, secure in her importance or not willing to accept one more hassle, she strode toward the service elevator. Without a second thought, she threw the keys over her shoulder. "Just move it before they come. I'm sure it won't be a problem. I'll come down before lunch to get them instead of you coming up. I know you're busy."

Out of the corner of her eye she saw the keys sail into his raised hand. Satisfied, she entered the elevator and pressed the button for the third floor when she saw the flash of silver fly through the opening to thud on the carpet. Her shoulders slumped as she gazed at her keys lying next to her purple suede shoes. One shoe was stained and she could feel the liner curling around her toes. My brand new Manolo's, she thought, sighing. I'll have to chuck them.

A sign read: SERVICE ELEVATOR IN USE 9:00 TO 5:00. She'd deal with her car later. The padded doors parted and she hurried into the muted elegance of Wilcox and Stein, Lobbyists. The receptionist never looked up.

Down the hall, Claire glimpsed the junior attorneys sitting shoulder to shoulder in the conference room. With a pad of paper under her arm, Claire threw her winter coat and satchel over one of the many empty desks. A wall mirror perfectly placed for last minute adjustments revealed her freshness, so she pulled out a wad of auburn hair from the clip and fixed a frown on her face. Unbuttoning her suit jacket, she mussed her collar and squared her shoulders before entering the meeting and another long, overscheduled day.

The table was full and as usual, no one offered to find her a chair. Her heart, still thumping from the race down the cluttered hallway, hardened a bit more and Claire looked around annoyed.

"Hey, Claire, I heard movers are using the service elevator this morning. It'd be a shame to get that nice 550 banged up," said Hampton Reid.

"What are you bullshitting about now? I've been in my office since seven."

"Really? I must have missed your car on P3. Have they moved your space next to Wilcox's?" There was rumble of laughter around the table. So competitive.

"Funny, Hampton. You'll get it before me," she said.

The week before, employees were told to pack their offices for a rumored move to Capitol Hill. The office hallway filled with boxes. Behind her, the sideboard was junked with supplies and a floral arrangement of paperwhites sat forlorn in the middle, their bell shaped blossoms calling to be claimed. Their stringent smell, like perfumed urine, belied their delicate place in the narcissus family. I should take them home, she thought, before someone throws them out.

Claire pulled a chair inside the room and struggled to wedge it into a corner, which became the second little miracle: the placement of her seat near the door. A heavy mahogany table for twenty, padded chairs, blank walls, and two exit doors faced the windows. Lanky Matthew Redden, wearing an ill-fitting three-piece suit, sprawled on his chair next to her. He looked at his watch and grinned.

Sweet-faced and dedicated to his pursuit of her, Matt leaned over with his hand on her back. Exasperated, Claire eyed him warily and busied herself with her cell phone, leaning away. She flashed a cramped smile.

"Made it just in time. Turning over a new leaf?" whispered Matt.

"What's the deal? How come nobody believes that I've been in my office?" she lied.

"Because you haven't. You inspire me."

"Yeah, like a panting dog."

Matt mouthed something that looked like 'I love you.' She snapped, "Stop it." He patted her hand on the table. Eyes followed. Claire moved her hands to her lap and frowned at him.

The floor registers gusted with a dry heat to ward off the chill from the glass wall overlooking K Street. Across the road, a bedraggled group of protesters harassed women attempting to enter the Planned Parenthood in the same building as her law office. The cold had changed their Wednesday morning ritual. They had propped three fetus signs in a hillock of blackened snow so they could warm their hands with coffee cups. They chanted toward the women's hunched backs and bowed heads. Claire looked away.

Hampton Reid's mouth gaped as he bit into a large croissant, scattering flaky crumbs. She was briefly envious and silently swore she would suggest hummus and celery one more goddamned time to the secretary who set up these meetings. No one ever listened to her. Balancing what was good for her figure and summoning the energy she needed to conduct her job search was delicate. Eating had become a chore, more like an assignment than a pleasure until she dished ice cream.

To Claire's disappointment, Jeanine Ferrell, the only female senior partner and her favorite, was missing. Jeanine was a short, squat woman, who had bullied her way up the ranks with quips like, "take your dick out of your mouth and pay attention." She wore huge pins on her lapel imitating Secretary of State, Madeleine Albright. Not afraid of office policies, Jeanine smoked cigarettes in the hallway women's room.

Claire glanced under the table one last time at her new Cartier watch, a Christmas present from her father. Nine o'clock. She sat back and pulled a pen from her jacket pocket to wait.

The Ultimatum

When Jack Wilcox, senior partner and head of the elite lobbying firm entered the room, it fell silent. Claire raised her chin, her brows slightly knit, thinking the man had lost his haggard look. His smile barely reflected in his eyes. It was unusual for the big man to run the show, so his presence couldn't just be about the office move.

"Good morning ladies and gentlemen. Georgia, is everyone here?" He boomed. Georgia Perkins, the orange-haired office manager nodded from her perch by the door.

"I should begin by congratulating everyone on your hard work, making six months in earnings highly successful. Client satisfaction is high, our influence in Congress continues to grow."

Through the plate glass, clouds parted and Claire straightened as the winter sun cast a white light across the assemblage as if they were all frozen in a Wyeth landscape. She saw the yearning spread across their faces. Money and influence were words to live by in Washington.

To Claire they looked desperate and lonely. She noted their uniformly dark suits, their collective Quaker-like appearance. They resembled a black funeral fan of yesteryear that unfolded with a splash of color in a man's tie or a woman's collar. She thought they wore their sameness like an ankle bracelet—the kind a judge imposes on those under house arrest. She looked down at her hands folded in the lap of her gray suit. She wore the uniform too. She scuffed her stained shoe against the table leg. I want out, she thought again.

"We are making changes that will affect everyone in this office. We appreciate each of you," said Wilcox.

Flatter us, then sack us, she thought. Not possible. There was too much work and strangely, too many had already been let go. She couldn't get used to the rise and fall of management's expectations: bigger contracts, increasingly intolerable workloads, or more layoffs. Her empty stomach growled. The smell of coffee and expensive body scents mixed with the sharp odor of the paperwhite blossoms. She felt a little sick and reached for a cold bagel, thought better of it and pulled back empty-handed.

Six years had passed since she graduated cum laude from Georgetown Law, starry eyed and bent on changing the system. The boutique conservative firm lured her with a promise that her liberal perspective would fit with their practice. Later, when she suspected she was hired because of her father's friendship with Jack Wilcox, she mustered the nerve to ask Jeanine. Her suspicions were confirmed. Jeannine barked at her, "If you don't want to be an office drone, define yourself. Go after your dreams." Claire blamed herself for living a prescribed life. Her father's words haunted her even today. 'Take a secure government job or work for an established firm.' She was done dodging the friendship between Wilcox and her father, Abraham McIntosh, done with men deciding her future and instead fed her fledgling sense of independence with quiet mantras.

Claire held her cell phone beneath the boardroom table, scanning email for a response to one of her feelers in Civil Rights and Immigration. Nothing. She looked up.

Jack Wilcox stood facing the windows. It was the first time she had seen him since the holiday party. His forehead appeared to be an unmovable brick. Botoxed? His dewy skin had to be the result of a recent chemical peel disguised by a spray tan. Gazing at his jug-shaped jawline, carved but a bit swollen, she smiled inwardly at his youthful resurrection. A new girlfriend? Or a new contract? Then she understood.

"As you know, it's a complicated time for the K Street economy but in light of anticipated government action limiting the influence of lobbyists, there will be more downsizing. Many of you will have to make some decisions and we are giving each of you an opportunity...."

Downsizing? This could be her chance. No more false pride in a job she'd grown to hate. Why Dad, I had no choice, she thought. They let me go! Could she avoid her father till the right job came along?

Wilcox waved a hand over their heads and continued with supreme confidence, "Our new address on Capitol Hill is smaller. However, we will be closer to congressional action which..." Could he speak any faster?

She glanced at the door. Georgia sat next to it holding a pile of colored folders. Dark blue, yellow and green, not the logo-embossed ones. Claire drummed her fingers on the back of her cell phone. Were the contents color-coded as well? The firm could've severed ties by email but that would be too simple. These letters would be tailored to each individual. That's what clients liked about Wilcox and Stein—old-fashioned and personal.

Nervous, she straightened in her chair, twirling a diamond earring and glanced around the room. She wondered how Stein would make the cuts. Seniority? Quality of work? Pedigree? Race? Some faces were self-contained, others stricken with worry.

Claire tapped her foot unconsciously. Hand out the folders and cut the feel-good speech, she thought. Was Wilcox wrapping up? "Ms. Perkins has your information. Jeanine, Albert and I are available to speak with you personally."

Matt appeared subdued. The clock over the door read 9:17. Her car, Sam's after-school snack and her desk waited. Worries were layering up like a pulled venetian blind. She wondered if she got a new job, would she be starting her career over? Could she continue to afford St. Dunston's tuition? She made too much money for Vance to pay child support. Would her dad help? She blinked and dropped the blind. Counting on him for everything had become a bad habit. Vance needed to sell their home. She was sure he needed money too. The divorce had been expensive.

She looked around the conference room, detached, no longer hearing the speech. She let her hair shield her face, her fingers at her throat. Her palms grew damp remembering how angry and impulsive she had been the day she left. Her words reverberated in her head. "You're a lying pig, Vance."

God, I'm such an idiot, she thought. I never should have stormed out. Dad should never have gifted us a house and Vance should have been the one to leave. Her words taunted, "I'll make you pay for plowing Rebekah on my sheets." He had pleaded with her. "...mistake...counseling," he said. "It's you I love." Lies. Lies. Lies. In a flurry of poor decision-making, she moved with Sam into a tiny retro apartment at the Kennedy Warren on Connecticut Avenue.

By Christmas the divorce was final and Vance had squatter's rights in their Chevy Chase home. Her divorce attorney had said, "You aren't moving back in and moving him out. *You* abandoned *him*. The courts don't look kindly on that. You don't want to lose Sam, do you?" In guilt, she lined the living room with presents for Sam and drank red wine.

Now it was January, a year later and the market had gone soft, especially in the upper end homes. Her thoughts persisted—I'm not taking one more red cent from my father—too embarrassing. Squeeze Vance until he sells....but how? The one good thing about being locked in this damn boardroom, she thought, is not having to listen to that effing news feed on the mortgage crisis.

Her phone buzzed in her hand. Claire opened an email with a start of excitement. Misreading her as being upset, Matt dared to pat her knee under the table. Riled, she crossed her legs avoiding more contact and glanced furtively around the room. Wilcox droned on, "Those who stay will compete and interview for seven positions in research."

The faces of her coworkers were crushed, ambitions dashed. Looking down at her phone, she was thrilled to see an offer to interview for an entry-level position. "Immigration lawyer.... A non-profit." It would be a bare bones salary. Would she interview? No question, she thought, and tapped an email back.

She knew the field of law didn't mean freedom, certainly not leisure time. But Claire was desperate for balance, a way to earn money and still not miss anymore of Sam's childhood. She was desperate for clients who might throw her a dog bone thank you and coworkers who could put their egos aside once in a blue moon. Somewhere in the distant future, she would find the right man. But not now.

Drifting miles away from Wilcox's words she realized she was smiling in the face of everyone's disaster, Claire pressed her lips into a straight line and tried to pick up Wilcox's thread, "I am asking that each of the potential candidates meet with Mrs. Perkins to organize your preliminary interviews. Over the next three weeks, we will...."

Georgia handed out the folders. Claire's was green, one of two at the table. She opened it and quickly read the first paragraph. The second paragraph was short, "Your job will follow you to our new location on Capitol Hill." Claire peeked at Matt's letter. A long paragraph. She bit her lower lip. She rubbed her forehead. No more, she thought, determined. No more arranging congressional trips or catered champagne and lobster. No more research or kowtowing to wealthy clients who thought they owned her. She would go to Wilcox. Someone else deserved her job. Would he call her father?

Wilcox was asking them to make decisions. There were generous severance packages that included accrued sick, personal and vacation leave. "The office will close on Thursday and move to smaller digs on Pennsylvania Avenue. We reopen after the MLK holiday. Decide by then, or the severance package will not be guaranteed. It would behoove you to take this offer seriously," he said frowning.

Blackmail. If they dawdled on their way to another job, they would get nothing. With a sigh she decided to tell her father she was leaving. Stand up to him! After work on Thursday she and Sam could head for the family home in Oxford to speak with her dad. Poised and poker-faced, she closed the folder and put it in her lap under her phone.

Suddenly Claire's vision seemed to pixelate when she felt a loud burst of pressure on her face. The lights flickered and went out. The coffee mugs and plates of Danish danced on the table. People palmed the edge of it, unsure. Wilcox took a step then another. Everyone was silent waiting for another shutdown. Was it the old heating system or a bomb scare? The light from the windows seemed to gray.

Alarms beeped in measured tones and the emergency backup lights came on, dimly. A collective groan swept around the table, and Wilcox said, "Again. And this, ladies and gentlemen, is why we're moving out of this building. Get your coats." He turned to walk out the door. People cursed. The familiar synthetic voice droned insistently over the building speakers in a calm vein they ignored. They knew the drill.

"Attention. This is not a test. Everyone must evacuate the building immediately. Please proceed to the exit stairwells. In the event of fire do not use the elevators." The recording would repeat and repeat until the fire marshal gave the all clear.

Claire muttered under her breath, frustrated. "Jesus. Great timing."

"Right? Can't bill for the next three hours and I've lost my job. How does this shit happen?" responded Matt.

"I'm going to get my laptop."

"If we get out of here fast maybe we can find seats at Starbucks."

The coffee shop across the street would be packed and the parking garage would be on lockdown. Matt was right. The day would be worthless.

As Claire pushed back from the table her phone fell near her shoes and tumbled under the table. She bent low to pick it up, stretching her arm out, her fingertips barely touching it. The third miracle was a split second of grace. A gift of momentous porportion.

She heard a sizzle, then a sonic sized crack detonated on the shared wall with the women's clinic. Opposite her, the sound built, expanding around the walls. She tilted her head in the tiniest movement beneath the table and then instinctively tucked her chin to her chest and fell to her knees. Something was wrong.

The room's contents blew at lightning speed across the conference table above her in a fusillade of papers, mugs, and bodies, some parts and pieces, toward the windows. Claire was thrown on her back from the force, hitting the floor, her arms and legs flailing. Debris blew toward her, and she felt pressure push her hair, her clothes, her skin toward the windows—everything happened in one long held breath. Then the glass exploded in a loud *bwooosh* into the gray sky.

She lay like a stone, deafened, rooted to the floor, watching as dust eddied and heard ceiling tiles with their curled metal grid crash in slow motion onto the table that acted as a partial shield. A single recessed light, tethered to a wire swung inches from her face. Gray particles fell like snow. She was rooted to the floor her arms flung out as time stood still. Slowly a pounding surfaced in her ears, and her hearing echoed with the sound of moans and hushed voices as if muffled under a blanket, swirling around her. Then another explosion blasted in the distance. She tried to move but was tangled half on, half off her tumbled chair, her hips strangely twisted.

Claire shut her eyes tightly trying to blink away the grit. She heard a light bulb burst nearby and flecks of glass sprayed, so she turned her face. Blinking repeatedly, she wanted to see but her eyes watered. What was it, what was around her, what was beside her? She willed her arm to wipe her eyes. Turning her hand back and forth, trying to focus, she saw it begin to shake imperceptibly. I'm alive, she thought in disbelief.

She wiggled her feet and pushed with her elbows, rolling over gingerly onto all fours and tensing every muscle. Stunned, she realized everything seemed to work. Saliva streamed from her mouth and in a horrified reflex she sucked in and gagged. Quickly she scrambled farther beneath the table, cowering. She cast her gaze here and there, the blood pounding in her neck and ringing in her ears. Bodies, soft rounded shapes lay about the edge of the table some moving slightly. She opened her mouth and an acrid dust seeped in her throat. She gulped air but choked and in a strangled voice, croaked. No response. Coughing, she covered her nose and mouth with her scarf.

The snow-like powder thinned and she could barely make out the ghostly shadows of people who began to crawl away. Three more blasts hammered in the distance. It was then she began to feel the heat of fire on her left side and a bitter cold where the window had been on her right. She blinked over and over, trying to see which way to go.

She heard whispers. "Got to get out. Get out," and slowly realized it was her own voice. Whimpering, she compelled herself to move. Crawling across broken ceiling tiles and bits of metal, she pulled herself up. Her hand gripped the doorjamb and she glanced over her shoulder at the wreckage. Matt's bloodied face turned to hers, their eyes meeting. "I'll be back, Matt. I'll get help." She stumbled into the hallway.

—◆—

A Message from the Past

Shielding her face with her arm, Claire scrambled to where the lobby doors should have been. Reaching the elevators, she caught up to a knot of people who pressed and pulsated into a corridor that seemed impossibly narrow.

The heat expanded like the hot summer sun and she could see a man separate from the rest to greet her. He grabbed her by the arm, swung her closer to the elevator doors that gaped open. Confused, Claire thought he was going to help her. Inside the cab she saw a white plume of fire spurting from a container. Sparks sizzled in the air. Searing hot, the fire sucked all the oxygen from the tight little hallway. Frightened, she saw a body clothed in white lay next to it. Claire turned and struck at the man who pushed her nearer the blaze and in a rising panic, she pummeled and clawed his face, reaching for his eyes. Disoriented, she heard his guttural snarl that split her fog.

"Bitch. You're going to die today."

Look at me, she thought. *I don't know you.* You've confused me with someone else. "Let me go. Let me go."

"God will make you answer. The hell fires await."

This couldn't be. Slowly, her determination grew and it became a concrete decision; she would beat him, beat him down. He didn't know her.

His eyes were wild, fanatical and his singed hair stood on end. But he was small, a coat rack of a man not much taller than she. In the light from the fire she could see that one side of his face and neck was burned raw. In one swift motion, she brought her fist up hard connecting to his chin. His head snapped back and he returned the blow, socking her in the gut with something hard. She lost her breath and crumpled.

The fire inside the elevator grew hotter and sparks burned holes in her suit, but when they reached her skin she felt nothing except a steely, single-minded resolve. Terrified at the man's purpose, she clutched at him, sinking her nails into his bare arms. She kicked and brought the heel of her hand up in one well-placed stroke aiming for his nose. Making contact, she pushed with all her might and he reeled backward toward the fire, one hand to his face and the other swinging. A glancing blow, hard as a baseball bat, cracked her skull. Her sight faded. She faltered, but not before she saw him flailing into the fire.

Moments passed and in a stupor, sprawled face down, Claire woke, raising her head shakily. In growing horror she recognized through the haze of smoke that the elevator doors had closed but were engulfed by flames that licked out into the hall. She felt the heat cooking her skin through her clothes. Pinpricks of light gradually disappeared into shimmering charcoal. The air scorched her face. She stumbled, trying to get up. The smoke burned her nostrils and throat, deep into her lungs. It permeated her body making her slow and heavy-footed. She was dizzy, off balance. She had lost her bearings and couldn't remember what had happened.

She coughed raggedly in the pitch dark and bumped into someone. She recognized the voice of Georgia Perkins, the office manager. The two clutched at each other. Georgia shrieked in her ears, "This way, this way." In the blackness, Claire tripped against a lump on the floor and lost her grip on Georgia. Her one eye coated shut with blood, she reached about but Georgia was gone. Her head throbbed. She wanted someone, anyone, to grasp her hand to lead her out. Hearing a groan, she reached down, fumbling at a stirring body and clasped a jacket collar with both hands. A large jewelry pin came loose in her palm.

The woman mumbled, "Can't breathe." Pull her up, Claire thought, and clasping her lapels, she heaved her against the wall.

"Please," the woman croaked, "can you see?"

She was not alone. "Come on," Claire whispered, afraid to gulp the poisonous air. Sticking her face inches from the woman's, she saw it was Jeanine Ferrell. Claire pulled her scarf from her neck and wrapped it around Jeanine's head and over her mouth. She tugged at her waistband. They bounced against the adjoining wall to the elevator shaft. Claire yanked her hand away from the searing heat. She heard the wail of sirens in the distance. "We have to get out."

Struggling around the corner she could see dim yellow lights flashing. A few feet away, a red light gleamed above through the dense smoke. An exit light. Her breathing grew thin and she wavered. Jeanine was becoming dead weight and nearly unconscious but Claire pushed the fire door open. The stairwell. Fresh air. Below there was light, garbled voices, and she heard the blessed sounds of authority.

Claire stepped onto the landing dragging Jeanine with her. A gritty smoke oozed around the door as it clicked shut behind them and Jeanine slumped downward. Claire yanked her up and looked at her hard. Jeanine's face was covered in soot and her eyes were reddened, her nose runny, but she met Claire's one-eyed stare. "Jeanine," she yelled, her voice sounding like sandpaper. "We're going down these steps." She shook her. "Do you hear me?"

"Don't leave me. Please, don't leave me," said Jeanine as she scratched at the neck of Claire's blouse. In a flash of frustration, Claire slammed her against the wall. Maybe it would knock some sense into her. We've made it this far, she thought.

In her mind, she saw Sam. "Mommy?" She imagined him, his shirttails hanging, standing in the cold, alone, his face stricken with grief. She thought, I'm here. I'm not going to leave you.

She banged her fist against the wall next to Jeanine's head. "I can't carry you. Hold on to the railing." Jeanine nodded, her movements clumsy. Below the voices became louder and some were calm. Control was within reach. Claire began to shake, her legs growing weak with relief and she could see a yellow coat, a helmet, and a face through a clear gas mask. Another followed, coming toward her fast up the steps. She stumbled. Safety. She felt herself being passed from one set of hands to another.

Bright sunlight. Freezing air, but clean. Claire sucked in deeply, coughed, hacked, wringing out her lungs. A warm surge of blood blanketed her right eye and her head pounded. Sirens blared and blue lights flashed off-kilter. Jeanine fell away from her as they stumbled on the concrete steps in the alley. Claire gripped the cast iron railing, its cold penetrating her hand, up her arm, waking her.

Emergency personnel channeled her through the maze of police cars and fire trucks toward a cluster of waiting ambulances. She looked up to the winter sky on K Street where a gooseneck crane delivered a wall of water near the top of the building six floors up. Overhead, she heard the whap, whap, whap of helicopter blades. Adrift in a sea of people as far as she could see, she felt disembodied until someone slapped an oxygen mask around her face and tightened it, pushing her onto a wheeled stretcher. Her vision stopped whirling. A blanket was tossed over her shoulders and she sat up on one elbow taking it all in, every last detail, hungry for more. The pounding in her head began to slow and a sliver of calm trickled through her veins. Could she let go? She began to tremble all over and thought she stopped herself from crying until she realized the quiet wail she heard was her own. Oh, my God. My God.

"Ma'am. Look at me. Follow the light with your eyes." An EMT, his brown eyes intent on her face, was flashing a penlight at her. Off balance, she wanted to fall back on the gurney that seemed to twirl slowly in circles. She was going to fall off. Sudden nausea gripped her. She looked down and realized there was blood all over her blouse and the skirt of her suit, running down her leg. Her feet were bare... My shoes. Where the hell are my heels? Blackness.

———•———

The Van

José Robles glanced over his left shoulder at the sleeping faces jumbled together in the back of the van. The baby whimpered and shushed against her mother's breast, stirred her tiny fist while nearby her two school-aged brothers sprawled upon each other in the narrow space. Five others leaned and rolled, somnolent in the van's cradle.

José opened his window and a chilly breeze blew inside waking the van's occupants. Thick armed and ham-handed, the driver gripped the steering wheel and muscled the heavy vehicle behind the gas station, past the security lights, and into the waiting darkness. When they had begun the trip across the U.S. border, José had privately dubbed him The Bull for his flat face and square chin. In the moonlight, José stole a look at his scarred cheek that glistened silver and wondered how he had come by such an ugly wound. He watched as The Bull's foot hovered carelessly over the brake and thought the man was too tired or possibly too stupid. But José had no choice in the matter, as he didn't hold a license and the driver spoke only rudimentary English. Their destinies seemed inextricably tied. They had a deal to make, a commodity to sell.

"Wake them. It is time," said The Bull.

"Make sure it's safe."

"*Que nada.* You make too much of this."

José sniffed and spit out the window. A seed of a plan grew inside him. He would not be arrested, or shot. A rifle rested behind the seat and he was mindful that the driver would use it. He tapped his right foot unconsciously as his hand hovered over the door handle.

At the other end of the parking lot the buyers remained undetected in a dark car. They flashed their headlights. Uneasy, José shifted in his seat. He ached and after thirty-three long hours, everyone, including the van, was running on empty. They were fifty miles from D.C. where José could hide in plain sight if only he could escape his tether to The Bull.

In a hurried decision that José feared would unleash waves of misery on everyone, the driver said brusquely, "Unload the boys." The mother raised her eyes from her baby's face in alarm.

José murmured again, "Wait," and scanned the parking lot. Only one car. A plastic bag ballooned in the breeze and skittered across the pavement. At the corner of the building, a black form with an outsized head caught his eye. The helmeted figure tucked into the shadows. José held his breath knowing the night would not end well.

The driver's foot slipped from the brake and the vehicle rolled a few feet toward the trash-strewn woods. Hitting the curb, the van jostled the huddled bodies inside. Mutters of insult rose.

"Help us, please. The bucket spilled." The voice of the mother was heard above the rest, reedy and thin like the scream of a deer. Her baby began to wail.

The driver cursed and said, "Shut that baby up or I'll strangle it."

A stifled sob escaped her lips and then she was quiet.

Seeing his chance, José turned and offered a dirty engine towel. They had orders to sell the boys to pay for the passage of her family but he would end his involvement now. "Give me the bucket. I'll empty it."

"No. Boys first. Get the money. Now!" said The Bull.

"Fuck you. You get it," replied José. The bucket handle crossed his upraised palm slopping its contents on the console between them.

The driver stared him down. José knew the man was exhausted and impatient and therefore at a disadvantage. More than that, he could see raw hatred in his face. Hatred for José's blue eyes and brown hair, hatred that he could pass for a gringo.

The smell of human excrement permeated their nostrils and the driver turned away with a curse. Grabbing the Bushmaster from its spot behind the seat, he stepped out and walked to the rear of the van. He held the back door wide and glared at his human cargo. He shouted, "*¡Órale y silencio!* Let's go!"

The mother screamed and grabbed at her sons but the driver yanked them from the back of the van, tossing them to the pavement. José wanted to reach for her, to pull her back, but the bucket was in the way. The driver yelled at the other passengers, "Hold her or I will slit your throats like the goats you are and leave you in the woods."

In the end, this ruckus was all he needed. José opened his door and stood behind it, holding the dripping bucket away from his side. He heard the rear doors slam, and the boys shuffled across the pavement, their meager belongings sagging in duffle bags anchored on their skinny backs. The driver walked behind them gripping the semiautomatic across his chest.

Two dark figures emerged from the car and strolled confidently toward them, the outline of a rifle held casually by one man's side. The other figure carried a small briefcase. The bull-faced driver was fool enough to believe that he had the upper hand and waited as they squared off. Quickly, José stepped over the curb and into the low brush of the woods, pouring the bucket's contents across his footsteps. The smell would confuse the dogs if they had brought any.

He watched from behind a tree. The Bull nodded at the open briefcase, grabbed it and nudged the boys toward the car. The buyer raised his rifle and moved quickly toward The Bull. Shouts came as José darted deep into the woods covering his scent until the bucket emptied. This time, freedom was close and he would find his mother. This time, no one would take him. This time, no one would send him back to El Salvador.

Bright lights clicked, flooding the parking lot. Their glare lit up the edge of the woods. José threw the bucket aside and scurried through the underbrush sliding in the leaves and mud, his arms swinging for balance and his head tucked down. He had run many times and had a second sense for escape.

"Immigration! Drop your weapon! On the ground!" A rat-a-tat-tat echoed and he could see in his mind's eye, blood dripping from the driver's face and pooling on the cold pavement. José slid down an embankment toward a creek as bullets whistled overhead in the trees. He was safe. They were too far away and he probably didn't matter enough for a chase but he cursed under his breath as he ran. He had left his coat in the van. It would be a cold night.

———

CHAPTER 2

Ophelia

A shard of bright light split the blackness. Was this a dentist's office? A rectangular mirror hovered over Claire's face emanating reflective beams that shimmered about. He needed to give her more gas. She hated the dentist.

No, she had it wrong. Someone was digging away at the inside of her chest. It was dark and people stood around her. A shadow-visage peered at her from under a Sampan hat. He carried a hoe. Others stood by. She was floating in shallow water like Ophelia, but safe and clean, and they didn't see her. Someone called to her but she couldn't rouse herself to care. Claire felt mild worry but it passed. She didn't answer or maybe she couldn't. She swam away from these strangers.

More voices and whispers. She thought, if I listen carefully, I'll find out what the secret is. It must be something earthshaking because she could hear her father's voice and was that Sam? Dreamily, she heard that sweet, high-pitched baby voice as if he were a toddler. She sensed that she hadn't seen her boy in a long time. Days, even. Someone needed to move that light before she went blind. Blackness returned but voices still pulled at her.

"Ms. McIntosh." Then more sternly, "This is Dr. Janana, Ms. McIntosh."

She heard beeping, measured and soft. The voices again and tugging deep inside her. She struggled to breathe. Her face felt hot. What was wrong? Was she dying? No, she was choking, gagging. She heard tapping and clanking kitchen sounds.

Bright, white light overhead. Scrabbling deep inside. Breathe, breathe, breathe. You are ripping out my lungs. Please, give me air.

"What's happening, girlfriend? Your face is all red." The woman's voice was sharp. Familiar.

A softer voice prodded, "Don't mind her, Claire. You look fine, honey. Try to wake up now."

Leave me alone, she thought.

"Hey, we have some partying to do. Naomi's right. You gotta wake up." Gentle Naomi and Britt. Annoying Britt. Were they going to a bar? She didn't want to go.

"That's working, ladies. Keep talking to her," said the doctor. She was strangling. She couldn't answer.

"Ms. McIntosh This is Dr. Janana. You're at George Washington Hospital Center. Work with me. I'm pulling out your breathing tube. You'll feel better in a minute."

Days passed. Claire's vision narrowed to a paper towel tube. A calendar, black and white, read: February. She heard a male voice overhead. A dark face floated into view blocking the light.

"Tell me your full name."

She tried to wet her lips. Her mouth was a dry sponge. "Claire Marie McIntosh."

"Where do you live, Claire?"

"Chevy Chase, Maryland," she croaked. She could see the house, the red door. So pretty, so welcoming.

"Who is the president?"

"George Waaaa..." That wasn't right, but she couldn't grasp the name.

"Okay." The man said, "What year is it?"

"1998." That slipped out confidently but he frowned. He must be a doctor. He had on a white coat.

"Let's try again. What year is it?"

She paused. Now he was stern and she wanted to answer him but she didn't know how.

"Do you know where you are?"

"...George Washington Hospital."

"That's right. You suffered a head trauma and a pulmonary embolism. We induced coma to protect your brain. Do you remember how the trauma occurred?"

She waited. Smoke. Tilted, off balance. Staggering. Were people screaming? Scattered images appeared one second and were gone the next. The face loomed over her. Who was it? Where was she?

"Claire," the voice was calm, understanding. She had met this man before.

"Try again. I'm Dr. Janana. Do you know why you're in the hospital?"

"A fire. At work. But everyone got out." Why couldn't he give her some water? Didn't he see how thirsty she was?

She saw herself slide toward outstretched arms. Frustration built; her memory was at the outer edges of a whiteout. Shut down. She gathered her forces seeing the doctor waiting. What did he want again?

"Do I look familiar?"

"Are you Dr…? I'm sorry."

"That's all right. What year is it Claire?"

Hadn't he asked that before? She was going to get it right this time. "2008."

"That's right. Tell me what you do for a living."

She had to get back to work. Papers on her desk would be piled high. Had she been on vacation? She was so hot, sunburned even. She had wanted to go to the river house to see her dad. She knew better than to go sailing without sunscreen. Where was Sam?

She woke again later to a wider view: green walls, soft lights, an English garden undulated in a ribbon next to her. She lay abed, propped up but utterly still. She tried to turn her head but it was too heavy. A nurse approached with a paper menu and told her she had to eat. The words were a jumble and the woman took it back and began to read. Words forgotten as soon as they were uttered.

"Soup would be best. There's a nice potato soup," the nurse said, the lights reflecting in her glasses. Where were her eyes?

A tray was pushed across her lap. The nurse spooned a small sip and Claire spit it out. Salty, salty.

"What else can I get you? Lemon ice?"

In a flash of first want, Claire remembered, "No. A bacon, lettuce and tomato sandwich.

The Family Calls

Nearly a month had passed since the bombing. Claire sat at her laptop in the living room of her two-bedroom apartment. A February snow fell, blanketing the canopy of trees in Klingle Park and muffling the traffic noise on Connecticut Avenue.

Her thoughts were cloaked as well and she trembled with cold as she recalled broken thoughts, incoherent words that floated, spoken by the hospital neurologist.

"A shutdown," Claire said. "A vacuum. I can sense it coming. It's worse when someone asks me question."

"It's a lack of what we call working memory. Recent events don't want to stick."

"I can feel my brain crinkling up, shrinking even."

The doctor tucked the file beneath her arm, relaxing against the counter as if ready for a long discussion. "I had a patient liken it to a newspaper wrinkling when lit by a match."

Claire decided to confess the truth no matter how embarrassing. "I know we've talked before. You're familiar but I can't remember your name or what you look like. I get anxious and everything goes blank."

"It will get better in time, Claire. Like playing checkers but forgetting the strategy, keep playing."

Playing. That was what she did with Sam but it certainly wouldn't earn her a living. How long would it take to be part of the sentient world? At daybreak before she sent him off to school, she and Sam watched with a thrill out the living room window as an elusive bluebird, the bird of happiness, darted through the gigantic holly tree. Now, in the quiet of Sam's absence, she had time to read about her diagnoses, and Claire laughed out loud at the current state of American medicine. Witch doctor medicine. Blood thinners from rat poison. "Ridiculous," she said to no one.

In the hospital, the initial diagnosis had been head trauma. The second was Factor V Leiden, a genetic predisposition for killer blood clots. An army of stern, Asian, nurse-clones woke her rudely day and night, flipping on the fluorescent light that blinded her. She would turn, shielding her eyes to glimpse them holding up a huge, empty syringe as if she were locked in some Transylvanian castle with a mad doctor.

Her blood surged, watery and pink. When they wore out one arm, bruising it purple, pink and green, they went to the other. They shot her belly with Heparin to thin her blood. To her immense relief, they sent her home with a standing order for blood tests every two weeks and an oral prescription for warfarin, the rat poison.

Just as her father was ready to wheel her out of the hospital, a doctor arrived and said, "Also, no birth control pills. Ever. Blood clots, you know? You'll need another method." Claire had smiled and said, "Nothing happening in that arena."

She slapped the laptop shut thinking she'd like to crawl back to bed. Doughy sleep. Wanderlust sleep. Her blessed bed had taken on an aura of sanctity. A nurse's explanation came back to her, "Sleep is your brain's desire to repair itself." It was true; after a good sleep, she always woke more capable. But didn't she have something to do this morning? An obligation. A piece of paper on her desk read 9:30 in her own hand. Below, she had written *FBI/Sam home early*.

The coffeepot buzzed in the kitchen. She was pleased she had written a reminder that the schools were closing early due to snow. Time didn't exist for her in sequence, and she drew a clock face, touching the pen to the numbers, counting the hours before Sam would arrive. She crumpled the paper and wrote 1:00 on her palm. That was it, after lunch.

She would wait inside the lobby of the Kennedy Warren and the door to his yellow bus would open. He would run to hug her, animated and smelling of crayons or poster paint or little boy sweat, always with graphite under the tiny nail of his forefinger. He loved third grade and his mom. She felt his adoration. She, in turn understood why she was alive. They pretended everything was the same but it wasn't.

One night after Carlotta left, they finished dinner and Sam grabbed his backpack from the kitchen counter, uncovering the stack of orange prescription bottles. One tumbled to the floor. He picked it up, rattling its contents before she could reach to hide them. Solemn, his blue eyes caught hers and he asked, "Mommy, are you going to be okay?"

"Yes, of course Sam. I'm okay now. I just need to take naps."

"But why do we have Carlotta cook when you're home all day?"

"Because you know my cooking's a joke. She's just here to make it easier. Maybe she'll work for us after I go back to work. You'd like that, wouldn't you?"

He leaned his arm on the table in front of her and tilted his head sideways as if looking at a creature under a magnifying glass. "Okay. But she said I need to be in bed in another hour and she's wrong. I don't go to bed until after we watch Power Rangers."

"Really?" So smart, she thought. He was testing her. "Since when have we been watching Power Rangers on a school night?"

He crawled into her lap and said, "Last night, Mom."

"We did not. We watched it in the hospital," she said, pushing his hair from his eyes.

"Well how come *Power Rangers* is on at 8:00 and you let me watch it if that's my bedtime. I can tell you every show we watched since you've been home. Can you?"

Claire paused and looked away. Sam went to bed at eight every night, didn't he? Or had she set it at eight-thirty after the winter break? She couldn't remember. She had broken her own rule: no TV on school nights. That much she knew and defaulted to a change of subject. "Did Granddaddy let you stay up while I was in the hospital? Is that what's going on here? Because if it is, this is not a good habit."

Sam reached up and his fingers traced the fresh scar under her bangs. "Mommy," he whispered, "How come they wouldn't let me see you in the hospital?"

She pulled his hand to her lips and kissed it. "You came to the hospital once I was awake, my little man. Before that the doctors were working on me so I'd be a better mommy. You can't know all the secrets. Let's do your homework and then bed."

"Aw, Mom." He knew he was caught and they laughed, her fingers lingering around his waist until she tickled him, catching him by surprise.

They hadn't told Sam of the bombing or the fire. Claire was sure he had seen it on television, but when her father told him Claire had been in a car accident and was in the hospital, Sam never made the connection. She thought he accepted the lies they told, because the truth, when he was close to recognizing it, was too frightening.

Claire rejoiced in his singsong voice, his stories of food trades in the lunchroom and his bragging about victories on the muddy soccer field. Mothering was automatic. Love compensated for her every little lapse. Alone, a prayer rose to her lips, "Deliver us from evil, now and at the hour of our death." They were automatic words. Ritual. She couldn't find her own so they would have to do.

The Post-it note read 9:30. Claire reached for her parka and rose slowly from her chair. The FBI waited. Anxiety niggled at her and she tried to calm herself, knowing her father would be near. She paused at the hallway mirror.

Claire thought she looked the same with the exception of her right eye where blood had pooled. The doctor had said it would reabsorb but it looked no smaller. She was always overly sensitive about her eyes. Blue-green with a splotch of brown at the outside corner of her left eye, they had earned her the nickname "Collie" at the Cathedral Girls School. Now, the right iris was dappled red. Peering closely in the mirror, she tried on a smile, a crooked one that grew in tentative confidence as she recognized the woman staring at her.

"Hello, you. Are you coming back to me?" she asked softly. Her heart-shaped face was thinner but her cheeks rounded as the smile spread. Her hair was too long and unkempt, a mess of ripples that she ran her fingers through and pulled up in a half-hearted effort at style. She poked two chopsticks through the bun to hold it in an X but it made her look more fragile so she let her hair fall past her shoulders in a thick cape. Brushing her bangs back, she inspected the tiny scars sprinkled across her forehead and the one that snaked back into her shaved hairline. Purple and hard, it was a token of something she couldn't remember. Hospital staff had asked how she had come by such a significant head wound but she had no answers.

Self-consciously, she smoothed her hand over her legs evaluating the web of hardened scabs covering her knees and shins. They were crusted and ridged in dark welts that were annoyingly resistant to the vitamin E cream she applied night and day. She couldn't go out like this and decided to wear tall boots.

Claire glanced down the hall at the little pile of pills that were clustered on the kitchen counter with a small glass of orange juice to chase them. They turned her into a lap dog, circling for the softest spot. Red, white, and green candy colored dots. One for this and four for that. Another one to thin her blood and shiver her bones. "Nasty stuff," she remembered the nursing volunteer saying. She had tested herself to see if she could research and found the woman's words true. "You know it was used as rat poison in the fifties before Big Pharma figured out it could dissolve blood clots. They're working on a new drug that doesn't require blood tests." Claire had smiled vaguely and the girl wandered away.

She looked up. The snow was thinning. She walked back to the kitchen and downed her pills. It was time to see the FBI. She studied the list she kept by the door. Keys, purse, phone, watch, coat, hat, boots. Every checkpoint took forever to process. She walked to the lobby of her apartment building and climbed in the black Suburban her father had sent.

Her dad's offices were at the top of the four-story Hebrides Building. Tosh Enterprises, Inc., had history in D.C. as the oldest and largest real estate developer and commercial builder the city had ever known. As she walked through the lobby, for once she felt the pride her family's 150 years had stamped on the Washington landscape.

Pictures of her earliest Scottish relatives lined the walnut paneled walls of the lobby. As a child skipping down the hall to the elevators, she had been oblivious to them. As a teenager they embarrassed her. At twenty, the portraits disgusted her as emblems of big business grown on the backs of the little man—black, white, poor and working class.

Claire stopped before a new photo of an H Street excavation carved down to the bowels of the city, dotted with the faces of Hispanic cement workers. The raw freshness of the cold outside had followed her. She felt more alert. The confusion of the past few weeks fell away. She inched along as if seeing the family history for the first time.

The pictorial tribute of McIntosh men, the industrialists, the wheeler-dealers, the builders, and a senator ended with two tiny daguerreotypes of early ancestors framed in orbs of worn red velvet, husband and wife tobacco farmers on the Tred Avon River in Oxford, Maryland. A small brass plate read "Aquilla McIntosh" in flowery script. Below the woman's, "C. McIntosh," her first name insignificant. Aquilla had made his money through hard work and the even harder work of his Negro slaves. With four wives, he fathered fourteen children.

His first wife, C., the only woman on the entire wall, had sloped bare shoulders rising from a sweeping collar. Her neck was long and curved up to reveal a delicate face and abundant hair pulled into a tight bun at her nape. Perfectly spun spaniel curls dangled beneath her chin like trailing roses above her décolleté. A hint of lashes across her downturned eyes painted a demure woman, private and secretive. The perfect woman for a McIntosh man. Claire looked closely at Aquilla's eyes for some hint of kindness but saw only the gaze of a tough, determined Scot, clean-shaven, with a high forehead. His poor wife.

In the center of the room, under preservation glass, was a lighted display case with the one item she had always cherished, a letter from the financier of the American Revolution to Andrew McIntosh asking him to contribute to the rebel cause. The request was made to rout the British from the Chesapeake Bay by *"joining forces with the French ships at the mouth of the James River. -- Robert Morris, June 25, 1781."*

Claire gazed toward the light from the entrance doors. Thirty feet of fame ended with plaques celebrating philanthropic acts—the hospital wing in Easton, Maryland, donations to the Kennedy Center, the Reagan Building, and the Chesapeake Bay Foundation—recorded for posterity and to impress clients of any political persuasion.

Family history like this held on to a person like marionette strings. Shamed at her belated sense of pride, Claire stared up and down the lobby. Tosh Enterprises was her heritage, and she thought perhaps she had been resisting too long. Maybe it was time to take her place on the wall.

———

The Great Scot in Charge

"Good morning, Ms. McIntosh." The man pushed an old-fashioned paper log across the desk. "Would you sign in here?

"How are you this morning?" she asked.

"Great. Another round of snow. School lettin' out early. My Dorothy said the kids aren't going to learn a thing if this keep up."

Should she know him, and who the hell Dorothy was? Claire scrawled her name and stared at the unfamiliar signature. Was there anything left of her old self? Smiling stiffly, she strolled over to the bank of elevators and pressed the button. The door opened but she did not move. She pressed again and the cab returned only to close again as she stood transfixed, a drip of perspiration coursed down her cheek. A whiff of smoke, a tendril of white-hot fire, a distant whimper. Her thoughts melted and then her mind went blank.

She sat down on the bench. The security manager appeared. He rode the elevator with his hand on her elbow, chatting cheerfully, his voice echoing as if from the bottom of a cave, as he escorted her to the doors of Tosh Enterprises, Incorporated. Leslie VanAnden, arms outstretched, swooshed across to greet her. So cool and calm, blonde hair swept up in a chignon with her signature sapphire earrings that matched her eyes. Her elegant demeanor disguised her warmth and she complemented her surroundings like the perfect piece of jewelry. For twenty years Leslie had worked as Communications Manager for Tosh. Claire was instantly relieved in her presence.

"You should have called to say you were downstairs. How are you feeling?" VanAnden asked.

"I'm fine," she lied. "Taking a little time off from my killer job." It sounded like self-promotion but underneath the bravado, Claire was worried she wouldn't have any job waiting. Brain trauma. Had they heard about it at Wilcox and Stein? She felt a need to hide the truth knowing her performance would suffer. Suddenly, more questions arose. How much sick leave would her bosses allow? Would she be able to do anything more than simple research? Better yet, would she be able to handle conversations? Surely the non- profit job was gone by now.

She felt a presence behind her and turned to see a familiar face, one that she had known for years yet she couldn't recall the name. He was bald, with thin eyebrows and a strong nose beneath strangely unfocused eyes that would lead one to think his mind was distantly occupied. She remembered that was the way he fooled you. He always knew, always had a prescient finger on the pulse around him. A vision of him instructing her in self-defense and target practice surfaced. This bullet-shaped man followed her father quietly in public and had taught her the steps to disarm the security system here at the office. Why couldn't she remember his name?

He reached around VanAnden to take Claire's coat and she marveled at how he moved so quietly. Claire opened her mouth to greet him. He spoke first.

"Ms. VanAnden, Ms. McIntosh." He nodded toward each of them with a contained smile. "I hope you don't mind if I sit in on the interview." So polite. Claire remembered these polished conventions hid the heart of a mercenary who kept in his breast pocket a short list of those who had earned his loyalty.

"Of course not, Mercer," said Leslie. Lloyd Mercer. The man had worked for her father for a decade and had taught Claire eye gouging, throat punching and chin slamming.

Leslie continued, "I expected Ham would have you in there."

Her father's office was a canvas of slate blue and cream. To Claire, it was stuffy, formal, and a vestige of her grandfather's era. Decorators were not welcome. Her dad had thrown out the one her stepmother hired with a, "I'll be goodgoddamned if he's going to turn my office into some New York pansy's espresso machine."

A large Kerman rug in pale blue and green, the colors of the former Shah, anchored the creamy upholstered couch and chairs. His office valet, a burly man in a three-piece Brooks Brothers suit, heavy black glasses, and tasseled wingtips, stood by an antique British teacart, ready to dispense coffee. Framed by the window, her father stood with his back to his dark oak desk that was devoid of any paper. An oil painting of Tred Avon House and a turbulent Chesapeake Bay graced the wall behind the couch. Outside, snow had begun again in earnest, blowing sideways across tree-lined Wisconsin Avenue.

Her father crossed the room welcoming her with a kiss and a hug, his electric blue eyes scanning her up and down. He was an oak of a man, with a Twain-like face and burry eyebrows partially obscuring that piercing gaze that could make conversation wither and die mid-sentence. Aware of this power, he laughed from his belly or snorted to disarm those in his gathering. If some dolt, in his estimation, was too invasive, too flattering, or too bubble-headed, he would fix his eyes upon the individual until conversation died and change the discussion to his liking. He was wildly successful, suffering a town of politicians with private sarcasm and public cleverness. "How's Red?" he asked. "You're looking well today. A little too skinny, though."

Oddly, Claire couldn't help but notice his face looked seamed and his shoulders sunken in his dress shirt and tie. "I might say the same about you, Dad. What's up with that?"

He reached a long arm across the back of his desk chair, grabbing his tweed sport jacket. Had she offended him? She hadn't meant to and backtracked quickly. "I hope you aren't worrying about me," she said. "I'm doing fine. Let's get an ice cream after this." A smile split his craggy face and he suddenly looked like her old dad. When he threw an arm around her shoulders, she felt a boniness that was new.

"There are two agents outside," Mercer interrupted. "My advice is for everyone to be honest, but do not offer irrelevant information about Mrs. McIntosh. Stick to their questions. I suspect this is mostly about Claire's car but it could easily turn into an ongoing investigation of her mother's involvement with Army of God."

Her mother? Her car? Claire's mind swirled like the snow outside. She tried to remember what she had heard, the bits and pieces gleaned from TV. The cable outlets, Sunday talk shows and internet news were still trending nearly a month later.

The glass façade in her office building had blown out, leaving people injured on the sidewalk, Farragut North Metro closed, and Washington Circle traffic stood at a standstill for days. Then Cathy Lanier, Chief of Police, said, "I will reserve comment about who is responsible until the work of the FBI has been completed." Erratic and scared, Claire shut herself off, not wanting to know more.

Ham McIntosh focused intently on his daughter. "They may bait you about your mother. We don't want to rehash any of that."

"I—I don't understand what mom has to do with the explosion. She stopped that nonsense years ago."

"It's a formality, honey. They have to ask."

"They'll be checking to see how estranged your mother is from the rest of the family, specifically, you," said Mercer. "The running theory is that whoever set the bombs was involved in Army of God and may have known your mother at one time."

Deflated, Claire plunked herself down on the couch, entwining her fingers and twisting. Her dad was right: rehashing. They would find out that she visited her mother at her home in Spring Valley, that she made sure the refrigerator was stocked, that her bills were paid, that she asked questions to see if her mother could answer despite her ever-present alcoholic fog. Would her father be livid? Years before, he had cut his first wife out of his life and had demanded the same of Claire.

A Metro bus horn sounded on the street below. Claire looked around at her father's surroundings wondering what to do. Her gaze fell onto his shoes, a pair of Barker Black ostrich wingtips in brown with the added stitching on the toe. No black oxfords. Studied casualness. And the sport jacket instead of the pinstripe. He was dressing down for the FBI. Everything planned ahead of time, he commanded the moment.

Claire debated for seconds, looked up at her dad and confessed, "I do see Mom once in a while. She keeps firing the housekeepers you hire, then she calls me. I go over and make sure she's eating and poke around."

"Bleeding heart Claire," said her dad, walking over to the couch to sit. He fooled with his top shirt button and straightened his tie. "And?"

"I find empty bottles and scripts. There are fresh ones hidden."

"That's information you can share. It makes her an unreliable witness," her father responded and he patted the cushion next to him, beckoning her to slide over. "Mercer, a reminder that we'll handle this as we always do," he said. "When I nod twice, the conversation is done. They can reschedule if they want more."

<hr />

Bust a Rail

It was a Sunday in early February, a snow white day with a blinding sun that streamed in a single beam across a brown head buried in a dirty pillow. He could feel its warmth but he lay still, face down, splattered across the bed. A bare shoulder twitched at a bad dream. He woke in a sweat gasping for air.

José sat up and held his head rolling it back and forth as he tried to wipe the memory from his mind. He had run like the gray coyote into the darkness, never looking back for fear the shadowy figures would be closer than he thought. He met them again and again as they chased him across the asphalt in front of a half abandoned mall. He slowed to read a street sign that said New Hampshire Avenue and they caught him. In his nightmare, they were determined to kill him. In life, they had only wanted to maim him: part of the initiation.

He limped over to the kitchen sink and ran the water. He drank from the tap, slaking his thirst, and then pooled it in his palm to splash his face. He opened the small refrigerator door and bent to see if there were any pupusas left. One. Its foil glistened on the shelf. He devoured it and went to the toilet.

His calf ached and he opened the mirrored cabinet for pills. Bootleg oxcy. OC. Bust a rail. Just two. He had to make them last because when he wanted more, he would have to work for them.

He lay down atop his damp sheet and crossed his mangled calf in front of him, massaging the rippled muscle tissue until the aching and burning stopped. Then he threw his hands to his pillow and waited for sleep to return. It didn't but he refused to take another pill.

He had suffered a beating that night in addition to the knifing. They had sent him to Langley Park to meet a dealer and run some drugs across the Bay Bridge to the coast. Hector was to meet him at the abandoned mall with a car. When José arrived, he met five other gang members he didn't know. Friendly at first, but drinking and hyped with crank, their eyes were crazed. They were ready for trouble. José stayed quiet and wary, waiting for direction. Then Hector drove by in a broken down Honda, nodded silently through the window and drove off. That's where the nightmare always began.

A day later he woke in this strange room. His leg was bandaged and his body sore and bruised from repeated blows with a baseball bat. Bleary eyed, he had taken in his surroundings. One crutch leaned against the wall near his bed. Across the room, near the ceiling a small square window lit a makeshift kitchen. Four cabinets, a counter, a hotplate, a sink, and a short refrigerator like the ones in El Salvador. An open door beside the bed led to a bathroom. He rolled his eyes above him and saw MS 13 sprayed on the wall in red paint. A handful of pills sat on an old wooden crate. He was theirs, wholly owned. He wanted to see his mother.

CHAPTER 3

Fire in the Hole

*A*t 10:10 the FBI agents entered her father's office. Agents Pumphrey and Norwood were the same height, same build, and wielded strong handshakes. The resemblance ended there. Pumphrey, a bold black man, obviously the leader of the two, unabashedly took in his surroundings and his gaze lingered over the teacart. He made introductions and Norwood, the whitebread FBI archetype, waited to be shown a seat. Claire sat across from them, next to her father as coffee was poured into black Tosh mugs. Mercer began by inserting a quick statement that they were going to record the interview. She looked hard at the agents hoping she could read their response. They appeared briefly disconcerted, one squinting and the other raising his eyebrow.

Pumphrey ignored Mercer and spoke directly to her dad. "This isn't an interrogation, Sir. We're here to ask what Ms. McIntosh knows about that day." He looked over at his partner. "We like to jog our memories when we get back to headquarters, so Agent Norwood will be taking notes for our internal use." On cue, Norwood waved a small notebook in the air.

Claire glanced back and forth relieved. She hadn't lost all of her old skills and knew this was their typical low-key procedure. She knew her father would record the meeting and, in fairness, Mercer had given them a friendly warning.

Ham McIntosh said, "No problem, gentlemen. Claire is fresh out of the hospital. When she tires, we're done." Claire sank into the cushions but was stunned at Pumphrey's next statement.

"Ms. McIntosh," he began, "the doctor, a patient, and a nurse died in the clinic examining room on the shared wall with your office. Where were you when the explosion occurred?"

As he spoke, Claire realized if she had been in her office that morning, she might have perished. She felt the blood drain from her face. "I was in the conference room. Wilcox told us that they were downsizing and he was pink slipping people."

"Take a sip of this," her father said and handed her a Pellegrino.

Pumphrey glanced at Norwood and steered the conversation away from the casualties. "Do you remember how many blasts you heard?"

"Two, I think." She adjusted her skirt aware of the scars on her knees. "The first was this low boom deep inside the building. When we were getting ready to evacuate, a bigger explosion hit. The conference room wall blew out."

"What did the explosion sound like? Do you remember?"

"A sizzling noise like cicadas and then the blast hit. It was right beside me, I think. There was an unbearable pressure in the room, and at first I couldn't hear anything. Then the window blew out."

"Can you estimate the time?"

"The HR meeting started right at nine, so after that. My phone fell off my lap and I bent down to pick it up off the floor when the sizzling started."

Pumphrey studied her face, and asked, "The other blasts followed when?"

"I must have been in the hallway. I just have bits and pieces—people crying and screaming. Someone grabbed me and I pulled Jeanine, I think. I was terrified." Both stared at her, waiting for more. "I'm sorry I can't be more helpful."

"You're being very helpful," answered Pumphrey. "How long have you known Hampton Reid?"

"Three years. He came in after me."

"Do you have a good working relationship with him?"

"Sure. Everybody wants to get ahead. He's highly motivated."

"Do you want to get ahead?"

"Attorneys are competitive. I'm no exception."

She remembered a small detail. He had the same color folder as hers. The favored son was a keeper. But then so was she.

"He mentioned that you were late to work that day," said Pumphrey.

"Late at Wilcox and Stein is relative. I made it for the meeting. Nine o'clock," she said and shrugged.

"He thought you weren't paying attention. Was something else on your mind?"

The asshole. Always presenting her in a bad light. "I don't remember exactly what was on my mind but I suspected I wasn't getting canned and he wasn't either." At least Reid was alive, she thought. She wondered who else had made it out but her mind was porous, a sieve and nothing would stick long.

"Ms. McIntosh, why was your car parked in the no parking zone by the elevator?" asked Pumphrey. "Your assigned parking is on P3."

She could feel her face color. "I didn't want to be late for the meeting. My ex-husband had our son for the weekend and at the last minute he called me to take Sam to school. The traffic was heavy."

Pumphrey stared at her poker-faced. "And?"

"So, I park there if I'm rushed. The building super makes sure I don't get towed... most of the time." She glanced at Norwood who scribbled. Son of a bitch, she thought. Do they have to write down everything?

"D.C. traffic. I understand," said Pumphrey. But she thought he didn't. He raised his eyebrow again and she knew he thought her privileged.

He looked down at his coffee and rested the mug on the table between them. "How long have you worked for Wilcox and Stein?"

"Six years."

"Did you ever notice anything, anyone out of place at the clinic?" He looked at her quizzically, "The reason we ask is that the explosions triggered multiple incendiaries and thermite fires. Super hot. They traced them to the biohazard boxes in the examining rooms."

She put her water down on a napkin. "Thermite?"

Her father answered, "A welding material that's impervious to water."

"That's right," said Pumphrey. "There was an accelerant. Gutted the third and fourth floors of the building. And the elevator shaft" He glanced at her dad as if asking permission. "I'm sure you've seen the media circus around the perpetrator? He posted a manifesto online claiming responsibility."

"I read a little," said Claire.

"Then you know he was an anti abortionist. We wondered if there was a link to you. Your car was in a no parking zone by the elevators. You can understand our concern."

Claire took a deep breath and braced her hands on the cushions at her sides. "I was involved in an anti-choice group when I was a teenager."

They were painful years after her father had walked out and Claire had followed her mother, joining a radical pro life group. Mercifully, her mother's influence faded after she told her daughter that a bolt cutter was best to slice off the abortionist's thumbs below the second knuckle. Claire had tied up those memories in a neat little box, never to open again. "But all that's ancient history," she said.

Norwood leaned forward. Maybe he was the leader of the two, she thought as his subtle familiarity overwhelmed her. "Special interest groups look for scapegoats. We have to ask," he said with sympathetic eyes. "Did you ever notice anything suspicious when you worked late?"

Claire vaguely sensed a question had been asked but she was absorbed with analyzing the relationship between the two agents and wiping out an image of thumb-less hands. She took a deep breath. "I'm sorry. What did you say?"

"Your car, Ms. McIntosh."

A man's yellow case had alarmed her. It was a Friday night maybe five weeks ago. Sam was at his father's. She was too tired to meet her coworkers at the W Hotel bar. Thinking about nothing but catching up on True Blood episodes and slugging a bottle of wine in bed, she locked the office and saw the elevator door begin to close just as she made the lobby. She shouted. It reopened and she bustled inside. The yellow case had an insignia. Four menacing black circles that formed the face of a horned devil. It made her think of dirty needles and contaminated blood.

"Once, I asked the medical waste technician who took the stuff out of the building if his job made him nervous. He said they're trained for it." The agents looked at her intently. "He and his wife were going on a ski vacation in Park City. So we talked about Sundance, the indie movie festival? He was worried those filmgoers would interfere with his skiing."

"Do you remember what he looked like?"

Claire looked at her father for assurance. She couldn't remember his face, a face she saw nearly every day. "It's the same guy we all run into in the elevator every night. We call him Hepman. Hep C, you know? Everybody knows someone who has it." She was rattled and realized she wasn't answering the questions.

"Your building had good security. Did you see anyone the day of the explosions that you didn't know, that you didn't recognize? Maybe by the elevators?" asked Norwood in that quiet voice.

Images flashed. The elevator wall was scorching hot against her hand. So dark. Who was that body on the floor? The doors were partially open and a white-hot fire burned inside. Arms reached and she pulled. Or was she punching? Her mind went blank.

"I…I'm sorry. I don't remember anything much except sitting at the boardroom table with my folder and my phone. I had just gotten an offer to interview for a non-profit. I remember being excited but things are blank after that. Except—"

The room was silent. She had the uneasy feeling she had said too much. Her father's hand covered hers on the sofa. Warm. She looked at them crossed: his large hand, ropey with veins turned hers and grabbed to squeeze. She looked up at her dad's blue eyes. He nodded twice.

"Except?" Pumphrey asked softly.

An image of hands, grabbing at her and pulling, trickled into memory. "I think somebody reached for me. Jeanine Ferrell. I can't…" Her head fell forward. Her father nodded patting her hand in his lap.

His arms spread ready to shake hands, Mercer moved with authority around the couch, his voice cutting through the quiet. "Gentlemen. The interview is over now. We want to thank you for your service to our city in this terrible situation. If you have further questions we are always available."

He and VanAnden escorted the agents from the room. In the quiet that followed, Ham McIntosh pulled his daughter from the couch. "I think it's time to head to Max's for an ice cream. You want pistachio?" She hugged him, burying her head in his jacket. She loved his smell. Juniper berries. If she could just stay safe in his arms.

The door burst open and in a rush Uncle Alistair, Ham's younger brother, churned across the room. His face was lit like a drunk ready for his fifth round. He swept Claire off her feet and twirled her in his arms.

"Claire! How are you, Baby? Man, you create the drama in the family. My Facebook page is all about you. And I hate sharing the limelight."

"Alistair, she just got out of the hospital," said Ham.

"Uncle Alistair. Put me down. You're making me dizzy." Flustered but flattered, Claire held onto his coat sleeve while she regained her bearings. Then she hugged him. "Nobody can share your limelight."

Ham pulled open a desk drawer, muttering, "She knows her uncle." He tucked a black pocket pistol into his overcoat and reached for a folder. "We're going out for an ice cream, Alistair. Do you want to come?"

"And freeze my balls off? No, I need to protect the package for the ladies. I have a lunchtime meeting."

Ham nodded, grim faced, and slammed the drawer shut. "Louisa's party is Saturday night. Will we see you this weekend at Tred Avon?"

"So I can help you massage those fascist egos?"

"Those 'fascist egos' are our income stream. There is a recession and we need to be nimble."

"You always were a better dancer," said Alistair and he kissed Claire possessively on the lips. "I won't be there this weekend but give my best to lovely Louisa. She'll miss me, at least."

Ham frowned as he adjusted his coat over his shoulders. "Claire, would you excuse us?"

"Sure, Daddy. I'll be outside the door." She slipped out, wiping her uncle's kiss from her mouth. She pressed her ear to the door, ready for another battle between the brothers.

"I'll thank you to speak like a gentleman in front of my daughter, Alistair." Her uncle mumbled in response and she heard her father's voice rise. "Billing yourself head of Tosh Security are we? Keeping the company secure while screwing the congressman's wife? How many affairs have I covered up for you?"

"What are you talking about, Ham?" Alistair's voice was filled with innocence.

"This." Something slapped against a surface. "Pictures. You and Furgeson's wife, half-dressed. And you and Tom Wagoner, Regional Bank's president enjoying lunch." Ham snorted. "What are you negotiating behind my back?"

"Claire?"

Ham's secretary stood on the other side of her desk, a fresh cup of coffee steaming in her hand. Claire fumbled in her purse, "I was checking to see if Dad was finished. I left my gloves inside."

"I'll ask."

"It can wait. Don't let me bother you," she said and sat in a wingchair to wait.

Later, bundled against winter, she and her dad sat at the little parlor table in the window at Max's Best Ice Cream. Vanilla in a dish for her dad and a pistachio cone for her.

"Daddy, who died that day? You know, by the elevator? Was it somebody from the office?"

"Not from the office."

"From where?"

"The theory goes that a physician assistant grabbed one of the bio-hazard boxes when it didn't ignite and ran to the elevator. Do-gooder type. Died when it caught fire in the elevator." He glanced at her. "You okay?"

"Go on. I want to know."

"Then there's Herbert Randolph. An anti-abortion terrorist who set the fires. Found him in the elevator too. Identified them by their teeth," he said grimacing and taking a scoop of ice cream as if he could melt away a bad taste in his mouth. "Randolph knew your mother years ago, even lived with her in my Spring Valley house for a short time. If I'd known, I would've moved her ass out and sold it. May do it anyway."

Claire ignored this last bit. He spoke harshly of his first wife but he wrote checks for her care as he did to Catholic Charities. "Really? Mom and a terrorist? Hard to believe seeing her now, but back then I guess anything was possible."

"The world is never what you think it is on the surface, especially family."

"Scarey. I might have even had a conversation with that man at some point."

"So you had an offer to interview. What non-profit?" he asked.

That was it. The secret she revealed in front of the agents. She fell into a split-second lie. "Oh, it was nothing. Just a little job with an immigration attorney. I wasn't really going for it."

"Putting out your feelers?" He adjusted his topcoat over his knee. Maybe he was cold. He looked down and Claire wondered what was coming. "Stein has called me, you know. He wants you back when you're ready." His calculating blue eyes met hers. "You'll return, of course. We need to dampen this crap in the news about your car. Go about life as usual. I expect it to be resolved soon."

Claire couldn't summon the wherewithal to object. She feigned relief and asked, "Where is my car, Dad?"

"Destroyed. The service elevator burned and fell to the garage floor where the car was parked. The two bodies were in it. The doors blew out from another incendiary and, well, it was all she wrote for the car." He swooped a spoonful of creamy vanilla into his mouth and smiled at her. "Time for a new car, Red. You want another Mercedes?"

"Daddy," she said, chagrined. A new car and she would trudge through the doors at Wilcox and Stein. "I don't need another expensive car. What's the matter with a Prius? They're front wheel drive and get around great in the snow. Besides the gas savings."

"That's a car for the masses, not my little girl. You let me know."

"I've been meaning to ask you for a while now." She tongued the ice cream in a circle, leaving a comma of green at the corner of her mouth. "What would you think of me coming to work for Tosh?"

His eyes narrowed briefly and a slow smile grew on his face. Did it please him? She couldn't tell.

"That's something we should talk about. Not today though. School is letting out early. We need to get you back to meet Sam."

Claire looked at the palm of her hand where she had scrawled 1:00. "Oh, I forgot."

"Well, we can't have that. I'll call Carlotta and have her come over early," said her father. "We're flying out of the Gaithersburg airport Thursday by 3:00. You kids coming to the Valentine's party?"

"You're clearing out of Reagan National? How come? You love National."

"I just moved the Pilatus to Gaithersburg. The jet will stay at the hanger but for short jaunts Gaithersburg's easier. It's hell getting out there in traffic. The security checkpoints at National are too cumbersome now."

"Can Gus pick us up on the way? No car, you know," said Claire as she pushed back her chair.

Leaving the vestiges of their snack on the table, they moved past the trashcan to the door. "Sure. It'll be like old times, all of us going down to Tred Avon together," said her dad.

They walked outside in the deepening snow. The cold wrapped its arms around them, freezing them in time, one of their last warm moments together.

———•———

The Valentine Party

Claire stood motionless in her backless gown, partially hidden by date palms and trellises of bougainvillea. She thought the weekend after the lover's day was a foolish time to throw a party an hour and a half from D.C.—for anyone but Ham McIntosh. The copper and glass conservatory was buzzing with D.C. powerbrokers. The buffet stretched the length of the room, and behind the dessert table a wall of pink and white orchids and bromeliads spelled out TOSH LOVE. A band played jazz as a duo crooned in the background. Gas heaters, tucked behind palms of every size were spaced at close intervals, buzzing and glowing. In the middle of the room, Congressional types milled about chatting with the off-duty press, trying to breach the crowd around D.C. authors and theater stars.

The evening was going miserably. Claire had been anxious to test her conversational skills in the safety of her father's shadow. She was back in the family fold, ready to help him drum up business or knead connections as she had done so many times before. But her ability to schmooze had evaporated. She watched as her father warmed up a potential client and passed them off to Dean, the company attorney, who explained contract highlights. She should have been the next stop to close the deal, offering the client Hawaiian vacations or ski trips to Park City but VanAnden had taken her place. Claire found every time someone engaged her in conversation, the whole business of the bombing came up and she closed up like hibiscus at night.

She searched for typical Washington gossip—which conservative southern politician was secretly gay or which liberal maven had the most facelifts—but this too did not end in her usual campy jokes. The party mood was edgy and everyone turned instead to the economy, boring her infinitely. She had never felt the effects of a recession and this one had unfolded with a vengeance while she was in the hospital, still disconnected and unaware.

Earlier, Claire had caught her father's eye and he laughed merrily, lifting her mood with his confidence. He worked the crowd, waving at servers to refill champagne or laying a strong hand on a suited shoulder to whisper a promise of business. As the evening wore on he rearranged chairs for the older matrons and flattered them with attention.

Claire wandered away, suddenly too tired for words. She recognized the former British ambassador to Yemen, Geraldine Wyatt, who kindly asked how she was feeling. Claire opened her mouth and nothing came out. She paused and shook her head, whispering, "I'm just about cooked."

Gerry laughed, "Ah, smart women like us are never cooked. You just need a break, dear. Get out of Washington and find some work that thrills you. Come to London." The thought, intriguing as it was, filled her with regret. She leaned against the doorjamb and thought what she could have done if she hadn't been a lobbyist, if she hadn't married, if she hadn't had Sam so young. She scolded herself. Sam wasn't a regret, an inconvenience at times, but never a regret. What was the matter with her? She swore again she would never give herself up to a man the way she had caved to Vance.

The kitchen doors swung open and closed. Claire watched the parade of servers dressed in black patent leather pants and red satin shirts. She rolled her eyes, thinking how vulgar her family home had become since her stepmother, Louisa, came on the scene. On her way past the cupid ice sculpture that reflected pastel colors from a rotating light wheel, Claire thought, now that's just plain cheap. Her mother might be a drunk and a pill popper but at least she had good taste.

After eight years of her stepmother's parties, she had learned that Louisa's idea of refinement leaned toward mink coats over lamé slippers and probably nothing underneath. Claire stared at the lights whirling about on cupid's face and shook her head a little, surprised at her own bitchiness. She needed to stop but the evening had worn her down. An aura appeared at the edges of her vision in greens and violets and she thought it was the light wheel until the kaleidoscope spread across the room. She felt dizzy. Ten thirty. It was past time for bed.

Sam was dishing handfuls of toasted crab points at the buffet. God, he'll be sick with all this rich food and staying up so late, she thought. She tucked his sticky hand in hers and dragged him up the back staircase. Downing her pills, she snuggled with him in bed. They watched Disney's *Cars* until they fell asleep nestled in each other's arms.

Claire woke just before midnight, drugged and groggy. She could hear music still thumping below. Getting up, she rinsed her cottonmouth, took off her dress and put on sweats. She followed the narrow back stairs to the bustling kitchen and found Frannie, the family housekeeper, waiting. The woman's round face and blue eyes lit up at the sight of her.

"Frannie, it smells good. Are we going to eat some mac 'n' cheese?"

"You woke up. I was worried we would have to save it for tomorrow."

The casserole was dotted with crispy breadcrumbs. A smile split Frannie's face, baring the space between her two front teeth. Claire remembered sitting in her lap as a little girl and pushing her index finger into the space saying she wanted teeth like Frannie's. "Harder to eat your corn on the cob," she had answered.

"I swiped some of those grilled lobster claws from the caterer and folded them in. Let me find Gus and we'll have a midnight conference here at the kitchen table." A server breezed by, almost knocking the hot casserole out of her hands.

"See here, you idiot. Mind where you zoom in my kitchen." Frannie still supervised the mayhem and kept order. Claire's mouth watered. Lobster mac 'n' cheese. Nothing but plain elegance.

Below the table sprawled Compass, her father's golden retriever. Claire warmed her bare feet in his fur. They wouldn't speak of the night's events. It was a family habit, left over from the days of her mother's alcoholic rants. Better to talk cheerily of know-nothings than to beat unhappiness with words. She bent over to pet the dog and his massive head rolled toward her with one bleary eye open, hoping for more. He was only two years old but his puppy was played out from chasing the ball with Romeo, a fuzzy Jack Russell that ruled the neighborhood. Everyone had a place in the world—except her.

She didn't want to return to Wilcox and Stein. Her ability to remember, to multitask and feel like she wasn't drowning had not improved over the last month. She feared she would be stupefied in normal conversations and end up blathering nonsensically or worse, constricted and silent. Other than holding a desk at Tosh, she couldn't imagine where she could work. Would she be demoted? Fired? Working was not a hobby. Her mother had hobbies. Claire had direction. No doubt she could sit home on her father's dime but the fear of becoming her mother, an obsessive, narcissistic drunk, terrified her. Claire checked a phone App called Creative Jobs: cupcake decorator, stationery designer (real need for that these days), yoga coach. All jobs she could do but was that work?

It wasn't law she had practiced these past four years. It was selling her soul. Guilt followed like toilet paper on a heel. She had dealt in a sea of words…. implantable wireless heart monitors that exploded in airport security and next generation lithium batteries that caught fire. New uses for expiring patents on prescription drugs became all the more ironic after learning about rat poison turned blood thinner. Even she could be a victim now. She had to get out of her job before she was called back to work. Her dad had been strangely noncommittal but she was determined to talk about employment at Tosh after the party was over.

"What are you doing tomorrow, Frannie?"

"Gus and I are leaving around eleven to get back and set up the house for the week. Taking the Suburban. You want to come with us?"

"Oh, I wish we could. Vance is coming at three for Sam. Some evening political affair. Poor Sam. After this weekend, he deserves time with his friends. I guess Vance is playing the devoted father to impress somebody." Claire glared down at her hand where the diamond had been. She pushed at her cuticles.

She softened, rubbing her ring finger, thinking Sam was only eight and there were years ahead with more demands on both sides of the post-marriage aisle. She should stop getting her backside up every time Vance called. Life was short. They had been a family for a little while.

"Well maybe you and Sam can stop by the house. We've been missing you. You used to come over for dinner."

"I know, but sometimes it's easier to eat take-out while we do homework. The evening goes so fast."

"Well don't make yourself a stranger. Gus and I aren't going to be around forever, you know."

"Stop that nonsense. You can't leave us and you know it," she said with her father's old conviction. Lately, she wasn't so sure.

"Louisa and your Dad will probably sleep in after the party and fly home in the evening. You could fly back with them."

"Dad sleep in?" Claire chuckled. "When did that start happening?" A pained look grew on Frannie's face. "Is something wrong? I wondered why he isn't offering me a job all of a sudden. Maybe it's nothing."

"I don't hear everything, Claire. He's been worried about the recession."

Claire glanced out the window and searched the blackness of the night sky. She wanted to make this time special for Sam, not waste it watching more TV. A three quarter moon and the stars appeared to be cutouts in the black February sky. Wisps of clouds were strewn across, obscuring their faint glimmer, and she wished for summer and her child-hood when life was simple and full of her father's love and attention.

She would take Sam for a hike on the estate and weave stories for him the way she had heard them as a child. There was much he had never seen because she had never made time.

Frannie slid a plate of chocolate galettes next to a heaping pile of creamy noodles and Claire smiled at her wrinkled face. How had Frannie grown old and she hadn't noticed? She threw her arms around the old woman, tears welling in her eyes.

"Here, here, my girl. What's this? Feeling a bit sentimental, are we?" Capable hands pushed her back into her chair and Frannie mussed her hair, leaning close, "This will fix you right up, now. Have a fork and pretend you just finished your homework. Now where is that Gus?"

Later, on her way up to bed, Claire wondered if others needed as much mothering as she.

Moss O'Lee's Home

Claire and Sam sauntered single file down the gravel path into a dense woods. It was barely nine in the morning and the sun was a silver light that glowed through hazy winter clouds. They had awakened early while the others were still asleep.

Pines bordered the edge of the property from Morris Street to the river. Separating the woods from the glassed-in breezeway was Lover's Lane, a service driveway covered in a thick bed of oyster shells frozen in whorls of winter ice. Their feet crunched in the morning chill as they walked past the Victorian carriage house to a narrow path which led to an historic log cabin. They stopped, breathless at the view before them. Mother and child gazed out at the water, dark from a passing cloud and whipped into frothy peaks by the wind. Seagulls spread their wings wide, waiting for a signal, a morsel of food, and then dove headlong into the choppy waves. This was the conjunction of the Tred Avon and Choptank Rivers, and beyond, the great Chesapeake Bay.

Wordlessly, both taken by the wild beauty before them, they turned to face the broad lawn and the sweeping back of the clapboard house as if they might catch the Valentine party still in session. All was quiet, the dark windows holding sleeping secrets of generations past. Claire tugged at Sam's shoulder. "Come on. It looks like the weather might turn on us."

"Where to?" he asked, his nose reddening in the cold and his lashes clumping in wetness. They stepped off the oyster shells and into the scrub pine. The woods were the last bit of undeveloped land in the town of Oxford. Ham refused all offers to buy it. The McIntosh estate was fenced by miles of delicate white picket, but only the open lawn in front and back of their early nineteenth century house was protected with state-of-the-art security cameras. The white painted boards of the house gleamed wet in the morning sun and the hodgepodge of frosty rooflines was a testament to the additions made by each generation.

It was eerily quiet. Years had passed since any human had walked this way and the path had narrowed down to a deer trail, laden with needles and overgrown weeds. The going was slow, and Claire raised each thorned twig in her gloved fingers for Sam to pass.

"Where are we going again, Mom?"

"The mausoleum, where your ancestors are buried."

"Moss O'Lee's home? I never heard of him."

Claire laughed. "No, it's a house for the dead, not somebody's home." Orange moss covered a rock in their path. "Watch your step here."

The pine trees thinned giving way to ancient tall oaks and hollies. Unable to catch much light from the sun, the prickly underbrush disappeared as well. Ferns filled their place, lush and carpet-like, scrolled with a delicate morning frost. Compass bounded ahead, his nose to the forest floor, tracking invisible animals.

They were quiet, hearing an occasional mourning dove and Compass rustling about in frozen leaves. White stones bordered the widening path which led to a glade filled with winter bayberry and low evergreens. Before them stood the mausoleum, a story tall, covered in lichen and bare vines, its oak door hanging on one corroded brass fitting. On either side, iron rings to tie horses were riveted into the joints of the stone. The roof had a gaping hole from slate shingles that had fallen into the greenery outside. A carved cornerstone read 1823. Claire pushed the creaking wood door gently open. Hesitantly, Sam stepped inside grabbing his mother's hand. They looked at their surroundings illuminated by the beam of dusty light from the hole in the roof.

The floor was flagstone, and heavy wood roof beams peaked above. Five tombs were on either side of a central aisle—four large and one small near a marble altar. Before them, high in the triangle of the stone on the opposite wall, was a small round stained glass window of Jesus with a lamb at his feet. Sam snuck his hand under Claire's coat and into her waistband. He tucked his head, hiding under her arm.

"What's up, my man? Don't be afraid," she whispered.

"I'm not." His eyes were wide in the ghostly light, infinite blue pools in his white face. If he wasn't scared, he was certainly cautious.

"What is it, Mommy?"

"It's a tomb, Sam. A burial place where you can pray. I'll tell you a tale from Scotland about how our family fooled the whole British army." They sat below the window leaning against the altar; the stained glass reflected a blue and red matrix upon their faces.

"A long time ago, the McIntosh clan built a big mansion by a loch. That's a dark lake, and the only way to reach the castle was down a path through a woods like this, and across the drawbridge over a moat. From a tower you could watch for anyone who came down the path. They called it Moy Hall. So see, we come from a long line of great builders."

"I'm going to build skyscrapers," said Sam.

"Of course you are."

Impatient, Sam patted his mom's knee. "Tell me how they fooled the army."

"The British King George was mean to the Scots. Most of them were Catholics and he ordered them to practice his religion instead. Then he sent his army to fight them. But the Scots were fearless warriors," Claire said proudly. "The story goes Lady McIntosh of Moy Hall defeated 1,500 English soldiers with just five men in the middle of the night."

"No way!"

"Yep. It's called the Rout of Moy. She had a guest, Bonnie Prince Charlie who wanted to overthrow the mean King. A barmaid heard that the British were going to capture the prince. So she ran to Moy Hall to wake Lady McIntosh. The Lady sent a young blacksmith, about your age, to scout for the British soldiers. Sure enough, he saw them marching down the lane. They were loud and drunk, bragging how easy it would be to kidnap the Prince.

"The young blacksmith told her what he saw and the Lady didn't even wake the Prince. She gathered five of her men who went into the woods in front of the castle. They waited for the English army and then shot off their pistols and ran back and forth, banging on kitchen pots and calling the names of the clan chiefs to get ready for battle. The English forces thought all the clans were waiting in the woods to slaughter them so they turned tail and ran."

Sam crawled into Claire's lap. He pulled the zipper of her parka up and down as he listened.

"So they won the battle because of a lady?"

"Yeah, but sadly a couple of months later at the Battle of Culloden, Bonnie Prince Charlie was defeated and the clan chieftains were killed or taken prisoner. That was the end of the Highland way of life and the clan system. King George sent the prisoners to live in America."

Sam tugged on her sleeve. "Is he *Georgie Porgie Pudding and Pie, kissed the girls and made them cry?*'"

"Maybe Sam. We'll have to look it up. Now, being sent to America was a stroke of luck because they were good farmers and fishermen and even good smugglers."

Sam walked around the smallest tomb in a circle slapping a stick against it.

"They settled here in Oxford in 1747. They were called the Scottish Redemptioners."

Sam stared at his mom. "I know this part. That's the sign in the town museum."

"Sure is, down the street on The Strand. They came on the sailing ship Johnson and our name is on the passenger list. If they wanted to live, poor as they were, they had to redeem themselves by settling here."

"I bet they brought their swords though," said Sam grinning.

"Maybe. The British took their belongings so they came as indentured servants and for their first five years they worked hard for their masters."

"Were they slaves?"

"How do you know about slavery?"

"It's Black History Month, Mom. Everybody knows about slavery." Sam sat on the cold floor and leaned against the little tomb, bored. Trying to get his attention, Claire said, "I want to show you the tunnel that leads to the cabin."

"A tunnel? Where?" He sprang up and pulled on her arm.

"It starts here and leads to the cabin."

"What's it for?"

"To help slaves around Oxford escape to freedom in the north. The Quakers were against slavery and they worked with this plucky little black lady named Harriet Tubman."

"Oh, I know about her. She was really old."

"She just looked old, Sam. Her life was hard. She took the slaves to Philly on the Underground Railroad. You know the railroad wasn't really underground or a train, right?" Sam nodded. Claire continued, "She led them at night through the woods and they would hide during the day."

"Mom, come on. What does she have to do with the trapdoor?"

"All right, all right. Hugh McIntosh liked the Quakers and he had a tunnel dug from the root cellar below the cabin all the way here." Claire rested her hand on the child's tomb. "At night, when Mrs. Tubman came for the slaves that were hiding in the root cellar, they crawled through the tunnel and climbed up into this mausoleum. Someone from a small ship would collect them and they sailed up the Chesapeake to Philadelphia."

"Where is it? Where's the tunnel?"

"That's what I'm going to show you." Only five feet in length, a marble lamb was carved into the tomb's lid. She picked Sam up and read the inscription:

Athol McIntosh
Sunshine passes, shadows fall,
Loving memories outlast them all.
June 17, 1834-February 7, 1843

"He was just a little bit older than me," said Sam.

Claire set him down and said, "Yep. Now watch." She pushed. Grinding stone against stone, pitting her entire weight against it, the tomb moved a few inches and Sam leaned in to help. "Watch out," said Claire as she pushed Sam aside. The stone gained momentum as it passed over narrow airspace below, and the grinding stopped. A three-foot opening in the floor appeared that led into a pitch black hole. Sam hopped around in excitement.

"Mom, is anybody down there?"

"No, honey. It hasn't been used in a long time."

They knelt down to peer inside. Covered in cobwebs, the entrance oozed the damp, putrid smell of dead animals. "Creepy, crawly, huh?" asked Claire.

With awe in his voice, Sam said, "Stinky! This goes back to the work bench?"

"Yes. I've never crawled through it but my brother Andy used to say he was going to lock me in so no one would ever find me. He was such a tease!"

"I forget how he died again?" asked Sam.

"Car accident when he was twelve. Remember, the story about your Grandmom Grace driving and that's she's never gotten over it?"

"Oh, yeah. And that's why she's a drunk," said Sam.

"Sam! Who told you that?"

"Granddaddy. It's true, Mom. Why pretend it isn't?" He stared at his mother intently and then said, "Maybe there are still people down there. We should go see." Sam leaned his head further into the hole and hollered a long "Helloooo" that echoed. Claire tickled him and he squealed. She ran for the door. He tore down the steps after her. She spun, slamming into a tree trunk to catch him. Sam's laughter pealed off into the treetops and filled the glade as they rolled around in the soft leaves.

Claire brushed herself off and walked into the mausoleum to push the tomb into place. Sam stood at the door, watching.

"Mommy, how come Granddaddy doesn't take care of this place?"

"I don't know. Maybe the little boy's tomb reminds him of Andy and how short life can be."

Sam was quiet a minute. "Granddaddy's old though. He shouldn't be worried about people in the past."

Claire walked out through the door, not bothering to pull it shut. Was Sam right? The past was the past and it shouldn't matter to the living?

"I think when you're a parent and your child dies before you do, it's something you never really get over. So, maybe that's why this place is hard for Granddaddy to care about it."

Compass, covered in burs and vines, sat at the edge of the woods, his tongue hanging out and his ears thrown back in the breeze. The three started down the path toward home.

"Well, when I own Tred Avon, I'm going to fix this place up and put a sign in it for people to read. I can charge them an entrance fee."

Claire laughed and patted his shoulder. "Oh my little entrepreneur. You're going to inherit it all someday."

The Carving Bench

They smelled the smoke pumping from the cabin chimney, welcoming them. Her dad was at his carving bench. She and Sam followed the path around the log building. Sam kicked the oyster shells under his feet, and Compass ran across the broad lawn, spying a deflated football under the giant magnolia. God, she thought, when does that dog ever get enough attention? He bounded toward them wiggling all over, and dropped the ball at her feet.

"Not now, Compass. Let's see what your daddy's doing."

Compass ran to the door of the cabin and waited for them, circling in anticipation. After all the dumb golden retrievers her father had owned, he had finally hit pay dirt with this one. He belonged on the show circuit. She paused before the security handset of the thick wooden door wondering if she could remember the sequence of numbers. Hearing the whir of the bandsaw, she shouted hoping her dad would respond. Sam put his finger to the pushpad, keying in the right combination and, mercifully, the door unlocked. Her little savior. He grinned at his mom and grabbed her hand. Her father was hunched over the carving bench, his back to them.

"Hey, Dad. You're up early. I thought you'd sleep in after the party."

He raised his head. "Well, I might say the same to you." He flicked off the power to the saw and turned, slack-jawed, surprised at their arrival to the cabin. "Where have you kids been?"

"We went to Moss O'Lee's home. Granddaddy, let's climb through the tunnel. Where does it start in here?"

Ham McIntosh rose slowly and stood in front of his bench and the gaming cabinet above, silhouetted by high intensity lights he clutched a sheaf of papers to his chest. His appearance was comical compared to the tuxedo'd entertainer of the previous night. He wore a black metal visor with LED magnifying lenses that obscured his bushy eyebrows and intense blue eyes. His white hair erupted like a potted plant.

"How's my girl? You okay after all that partying?" He asked and pushed the visor up on his forehead.

Did he realize how badly her evening had gone? "Hey, I'm a Tosh," she said with false bravado then asked, "What did Granddaddy always say, 'Our eagle has landed'?"

"I think it was our beagle has landed," said her dad grinning. "That was before we started with golden retrievers. He also said my mother was the pineapple of politeness. Quite a gift with words for a senator," he said laughing.

Ham was dressed in his favorite carving clothes: a shapeless, gray sweater and paint-stained corduroy trousers. The smell of linseed oil sharpened Claire's senses. She loved her dad's Southern Maryland good ol' boy attitude. In every corner, on every shelf and table were ducks, paddling, flying, and nesting in groups. Behind him on the left, a white light illuminated an almost finished green-winged teal, its wings spread in mid-takeoff from the carving bench. It was magnificent. This was what he needed to show, not Compass.

"Dad, when are you going to enter competitions?" Claire asked. It was more a statement than a question.

"Give me a minute and I'll show you the trapdoor, Sam," he responded, ignoring Claire. His voice was gravelly and he cleared his throat unsuccessfully.

Behind him, she saw an empty shelf with an open metal door. Upon closer inspection, she saw a cleverly disguised metal safe set into the back of the gaming cabinet. He tucked the bundle of papers into the opening, closed the door and spun the combination. He pushed a false wood panel shut. Then he loaded the shelf with a stack of worn game boxes.

"Hiding something for posterity?" she asked, amused.

"Exactly. For you, Red, when you need it most."

Ham took off his visor and set it down on the carving bench with both hands. His eyes caught hers, crinkling to a smile as if he had a surprise for them. "Now look here," he said. Ham knelt creaking on one knee and turned off an electric space heater. He tugged at the dirty prayer rug beneath his bench, revealing the wide plank, pine flooring of the cabin. One gnarly forefinger caught a metal ring and he pulled up a trapdoor, hooking it to a rope that hung under his bench.

Here was the entrance to the dingy root cellar. The top of a wooden ladder rested against the opening. Her dad reached inside to switch on a light that gleamed on the packed dirt floor below.

"Jeez, Dad. I don't remember it being so cold. How can you stand it on your feet when you're carving?"

"I'm just an old waterman in disguise, girl. Cold hands, cold feet, warm heart." He flashed that killer smile and Claire hugged him. He had his humble moments.

"C'mon, Grandaddy. Let's go down," insisted Sam.

"Not today. It's too cold. This summer, I'll take you down. But let me show you something." He reached under the wood floor joists and pulled out a small metal firebox. Claire and Sam gathered round. A key was taped to the bottom and he opened it revealing a pair of long stemmed clay pipes and a few old coins, one with an image of a kneeling slave, his bound hands upraised in supplication. Along the curved border read, *Am I not a man, Am I not a brother.* Ham dug around and pulled out a slip of paper.

"This is the combination for the safe in the gaming cabinet. Now you know where it is. Nobody else knows. Just you, Claire, and Sam."

Claire giggled, dismissing his words. "Wow. That's running under the radar. High tech, Dad." Her father's bad habit of hiding odd bits and pieces he thought valuable had been a family joke over the years. He would forget where things were, then enlist them to find his trove of goodies. The anticipation was more fun than the discovery. Worn baseball cards, U.S. Navy medals, or collars and tags of deceased dogs were full of fond memories but not of any value.

"It's a matter of whom you can trust. You'll count on this some day," he muttered, rising slowly from the floor. Sam's stomach growled.

"You hungry, boy?" Ham's eyebrows twitched in amusement.

"Yeah. Like starving."

"Let's go raid the fridge." He lodged the metal box inside the opening of the trapdoor and let it close with a bang. The old man gathered Claire and Sam in his arms and the trio made their way to the main house. Worn out, Compass trailed behind.

Frannie and Gus were packing the car to return to D.C. and had laid the kitchen table with a leftover feast. Louisa, in her pink silk robe, wandered around it picking at the vegetables.

Sam ran for the bathroom and Claire took off her coat and threw it over a kitchen chair. Pushing up her sweater sleeve, she inspected a large bruise forming around her elbow.

"Gross, Claire. How did you get that? Did you fall?" asked Louisa, staring.

"No. A tree tried to wrestle with Sam and me. Didn't think I would bruise from it. Must be the blood thinner." And I had two glasses of champagne, she thought. Would she ever get used to the warfarin? Limit the green veggies, the wine; the nurse said bruises and cuts could turn into a hospital visit.

"Lord. Be careful," Louisa said as her interest shifted to the shrimp. "Have you ever seen people eat like those hockey players? It's a wonder we have any leftovers."

"You and Sam are staying for dinner?" asked Ham.

"I am. Vance is going to swing by for Sam. He's speaking at some convention at the Cambridge Hyatt and then has some daddy event in D.C. this evening."

"Vance is coming here? Great. I'll prime the engine," Ham said, his eyes lit in anticipation.

"Oh, Dad. Be nice. I'm going to turn a new leaf and so should you. Vance is trying harder. He has to polish his image. He's running for the Maryland Senate."

"Ahh. My ex son-in-law, a senator. He always had pretensions to office. That's why he's coming here. To butter me up. He thinks I'll pull some strings. And that's where he's wrong. *You* have to be forgiving for the sake of Sam. Me, on the other hand, I can always shake him up a little."

Claire snorted at him and shook her head.

"You don't think I can make him see the error of his ways?" he asked.

"It's not like that Daddy. He made a choice, and it wasn't me."

"His choice was the house I bought you. When are you getting your money out of it?"

"As soon as it sells. Listen, let's not talk about this in front of Sam."

"You should've never walked out, Claire. He should have walked."

"I know. I know."

Sam came out of the powder room to silence, all eyes on him as he pulled up his zipper. He looked from one adult to the other, then down at his jeans. "Okay, okay. I know, I'm supposed to zip in the bathroom."

Hels Half Acre, Oxford

Carlos had baptized him with a new name, something more suitable, he said, to his new job: Underling. Carlos' men shortened it to Under. At first, he had goffered about like a woman, bringing Carlos his sunset drink that he sipped while Under polished his crocodile boots. But now months later, there was a task, a test to see if Under was trustworthy, if he had the stomach to move up in the clique. His light coloring, his travels around the coast, and his command of English had raised Carlos' expectations.

He had slid a gun, lightweight and cheap, across his desk toward Under and said, "Don't get caught. If you squeal like a spider monkey, you'll die." They had taken his machete saying it was too risky. "Study the house, the grounds," Carlos said. Then, "Watch the family. They will be careless about security after their winter party. The man named Mercer does not work on Sundays."

It was a good test. Under did not search for his mother any longer. For so many years he had taken care of himself in the absence of anyone else. Now he would have a family if he didn't disappoint Carlos. He was afraid of this man with his gentle doe eyes and slick, black hair. At first he thought his soft words and soothing hands were like a father's he never had. But when Carlos turned, a crossed dagger tattoo grew out of his collar and up to his ear. He was known on the streets as el Cortador, the Cutter. Stories of him loping off the ears and fingers of those who failed him spread like a sickness among the Latino vagrants. Everyone knew he gave as well as took.

Earlier, Under had penciled a layout of the compound, staying away from the rolling camera eyes but making little circles on the scribbled paper to indicate their location. His empty stomach rumbled and churned all afternoon as he watched the family in the glass room, their doll-like figures moving in the soft light. Why would anyone live in glass rooms in the cold, he wondered, and tried to pull his coat tighter. The temperature was falling and the freezing air gripped his chest like a vice through his thin sweater. The zipper had broken on his tattered jacket.

He had scrawled some words to describe each adult, the two men—one old, one young, and the women. The child, *chico pelirrojo*, the red-headed boy, was easy. He was eight or nine, the center of attention except when the room emptied leaving the older man who shook his finger in the young man's face. They were both angry. A door opened and the dog bounded out barking. This could be a problem. He folded the paper and stuffed it in his pocket to scurry away.

He followed the moss covered rock wall to the edge of the property where the gray water lapped at the shore. He spit and pulled his stocking cap over his ears. The wind had calmed but he shivered. A few yachts sat cradled in their boatlifts, wrapped warm in their canvases, zippered tight. His nose ran yellow and gummy and he inhaled, spitting again. Turning, he narrowed his eyes, spying a hump-snarl of vines a short run into the woods. Curious, he limped over, discovering a grate and what appeared to be an overgrown tunnel behind it. He began tugging.

It was sealed tight, locked as if for centuries against curious hands like his. He wished for his machete. Close by, he heard a fox screech, stop and screech again, following in the meter of a metronome. Its call echoed across the water, circled back in the wind across the wide grass, and slammed up against the crumbling rock wall that ended in the iron grate.

He yanked harder at the thicket, and his bare hands, thorn-bit and chapped, were so cold that when he sucked his wounds to stop the bleeding he tasted the iron of his own blood but couldn't warm his stiff fingers. The fox was close, only a few hundred yards into the neighboring woods, perhaps guarding her kits. Earlier in the afternoon, when he scuttled down the overgrown trail at the compound edge he had seen her, red-haired and black-socked, not like the gray ones of El Salvador.

Now, he looked up. The winter sun hung low and a horizon seam sewn across the calm waters of the Chesapeake Bay barely distinguished the water from the sky. His gaze passed over the long shadows from the oak trees and he knew he hadn't been seen.

Was this an entrance to the compound? He could see the tunnel was partially collapsed. He would not find out today. He would tell Carlos of the grate and that it was rusted shut, tentacled with vines. Certainly his hands would tell the tale. He gave in, gave up and scrambled over the rocks wondering if Carlos would make him suffer for not finishing the job.

The rock wall ran the length of the property from the quiet street to the water. If he was going to meet Hector he needed to be quick. Digging his hand into his coat pocket he nudged the plastic grip of the Beretta till its nose touched the top of his thigh and he loped up the path, stopping to hide when he heard voices on the driveway of the big house.

He peered through a break in the rock wall. The red-haired woman stood without a coat at a door. Her body pleaded with the man who lifted the child into the back seat, hurriedly buckling his belt. The man drove quickly, the black bumper swung heavily on the driveway apron as its tires spun but then he abruptly jammed on the brakes and got out. He yanked open the back door and stared at the boy, yelling, "What now?" Under thought this man had no respect for his car or the child.

It made him angry to see a father treat a son so curtly. Reaching into his pocket Under felt the gun's cold metal barrel and was strangely comforted. He had never shot at a target, only into the air. He would have to practice. The father slammed the rear door and got back in the car. Under slipped into the treeline, walking out of town.

Hector was waiting a mile away past a road called Hels Half Acre. Under ran, a hitch and a stride, one good leg against one bad, his breathing growing heavy, his mouth open and a mist exhaling around his face. He wanted food and money and someday to be *segunda palabra*, a lieutenant, like Hector. Then he would sleep without one eye always open.

At the sound of tires he darted into the trees. He didn't turn to look, didn't want to meet any expectant eyes, didn't want to be identified. But as the car passed, he realized it was the one from the compound. The father must have forgotten something and gone back to the house. He was driving slowly now. Under's eyes met those of the red haired boy in the back seat, blue to blue, both a little astonished, searching for more. Then the car passed. He cursed, but calmed himself, knowing the father had not seen him.

Ahead, the road opened up to cut cornfields and the dusky light of winter sun. Rows of humped stalks sat frosted and brittle. Pumping in one great stride, then a shorter one, the pain of his shredded calf muscle and his mismatched hips intensified. He would not be caught again, would not endure the questions, the lockup, the deportation. He belonged to something bigger, powerful, connected. Soon he would have stature.

Reaching the edge of the woods, he saw the ridges of corn were dotted white, covered from edge to edge with what looked like clumps of snow as far as his eye could see, but there was no snow on the ground or on the road. He squinted. Some clumps fluttered and he realized they were snow geese, hundreds of them settled in among the chopped stalks. He remembered them gathering on the farms of El Salvador and figured this must be how they made their trip from the north. They eat from the fallow fields on their migration along the Atlantic Flyway to winter in the cornfields of El Salvador. So this is what we share, he thought, the trash bird that the golden eagle attacks for fun.

It was then he noticed the BMW parked some distance past the cornfield. The father emerged zipping up his leather jacket, walking toward him, his face constricted with anger. He was tall and elegant. Carefully, Under moved into the shadow of a tree and watched as the man treaded stealthily away from the car into the field. He moved through the nestled birds and a few rustled taking flight. As they ascended, the rest rose with them until the sky began to fill in an inverted V, their silver tipped wings and deep yellow legs standing out against their white plumage. Sucking his breath in a snap, Under watched as the man raised his outstretched arm pointing a black handgun with a silencer, taking aim and he heard the muffled pop, pop, pop as the birds dropped onto the cold field in growing red stains.

CHAPTER 4

The Castle Walls

*T*he redline Metro train was single tracking during the morning rush hour. Raising her eyes from the octagonal red tiles on the platform, Claire gazed at the sea of people brimming with purpose and importance. She never found out what caused the enormous crowds that swamped the platform or what slowed the trains to glacial speed. Everyone accepted it with a shrug. She fretted and retreated to the back of the crowd.

She heard people bellyache over the lack of transportation funding, or political influence that failed to keep the infrastructure up to speed. She was worn out from the grumbling that surfaced everywhere. Strangers commiserated about the stock market slide, the job losses, and the immigrants taking their opportunities. Eventually, someone wondered out loud if the trains were slowed by a terrorist attack but when no evacuation announcement came over the loudspeaker, a tired voice commented that they wouldn't be so lucky to get the day off. Claire avoided eye contact, not wanting to talk.

On that morning in early March, Claire was attempting a dry run on the subway, timing the journey to Wilcox and Stein at the Capitol Hill location and thought all the riders were jaded. Her thoughts drifted and she saw a warning in every little thing that happened no matter how insignificant: the sparrow caught inside the cavernous station and the lost child who cried for his mother. A man put his briefcase down and took two steps away. She nearly panicked.

The warning lights in the platform flashed in their unsynchronized way and she sniffed at her own temerity. Claire pushed her way onto the train and stood beneath a man's warm breath, her shoulder against his suit jacket, both of their hands grasping the vertical bar for balance. Compression in a silver tube at high speed. All faces knitted tight.

A garbled voice announced the next stop and she looked for the Metro Center sign. The smell of wet wool and warm bodies overcame her and she wondered how she could face the office and the minutia of computer files, the tracking of emails, the memorizing of client details and boardroom conversations. Her recovery had been slow and neither she nor her employer knew the length of the shadow that followed her every step. Her father had not offered her a job at Tosh, baffling her, but she accepted his silence.

She pushed through the crowd and up the escalator to the open air. She would go back to work soon and wouldn't ask for help. She didn't need a car. Sam rode the morning school bus and stayed late for an after-school program for kids whose parents worked long days. He rode the sports team bus with the big boys, sweaty and swearing about their latest win or loss. Sam was their mascot who gloried in their attention. No longer her little boy.

Two weeks later in mid-March, Claire returned to work.

The Best in Washington

Wilcox and Stein had smaller office space and fewer employees. After the bombing, only a very few decided they wanted to return to a job with people who had a shared memory of their trauma. The skeleton staff welcomed her with hugs. They were a private club. Afraid, she asked few questions but the answers were whispered anyway.

"You didn't know? Georgia lost some fingers on her right hand. How will she ever be able to run an office again?

"Jeanine's at home with her husband. She always sounded like a coffee grinder but now it's full-blown COPD. She said she wouldn't be alive if it weren't for you."

"Hampton quit. You know how he is. He came out of it fine. On the Board of the Survivors' Fund. Doing the round of talk shows; got a book advance. He'll be a multi-millionaire over this."

And the worst news.

"Terrible about Matt. Multiple surgeries. The string of lights carved him up and the conference table collapsed on him. Should've been an easy surgery but he died under anesthetic. A weak heart."

Albert Stein was running the practice, alone. "Wilcox's gone to his home in Coral Gables. He's had four grafts already. He has a plastic surgeon in Florida he trusts."

By dribs and drabs, the news filtered out in the workroom or lobby. She ran to her office and hid until she could compose herself. The few coworkers with visible disabilities qualified easily for payments from The Survivor Fund, the charitable arm that had collected hundreds of thousands of dollars to aid those wounded in the bombing. Too afraid to describe her invisible defects, Claire had trouble completing the application. Exasperated, she stalked out of her office, stopping in front of Hampton Reid's former secretary who was in charge of processing claims.

"Terry, do you have a minute?" Terry looked up and smiled slowly.

"Sure. Anything you want, Claire." Claire winced internally. She had always called her Ms. McIntosh.

"I was trying to fill out the paperwork for victim aid. They want you to describe the nature of your physical disability. I, uh, wondered if I should put down every detail or do they want something more general?" Anxiously, she seesawed from side to side and realized Terry noticed. She stood stock still.

"Details. You need details and evidence. Doctor's reports, tests you've had, diagnoses. The medications you're on and anything that's pending. It's pretty easy if you go through it page by page."

"I didn't know to what depth they want the information. So, I need to bring my medical files?"

"Yes. Most folks are applying because they have serious disabilities and they can't work full time. A few scars on your legs won't mean much."

She thought Terry's lip curled. Claire was stunned into silence. So that's what I present on the outside, she thought. I cover up so successfully.

Terry continued, "I can help you, but you know, it's based on the severity of the situation."

Claire scanned the woman's face, embarrassed that she had asked. She wandered away and as she shut the door to her office she crumpled to the floor heaving. Her last clear memory of that horrible day was staring at Matt from the doorway as the string of lights swung precipitously over his face. He had stared at her pleading with his eyes and she had run away.

To what? Her half life, mired in confusing emotions was threatening to expose her. Her analytical thinking, command of conversation, and supreme confidence that had come so easily before escaped her now. She wasn't productive and so far no one had noticed. Or maybe they had and didn't complain. She lived in constant fear of discovery. A woman with half a memory, and Matt was gone. Maybe it would have been better if they had traded places.

She filled Post-it notes in her miniscule handwriting to remember details. She printed out documents rather than reading them in the glare from her computer screen, hoping the tactile sensation of flipping the pages would help her remember the information. The words were like mist. In the quiet of her office, the events of that day interrupted, bubbling with images of smoke, heat, darkness and hands pulling at her. Her hair began to fall out in clumps.

By the end of March she sought out a psychiatrist, pictured in a *Washingtonian Magazine* article as one of the areas "Top Doctors."

"Ms. McIntosh," he said, "You need a good doctor to coordinate your care." He handed her a printout of names. "I'm referring you to specialists in neurology, pain management and hematology. You have Post Traumatic Stress Disorder. I would like you to come for therapy weekly." He looked at her over his reading glasses, his brow wrinkled in concern and explained that she might be overly sensitive to light and sound, or aphasic when tired or stressed. "Your short term memory will be a challenge. Play cards with your son. It will help you to remember strategy."

Claire never completed the paperwork for the Survivor Fund, but found comfort in the Xanax the doctor gave her.

Walking up Connecticut Avenue one clear spring day, the smell of botanicals drifted toward her. Impulsively, she swung open the door to the buzz of hair dryers and odor of nail polish and asked if anyone had time. An hour and a half later, she bounded out the door with her hair cut above her shoulders. This was all I needed, she thought amazed.

She got her blood tests when she remembered, misplaced her keys and phone often, and one day left her purse on the Metro. A Good Samaritan returned it in the mail, her money gone but the credit cards intact. In a real challenge to her budding skills, she let Carlotta, her cook and housekeeper, go. She and Sam ate out or ordered in their favorites like Nanny O'Brien's spicy Old Bay wings dipped in ranch dressing. But she gained some small measure of confidence by not relying on her dad's money.

Finances were easy, or so she thought. She kept a list of all her bills on her phone. She never looked at balances and blindly assumed there was enough money to cover whatever came her way. When her bank statement came in the mail, she worried briefly about expenses and then forgot. She had a fleeting concern that the marital investments had not been separated. She couldn't remember. On second thought, she wasn't sure what shares they had purchased. She needed to contact the attorney one last time but never found the desire.

The Yellow Brick Road

Claire leaned against the brass railing overlooking the Potomac River and the wide allée lined with young Sycamores. She tapped her toe behind her, enjoying the view. A full moon hung low, competing with shore torches and strings of yacht lights. She wasn't there for drinks or the views of the Kennedy Center, the Watergate, or the arched span of Memorial Bridge mirrored in the river lights.

She was there for Vance. She was on time. He never was. Her watch read nine-thirty and she gazed up at the sapphire blue night sky. She wished for a romance instead of a face-off but the attorney had told her there were no investments to split. Money was growing tight.

She had slugged two quick glasses of wine and girded herself for battle. The smell of a cigar wafted toward her. Vance. She saw him sitting on a promenade bench with Rebekah who apparently tolerated cigar smoke. Nauseous lovers. Deep in conversation, heads tilted toward each other, they weren't looking for Claire. Her hands constricted on the railing.

Vance loved the details of the divorce. This is mine, that's yours; carry your debt, I'll carry mine; I'll take the BMW and the roadster, you can have the Mercedes. Not this time. She would tell him her plan and leave.

It dawned on her that he was adept at pretension, a self-serving chameleon. He handled the household, the money and the investments. Growing suspicious she had once opened his credit card bill and found a zero balance but when she opened hers she owed thousands. When she questioned why the bank account was so low he said it was expensive to live in Chevy Chase, not to worry. The money came and went like the tides. Sweet acid rose in her throat.

Claire straightened her back and walked down the broad staircase to the bench where Vance and Rebekah sat beside the fountains, their hands nestled in her lap. As she approached he rose, smiling affably and walked to her, his arms outstretched. He didn't look like the same man. His dark hair was perfectly finger-combed and his face had changed. The mole on his cheek was missing. Was Rebekah better for him? She stared at him coldly. The smile died on his lips.

"Vance, I have to get back to Sam, so you need to listen and call your attorney tomorrow."

Ignoring her urgency, he cajoled. "Claire, you're looking particularly beautiful tonight. Your hair's shorter. I've never seen you with so many waves."

It was just like him to needle her over a flaw. Embarrassed, she fluffed her thinning hair nervously with one hand. "Stop it. We both know you don't care about my hair."

"Au contraire. I care about everything that affects you since we know it will affect me in the end."

"Fuck you, Vance. We're here about the house because that's affecting me."

"I'm hurt. One would think you don't relish talking to me. I brought Rebekah. Have a drink with us."

"Jesus, Vance. Don't take this the wrong way but why would I want to talk to the bitch who broke up my family? I barely want to talk to you."

"Stop," he whined and pursed his lips. "There's been enough hostility. We need to develop a working relationship if for no other reason than our son."

"We have a working relationship. It's been laid out very clearly." The Xanax and two glasses of wine loosened her tongue. "I've always wondered how long were you fucking her before I knew."

"My goodness, Claire. So negative. And jealous."

"Negative? That's a high bar! You're shooting her the juice in our marriage bed and I'm jealous?" Her chin came up in a challenge. "I could be so much more."

"You have been. Are you threatening me again? "

That was a warning shot. She couldn't calm herself and the wine heated her neck and ears. Impulsively, she added, "Yes. It's payback time."

"Be careful. There's evidence that you are incapable of raising our son now. Some mental issues, I hear." Casual words, a sardonic smile appeared.

"You wouldn't dare."

"You know me Claire. Of course I would."

She backed down, crossed her arms. "That's a two-way street. Your campaigning makes you an absentee father. Never mind your reputation as a punitive state's attorney. People call you the jailor behind your back."

She watched his practiced transformation as his face softened purposefully in a politician's smile. He hates to be disliked publicly much less reviled, she thought, even by me. He reached to put his arm around her shoulders but she shrugged him off, her eyes blazing.

"Don't touch me."

He set his shoulders and cocked his head questioningly. "Why are you like this? We have an agreement. Things are good with Sam. You said yourself that joint custody was working."

Don't bring up Sam. It wasn't about Sam. The house. Get to the house. Please God, do not let me screw this up more than I already have. She had arranged this meeting for one reason. She seethed with frustration, stage-whispering, "Happy? I'm talking about the house. What's happy about a tenants-in-common agreement that has no end date?" Her skin prickled on the nape of her neck. "I've waited for it to sell for over a year. You're forcing me to take further action."

Vance's face transformed to the wounded puppy dog. I won't be suckered again, she thought. From her peripheral vision, she noted others moving away.

In his best conciliatory voice, he said, "Claire, come now. You don't need to be so contentious. You know I have Sam's best interests at heart. The market is soft. We'll lose at least a million."

"I get it. There's a For Sale sign in the yard but no one ever shows the house." His eyes widened slightly and she waited for him to respond. "Yes, I called the realtor. She said you aren't making the house available." Her voice was strident. "You have no intention of selling it." Her finger rose and she stabbed at his chest. "I am going to force the sale with a judicial partition. Papers, your way, next week."

Vance blinked, a slight grimace played around his mouth. He leaned in and grabbed her elbow walking her toward the river's edge away from the crowd of partiers. Claire looked over her shoulder. Rebekah laid her cell phone down, crossing her leg and turning her head away. Claire looked up at him, his face contorted with rage. She wondered if he was going to throw her in the Potomac.

His voice was gritty. "You fucking bitch. We will wait until the market improves."

She yanked her elbow free. "I left seventeen months ago. The divorce has been final for five. It is what it is, Vance. The only person who has a loss is my father."

"No. This is what it is: your holier than thou father is directing everything from a distance. You tell him he lost it when he put it in our names. This is a fifty/fifty split. You're pissed because you can't assign fault and you never had a prenup." His facade had disappeared completely and his menacing face neared hers. Around his shoulder, Claire saw Rebekah slide down the bench the phone held up. Suddenly she wondered if she was being filmed. She fought for composure.

"I have the same credentials as you, Vance. I may have made mistakes in the past, but no more. You screwed me on our investments. Our financial manager says there's no cash. And now you're going nowhere selling the house." She was steady, calm, and determined. Narrowing her eyes, she faced him. "Get ready. When I see you in court, you'll have to demonstrate that you're actively selling the house, or you'll be making payments to me after I win a partition lawsuit."

Claire arrived home to find Sam still up and the babysitter talking on the phone in front of the TV. Sam's pajama shirt had a waterfall of Doritos crumbs down his front. He kissed his mom and she saw chocolate in his teeth. She looked at her watch and dismissed the sitter with three twenties which was probably too much but she didn't care. She took him to brush his teeth, tucked him in and read another chapter of the *Chronicles of Narnia*.

Wired but satisfied, she poured herself a glass of cheap Reisling and plopped down on the couch. She had gotten her message across but had not restrained her temper. What had that doctor said? Watch out for impulsiveness? Write out what you want to say ahead of time. She had done none of it. I've always been a planner, organized, a step-by-step person, she thought. She had to get out. Out of town. Out of her job. Out of her life.

The Contract

The kitchen was hot, gas flames flickering on the line of stoves and the cooks wiped sweat from their faces with kitchen towels. Standing alone in a corner removed from the action, Under watched a cockroach nudge about on a dark edge of the counter. He watched for a few seconds before he brought the heel of his hand down to crush it.

Through the back door, he saw workers bundled in their jackets, sitting on egg crates in the loading zone. They were Hispanic day laborers as he had been once, but now he was someone. Their aprons were smeared with grease, and they bantered about loudly as they ripped the leaves off cabbages that had been trucked in that afternoon. Bored, Under looked around the bustling kitchen. It was the dinner hour on a Saturday night at an upscale Penn Quarter eatery in D.C. and good cover for the gang.

He lurked outside the office waiting for Hector. Through the glass he could see Carlos, attentive, respectful, his fingers pyramided in front of his face. He nodded to a man whose back was to the door. This dark-haired American spoke with his hands, waving them like a woman and wore expensive cuff links. Hector had called him a "client" and told Under to make himself scarce. Probably, Under thought, he wanted something from Carlos, something he wouldn't do himself. It was the way of the world to make money so you could pay peons to do what you found distasteful. He would do the white man's work until, one day, he would be like Hector.

The door opened a crack and he stepped back into the shadow of the storage room. He couldn't see the white man's face but he would remember the falsetto voice.

".....as soon as the deposit is made. We have the information we need," said Carlos.

"There can be no mistakes," said the white man.

"You ask for excellence, you get excellence."

"And the boy won't be hurt. Guaranteed?"

"Of course. Rest assured, my friend."

Hector escorted the man in the suit out the back door and returned. As he reentered the office, Carlos' voice came from inside, "Stupid Americano. Paid a religious fanatic to make bombs."

Under frowned, curious. Carlos did not deal in messy bombs and he certainly wasn't religious. He was a perfectionist: tidy about his dress, his manners, his deference to his employees. He never failed in his contracts. But he was a killer.

CHAPTER 5

Seals, Sea Otters and Tattoos

A Saturday morning in early May broke clear and warm. Over breakfast, Claire and Sam planned a bike ride around the corner to the National Zoo. The phone rang as Claire cleared the table. Only two types of calls came on the landline, telemarketers and Vance.

"I'll get it Mom."

Claire turned down the TV and cocked her ear to catch Sam's lilting voice describe the seal he had named Gabby. The seal delighted them both, clapping its fins and barking before a dive in the clear water. Sam returned from the living room.

"Dad's coming to my soccer game Wednesday. He's taking off from work."

Claire closed the dishwasher. "Does he know where it is?"

"Guess so. I told him about the seals and he wants to see Gabby too. Maybe we could go together sometime?"

"Or maybe I'll see him at the soccer game," she answered. Claire ached seeing Sam's blue eyes crinkle up in hope. Vance never went to a game. Or to the school. Why would he set false expectations? She wondered if he wanted to make good on his promise to take Sam away from her.

She insisted that they organize the apartment before they left, and Sam whirled around picking up toys and dirty clothes, talking like a magpie while Claire pondered Vance's promises. There was no answer to the questions and she decided not to let these thoughts ruin her day. The job done, she locked the door and they went to the basement to get their bikes out of storage. The sun was high in the sky as they pedaled the short distance to the zoo entrance.

Sam sped through the broad, Oz-like gates with Claire close behind. They hurried over to see the pandas, black and white puzzle pieces hiding in the vegetation, chewing on bamboo lollipops. They found a bike stand and decided to walk the paths. Families floated around, pushing strollers or minding toddlers. The smell of popcorn at the Panda Café lured them close. Claire bought boxes and lemonades but Sam pushed his into her arms and skipped the steep walk down to the sea lions and seals.

"Stay where I can see you." Claire walked slowly absorbing the warmth. The sun's rays dappled through the trees, fooling her vision. The path zigzagged against a stone retaining wall on one side and an iron railing bordered by dark evergreens on the other. Sam broke out running.

"Hey Sam, slow down," she called but he was fired by anticipation. He shouted back, "It's okay, Mom. I gotta go see Gabby!"

She hurried around the corner and pulled up sharply. Out of her sight for thirty seconds and Sam was surrounded by a group of rowdy Hispanic men in front of the seal pool. They were in their mid-twenties maybe older. A cluster of baggy jeans and baby blue wife beater T-shirts almost hid her son. She was horrified at the sight of one man, older than the rest, his broad cheek tooled with two long-nailed fingers. He grinned at her as he held his hand in the air for Sam to high-five. Sleeves of tattoos covered his naked arms in red and black but she couldn't read them in the blinding light. It dawned on Claire that these men were gang members. She caught her breath and hurried into their midst to gather her baby.

"Hola. Hola. Buen dia. Perdoné mi," she said nodding and smiling. No one else was around. To the left, the path led to a parking lot. Uphill to the right, the path was a blind corner.

"Lady, you have funny boy."

Sam held his arms in the air, striking his wrists together and barking like a seal, "Arrf-arrf, arrf-arrf." Claire's smile faded as one man raised his cell phone and snapped a picture of Sam.

She dropped the popcorn boxes, white kernels spilled at their feet. Her protective juices flowed and she called out, "Sam!" He turned to look at her and another man bent down clicking his phone in a full, animated portrait of her son. Alarmed, she wrapped Sam in her arms holding the lemonade across his chest. She turned him away, whispering in his ear, "You forget the rules Sam." Hearing voices around the corner, she walked him in that direction. Claire glanced over her shoulder, satisfied that they were in a safe zone as she watched the cluster of men move back up the path talking cheerily. One waved back to her.

"Mom, they were talking to me about Gabby the Seal."

She fairly screeched, "They knew her name was Gabby?"

"Yeah. Isn't that awesome? My name for her has caught on with everybody."

She squinted at him. One minute he was so grown up and the next a mere innocent. There was no possible way those men could have known Sam's name for the seal. "Listen, you weren't obeying the rules. You could have been in trouble, Sam."

"You were right behind me. They're nice guys."

"I'm sure they are. But the rule is you stay in my sight." Sam's brows knitted in confusion or sudden fear. Good, she thought. You need to be a little afraid in this world. He had shouted that he had to see Gabby. But weren't they too far from the seal pool for him to be heard?

"They weren't out to get you, honey, but you need to stay in my sight. What are the other rules, Sam?"

"Don't talk to strangers. Don't take presents from strangers. Keep a distance. Yell, 'I don't know you,' if someone touches me," he rolled out dutifully. "I'm sorry."

"I love you, Sam, but you have to listen to me. Don't do it again."

———

Deaf in One Eye, Blind in One Ear

"Why didn't you ask them why they were taking pictures?" asked Naomi. The women lolled on the couches in Claire's living room the following weekend, ready to watch Saturday Night Live. Each held a pint of ice cream. It had been an early evening at the Birchmere listening to Jump Blues, New Orleans style. As Georgetown alumnae, they had dropped their weekday suits for torn, bleached jeans and going-out blouses. They dangled bare feet, their makeup was smudged and their hair tangled. They were tipsy.

"'Cause I wanted to get us out of there. Why take a picture of a kid you don't know?" asked Claire.

"The kid's doing something unbelievably cute or stupid. Then you go post it on Facebook or You Tube," responded Britt, wiping ice cream from her ample chest. "And hope the parents don't sue you."

"Sam has that sealed up. Get it?" Naomi said, slapping her knee. Britt threw a chip at her. "Don't worry," said Naomi, tossing it in her mouth.

"They looked like they might be gang members. Everything worries me these days," said Claire.

"Oh, you mean you realize it? I didn't want to tell you but your two best friends are a little worn out listening to your whining," said Britt.

"Like I haven't listened to *you* enough over the years," said Claire faking hurt, a palm to her heart. Then, tipping her head side to side imitating Britt, " 'Jason is so good in bed but he doesn't make enough money.' Or, let's see: 'I wanna go to Paris but Ben has to help his parents move into assisted living.'" She accused her friend, "At least my worries have been real."

"Yeah, but you're talking about Britt," said Naomi.

"You're just jealous you don't have my luck in men," said Britt, flipping her long legs over the chair's arm and nestling in. "I'm not ever giving you any spicy news again. And, I don't want to have kids. It's too much responsibility."

"I'm going to have kids. Two. I'm finding me a handsome black man who loves the blues and adores me," said Naomi.

"How's that going these days, Nome?" asked Claire.

"I'm out with you on a Saturday night. That's how it's going."

"Not for lack of trying," said Britt. "You've been dating like it's a job. She's wearing out her Black Christian and Match accounts. Goes for coffee at Starbucks with one, has lunch at Cosi with another and dinner with somebody else. It's a miracle you're not 200 pounds."

"It's called good genes and the gym. I just can't find a man who's interested in anything but his career. Beat it to death. I may have to go home and find a keeper on the coast," said Naomi.

"You wouldn't dare—not after toiling all these years to get your J.D. and a good job. You'd live in chicken country?" asked Claire throwing the empty pint of Belgian Chocolate onto the coffee table with disgust. She stood before her friend with her hands on her hips.

"No, I'm just talking," said Naomi licking her spoon. "But seriously, I miss it sometimes. Lower slower Delaware. There's not much in the way of educational opportunities and you can't find a decent job. But they're good people. There's respect. And for God's sake, you sure don't worry about anthrax or Metro. Or politics. The biggest worry is the price of broilers and…maybe flooding."

"Sounds wonderful," said Claire as she slumped back into her chair.

Britt laughed and drummed her feet on the chair. "That's it. The princess wants to move to the country and rub elbows with the common folk. Gonna give up her Vineyard vacations and skiing in the Rockies. You'd be better off getting daddy to build you a farm with some sheep to tend so you can play Marie Antoinette. I'll come over and drink a few French 75's with you."

"Oh, zip it Britt. I need a new job."

They fell silent, watching Amy Poehler looking like a young Hillary Clinton tell the audience that she would be a sore loser and her supporters were racist. Britt and Naomi roared with laughter. Lost in thought, Claire stared solemnly at the TV.

She got up and cleared the spent ice cream cartons taking them into her tiny kitchen. She missed Sam and wished he were curled up in his bed so she could sneak a peak at him. Suddenly, she was surprised to see both her friends standing in the doorway looking at her.

"What?"

"We're going to Ocean City next weekend. Naomi has a condo lined up and there's room for three. We can do some sunning and Seacrets. It'll be fun. How about it?" asked Britt.

"That's really nice you guys, but I have Sam next weekend," said Claire.

"Oh, come on. Trade weekends with Vance for once. He'd like to have two weekends off in a row. Ask him."

"I can't do that on such short notice. The schedule's set in stone. You don't understand."

"Sure we do. We also get it that you're shriveling up socially," said Naomi.

Claire looked back and forth between her friends. She was cornered, yet the idea of beach fun spun out before her. It would be like old times spending a weekend with her college girls, before Vance, before Sam. She had only been to Ocean City once when she was a kid. The crusty boardwalk on bare feet, the Ferris wheel swinging wide over the ocean and those french fries stacked upright in a cardboard cup, doused with vinegar and salt. All those sunburned bodies and beer bellies. Firemen, high schoolers gone berserk and cotton candy. Another world. She wanted to go.

Double Vision

Another margarita and the transformation began. Hairdryers, curling irons and makeup spilled onto the bathroom counter as Naomi, Claire and Britt tarted up before the mirror, twisting and turning in their thongs and push-up bras. Sandwiched between her two longtime friends, friends who had stood by her in divorce, the hospital and her recuperation, Claire felt cherished. Under the garish makeup lights, Britt was a confident, fleshy blonde; the more refined Naomi was taut, athletic and brown. Claire was amazed that she didn't feel more self-conscious.

The wonders of mixing pills and alcohol. She had gained five pounds so her hips bones no longer protruded but she was still unnaturally flat like a prepubescent teen. Fair skinned, freckles speckled on her chest, upper arms, and nose, she thought she looked as if she had been poured out of a milk jug. Evaluating the woman in the mirror, she decided her eyes still took up too much of her face, like an animé cartoon.

She leaned in closer and pretended to check her teeth, watching as her reflection split in two. She needed to slow this show down. She would never make it through the night if she kept pace drinking with her friends. She wanted the security of home and Sam. Maybe it was better for her to stay in and watch movies alone.

Britt slipped on the requisite little black dress and sealed her sizzle with bright red nail polish. She flashed the hair dryer back and forth over her nails. Claire's ears sang with an uncomfortable vibration.

"You know, maybe I'll just stay here tonight," she said in all casualness, laying the curling iron down like a gunslinger conceding the fight before it began.

Naomi and Britt froze, staring at her in the mirror.

"No you don't, girl. You coming with us." Camping, Naomi threw her hip out and waved her finger back and forth. "You not slipping out of this show. You're the whole reason for the mission."

Claire crossed her eyes at her.

Britt grabbed Claire's dress and tossed it to her. "Put that on."

Laughing at their bossiness, Claire stepped into the shiny copper bandeau that left her shoulders bare and exposed her long legs. She glanced at her image. Deflated by the whole process and weak with drink, she sank down on a bench in the bathroom.

"I can't do this. It's just so alien. I'm worried about Sam. I'm just not ready. This is different from Friday night happy hour with the office. It's–predatory."

"It's just like Friday night happy hour. Get up before I slap you silly," said Britt.

"You don't understand...."

Britt, indignant and forceful, said "I'm not listening to this garbage. You have to do this *for me*! You don't understand how worried I've been about you for the past year. If you don't owe this to yourself, then you owe it to me. If you aren't having fun by the time we watch the sunset, we'll come home. Right Nome?"

Naomi nodded, pulled Claire off the bench, and twirled her around to zipper her dress.

"Jeez. All right. Sor-ry." She had been so oblivious. Living in a constant state of self-absorption, Claire never thought that her worries were spilling over onto her friends. She had no energy to fight them.

By seven, Britt and Naomi had established their beachhead on the last two seats at Gallagher's bar and Claire stood next to them, reeling in the bar noise. Ordering a sparkling water and lime against Britt's fourth margarita, she whispered to Naomi, "Are we both watching her? 'Cause I've already had too much."

"It may take two of us." They both eyed their friend with suspicion. Claire plowed her hand into a dish of Goldfish, barely chewing before swallowing. She wiped her lips with the back of her hand and hit them again.

The bartender, swamped with requests, brought back the drinks and shouted, "Want to start a tab?"

"Sure. We're just waiting for our table."

"Name?"

"What?" shouted Claire forgetting the bar conventions. The bartender leaned closer to her. The only black man in the place, his green eyes stood out against his dark brown skin and shoulder-length dreadlocks. He grinned slightly. She reached for her purse but then realized he had asked for her name not her money. Feeling goofy, she thought he was summing the tab mentally when he said, "My eyes are prettier than yours. What name do you want this under, Red?"

She paused and realized the man was flirting with her. "Ya think? Well I bet yours are contacts. Put it under Claire."

"Okay, Claire. Can I get you and your friends anything else?"

Britt was toying with two men, business types in expensive white shirts, open at the neck. Very tanned. Claire wondered if they had just returned from the Caribbean. They each had an IPA brew in hand, and one chatted intently with Britt while the other eyed Naomi from a distance. She looked out over the bayside panorama and wondered where the sunset pier was. Claire turned to the bartender. He had moved on to the next customer and her question died on her lips.

"Claire, honey, I want to introduce you. This is Demitri and this is Cage."

Britt had one hand out playing door number one and door number two. Both men wore cursory smiles.

"Hi, I'm Claire. Nice to meet you both." Something about them irritated her. It wasn't the gold bracelet on the Greek or Cage's oily black hair. They looked like runway models, just more muscular. No, it was their eyes. They were hard, distant, as if they were waiting for something. Vance's eyes.

Naomi shouted out to a man she knew and strode across the room. Claire waved her long white arm. My God, she thought, don't leave me here alone. The men turned away from her and leered at Britt. It was time to order a drink. She slapped her hand across the bar in frustration and the bartender glanced her way.

"Want a real drink now?" he asked.

"Why do I feel like I've been here before?" she asked with a slight slur.

He glanced at her friends and said in a deep baritone, "Woman, them boys don't know what good lookin' is 'cause I'm staring right at her."

She was a sucker for an easy, crooked smile like his. He laid an open hand near hers. "How 'bout I fix you a special drink?" he asked.

Leaning over she said, "That's what I'm saying! I'm in Ocean City for the second time in my life. I should enjoy myself, right?"

"Yes ma'am. And under my tutelage you will have a good time tonight," he answered. "Your first time to Gallagher's? In about an hour here we're gonna show you what a real sunset is."

"Yeah, I heard this is the place to come." He turned his back to fix her drink and Claire took in his broad shoulders and fighter arms encased in a skintight polo shirt. She felt a flip in her tummy. Nice guy. Too bad he's a bartender. He'll be busy all night.

He set a goblet before her. "Beautiful drink for a beautiful woman," he said.

It was a perfect shade of deep burnt orange. "Pretty! It can't possibly taste as good as it looks," she said.

"That's what I'm thinking," he answered, staring straight in her eyes. Claire blushed and he laughed softly, clearly disarmed. "Tell you what," he said, "I get off in a couple of hours. Why don't you let me take you up to Northside Park for a walk?" he asked.

Claire sputtered on her first sip, "We're supposed to eat dinner. I don't think that would work out time-wise." She smiled.

The red lights flashed on the dinner pager. She wondered what his hands would feel like pressed against her back. I'm drunk, she thought and asked, "What's the name of the drink in case I want another?"

"It's called a Redhead. On me. Enjoy your dinner, okay?"

Claire grinned and turning toward her girlfriends was disappointed to find them negotiating a larger table to include the Caribbean Boys. Goddammit, I'll be the fifth wheel, she thought. The walk in the park sounded more enticing.

They were escorted to a round table near the large windows. Disappointed, Claire found herself seated with her back to the view facing the rest of the dining room. The waitress asked for her drink order and she replied, "Oh, I think he called it a Redhead."

The waitress laughed. "Actually, that's a Redheaded Slut."

Britt thumped her hand on the table and shouted, "Ha, like that would ever happen."

"I'll just have a Pellegrino, thanks." She eyed Britt, thinking she'd like to spill her drink right down her plunging cleavage.

The sun lowered in the sky, the background music stopped, and the faces in the room grew expectant. A snare drum beat softly accompanied by a flute playing a whimsical melody that repeated like rushing waves on sand. "Here it is," said Naomi.

"Listen, it'll get louder," Claire heard from another table. The drum continued its march and heads began to bob. Naomi hummed. The strain of notes became more insistent, adding a clarinet, a saxophone and piccolo to the cello and violin. Fingers drummed on tables and Claire recognized Ravel's "Bolero."

Fiery oranges splashed across the sky and melted into the room as the music built. Couples danced and swayed. Claire looked over her shoulder at the bright orb slipping under the blackened waters of the bay and she wished for the strength of a man's arm wrapped around her, his warm breath upon her neck. The night exuded sex and she never felt more alone.

Britt sobered up as dinner progressed, but Claire thought she hadn't heard the end of her friend's penchant for embarrassing her. As she expected, Britt morphed from brusque party animal to coquette. Dinner plates were cleared.

"Why don't we head over to Seacrets? I have a limo waiting out front," said Demitri.

"Perfect. They have lots of dance floors," answered Britt. Naomi shot looks at Claire, who was growing increasingly sleepy, and propped her chin on her fist. Distantly she heard Dimitri say, "The night's on me." Following her friends, Claire dragged herself across the dining room, wishing for bed.

As the group passed the bartender Claire noticed him watching with a deep frown on his face. She waved goodbye and he saluted with two fingers, beckoning her over. She slipped to the end of the bar and his warm hand touched her bare arm giving her a tingle. He whispered in her ear, "Be careful."

"Claire, c'mon," yelled Britt from the door, stamping her foot.

She ignored her. "Why? What's wrong?" she asked the bartender.

"Lose them. Trust me, I know what I'm talking about."

Claire nodded and lingered near the door as the bartender eye's followed her. She didn't think this was a game he was playing. He was serious.

Outside, she walked across the warm pavement between two lines of cars. A chauffeur leaned against the front grill of a limo. Claire caught up with Naomi and tapped her lightly on the back. "Nome, what are we doing?" she asked. Britt continued on between the two men.

"I don't want to go out with these dudes either. They got bad shit written all over them. That Demitri guy was bragging about his connections in Costa Rica. What the fuck is that about? "

"No kidding. The bartender just warned me."

"Really? Yeah, you saw him taking calls on his cell like this is New Jack City."

"Well, we better move fast or Britt will be in that limo."

The cool salt air had cleared Claire's head but the food sat heavily in her gut. Pushing herself, she jogged over to Britt and laid a hand on her elbow. "Oh hey, we've had a great time. I hate to do this but we have to get home now."

"Booyah! There you go. The redhead's going to spoil it all," replied Cage as if he had been waiting all night to make this prediction.

Demitri stood stock still between the rows of cars and stared squarely at Claire, the wind riffling his hair. "It's early yet. Why don't we take you back to our condo? I'm sure we could find something to do after a drink on the balcony."

"No question you could find something to do but it's not something we want," Claire responded sharply. Britt was moving her hips against Demitri's crotch in a rhythmic sway to the music that filtered over from the pier proving her wrong. His arm circled her back, his hand massaging her ass.

He answered by bending Britt backward. She slumped like a rag-doll in his arm and he kissed her forcefully, looking up at Claire like a smug conqueror. Straightening with great assuredness, he said to Britt, "It seems you're going to disappear. I have work to do tonight so I'll see you tomorrow. We'll go for a cruise on my boat. You too, Red, if you can get rid of the goody-two-shoes act."

To Claire's relief, Naomi pushed into the group and spoke up, "You guys have a great time tonight. Thanks for dinner but we're outta here." She bent to pick up Britt's purse from the ground, and the women dragged her along.

Britt pulled back and sniveled at them, "I wanna stay. Let's invite them over."

Demitri answered, "Tomorrow. Get rid of the cockblock bitches though."

"Hey," said Claire. "No need to insult." Naomi and Claire dragged their friend to the entrance of the restaurant and huddled under the portico in the darkness while Naomi called a cab.

Britt protested, "You ruined my night. He's got a cigarette boat. We have to go tomorrow."

"Yeah. Well, you're plastered and I'm not taking care of you all weekend," said Claire as she yanked Britt's bra strap over her shoulder. They heard police sirens that clipped off, one after another, "whup, whup, whup." Raising her eyes, Claire saw blue and red lights stroking the darkness and she craned her neck to see if there had been an accident. "Oh great, now we'll never get out of the parking lot."

"Yes, we will. I told the cab to meet us at Dumser's Ice Cream. We can walk over there."

"No ice cream. No walking," said Britt. "I'm going back to the condo and have a margarita."

"God, Britt. Have you ever thought you're too old to behave like this? Your liver probably looks like Swiss cheese by now," said Naomi.

"Oh shut up."

"You ladies dodged a bullet." A deep baritone voice came from the darkness behind them. The bartender leaned against the entrance railing holding a cell phone in his hand. Those bright white teeth gleamed in his crooked smile. He moved into the light and said quietly, "It's a drug bust. Your gentlemen friends who bought you dinner are being arrested."

The night ended with Naomi and Claire watching their friend descend into a stupor on the balcony, first sucking down margaritas, then a six pack of beer. When the glow of a cigarette fell from her lips as she yammered away on her cell, Claire quickly pushed open the glass door to dust the live ash from her lap. The ocean air immediately chilled Claire, but Britt seemed immune to the cold and angrily grabbed at her cigarettes.

Shortly after 9:00 in the morning, Naomi's father picked her up and offered to return for Claire at lunch. They didn't invite Britt, but it wouldn't have mattered as she lay sprawled asleep on the bed. Claire squeezed toothpaste on her brush and bent over the sink. A muffled cough came from behind her. Britt stumbled into the bathroom and sat down to pee. She leaned against the sink and groaned. "Oh my God. Why did you let me drink so much? I've got to sober up before we go boating."

Claire spit into the sink. "They got arrested last night. They aren't going out on any boat today."

"What do you know?" She trained her bloodshot eyes on Claire. "Demitri texted me. They got released. It was a mistake."

"You aren't still going?"

"Of course I am. Maalox and makeup. I'll be fine."

"You're on your own Britt. I'm going over to Naomi's house to see her parents."

"You're what? Na-uh. You have to come with me. I need backup."

"No," Claire said patiently as if speaking to a stubborn toddler. "I'm not in for your escapades. It was okay in college. I figured once we had jobs, you'd eventually settle down. It's been six years. I'm not babysitting you anymore. Go by yourself or don't go."

Britt flushed the toilet and tossed her mussed hair as she swept by Claire and knocked her into the sink. "Whatever. You were never really my friend. I wasted time trying to show you how the real world lives. Nobody likes you, Claire. You're a snob and a bitch and you think you're better than everybody. Go fuck yourself." Britt stormed into the bedroom, slamming the door on her way.

Claire carefully packed her overnight bag, taking comfort in the order of the little pockets and straps, smoothing the shiny cloth of her dress and thinking the next time she wore it would be for a man who could appreciate her. She left the case by the front door and went for a walk on the beach.

The ocean waves lapped gently on the shore but the water was freezing and her feet sunk deep in the soft sand as she stood glued to one spot her eyes on the horizon. Her thoughts bombarded her tearing away at her fragile confidence. She wasn't a bitch, maybe a bit of a snob but how could she be anything else? Did she need to apologize for her upbringing? Fuck that. Britt was a drunk just like her mother and now Claire was mourning the loss of a friendship she had long ago outgrown. What was important? Sam, her dad, and living her life with happiness when she could find it. It certainly wasn't guaranteed. She trudged back to the condo determined to enjoy the rest of her weekend. She opened the door to find Britt gone and Naomi and her dad, Albert Gleason, waiting.

Cooky

Down a narrow country road, Naomi's family home sat amidst fields of early soy. A chicken house loomed in a near field. Her mother, Lydia Gleason, hugged Claire in welcome. Once they had chatted about the rains and the price of broilers, Albert left to tend his asparagus patch. The women sat in the kitchen, eating tuna sandwiches. Claire thumbed some real estate flyers and asked if they were planning on moving.

"No, Albert's a realtor but lately he spends more time evenings playing in his band."

"What fun," Claire answered, smiling.

"It's a living, girl. This isn't a picnic around here." Mrs. Gleason sighed and wiped some crumbs from the table into her hand. "We have chickens, I grow vegetables for our roadside stand and keep the books for a pet store." Then she added, "Albert's the only black realtor on the beach."

Claire followed her wrinkled hand to the center of the table where a ceramic cookie jar of a portly black chef sat. His pink lips were fattened and the whites of his eyes fearful in an "Aww, Lordy," expectation of a hand grabbing his poofy hat. Across his chest read his name, "Cooky." Claire felt as if she were in another world, like the home Franny and Gus might have in retirement.

Lydia saw Claire studying the cookie jar and asked, "You want one? They're chocolate chip, homemade."

"Oh, no thanks. I was just thinking that must be pretty old."

"The cookie jar? 1940s. Albert and I collect black memorabilia to remind us how far we've come. And to keep it out of the hands of white folk who aren't as nice as us."

"It's so disturbing. *Like Little Black Sambo* who was Indian not American. And that all blew up when the world became politically correct. I had never seen black collections until I took an African American History class."

Naomi put her sandwich down. "That's where we met, remember—Dr. Burton's class."

Claire brightened, smiling at Naomi, "Right! And you said that today Sambo would be called Little Black GT."

"GT like in the car, going fast?" asked Lydia, confused.

"Gay and Trans," answered Naomi.

Lydia snorted. "Well, you girls live in the city. We don't see that here. Mostly our good black men in chicken country are marrying fat white women."

"Mom, how can you be so oblivious? What about Rehoboth? It's not like there aren't plenty gays, trans and fat tourists of every color among the D.C runaways. You gotta feel the love."

"I don't have to love everything. You best take your own advice. Look at you. So smart you can't find a man."

Naomi rolled her eyes so Claire piped up in defense of her friend. "It is tougher to find a decent guy in D.C. Everybody's so opinionated and stuck-up."

Lydia softened toward her daughter. "Well, guess who's back in town?" she asked.

"Do we have to play this game every time I come home?"

Claire reached for Cooky and was astonished to find under the chef's hat that his hair was blond. It really was blackface. Deflated, she pulled back and listened.

"DeWayne is visiting his mom this weekend. He's back from Sudan. Going to work in the U.N. liaison office in New York."

"Of Doctor's Without Borders? He doesn't want to do field work anymore?"

"They need someone with first-hand knowledge. He asked about you. They're looking for a staff lawyer."

Naomi grew quiet. She pushed her half-eaten sandwich away and folded her hands on the table. "Really?" she asked and pressed her lips together.

Between bites, Claire asked, "May I ask who DeWayne is?"

"My high school sweetheart. He went to Hopkins. We kept it up for a year but it was too hard. He left to do his residency at Mount Sinai in New York. Next thing I knew, he emailed me from Kassala every once in a while. Awful situation. Next to Eritria."

"He's in New York now? What an opportunity. You should reconnect."

"Hold on," said Lydia. "I got another one for you. Odessa Solomon told me that local guy, Pembroke, is looking for an immigration lawyer right here in the County Seat."

"Mom. Get real." Naomi shut her eyes and weighed upraised palms as if she were the Blind Lady Justice. "New York or Georgetown, Delaware? Hmmm. That's tough."

"I'm speculating. You could be close to your mom and dad," said Lydia.

Claire dusted her chest of crumbs and spoke to the cookie jar black man. "Well how 'bout I move to Delaware for the immigration job and you and me become an item?"

Lydia looked at her in surprise.

"Well, that would be something different for mom to gossip about. The fat black man and the skinny white girl," said Naomi.

The Initiation

The door shut behind him and he scanned the room. It stunk of alcohol and sex and something else—blood. A young girl lay naked on her side on the floor, her wrists tied to the bed leg and her long black hair strung across her bruised and swollen face. She moaned softly, "Por favor, leave me."

He kept his silence and looked around. Red plastic cups spilled their contents on every surface and the sole sheet was torn from the bed like a Roman curtain in those 1950s faded color movies he had seen as a child. A tray on the dresser held a plastic spoon, a lighter and gelatin capsules, broken open spilling their white magic. A half-used syringe sat next to it. I won't be her thirteen, he thought. It may be an honor to them but it's an insult to me. It was her choice to be sexed in. She could have taken a beating. Only 13 seconds. I survived.

She already had twelve men. Taking in the whole of her body, Under was repulsed. She had done enough and so had the rest who carried on in the next room. In the end, they wouldn't know anyway. They were too drunk, too high and too loco.

They had called her Lolita but he knew her as Dolores. In Spanish her name was short for the Virgin Mary of the Sorrows, Virgen María de los Dolores. Lola, Lila, Lolita. Whatever, she would not remember her given name after tonight. Like him, another who had lost the name a mother had given in baptism and God had blessed, she would be nothing to anyone. Once, she had been a thirteen-year-old Venus; now she was theirs.

He bent to pick her up and untied her first. Her moans tore at him so he shushed her and placed her gently on the bed. He took a corner of the sheet and dipped it in a cup of water wiping her face, legs and feet. He dared not touch anything else. She eyed him with suspicion and asked him why.

"You have done your thirteen. You do not need me."

In her little girl voice, she said, "You don't want me? I be ardienté. Watch." To his horror she writhed across the bed in a childish imitation of a sex slave. His feelings must have shown on his face for she hurled at him, "Maricón. Faggot."

She grew louder and he panicked but said nothing. Coldly, the back of his hand came across her jaw and she fell against the bed, moaning again, her eyes rolling back in her head. Quickly, he found the syringe, tied off her upper arm and tapped the vein till it popped. He pushed the needle in giving her dreams and him salvation. But some splinter of her consciousness must have been aware for she raised up and spat at him loudly, "Beast, beast." These last two words took everything from her and she collapsed.

He whipped his belt out and tied one wrist to the headboard and pulled the rope to tie off an ankle. The doorknob jiggled and there was banging and shouting. He twisted the sheet around her other leg and unzipped himself just as the door exploded and the real beasts stormed in. He was breathless from hurrying and panted slightly but did not speak. They would not hear the tremble in his voice. They flooded the room, yelling, pushing, and stood around the foot of the bed. They looked from Lolita to Under and back again. Guttural laughter broke from the group and congratulations were given. They slapped him on the back and pushed him out the door. He did not look back at the little Venus. He left the quiet behind him and there were no worries. He was her number thirteen.

—————

CHAPTER 6

Will Someone Please Tell Me?

*J*une broke with the news that Pakistani soldiers had been killed in an American airstrike on the Taliban. Congress issued a hue and cry about mistakes and members called for increased defense spending. In short order Wilcox and Stein, in a show of comeback power, increased their lobbyists on staff. Claire became the liaison for Lockheed Martin drone research. In the months after the explosion, she knew her memory had improved although she couldn't place faces with names. She spent hours memorizing everything about the fledgling Transformer TX program, the ARES design concept and the "quick, quiet and quality" mantra of Lockheed Martin's Skunk Works.

She had little time to spend with Sam. The school year drew to a close and she almost missed his third grade celebration. Belatedly, it occurred to her that she should check if Franny would watch Sam at Tred Avon for three weeks until summer camp began after the Fourth of July weekend. Franny had delighted in babysitting the previous summer and Claire expected it wouldn't be a problem.

She called late on a Friday night. Louisa answered and Claire was met with silence on the other end of the phone. Louisa's hand covered the mouthpiece and Claire listened closely to a furious but unintelligible interchange. When her father finally came to the phone, his voice was gravelly and worn. He explained that they were too busy in Washington to have Sam at Tred Avon House but said distantly that they would be in touch soon to see them both.

Stunned, Claire asked, "Daddy, what am I going to do?" She realized a seismic shift had occurred in her relationship with her father.

"What did I just say? We need Franny and Gus here in town. Not everybody says how high when you say jump."

He was angry, or maybe annoyed, but now, so was she. And a little panicked. "But it's only three weeks. I guess I can find daycare for him. I thought..."

"Claire, grow up. Call Carlotta. What would you do if I wasn't here?"

"I guess I'm going to find out." This was a little snippy but she felt as if he should've told her or had Franny call. How was she to know?

"It's hard being an adult, isn't it?" Harsh words from her father. He had been avoiding her. They hadn't talked much; a phone call here and there but her dad always seemed preoccupied. She said goodbye and laid her cell gently on her nightstand. He was right, she should have asked. The next morning she called Carlotta, who was grateful for the work. After the Fourth of July, which they always spent at the river house, Sam would rev up for summer day camp. Carlotta would meet Sam's bus in the afternoon and watch him till Claire arrived from work.

They left D.C. in a hurry late Thursday evening the weekend of the Fourth and met a crush of cars before the Bay Bridge. The great Washington Exodus, she thought. Claire watched the sunset in her rear-view mirror as Sam dozed beside her. The waters turned salmon pink, glimmering in the heat. An endless two hours passed before they turned on Route 333 South and blackness closed around them on the empty road. She fumbled for the window levers on her newly purchased Mini Cooper. Try as she might to learn the quirky dashboard on the used car, she struggled to remember little things like how to open the windows. The sound of crickets sang through the car. She had not called ahead and fumbled for her cell.

Stirring awake, Sam grabbed it from her hand in alarm, saying, "Give me that, Mom. No calls or texts in Maryland."

"You call. Hit number three." Sam cleared the password but couldn't get into Contacts. "Never mind, Coppertop. They'll be expecting us." But a needle of worry struck her. Stupid. When did her family stand on ceremony for the Fourth of July? The house would be full of guests, and her only regret would be having to share her dad.

It was after ten and dead quiet when they arrived, and she was surprised to find no cars parked on the circular drive. She opened the front door and saw a kitchen light reflecting on the wide planked chestnut floors of the hallway. They left their overnight bags at the foot of the wide staircase. No lights shone upstairs.

Claire and Sam giggled uncomfortably at the quiet and tiptoed into the kitchen. Franny rose from her book with a look of surprise. At her feet lay Compass who bounded up and wiggled with delight.

Claire ruffled his broad head and rushed over to kiss Franny. "Where is everyone?"

"I haven't seen you two since February. Samuel, come over here and let me see you in the light. Look how you've grown." Franny smothered him in hugs.

"What's going on?" asked Claire. "This is too weird. I call Dad, he's too busy to talk, he puts me off when I ask to come over, and now nobody's here this weekend."

"Well honey, you better ask Louisa. I don't tell tales and I'm not going to start now."

"That's too cryptic, even for you Franny. Tell me."

A click, click, click tapped on the wood floor behind her. Louisa leaned against the doorjamb in a silk robe, her feet ensconced in feathered pompon slippers. What a vision, thought Claire. "Hi Louisa. How are you?"

"What are you doing here?" she asked.

Claire smiled at her father's wife and Franny scooted Sam across the kitchen. "I'm taking Sam up to bed. Goodness knows you got to be tired, mister." They rattled up the back staircase, chattering away.

Claire approached Louisa to give her a kiss, and the woman barely tilted her cheek. Claire stood back.

"Is there something wrong, Louisa?"

"Did we invite you down?"

Claire took a deep breath. "I didn't know I needed an invitation."

"That's right. You just assume that your father and I are at your service. This weekend isn't a good time. There's no party as you can see."

"Do I need a party to come visit? I'm sorry if I interrupted private time between you and Dad. I thought it would be a normal Fourth of July as it has for the past two decades."

"Yes, the only world you've ever known, your entitled life."

"Wow, sorry. You seem really pissed. All I did was come down to my family home."

"You are a rude young woman, Claire. There is such a thing as a phone call."

"I've called, Louisa, and no one tells me anything. What's up? You seem more hostile than normal."

"That's what you think? Well, things are going to change for you, Missy, and change big time. You need to wake up."

"For Christ's sake, Louisa, what the hell are you talking about? Where's Dad? I want to talk to him."

"He doesn't want to see you. After you two wake up tomorrow morning, head back to the city."

"You are out of your living mind. I'll see my father whenever I want."

"Nobody talks to me like that in my home. Go get your little prince and get out of here!"

"Your home? Since when is Tred Avon *your* home? You hate it here. This is *my* family home and he's *my* father. You can't change reality."

"Oh, yes I can, my dear. Just wait." Tossing her blonde curls, Louisa turned on her heel and clicked along the hallway and up the grand staircase. Claire followed her in silence. "You'll find out you spoiled brat," Louisa said. Her stepmother eyed her from the door to one of the guest rooms. She wasn't sleeping with her husband and the doors to the master bedroom were closed. Claire wouldn't wake her father.

She returned to the kitchen, bewildered and angry. "Something's rotten in Denmark," came Franny's voice from the darkness. She emerged from the shadow of the back staircase and took her place at the table, her hand on the open pages of her book.

"What on earth was that about?" asked Claire.

"You haven't been around. Things are changing, girl. You best get on board."

"Gladly Franny, but I'm getting a little tired of asking what's going on."

"Your Daddy's got bladder cancer. He's dying. A month ago he started carrying a bag and he's been on radiation for months. They finally ended it because the treatment wasn't working. I asked him a week ago to tell you. Louisa heard me talking to him and ran me off. The woman's gotten it into her head that nobody should know. Especially you."

"What, Franny! What are you saying to me? Dad can't be dying. He hasn't talked to me. How was I to know? He won't talk to me." Claire slammed her fist on the table. "This can't be happening. It can't." She cast her eyes about the kitchen, and when they rested on Louisa's 18th Century faux tea caddy something broke inside her. It was one of those items that her stepmother purchased to rewrite family history, to brag to guests of the McIntosh wealth arriving from Scotland to the New World as if the truth of their poverty and struggle centuries ago was embarrassing. Claire picked it up in both hands, raised it above her head and hurled it across the room. Franny, ever the peacemaker, absorbed Claire's anger, wrapping her arms around her, and they wept on each other's shoulders.

"Why Franny?" she whispered. "Why am I not supposed to know?"

"Money and property. When a man of your father's stature dies, the family philistines make their play."

"For what? Daddy would never allow us to be hurt."

"He won't be here to protect you."

———

Out of the Woodwork

The next morning, Claire woke to the sound of a dog barking and ducks quacking furiously. From the comfort of her bed, she imagined them taking flight as Compass ran to the edge of the river, incensed that winged strangers had landed in his yard. She pushed her arms above her head and froze mid-stretch, remembering the night before. It was barely dawn and the gleam of soft light around her blinds told her to get up. Quickly, she hopped from the bed and ran to Sam's door. She wanted to explain, to see if he had overheard, to know what he knew. Pushing it open a crack she saw the bed was empty.

She felt the pull of her father's room. At the other end of the hall, his door stood slightly ajar and as she neared, she heard the music of their voices: calm, one hoarse, one singsong. She stood outside and listened.

"I've been waiting for my grandson. Where's my high five?"

"Granddaddy, this is like Mommy's bed in the hospital. You're sick, huh?"

"A little. But now that you're here, I'm better. Where's your Momma?"

"She's sleeping. We got in late last night. Franny said we couldn't wake you."

"Aww, you shoulda come in. All I do is lie here and wait for somebody to talk to," he wheezed. "Get me some water there."

Claire peeked around the door. Sunlight from the shutters cast oblique lines across the blanket. The bedsheets enveloped her father's wizened body, and his face appeared to be a wrinkled walnut sunk into the white pillow. Sam perched next to him on the bed. He reached across the railing and grabbed a lidded water glass punctuated with a straw.

"Can you raise your head, Granddaddy?"

Her father grunted and sipped while Sam held the glass. His head fell heavily back into the pillow. "That's better," he said. "Let's talk about you. How did school go? Did you get good grades on your report card?"

"Straight Outstandings. Next year they're going to give us letter grades. I won most valuable player in soccer for the year."

"That's my boy. A man the team holds dear. That's what it means to be a Tosh." He cleared his throat and said, "I have something I want to tell you."

"Do you want me to get Mommy?"

"No, no. This is between the two men of the family. I want—I want you to be strong for your Mom. She treats you like a baby like any good mom but let her know how old you are. She has a big job and she tries hard to make everyone happy. That's not wrong Sam, but sometimes you can't make everyone happy. You can only make things right."

Claire's eyes filled and tears spilled onto her hand. She was afraid. Stepping back, she tried to choke away sobs that wracked her. How could this be happening and she was so oblivious? She should have pressed him for the truth. She should have dropped work and Sam and gone to visit. She swallowed, strangling the words that wouldn't—couldn't come. She didn't hear everything. "...the trapdoor. Don't forget, okay?'

"I won't. But we won't need that Granddaddy. We have all of Tred Avon."

"Of course you do but the world of adults is very confusing, Sam. Tell your mother to be patient and time will heal everything. Remind her of that for me, will you?"

"I can, but don't you want to tell her?"

"Of course. But I don't know how things will work out. Listen to the adults and don't let on what you know, especially the ones you want to trust. Make your own decisions with your mom. You just don't know until—some…."

Claire heard him cough once and then again, more croupy this time. He fell silent, breathing raggedly. She wiped her cheeks and decided to go inside.

Compass rose from the floor next to the bed and came to her. She patted his head and stepped nearer. Her father's deep blue eyes followed her. He was exhausted, as if he had fought a war all by himself. He wouldn't take his eyes from her face. "You're so beautiful, Claire."

"Daddy, don't worry. Sam and I will be okay. I love you. You've done everything for us. We can handle things on our own."

These words seemed to embolden him and although his body was still, he smiled and his eyes twinkled in response. "Of course you will. Don't mind me. These are just the musing of a sick, old man." He looked at Sam and said with some amusement, "Has Mom been treating you like a big boy or a baby?"

Sam grinned, as if they held a secret pact and said, "Yeah, you know, Granddaddy. She's always making me follow her rules. It's okay though. I still love her."

Claire and Sam did not return to Washington that day. They didn't attend the Fourth of July parade on The Strand or the fireworks at the town park that evening. Louisa sat in her room afraid to come out while they talked in hushed tones to Franny. When he was awake, Claire and Sam wove stories for her dad and eventually he was unable to respond, only his eyes softening told the tale of his suffering. Claire tried to make sure his last hours were comfortable and filled with words of love and promise. The priest arrived to administer the Last Rites, and Claire and Sam removed themselves to watch a game show on morning television. The show's bells and whistles blew and they cuddled on the couch aware that Ham McIntosh was making his peace with God.

Half the day passed, the hours and minutes dragging. At noon, the hospice worker announced that time was short. Claire spied Louisa outside the door but she disappeared only to return, hovering, alone and expectant. Two hours later, her father's brother, Alistair, the corporate reps, Campbell and the lead accountant, Ross, lined the walls of the bedroom. The lovely VanAnden arrived last with an old Scottish recording of My Ain Countrie that Claire's father played in his D.C. office. Louisa disappeared again. Franny took Sam outside to help Gus cut the spent white rose blossoms. When she returned, she placed her hands on Claire's shoulders as she sat folded over next to her father, holding his hand and watching his labored breathing.

"I'm here, Daddy," she whispered.

Louisa stood at the door outlined in the afternoon sunlight. In her fist, she clutched a hanky to her lips as if trapped in a Hollywood melodrama, her eyes streaming crocodile tears. "Daddy, Daddy," Louisa screamed. "Don't leave me, Daddy." She threw herself upon him, slapping the pillow with her fist. "Don't leave me."

Claire rose, still holding her father's hand to her chest and laughed uncomfortably. "My God, woman. Don't you have any self-respect? Can you give him some dignity in his last moments?" she asked. But he was already gone.

<hr />

Come to Saint Peter

"Louisa, we're all waiting outside. Are you ready?" Claire called up the stairs of her father's Embassy Row home. Sam had followed her inside. She shuttled him to the front door and into Franny's waiting hands. Five black limousines lined the circle in front of the house. Claire shoved the papers, the biography and funeral program into her purse.

The air was heavy with the threat of afternoon thunderstorms rolling through and she felt a film of perspiration across her cheeks; her silk blouse stuck to her back under her suit jacket. Claire lead-footed up a few stairs to gather Louisa. She pushed her sunglasses up on her head and blinked, adjusting to the interior light. Behind her on the driveway her mother, Grace McIntosh, climbed out of her third-in-line limo, her face contorted in anger as she rushed into the foyer.

"Claire. Claire. I see no reason to wait for that bitch. Would you please direct these limos out of the way so that mine can proceed?"

"Mom, please get in your car. We're all going over in a procession. If you get in the car, you won't even have to see her."

"See her? I was the first wife. My limo should be first."

Claire felt someone beside her and realized Dean Campbell was ready to intervene. She exhaled slowly and waited, knowing he would take command. He knew her mother well.

"Mrs. McIntosh, Grace, let me escort you. You shouldn't be riding alone."

He took Grace by the elbow, and Claire watched her deflate like a punctured balloon. She started up the stairs again thinking the faces in each car marked a different and competing stage of Abraham McIntosh's life.

"Louisa…," she called again.

"I'm here. I'm here."

Claire was dumbfounded at the vision that appeared at the top of the steps. Louisa wore a red silk shantung suit and spiked red heels. Claire pressed her lips together and her nostrils pinched in a tide of anger that died thankfully in her Xanax-filled blood. It was too late to protest. Louisa tottered down the steps clutching the banister. Ross had followed Dean's lead and met them both at the arched front door. He raised his eyebrows in alarm at Louisa's appearance but said nothing and offered her his arm.

Claire climbed into the second limo with Sam, Frannie and Gus. She shuffled the funeral script in her trembling fingers, reviewing the steps. The line of limos turned up Massachusetts Avenue led by police escort.

While the family had not outgrown the parish church in Northwest, the family business had. Long before he passed, Ham had anticipated the need for a more public venue, something that would be equal to the family history of government service and city development.

He had quietly negotiated a Catholic-Episcopal service at the Washington National Cathedral. Wanting intimacy, Claire had pulled the funeral director aside, objecting to the plan. She had in mind a small family service, but when Louisa stepped in, Claire's words died out unheard. The interchange released a torrent of demands and unfiltered remarks from her stepmother to anyone who would listen.

"I want the funeral covered in the *Post*," or "Make sure there are enough limousines." Then, "The attendants will wear white gloves and morning coats." And, "I want those lobster crepes and asparagus tips at Congressional. And a harpist. Tell them to take down those awful tapestries in the dining room. Hang the oil paintings of me and Ham."

Inside, Claire's exasperation grew; on the outside, she graced Louisa with concern and deference as she promised her every wish. Then, while standing at the hallway mirror after they returned from the second night of wakes, Louisa evaluated herself detachedly saying, "I knew I should've gotten that neck lift the minute he was diagnosed."

"Oh, my God, save me," muttered Claire as she followed Franny into the kitchen. She poured herself two thumbs of scotch and wondered exactly when a diagnosis was made. She decided that a service in the Episcopal Cathedral was the least of her worries.

Trying to be inclusive, Claire had asked her mother to appear at either the viewing or the funeral, and initially, her mother had said she wouldn't be caught dead in the same room with Louisa. The next morning, strangely sober, Grace had called saying she would attend the funeral and didn't want to be shoved into the background. "I want my own limo. I want my own row in the Cathedral and at the cemetery. I want my own table at Congressional. And don't forget I have to be driven home."

It was a moment of great clarity that Claire hadn't seen in her mother for years. But it added to the demands, and she wished she hadn't opened that door. It was Claire who met with the funeral director, the priests, the house caterer, the limo service, the cemetery, the country club and lastly, the maître d' for the evening tribute. It was Claire who planned the entire funeral service according to her father's wishes. She made long lists of details, checking them off as she finished each one. Her trusty Post-it notes covered her paperwork in layers, like the wings of butterflies covering a field. After dinner every night, she called Dean for advice and he gave the final word. She was exhausted but had not experienced any moments of whiteout.

At the Cathedral, Claire paused to make sure the scripture readers were ready and the Catholic priest was satisfied. Even though the Cathedral's mission was to be the people's church, it wasn't a Catholic church. There would be no funeral Mass, only a shared benediction and communion. Monsignor Cafferty mumbled under his breath about this being the last time he would participate "in a celebrity funeral."

He pulled her into the vestibule before the service. "I hope you'll hold a proper Mass for your father after this fiasco is over."

She fixed a smile across her face and said, "Monsignor, we so appreciate your kind presence and leadership at this very sad time for our family." Privately, she wanted to spit on his exclusive polished shoe.

She walked outside where a small group of reporters were clustered at the west entrance under the great rose window. She trotted down the steps ignoring them and their long nosed cameras that pointed here and there as the mourners emerged from their limos. As the funeral attendant pulled the casket from the back of the hearse, a quiet sob escaped Claire's throat. Get it under control, she thought and followed the pallbearers up the limestone steps to the broad central door. Dad had wanted it this way: so public.

She had ticked off every demand of the living and the dead and thought if it was her father's choice to not see Tred Avon House again and instead be buried in Washington, she had done her best. It seemed wrong, as if he bowed to business interests even in death instead of his love for the river and the family.

A reflection caught her peripheral vision beneath her sunglasses. Claire looked at the knot of reporters. A cameraman was training his long telephoto lens over her head. The camera aimed at a stone carving of St. Peter, the fisherman, who stood between two massive entrance portals. And in a moment of reverie, the image wiped her morbid thoughts away.

The statue's face was not a delicate European vision of the first apostle, nor the older, balding version of the sainted man who became the first pope. He was young Simon, the common man with a net thrown over his shoulder and his eyes wide open with awe. He had broad cheekbones, a heavy brow, rivulets of long hair, and full lips. This was Simon, fishing the Sea of Galilee when Christ called him into service and renamed him Peter. Rugged and virile, he had just met his Prophet and had not yet denied

Him three times before the cock crowed. Otherwise clothed in a T-shirt and jeans, this man could have been a rapper. Good, she thought of the cameraman. Take his picture—better St. Pete than me in the news.

An usher tucked her hand in his arm and they walked down the broad center aisle. He handed her the Mass card her father had chosen of an eagle flying beneath the hand of God; 'In Loving Memory' was printed on the other side. Still selling his image, she thought, but it should have been a beagle landing. Perhaps Monsignor Cafferty was right. Was the funeral a fiasco? From her viewpoint, it appeared that about six hundred were assembled but they were dwarfed by the immensity of the nave. Some were local government dignitaries, others hailed from Congress. Some were construction workers dressed in work clothes. Her father had been a man of the people. As she passed arched portals, leading to darkened spaces that sheltered raised tombs and statues, the sound of violins and bells echoed through the stone archways.

Hearing the tender sopranos of the Cathedral Boys Choir rise in a tide she grew lightheaded and gripped the usher's arm tighter. A medieval funeral song, the music wafted upward. Her eyes took in the flags of nations hung under the high stained glass windows that cast red, blue and green kaliedoscopes upon the assembled faces. Her heels tapped across the stone as she walked behind the pallbearers. She was the last to be escorted down the aisle.

Claire entered the row of chairs and Sam looked up at her, searching her eyes for comfort. She slid an arm around him and smiled wanly at her Uncle Alistair. He gave her a calculating look, as if evaluating her pain without wanting to be a part of it. He must have read her surprise because he warmed, and smiled back, nodding. She settled in to wait for this last piece of her father's life to be constructed. Within seconds, she caved to her exhaustion.

Her neck woke her, sore and achy. Barely conscious, she heard the priest intone, "...Lamb of God, you who take away the sins of the world, have mercy on us. Lamb of God, you who take away the sins of the world, grant us peace."

The Agnus Dei. How long had she been asleep? She had missed the eulogy. Claire stole a look around to see if anyone had noticed. Alistair patted Sam's knee. Sam looked at the high altar and patted Claire's thigh. A chain reaction.

The faces around her were set in stone. Such a dignified collection in such perfect harmony that she wondered if they missed him at all.

Perhaps she was being too hard on everyone or it was too early for tears or even a polite sniffle into a hankey. She felt adrift on a rolling sea. Her father was gone, and she had a growing worry, an amorphous anxiety, that she was no longer defined as part of something. No one was left to love her. No one but Sam.

The five limousines, the burial at the cemetery and the catered food followed. She endured embarrassing tributes to her dad, expressions of drunken sympathy from some and watery-eyed sentiments from others. Walking out of the country club in the late afternoon, Claire was surprised that the rain had held off. She looked up into the summer sky seeing white clouds shirred like a petticoat while others twisted like bunches of string. Storm clouds were distant, and a strong breeze ruffled the hem of her skirt. She again thought of the river and Tred Avon House.

As a child, when she and her dad sailed out into the windy Chesapeake he would warn her, looking up at the clouds, "Horses tails and mackerel scales make tall ships reef in their sails." Words of caution immortalized for sailors and their daughters.

———•———

Pickup or Limo?

Details about the family had been collected by Hector, some by Carlos but most by Under. The funeral had been a grand affair with many important people, or so he thought. The only thing that confused him was that the women didn't keen in sorrow. In his country, the women would have swollen faces from days of weeping. Though this McIntosh man had wives and a daughter, none of them shed a tear.

Perhaps, he thought as he watched them enter the gates of the country club on River Road, this is where they wept. He could not find a way to follow the parade of black limousines without being discovered, so his report relied on the funeral at the Cathedral. Many Mexicans were present, some dressed in construction clothes who didn't look as presentable as he. Humbled by the size of the great church and the congregation, he limped down the broad center aisle, trying to appear as if he was not impressed with the surroundings, as if he had done this many times.

He had, in fact, been to many funerals in El Salvador. He always rode, crammed in the back of a pickup truck with others, where he carried a shovel to dig the grave, and where family men shot guns and shouted loudly while the old priest read from the missal. He had ignored the women whose job it was to wail throughout the service. He had prayed that he would not go the same way: by the cartel's bullet or machete.

He found the view from the side altar perfect. The child stood near his mother and looked up into her face often, watching for cues. The redheaded boy was dressed like a small man, in a dark suit with a pale blue tie and black shoes, not sneakers. Such an image was so foreign to him that Under thought it was a costume, as if the adults were making a statement that this child was really his grandfather's holy spirit. And it seemed that this was true, since the mother and uncle held the boy's hands between them as they walked to the casket. They knelt before it, each reaching to lay a hand beneath the blanket of white roses, bowing their heads in silent prayer. What would they say to their God? Did they ask for the man to return?

The man had been sick for months rarely leaving his home on the river. Probably he had cancer and Under thought people all over the world accepted the fate of this disease, helpless in the face of its progression. One could not escape once it had you in its clutches. Much like the cartel. Much like Carlos and Hector. Their bidding was his life now.

CHAPTER 7

The Fall of the House of Tosh

*T*he next morning, her alarm rang and she punched the sleep button repeatedly, until she heard Sam's voice at her door.

"Mom. Aren't I going to camp today?"

Claire dragged herself from bed, fed him and gathered his backpack at the front door of their apartment. She threw on a bra under her shirt and straightened the waist of her pajama shorts. At the door, she slipped her feet into flip-flops. At the hall mirror she ran her fingers through her hair. It had grown past her shoulders, thick and for the first time in her life, wavy. In the light of early morning, Claire and Sam walked two blocks up Connecticut Avenue to his bus. She kissed him good-bye and turned making a beeline for home.

All she wanted was more sleep. Pedestrian traffic was light and Claire kept her head down hoping she wouldn't run into anyone she knew. She hadn't even removed her makeup from the day before and her eyes felt like boulders rolling in her head. She wished for her sunglasses.

As she circled the fountain at the front doors of the Kennedy Warren, Claire decided it was time to extend her six-month lease in the historic Art Deco building. She didn't need the stress of moving again. A short nap would revive her and afterward she'd call the realtor to find out if there had been any progress on selling the Chevy Chase house.

She passed the stone Aztec eagles that guarded either side of the glass entrance. They always weirded her out and she was so absorbed that she didn't see the man in dark clothes who separated from the holly tree. A camera was slung around his neck. Appearing flustered and apologetic, he held his hands out to her sides while a slow smile grew on his face. "Ms. Mcintosh! I can't believe my luck. I was hoping I could interview you. I'm Josh Bigelow with WKKG News. Do you have a minute?"

"What? No. I can't talk to you now." He walked backwards as she pushed forward.

"Please, just one question. What do you have to say about the article in the *Post* this morning? Ms. McIntosh, can you tell me what the future of Tosh Enterprises is since one of your signature properties is going to foreclosure."

Claire backed up and tried to move past him to the right and then the left but he blocked her. "I'm sorry. I—I don't know what you're talking about."

"Foreclosure. The *Post* is saying that the southeast waterfront property your father purchased two years ago is going into foreclosure. Does this spell the end of Tosh Enterprises in the District?"

He was so close she could smell his aftershave. Claire pushed the man and ran for the front doors. He pursued and raised the camera lens as she slipped inside to the cool safety of the lobby. She clipped down the hallway on the blue carpet, her flip-flops slapping her heels to move faster, faster. Her hands shook as she struggled with the key. What had the man said? She burst through the door. What did he mean, "the end of Tosh?" She fell onto her bed, her heart beating wildly.

Unable to rest, she made coffee and opened her laptop. The *Washington Post* feed popped up in her mailbox and she scanned it until she found the article in the Business section. "Foreclosure of Tosh Properties on Southeast Waterfront." Apalled, she read in snatches. "On the Washington Channel—27 acres—purchased by Abraham McIntosh of Tosh Enterprises—peak of the market—falling values—project goals fade for business and residential development. Scion of D.C.'s oldest and largest development corporation dies leaving questions for investors—inheritance conflicts...."

She jumped when her phone rang. It was Dean. "I guess you know why I'm calling."

"God Almighty, Dean. I got ambushed by some intrusive reporter at my front door." Claire tapped a pencil on her desk.

"I know. Me too. They were at the doors when I came into work this morning."

"What's going on with the development project?" she asked wiggling her foot.

"Somebody leaked inaccurate information. It's being refinanced. We have investors, solid investors we need to keep."

"Well, how do we get ahead of it?" Her voice sounded tenuous. She slammed the pencil down. "I'm not the person to handle this, Dean."

"VanAnden is writing a press release now. We want to correct the story before the stock declines any further. Hell, everybody's stock is plummeting, but construction is hit the hardest. Your father made the promise to buy the property two years ago. It's always been a crapshoot. Some of the early investors want to back out. He was in the process of buying out their seed money with his own. He really believed in the southeast waterfront. We aren't going to lose it now."

"So this is just fear mongering?"

"Well, there was some basis in truth a month ago, but we're very near a deal with the bank. The banks are afraid. They want to see us as stable, carrying on, so they're giving us a low interest loan. We need to get to the next stage. We need to have the will and trusts read so that we can lay the questions to rest."

"What 'questions to rest?'"

"Inheritance conflicts. The investors need to know there aren't any."

———

The Reading, The Reckoning

Stein had graciously given her a week off from work. She found she couldn't talk to anyone now. Louisa was erratic and self-absorbed. Her mother was glassy-eyed and paranoid, afraid everything would be taken away. Dean scheduled the reading of the will for the end of the week.

Two days later, in her father's office, she met with Dean and Ross, downing strong coffee and they laid out the folders on the small conference table for each family member. She had not eaten and wondered if there would be any croissants. Strangely, she felt that she had been here before and remembered the folders before the bombing.

"Dean, I don't think this is wise to read it to Mom and Louisa in the same room. Never mind Alistair."

"It's your father's wishes."

"I know but he was wrong. He wasn't thinking about how difficult it's going to be for me to deal with them afterward."

"On the contrary, he felt if everyone knew what the other was getting, there would be less jealousy and less of a chance for a lawsuit. He has been very fair."

There was no arguing with her dad now. So Claire greeted everyone at the door, bussing the air beside her mother's cheeks in the European way and kissing her stepmother's lips in her southern way. She wondered why she wasn't more annoyed, but the antidepressant and a double dose of Xanax helped. She figured this was her last performance. Impervious, untouchable, non-reactive. Her inheritance would solve her own financial hurdles and allow her to look for the job she wanted. She could quit Wilcox and Stein with a month's notice and never suffer the indignity of having to ask for money again.

Everyone moved without seeing each other, their conversation stilted. Her mother sat at one end of the table, Louisa at the other. Alistair and Claire sat in the middle across from Dean and Ross. Mercer hovered outside the door to prevent anyone else from entering.

Dean began by announcing that all properties he identified held no mortgages and that trusts were in place to pay the taxes on them in perpetuity until such time as the respective owner decided to sell or died. Louisa's Trust included the Embassy Row home in her name, the use of Tred Avon House, which would remain in the McIntosh Family Trust, and a balance of cash and investments that would pay her generously every month. Visibly relieved, Louisa said, "I won't be using that moldy old house. It's too far away from everything. Just close it up."

Under the fifteen-year-old divorce agreement, Claire's mother would continue to receive equal funds from a trust aptly named First Wife and was remanded ownership of the Spring Valley house. At this, Grace exhaled loudly raising her chin defiantly, and looked around the table, "What are you looking at? He wouldn't cut me out in death. I deserve this."

Alistair, who had never married and always fancied himself a playboy, received Ham's compounds in Park City and St. Lucia, where Claire speculated his peccadilloes would go unnoticed by the Washington press. He would continue to draw from the trust left by his parents in his name. "Nice of my big brother to provide for my entertainment," he said with a grimace of disappointment.

Dean spoke further, this time about the corporation. Like sunflowers turned to the sky at high noon, they drank in his words as if they were a lifeline. "Since we are a privately held corporation, we will continue to operate under the Board of Trustees as Tosh Enterprises. Ham wanted us to become publicly traded with an initial offering but that isn't going to happen now. Alistair will take Ham's place as Chief Operating Officer. The position of Chairman of the Board will rotate bi-annually between Ross and me as executive officers. I begin the first two-year term. Ham discussed this with us in a board meeting last March, before we knew he was ill. He told us at the time that he wanted to enjoy semiretirement and spend more time at Tred Avon. He did not tell us of his illness until it became obvious in May."

May? The word socked Claire in the gut. They knew in May? She had gone to the beach for the weekend before Memorial Day. She could have gone to Tred Avon if she had been told. Why was she left to find out days before— what seemed like mere hours before—it happened?

Her father had left Washington for the river house in April, he said, to spend time sailing and carving. As the assembled realized Ham McIntosh had lied to them, Dean's hold on the group wavered and everyone broke into separate conversations.

"I knew it in April. His suits were hanging on him," said Alistair.

"He called me around the first of May to have the house inspected. He never called me; always had Dean do it. I knew something was up," said Grace.

"We suspected something here in the office. He had been delegating things he loved to do, like calling the mayor," said Ross.

Louisa was silent.

Claire looked around the table. Louisa fingered her glasses. Grace sighed repeatedly, declaring that Alistair or Dean should have confronted Ham. Alistair caught Claire's eye. Quickly, he looked down at his fingernails.

Dean grabbed their attention with the wave of his hand. "Of the sixty-five percent that Ham controls, Alistair is left 7 percent, Claire is left 15 percent and Sam, 36 percent. Five percent is left in the McIntosh Trust to support the Tred Avon estate and provide a monthly stipend for Sam to continue his education, health care and anything else he needs. After he attends college, as his grandfather expected, and works in the corporation from the ground up, at the age of twenty-seven he will be offered a position on the Board. He may refuse it. If so, he will have to sell out his stock to another living family member."

Claire's mind was running at half speed. Bribery. Sam would be channeled regardless of his own desires. Dean had not mentioned anything about her future, only Sam's. Together they were 51 percent. Separately, neither had a voice. There was a new McIntosh Trust but she couldn't tell if she was included with Sam. She only needed enough to declare her independence from Wilcox and Stein, to buy a house, to find another job.

Dean paused to allow the older generation to express their relief.

"Now, I must caution everyone. The economy is soft, as you know. The company stock has been temporarily devalued based on our plummeting real estate holdings. This business with the southeast waterfront property is the tip of the iceberg. Ham's personal investments were moved a few months ago and we are still reviewing that money trail. The cash amounts in each of your trusts will have to tide you over until the market comes back at which time you can live off the interest. You must be conservative in your spending. No around the world trips at this time. Ross and I will meet with each of you to assist in financial planning. While there is a considerable amount of cash, I warn you that it's not unlimited. Ham was a fiscal conservative and in times like this he tightened his belt.

When was he going to get to her? She pulled her hair up and with a chin tilt she wedged a single pencil in the twist. It was a comforting move left over from her days in law school. And it brought Dean's attention.

Finally, his gentle eyes turned to her saying, "Your father was reluctant to provide you with a trust Claire. He felt that at your age, with your education and employment, it's now up to you to prove your independence and personal resourcefulness. Of course, you will receive your stock options and can draw from them in the future as the economy improves. We can discuss their use privately."

Everyone's stunned eyes were on Claire. Dean continued, "For a wedding present, Ham bought you and your ex-husband a home in Chevy Chase, Maryland. He understood that you are waiting for the proceeds of the sale. Therefore, Ham decided that he would supply you with enough money yearly to ensure Sam's private education through his college and post-graduate years and support him as a member of this family. That exact amount must be requested each year from the McIntosh Trust, which Ross and I administer.

"If either you or Sam develop a health issue that the company insurance does not cover, your father will allow you to tap the family trust. Ross and I must approve each request. "As I said, at twenty-seven if Sam decides to become an officer on the board, the amount he will earn will be based on a preset formula indexed to inflation. Your father's expectation was that Sam would be Chairman of the Board in a non-rotating position.

"Upon his death, your father wanted you to take his beloved golden retriever, Compass, for you and Sam to raise. He also left you his vintage Patek Phillipe pocket watch as a token of his love." Dean reached in his coat and presented it to Claire with a flourish.

"Oh," Louisa said. "Isn't it nice he wanted you to have that, Claire? He told me that it was only worth $5000 but that it was inscribed on the inside. I'm sure that has great sentimental value for you."

Claire looked at her stepmother's sneer. The disdain. The room was silent. She blinked and took a deep breath. The watch? She remembered it was a gift from her great grandfather to his son upon winning his U.S. Senate seat. She felt a lump rise in her throat and with the first hint of acid her breathing grew faster. A cold sweat broke out on her forehead. Her vision swirled slightly. She was going to be sick.

Quickly, she pushed up from her chair and darted down the hall to the women's room where she fell to her knees in front of a commode, retching. She slumped to the floor, hot perspiration covering her face, and leaned against the stall wondering what her father had been thinking. Why had he not said something?

One hand propped her up but her elbow began to shake uncontrollably from the pressure. She wiped her mouth with toilet paper and crawled out of the stall to see VanAnden's pointed black shoes in front of her. She looked up, ashamed.

"My dear, let me help you."

She stood and stumbled to the sink. Leslie produced a cold, wet tow-el and held it to the back of Claire's neck. She began to cool off. After some comforting words, Claire followed VanAnden back to the confer-ence room. It was empty, except for Dean who sat waiting for her return. VanAnden slipped out and shut the door behind her.

"Dean....I don'...?"

"Claire, let me explain."

"Wait, wait. Dad loved me. I know he did. Why would he do this? Especially now when I need cash."

"Stop it. You are not destitute. You are not homeless." Dean rose and took the chair next to Claire, smothering her hand in his.

"Well, I could be." You see people everyday out there newly home-less. I should not be one of them. Me. I should not be one of them!"

"You sound like your mother. I've known you since you were a little girl and Ham even longer. Do you really think that your father would abandon you? I can see you aren't in your right mind."

"I'm devastated. And embarrassed. Humiliated in front of everyone. The dog and the watch. What was the point?"

"Your father was protecting you. It may not seem like it now, but believe me that entire scenario will hit the press. You will be seen publicly as 'rich girl, poor girl'—left out of the will even though you and Sam hold a majority of stock. That was exactly what your father intended, but it is not the reality."

"You said the stock is devalued. What does that mean?" Claire's eyes darted over his face searching for more. She was befuddled, tired and the whiteness seeped into her thoughts. She couldn't reason. Enough had happened. She had taken care of everyone's desires, as her father would have, yet when all was said and done she was left dependent on Sam's trust. There was no wiggle room to look for another job.

"The stocks are contracting. Cash is tight. Claire, let me be frank. You are ripe for the picking. You are Ham's direct heir, divorced with a great education and career. Your dad was well aware of how many gold diggers you have had to fend off in the past year. He and Wilcox were good friends and he spoke to him regularly throughout your divorce. There may not be sexual harassment from top to bottom, but nobody's stopping the rank-and-file employees from having affairs. He didn't want that to get any worse, especially now that you have a...now that you are more vulnerable. He also didn't want you to end up back in court with

Vance petitioning for more money. He had grown to dislike Vance who, in my judgment, has changed as he's climbed the ladder.

"Your dad has provided for Sam and you by extension. Ross and I will approve any request for funds that you make from the McIntosh Trust as long as it's within reason. Your father didn't want that to be public knowledge."

Within reason. Doubtful and still shaking a little, Claire mumbled that she understood. But this was a lie. She didn't understand why she was the last to know, or why her relatives looked at her with such condescension. But mostly she didn't understand why her father was afraid. What had Dean just said? "...especially now that you have a....." Maybe it was what he hadn't said,—that she was "more vulnerable." What the hell was that supposed to mean? Was he referring to her head injury, to her memory? What she wanted was to go home and be with Sam, her security.

Dean put his arm around her and led her to the door. It opened to a rush of air from the hallway.

"It's okay, Dean. Whatever. I'm done with all this. I need to find my own way," she said and waved her hand over the office. She stepped away from his protective arm. Brushing her hand across her face, she decided it was time to leave. With each step she became more resolute as if she had been touched by lightening. Her whole being was electrified. Her jaw clenched in determination. It *was* time to leave. This was her life; no one else's to make or break.

"Claire, don't forget the watch," said Dean.

She turned around to see his fist wrapped around the Patek. Dean tossed it, the chain trailing like flowers loose from a bouquet and she caught it midair. It filled her palm. A watch with a complicated face of numbers and hands, and a blue constellation. Heavy gold, it was close to a pound in weight.

"It's worth a lot more than $5000. But you need to get the box," he said.

She hadn't seen it in years, maybe not since she was a child. Her father had tucked it away in one of his hidey holes. It was perfect, not a scratch on it.

"Where is the box?" she asked.

"Don't know. Ask Louisa. Ham handed it to me like this."

Mercer and Alistair were huddled in conversation. They both grew silent and looked at her warily. She shouldered her pride, what little was left, and walked past them to the elevator, riding it down to the street without any fear for the first time in six months.

Claire dreamed her dad sat at the antique secretary in his study. She was still a child, small, and she looked closely at his new reading glasses perched on the end of his nose. They were tiny jellyfish and she had to save him from their sting or he would be blinded. He pushed back his chair and slapped his knee, calling her. She shuffled through the stacks of papers surrounding him in a protective ring on the floor and he lifted her onto his lap. He kissed her cheek and she reached to grab the jellyfish glasses but they evaporated in her hand. He pointed to each of the ornate cubicles of the desk's interior and told her what was in each. A thimble, a teaspoon, a miniature hammer and a shiny pocket watch.

The small drawer below the arched mahogany door had its own skeleton key. She bit her lip in concentration and turned the key. Inside were ancient, round wire-rimmed glasses, nicked and scraped but treasured in her father's hand. He reached for a leather-bound book, its edges worn, the cover brittle. Opening it, she saw lists of items scrawled in cursive on the left of each page with numbers to the right in neat columns. She was too young to read but he explained it was an accounting ledger. This was a good Scot's record of family frugality. A list of everything spent, everything earned.

A coin fell into Claire's lap and her father said, "Ah, there it is, my girl. The Nova Constellatio." A rough silver circle stamped with an eye, 'of Providence' her father said, with thirteen rays divided by thirteen stars floating in front of her face. One of the earliest coins of a new nation, he said, minted by Robert Morris, the financier of the Revolution, a landowner of Oxford, Maryland, and friend of the McIntoshes. It was scarred and blackened by time. She tried to grab it but it floated to her father's hand. His wonder was infectious.

She woke thinking she hadn't seen the coin in years and thought it had probably gone the same as the watch. Talismans lost or given away.

———

Planning and Execution

During the mid-August vacation days, Claire stayed in Washington suffering through the swampy humidity. She had a plan. She gave notice at Wilcox and Stein to few objections and the Lockheed Martin contract slipped off her desk. Her coworkers did not ask about her future plans. Too wrapped up in their own mess, she thought. Wilcox, Jeanine and Matt were gone. Hamilton would have teased her until she spilled the news.

As much as her personal life had eroded, oddly just when she was ready to say goodbye to her life at work, it improved. Commuting on the crowded Metro, remembering office security codes and passwords, and riding the elevator without flashbacks were her only real ways to measure her comeback. She could remember the finer points of a contract if she had a trigger or had written detailed notes. She could carry on an in-depth conversation if she rehearsed but she still failed miserably with names and faces.

Time was of the essence: time with Sam that her job took from them. The promise of practicing immigration law in Sussex County for those who actually tilled the soil, picked watermelons and peaches or worked in the chicken processing plants was a far cry from K Street and the millions of dollars that were traded each day. She imagined herself and Sam escaping to something better.

Impulsively, she broke the news to him that they were moving. Sam barraged her with questions that she promised to answer only if ("Shhh!") he could keep the secret from his father. Too late, she realized she had no concrete answers and made up fantastical stories about where they would live. Sam laughed but she knew he was worried. Secretly, she packed boxes and hid them under her bed, in the closets and behind the couch. She would tell Vance herself and remain stalwart in the face of his protests. He disagreed with everything she proposed and discussing it with him would only make her look crazy. Sam's summer camp was over, and in the two weeks left before he entered fourth grade, Carlotta would babysit.

Shimmering Washington heat added to her determination to leave. Scribbling at her desk one day, the sunlight streamed across her face almost blinding her and she began a list.

Traffic, people everywhere, waiting, no time, where's our quality of life?
Bombings, taxes, money, threats on Metro, was that a gang at the Zoo?
Friends… family—gone. In frustration, Claire erased the last words, smudging the paper.

She lowered the shade over her desk and in the shadow looked over the list. Putting the pen to paper she wrote slowly, *Will I ever find another man to love?*

The television was on. Stein had them installed in every office so that breaking news was ever at the forefront of their minds. The constant cycle irritated her. Congress bickered, the federal budget stalled, and the media predicted a firestorm if the government shut down in October over a spending gap. The mortgage crisis had expanded. Small banks closed their doors, but the rumor was that WAMU, a large mortgage broker, had also failed. A reporter on the floor of the New York Stock Exchange droned on about the bond market and safety nets. Claire knew she had one but she refused to ask Dean for money from the trust. She had her pride. Instead she called her attorney about the partition lawsuit. Vance had ignored every query to sell the house. The judge ordered them into mediation. "We should have taken care of this before the divorce was final," she said to her attorney. "When will this be over?"

"Slowly," he said. "You know these things take time."

She prayed at night on her knees for strength to stick to her plan just like her father had for all his years. When Dean called she let his message go to voice mail, afraid that a discussion with him would derail her. In the shelter of her bedroom, she listened to his messages. He wanted to discuss financial planning, and the Chevy Chase house and the missing investments from her marriage. She deleted the messages.

Claire searched the internet for the immigration attorney in Georgetown, Delaware, but couldn't recall the man's name they had spoken of at Lydia Gleason's kitchen table. She called Naomi.

"The job with that guy Pembroke? Are you out of your mind?" asked Naomi.

"Sam and I want to live in the country."

"Where's he going to school? Where're you going to live? You know there aren't any Art Deco revivalist apartments in Sussex County."

"Nome, give me his number. You think the job's still available?"

"I don't know. Who would want it?"

Naomi texted a day later with the lawyer's private number and her mother's as back up. Claire called Pembroke who explained there was a backlog in providing legal services to immigrants and asked her to come for an interview. The next Friday when Vance was to pick up Sam for his weekend, Claire drove across the Chesapeake Bay Bridge.

Georgetown, Delaware, was a fading oasis nestled in patches of farmland. Two major roads crossed paths at The Circle where the renovated courthouse sat opposite The Brick Hotel, both names so disingenuous that Claire thought it enchanting. Side streets were lined with dilapidated white Victorians and Georgian-roofed clapboard monstrosities. Seedy little 1912 cottages were interspersed, repurposed as law offices for the county seat.

Pembroke's office was in a vintage Sears and Roebuck bungalow. Industrial-sized cement steps led to a cracked front porch big enough to support five William Howard Tafts rocking away. The front door was thick with layers of paint, and inside, the floors creaked as she walked across the well-padded industrial carpet. It was a rabbit warren of little rooms that circled about nonsensically. A previous owner had knocked holes through the walls to shuffle legal papers back and forth. If it hadn't been for all the wired-in technology on Pembroke's desks, she wouldn't have been surprised to see a Model T Ford puttering down narrow Bedford Street.

Howard Pembroke was a one-man show and looked as hungry to fill the vacant desk as Claire was to take it. She made note of his hairpiece thinking his mophead would help identify him outside his office. He asked what volunteer work she had done in high school. Odd, she thought. Why didn't he ask her about her years working as a Washington lobbyist? He asked what Spanish-speaking countries she had visited in Central America. "Mexico, St. Maarten, the Caymans, St Lucia," she said. "Any paid jobs in high school?" She scratched her head and told him about interning at CBS' *Face the Nation*, about the clothes closet for the poor at Annunciation Parish and opening a chapter of Students Against Drunk Drivers at the Cathedral School. He seemed unmoved. Claire started on her recent job history, but he interrupted and turned to football instead. Would the Redskins finally have a winning season? She sparred with him comfortably about the future of the franchise. Pembroke told her he was a Baltimore Raven's fan and wore purple jerseys every game weekend.

"You aren't holding out for that 'Skins quarterback saving the team, are you?" he asked.

She didn't like assumptions that ended with a question mark. Was he trying to impose his thinking on her? She decided to stop him in his tracks.

"Mr. Pembroke, loyalty is a Charm City thing. Ravens fans can afford it. Not so much in Washington. Our football is similar to Congress passing legislation. Start out strong on one side, waffle a little, then vote for the winner."

"Is that what you do?" he asked.

"No. That's why I'm leaving D.C."

"Call me Howard."

"Well, call me Claire." The questions were random but she liked his old-shoe-leather appearance and his folksy conversation. She decided to ask him later for his employment criterion.

Afterward, she stopped at the Gleason's home. None of the roads looked familiar until she saw the brick rambler nestled near a peach orchard. Claire knocked on the front door. A tall black man dressed in a gray summer suit walked out from the carport. He had to be Albert but she wasn't sure.

"Hello, can I help you?" he asked.

Claire grinned and decided to go with her gut. It had to be him.

"Hi, Mr. Gleason. Remember me? Naomi's friend, Claire. I just stopped by to chat a minute with your wife."

"Sure. You're gonna get that job with that old coot Pembroke?" He opened the front door calling to his wife.

"In the kitchen, honey," called Lydia.

"She's making my favorite: chicken and dumplings. You want to stay?" he asked.

"That'd be great. It's been a long day. I just interviewed and he's hiring me. I'm headed back to D.C. but I wanted to see if you knew of any rentals. You're in real estate, right?"

"Yep. But the rental market is tight. People can't get financing to buy so everybody's renting. Have you thought about buying?" He threw his car keys on the foyer table and pulled off his suit jacket.

"I'm not ready for a purchase."

"Lydia might know of something." Then he raised his voice, "Look who the cat dragged in, Lydia. It's Naomi's friend, Claire."

Sweet ripe fruit perfumed the air inside the kitchen and a golden light shone through the windows. Lydia Gleason threw out one of her ear-to-ear smiles and kissed Claire on the cheek. Her hands were covered in flour. Claire remembered the smile and the cookie jar that sat confidently on the table.

"So you're going to take the job we wanted for Naomi?"

"Yeah, I'm sorry, Mr. Gleason."

"It's okay. Did Naomi tell you she's moving to New York?" asked Lydia.

"No way! She got that job her old boyfriend was talking up?"

"DeWayne. Yes. Now we really won't get to see her," said Albert.

"New York's not that far. But she'll be really busy," said Claire. "That's what I'm trying to ditch. I want to be home with Sam in the evening, and I can't do that with a high power job."

"I'm glad you'll stay for dinner," said Lydia. She dusted her hands with a dish towel. "Peach pie for dessert. I picked 'em myself this morning."

Claire set the table. The steaming casserole covered in browned parmesan coated dumplings made her mouth water. Albert and Lydia bowed their heads and Claire took her cue. "Bless this food to our use, and us to thy service, and make us ever mindful of the needs of others. Amen."

Albert directed Lydia where to spoon food on his plate. Claire could tell something was on his mind. "I worry Naomi will get to New York and find out her job isn't what it's cracked up to be. She has a good job now."

"I'm sure there's no glass ceiling. Government jobs are good for women. A U.N. opportunity like that will open international doors for her."

"I hope you're right."

"She just won't have a lot of free time so you might have to visit New York."

Lydia stopped, the serving spoon suspended in her hand. "Albert, that would be so much fun. We've always wanted to see the Big Apple."

Albert looked doubtful. Claire wanted to reassure him. "You can get theater tickets and eat out with Naomi. I'd take the train into Grand Central. It's easiest." Claire waited for Lydia to take the first bite.

"Don't wait. I forgot the jelly," she said getting up again.

"If I were single and didn't have Sam," said Claire, "I'd be thrilled with an offer like Naomi's. I just want to raise Sam in a simpler world."

"Well, we may be simple but we're not stupid. City folk come down here and think we locals don't know shit from shinola," said Albert.

"Albert!" said Lydia. "Watch your language."

"Oh, come off it, Lydia. Like she's never heard it before?"

"This area is safer and more laid back," Claire said. "Sam needs to learn the value of work and money."

"We worry about money just like city folk, probably more. We just eat better," said Albert, raising a spoonful of dumpling. "Solves a lot of problems."

Claire laughed. "I'm going to learn to cook finally."

"Lydia can help you with that. She's got every church recipe in Sussex County."

Later, while she was helping with the dishes, Claire looked up realizing she had forgotten the reason for her visit. "Lydia, I meant to ask if you know of a place I could rent."

Lydia rinsed a gooey plate. "I was talking to Odessa Solomon this morning. They have an old farmhouse they want to rent so someone can pay attention to what's broken." She paused, thinking. "You might not want to live in that drafty old place."

Amazed at her luck, Claire sputtered, "We'd love it. I'm not any good at fixing things but I can help. Not another apartment, but a real house?"

"Don't get your hopes too high. Odessa's complained that her son isn't keeping it up the way she wants 'cause he's so busy. Man's working two jobs and has no time. If you lived there, maybe you could make a list of repairs and she could organize his spare time."

"May I have her number?"

On the way home Claire called Mrs. Solomon. She sounded formal and distant. Or was it doubt that Claire heard in her voice? She told Claire that she could rent it month to month and if she wasn't happy she could leave anytime. Odessa Solomon cleared her throat and said firmly, "I don't want any complaints about repairs not getting done fast enough."

"I understand. Could you send me an email with the location? Maybe I could come up and take a look." Mrs. Solomon agreed.

Claire arrived home at eleven. As she pulled in the parking garage and gathered her purse, her phone buzzed in her hand. She opened the email to find a picture of a white frame farmhouse on the water outlined by a breathtaking sunset. The message that accompanied it said, "It's old but I loved raising my children here." Claire's eyes watered and she caught her breath, not believing her luck.

She made her way through her darkened apartment and threw herself across her bed. It was time. In the quiet, she called Dean. When he finally spoke, he made a strange request. "Claire, your father wanted Ross and I to watch out for you. It's going to be harder if you decide to take this job, because we won't be around the corner. I want you to stay in touch with us."

"Of course. It's not California. It's one state away," she said.

He breathed through the phone as if she was being obtuse. "Will you consider not using the McIntosh name? Maybe your mother's maiden name instead?"

Stung, she asked, "Why would you want me to do that?" She felt blindsided. Her name was her last vestige of family. It was who she was. She had fought that battle marrying Vance when she told him her J.D. was awarded in her name and that's how people knew her.

"McIntosh is widely known, I'm sure in Delaware. You could be ripe for a shakedown if you share your real identity."

"Haha," she deadpanned. "Like I could empty the trust."

"Don't be naïve. There are consequences to inheriting that kind of money at your age. Sam is too young for anyone to consider him a commodity. Besides, he has no control over it now. You, on the other hand, are a sitting duck."

"Pembroke knows me as McIntosh so he has to be in on any change. I can trust him."

"Remember, we have your updated profiles here in the safe. The dental records, the body mole pics, blood types and DNA tests. It's after-the-fact security that I'm sure we will never need. I can talk to your employer if you like," answered Dean.

"I appreciate that, Dean. But you're overreacting. This is my deal. No more interference. Dad didn't have confidence that I could handle myself, for whatever reason. He thought in his most paternalistic way that I need to be sheltered," she said, her voice hollow. "I'll go with mom's name and be Claire Lamar. It's my middle name anyway."

"There you go. Don't be a stranger. If you need money or help with anything, anything at all, please call me." His voice was sincere.

Claire snickered. "When was the last time you helped someone move?" she asked. "Are you available next Saturday?"

Part Two

CHAPTER 1

Bug Dancing

September beach mornings were different. Waking slowly didn't work. Darts of orange clicked across Claire's inner eyelids until she squinted open, shielding her eyes with her arm. The light enveloped the room, splashing against every wall and into every corner. No debating sleep. She sat bolt upright in the old iron bed. Bewildered, incredulous, she wondered if her entry into the day could be taken at a slower speed. She succumbed to the warm yellow sun, humming tentatively and testing her voice against the other sounds.

Birds. Many, on the tin roof. Peeps, squawks, soft hoots. The roof creaked and the metal lining of the chimney banged. Was it a seagull? No, maybe a pelican or an albatross, she giggled. These birds claimed the morning.

She rubbed her upper arms, achy from carrying boxes. A brief vision of the rented moving van sitting outside in the rutted driveway yielded to a wild urge to run to the windows and sing out loud. She was ready to explore what she hadn't seen at night. Everything seemed so different from the city, so open. Looking at the farmhouse windows, she realized not even blackout shades would keep this sun out. Her watch read 6:20.

Blue skies beckoned her. She wiggled her sleep shirt past her hips as she padded over the linoleum floor. She had gained a little weight since the bombing and felt sturdier as she stared out the nearest window, captivated by the dark blue waters whipped by a breeze. Waves slapped at marsh grass a bare fifty feet from the back porch. Different waters. The

Tred Avon was bigger, wider, deeper. Here, she saw mudflats and islands, their grasses flattened by the action of wind and waves, and other tall grasses that resembled cattails with a feathery tip.

She placed both palms against the wavy panes of glass and pressed her forehead to the sash. Her fingers fluttered over the lock and she threw it wide open, breathing in the salt air. Sheer curtains grabbed the breeze and bubbled upward.

Tantalized by the view, she decided there was no agenda to keep but the one she made. But perhaps it was more than that. This day would fall into place on its own. For the first time in her life, no one else stood in her way. She twirled on one foot, spinning, until it dawned on her that she wasn't alone. Sam stood in her bedroom doorway. Barefoot, in a T-shirt and pajama shorts, he didn't look any different and yet he was. He grinned crazily, eyes flashing under his tangle of dark red hair.

"Mom! Mom!" he shouted as if she wasn't paying attention. In a play-dance learned during his preschool years, he circled like a praying mantis and Claire mirrored him, ready to pounce, connected in a childhood dimension that would evaporate instantly if they thought the wrong thoughts or said the wrong things. They broke into loud raucous giggles and hugs and Claire scooped Sam up, whirling him in her arms, leaning backwards in counterweight to him, his feet and legs radiating out in a circle of oneness. Breathless, she put him down and he ran over to the door. "Come on…we gotta let Compass out!"

They ran down the old oak staircase careful not to lean too hard as it wobbled and raced each other to be first. Together they peeked around the doorjamb into the kitchen. There sat Compass inside his kennel, trembling and wild-eyed. Sam fumbled with the lock. The dog stood up, snorted and stamped from paw to paw as the gate opened. He jumped on Sam, knocking him to the floor. There they lay, boy and dog, wrestling across the peeling linoleum.

Claire skipped by them sideways, around the Formica table to the old 1940's porcelain sink cabinet. A box of dishes sat on the imbedded sink drain. A flash of regret hit her. Tuscan, from her Chevy Chase house, wedding presents. She grimaced fleetingly thinking she might like to break every one and buy something else at Walmart. Begin again with a clean set. She sighed letting the recriminations go. She would not be angry and bitter. That was over. She would be careful with her money and not waste it ever again.

She had set up the coffee maker on the chipped counter the night before. Claire unwrapped a large soup cup from the newspapers and poured a cup of strong Javan. The sun was streaming in so brightly she looked around for her sunglasses. Blindly, her fingers located them among the silverware and she slipped them on still squinting at the glistening water.

Sam giggled. "Want your ball, Compass?"

"Let him out, Coppertop. He has to go."

They had arrived at dusk the night before and barely had time to unload a few boxes and make the beds before darkness had fallen. There were no streetlights and they gazed at the full moon and the stars that blanketed the sky, casting their gleaming reflections on the black water. Now, she took a closer look at her new homestead.

She opened the squeaky, window-paned door to the porch. Wooden chairs in need of paint lined the wall. Everything needed a coat of paint: the walls, the floor, even the ceiling. An overhead fan dropped its blades like a wilted flower into the room. Her immediate response was to replace it, but she cautioned herself. This wasn't her house. She looked for the switch and flipped it. The fan spun in perpetual wilt. She pulled over a splintered armchair and sat down on its cracked plastic cushion.

Sam and Compass returned through the squeaky screen door. He crawled across her lap and reached up to hold her cheeks in his palms. His blue eyes scanned hers, searching. "Mom, are you happy?"

She smiled and felt the corners of her eyes crinkle, "I am. Are you?" More words wouldn't come to her. Her contentment, her first real independence was so complete that she thought this was the happiest she'd been since his birth. He rolled around in her lap and nestled in, the two of them taking in the great expanse of water and endless sky.

The view from the farmhouse overlooked a wide creek that fed into the bay. Kitschy beach housing stood tall in the distance by the ocean. Her driveway led to a back exit through a trailer park where shoebox housing sat along an ordered lane, each graced with a pickup truck or an old Lincoln Town Car. Charmingly different. Achingly different. No stone colonials and manicured yards. No office buildings and traffic lights on every corner.

Sam jumped down and buried his face in the dog's ruff, murmuring in his fur. She turned to the water, her chest tight with sorrow, thinking it odd how her family slavered their dogs with affection but kept so much hidden from each other. Those secrets, that fear of engaging in difficult conversations had conditioned them to shutter their feelings. Compass went to the door and whined.

"Let him out, Sam," she said again. "He's part your responsibility." Claire put her mug down with finality.

"Can I go too, Mom?"

Such a good kid. He was checking to see if the rules applied in this great open space. "Go get your flipflops and I'll watch him till you get back." She put off emptying the boxes, deciding there was plenty of time for work and schedules later. She let Compass out and he flew across the yard to the edge of the water. There was nothing here to worry her, no bogeymen, and no predators. She could let Sam explore as long as he stayed out of the water. It looked shallow and mucky.

Claire wished all decisions were this simple. She had thought the same thing when they moved into the Kennedy Warren, when she had married Vance, when she had chosen law as her major. They had been decisions based on parental influence, or money, or status. Automatic decisions like opening Russian nesting dolls. No great discovery, no uniqueness just smaller and smaller changes.

Someone had recently mowed the back lawn where Compass was nosing around. The yard led to a rickety pier where a flat-bottomed fishing boat was moored. An old green and white Evinrude motor was attached to the stern. Further down the western shoreline a flashy fishing boat was moored to an updated pier. The water had to be deeper over there. She would find out who owned the boat and set some rules for Sam.

Compass was busy sniffing the grasses at water's edge when Sam returned. She gave him a hug and said, "Ten minutes and you guys have to come in for breakfast. Don't go in the water and stay in view of the back porch."

Sam nodded and charged outside. Compass ran to meet him and soon they were exploring every inch of the backyard. She began humming again as she returned to the kitchen to find some cereal. Glancing out the window at her child stooping at the water's edge, she heard a sharp rapping at the front door. Claire grabbed a jeans jacket to throw over her nightshirt and walked up the hall wondering who would be knocking at this hour of the morning. Opening the door a few inches, then wider, she hoped her face didn't register surprise.

"Morning. I'm Odessa Solomon, your landlord. Brought you some zucchini bread. Figured you wouldn't have much in the refrigerator and y'all probably could use something to eat." The woman studied Claire's face closely, then asked, "You got something wrong with your eyes you got to wear sunglasses inside?"

Mrs. Solomon was older. Her dark hair was pulled tight in a high bun and she wore heavy red plastic glasses. Her small face and pointed chin reminded Claire of her high school field hockey coach, a tiny powerhouse. Claire smiled at the thought. The woman eyed her carefully, maybe a little suspiciously, and offered her a loaf of dark bread and a stick of butter wrapped neatly in plastic wrap.

"No, I—um, I'm Claire." Embarrassed, she pushed her glasses on top of her head. "I just forgot I had them on. So much sunshine everywhere! Pleased to meet you, Mrs. Solomon," she said and shook her hand.

"Well, I figured as much. Just call me Odessa. Where's your son? Didn't you bring him with you? And you got a dog, too?"

Wow, Claire thought. In a strange economy of words, Mrs. Solomon got down to business quickly. The lady was friendly enough, she thought, but who brings you a welcome gift and gets nosy all in one sentence? "Why don't you come in? I'll call Sam and Compass to meet you."

"No, no. You probably tired from moving yesterday and I got lots to do. I want to let you know we live here on the property. Over there. My son and I," she said and pointed.

Claire glimpsed a rambling wood contemporary with huge windows that sat a good distance up a slow rise to the west. It faced the creek and bay but was protected from full view by a stand of trees that sat between the two houses.

"Bring your boy over for lunch this afternoon after you done some unpacking. I'll tell you 'bout the property."

She immediately latched on Odessa's words, "My son and I." This woman was in her late sixties, maybe older, so he probably wouldn't be a kid but maybe he had children Sam could play with.

"That's so nice! We'd love to come. Will your son be there?" asked Claire.

"Booker? Probly not. He work all the time." Her friendly tone changed to proud mother. "He was in Somalia, then went to work in Baldimer. Gave it up to come back here and take care of me. But I'll tell you 'bout that stuff later."

"What time should we come and can I bring something?" Claire thought a bottle of wine would not be the right gift. She wanted to befriend this lady and assumed it wouldn't be hard since Odessa was halfway there divulging so much personal information.

"Come over 'round noontime. I made a big ham yesterday. You eat meat, don't you? So many of the young people today don't eat meat no more," Odessa said, a little wonder creeping into her voice.

"I eat everything, except okra." Claire laughed. "I think maybe that's an acquired taste." Once her office had held an okra cooking competition at lunch and decided it was one of those foods that could not be prepared in any form that was appetizing. Odessa looked at her askance. Claire caught her breath realizing, oh my God, she likes okra. "Of course, I'm sure I just haven't had enough exposure," Claire said. "So we'll see you at lunchtime then. Thanks so much for the invitation *and* the zucchini bread. We'll really enjoy this, Odessa. I can call you Odessa?"

The woman humphed, nodded, and waved her hand as she turned to grab the porch railing. Claire watched her step carefully. Someone had thrown fresh mulch at the foot of the stairs. Probably her son, the phantom mower/Somali vet/Baltimore emigré. She wondered if she needed to get a lawn service or learn to mow. Life on her own terms was coming with new responsibilities.

She walked past the stacked boxes into the kitchen thinking about Naomi and their recent phone call. Claire had commented that she didn't want her law degree to define her. Naomi's splattered her with questions about the funeral and will, but Claire had put her off. That had piqued her friend's interest more and when Claire told her that she was moving and going by her mother's maiden name, Naomi had said, "I get it. Taking a break. Want to play in the sandbox with the rest of the kids. You'll get tired of Sussex and head back to D.C."

Despite Naomi's warning, Claire extended the rental of the 'security monitored-climate controlled' warehouse for her heirloom furniture, paintings, good china, crystal and silver even though it was an extra expense. She kept the large Naman photo she had purchased in a Bethesda gallery when she separated from Vance. A black and white photograph in counterpoint, it was a nude woman walking with her back to the camera along a railroad track. She held a hobo's rucksack over one shoulder on her way to the unknown. At the time, Claire thought it would be great to hang in the post-divorce home she was going to buy, maybe in the master bath. Now it had new meaning. No men, no belongings.

The Landlord

Later that day, Claire and Sam walked along the sandy road to Odessa Solomon's house. The road narrowed and turned into a path that cut through the trees. Sam watched his feet, being careful where he stepped. She pushed him teasingly to awaken him to their surroundings. The trees stood straight and tall, blocking out the heat and light of the midday sun. He pushed her back.

"Jeez, it feels ten degrees cooler in here. Somebody must have planted these trees because everything else is those scrubby looking pines," Claire said, looking around her at the silvery bark.

"Yup. Mom, look ahead." Sam wasn't interested in trees. Something else had caught his attention.

At the top of the path sat the Solomon home. Odessa was setting a table on the deck when she saw Claire and Sam.

"Oh, there you are. I lost your all's phone number or I would've called to see what was holding you up." She crossed her arms abruptly.

A little embarrassed for following her mother's rule (always be late, don't ever be the first to arrive to a social event), Claire felt herself redden and silently put "Be Prompt" on her list of personal makeovers.

"Oh, I'm sorry, I guess it is closer to one." Claire put a small Mason jar on the table thinking it looked tiny compared to the offering Odessa had brought them earlier. She continued in a tentative voice, "We brought you homemade chutney we found at that roadside market on Skeeter Neck Road. We went exploring this morning." Lifting her chin, she realized she hadn't brought any crackers for the chutney. She wiped her hands nervously on her shorts and said, "We so enjoyed the zucchini bread."

"Yeah! It was really good. Whoever heard of putting vegetables in bread? I told mom that's the way we should always eat them," piped up Sam.

Odessa smiled broadly, her eyes turning up at the corners in a web of laugh lines.

Relieved that her son had eased the conversation, Claire introduced Sam to Odessa and he extended his hand to shake hers. Sam raised his eyes to the sky obviously mulling her name over before he tried it out. A question seemed to be brewing.

"Miss 'Dessa, how come your trees on the path are different from all the other trees around here?" He was testing her to see if she would talk to him, if he counted enough for her attention. Little suck up, thought

Claire. She would have to warn him about challenging new people for information.

"Well, aren't you a smart one! My grandfather planted that stand of beech trees to provide some shelter for the animals 'round here. When he was alive, everything was farmland. All the pine, walnut and oak were being razed to the ground and the wildlife didn't have anywhere to live. So he got it in his head that they needed a new home, and he planted that stand of beech so they'd have a place to live and hide from people."

Sam rubbed his hand back and forth over the back of the deck chair. Claire smiled and waited for the next question, sure it would be about animals.

"What kind of animals?"

Odessa stood next to Sam and put her hands on his shoulders. Claire warmed immediately, thinking the woman might be short on social niceties but she definitely had a way with Sam.

"If you go back in that woods and look real hard in the morning and evening, you'll see white-tailed deer. And the rabbits come out to the meadow to eat 'round the same time. And we got grouse, porcupine and a woodpecker and an owl you can hear hooting at night." She patted Sam's shoulder as she spoke, quietly staring into the trees as if they carried the memories of her past. It was a thick woods indeed, and Claire thought it a good sanctuary for the wildlife, so different from living next to the National Zoo and all those caged wild animals. These animals were protected from prying human eyes.

"Mr. Sam, you come inside now and help me bring out the plate of ham so's we can all make ourselves a sandwich." She turned to Claire with an impish smile, "I got a surprise for you. I know you said you don't like okra, but I made some from an old family recipe and I think you going to like it, girl."

Claire fixed a grin on her face. Revolting, she thought, okra slime sliding down my throat is an automatic gag. She stepped through the sliding glass door off the deck and took in the flagstone floor of the kitchen and the deep luster of the wood cabinets. Odessa was ready for lunch. Breads, condiments and sides were all plated to carry outside. Glancing over at the ham and okra on the counter she caught her breath at the sight of a gun cabinet that held an array of rifles. Dismayed at the display right under Sam's curious nose she asked softly, "Is your son a hunter?"

Odessa put the bowl of fried okra in Sam's hands. She never even looked up. "Those guns belong to Russell, my late husband. He was the large animal vet in lower Sussex. And he hunted."

Claire wondered how long she had been a widow.

"My son don't hunt. Them guns don't get used no more. They been locked up for 'bout eighteen years."

Relieved, Claire took the ham plate when she heard the screen door slam in the front hall. She looked over to see the outline of a tall man framed against the light.

"Ma, why are you talking like you don't have an education? Who's here, Aunt Lydia?" came a deep baritone from the hallway. In the shadows he appeared dark as an old penny. He entered the kitchen and his presence filled the room. Claire's gaze ping-ponged between the two, realizing this was Booker. He stood beneath a recessed ceiling light, his bald head gleaming as the smile died on his face. He eyed Claire carefully.

"Didn't know you had company," he said to neither of them and both of them.

Odessa was embarrassed and muttering under her breath. Distracted, Sam tilted the bowl and Claire caught it before the okra hit the ground.

"Hi, I'm Claire and this is Sam. We're renting your farmhouse. Nice to meet you. Are you Booker?" She put the bowl on the counter to shake his hand.

"I am." He put his hand in hers briefly, looking askance at his mother. She couldn't tell if he was nervous or disturbed by something his mother had said.

"We're having some lunch out on the deck. Do you have time to join us?" asked Odessa.

"No, I'm on my way over to the church. Stopped by at six this morning and they're getting ready to start the framing so I better get going. Just came home to get a couple ham sandwiches."

"You should have left me a note. Let me fix it for you, and you can help Claire and Sam take the rest out to the table."

Claire noted Odessa's speech, so formal all of a sudden, and wondered if she had been conned on purpose. Whatever had transpired between them, they both recovered easily.

Booker took the lead, handing the relish plate to Claire. "Sam is it? Here, you take the chips and I'll get this potato salad." He strode out on the deck. Once a safe distance from the kitchen and his mother, he glanced over to make sure she couldn't hear him. "We sometimes play a game with newcomers. Ma's jive talk. I guess you caught us," he said.

"Please, it's no matter," she said. "My father and I did the same thing with clients. And actually it was way more aggressive."

His smile was crooked but big as the noontime sky and she relaxed as his brown eyes warmed.

"Do you come to the beach much?"

"No actually. This is new to us."

"Really? Where are you from?"

"The city." She began to feel anxious. She hadn't thought about how she would present herself to locals, and she was in the thick of it now.

"And you don't know the Delmarva beaches? I thought everyone from Baltimore came here for vacation," he said.

"Oh, we're not from Baltimore," said Sam, and then murmured, "and this isn't a vacation." Claire shot him a look and Sam frowned at her but sat down at the table, his chin in his hands.

"Where are you from?"

"Washington," answered Claire.

"Oh, the City of Light," said Booker. "Well, lucky you. You came to the right place. We treat our tourists right."

She decided not to tell him they weren't tourists on vacation. Best to put the focus on him.

"I heard you work a lot. What are you doing at the church, may I ask?"

"Building one, out on Route 17. It's the Latino church. They have a huge Hispanic population, most of them work in chicken processing. The steel framing starts tomorrow."

"That's a big project. What's your field of expertise?"

"I'm the quasi-architect on site. I didn't finish my degree at Maryland but I got enough to be hired as a subcontractor. It's better; they can afford me." He took a few steps away as if he was ready to go.

"My Granddaddy was a builder," said Sam, wistfully.

Booker looked down at Sam, perched on the edge of a huge porch rocker. Claire's hand shot out, her fingers running through his thick curls. He yanked his head away, casting his eyes at the empty plate in front of him.

"I bet he was a good builder too," said Booker quietly.

"Yes, he could build anything," said Claire. She looked up at this man who had learned too much already. "You'll be late if you stay and talk to us. Let's go see if your mom has finished those sandwiches."

Eyeing the Neighbors

Booker hadn't showered and felt gritty as the early morning sun beat down upon him. He was baiting crab pots, a dirty job, and he wanted to set them out in his favorite spot before he had to leave for his real job. The pots were shiny new, no seaweed, no muck. A plastic bag of bunker, the smelly baitfish crabs loved, sat stinking on the dock next to him. He could feel the sweat soaking the band of his Maryland Terps cap. Tight little brushes of wind came from the west, from the chicken farms, bringing green-head flies drumming toward any juicy meat. One laid a welt on his calf, and he slapped instantly at the sting leaving a patch of blood trickling downward.

The water was silver smooth and reflected the white contrails of fighter jets, making their early morning sorties from Dover Air Force Base to the naval base at Virginia Beach. Seagulls laughed raucously. It was Saturday morning, a workday like any other and one of the truly last steaming hot days of summer. Crabs loved the heat.

Booker wanted a shower and a power nap, but he wanted to catch the asshole who was stealing his crab pots more. His vision blurred as he checked his watch. He needed a couple of hours to complete his plan. The crabs would stop running in the next few weeks as the bay waters cooled. The population was down. Only diehard crabbers worked the end of the season, so he knew the culprit was a local not a tourist. His pots had been stolen in the middle of the night for the third time this season.

Pots weren't cheap anymore, and Booker was a frugal man. He tended his four pots daily, two with his name, two with his mother's labeled on the buoys. He kept only the male crabs, measuring them and throwing back the small ones. The catch had been good this summer because the water was cleaner and the low and high tides more extreme.

Booker fanned his fingers open and closed, working out the soreness. His knuckles were swollen and crusted with blood. His phone rang and he cursed when he saw it was Bandylegs, his Detective Sergeant. Christ, he thought, already this morning. Recently, work calls that came at any time of day or night had begun to wear on Booker. He thought it was time to retire, find another line of work. But it was money and this job had a pension.

"Solomon? You need to get over here. I want a debriefing on last night,"

"Yes sir. Gimme a couple hours, say nine?"

"You dog. You got a woman you got to take care of first? 'Cause if not, I expect you at eight-thirty."

"I'm not that quick," said Booker. "These things take time at my age." Bandylegs laughed his sharp staccato. The rest of the team wouldn't be in till ten o'clock but he always arrived early to massage his boss's ego. His Detective Sergeant was a rude country boy, but Booker knew how to get past the man's prejudices. A little ego stroking went a long way. Booker laid his phone on the dock.

He cursed again as the needle nosed pliers slipped out of his stiff grip. The Department of Natural Resources and Environmental Control required turtle rings on all crab pots. Damned government agencies, he thought, they couldn't clean up the water in Delaware but they passed laws for turtles.

Struggling, he finally got the little orange oval wired in. He grunted in satisfaction, stood up on his dock and grabbed the crab pot to dump it in his boat. Now I'm making progress, he thought and turned to pick up the next one when movement a few hundred feet away at his rental house caught his eye. It was the red-haired woman he hadn't seen in two weeks. She was between the back porch and the dilapidated dock, dressed in a skintight black leotard. She swung her legs up in slow motion, her whole body resting on her forearms and held the position. He watched entranced as her feet circled over and her heels rested on the crown of her head. He jumped in his boat and squatted down to check out the goods while hidden from view.

Suddenly, a large golden retriever went racing past her in pursuit of a rabbit, and the boy followed. Neither one broke her concentration. She brought one leg and then the other over her head slowly in an arc, and stood. Her dark red hair fell in a waterfall, sparkling like embers in the sunlight. She bent down to grab a towel, wiped her face and shouted at the dog who trotted back to her penitently, just like every other golden he had ever known. She bent over and scratched his cheeks with both hands.

He couldn't hear the conversation between the kid and his mom, but he could tell she was giving him directions. Booker hadn't had this much entertainment this close in years. Before she moved in, his mom had heckled him into caulking the rattling windows on the farmhouse, repairing the torn screens, tuning up the furnace and mowing the beach grass. He had been reluctant to rent it, speculating with what he knew about her that she wouldn't be satisfied. One more thing for him to tend in his schedule. Apparently she was from Washington, not Baltimore as his Ma had thought, and she was going to work for a bleeding-heart attorney in Georgetown. Another expat. There were plenty of them around lower, slower Delaware, but mostly they were AARP members. Man.... this one doesn't fit the mold, he thought, as he admired her yoga pants.

He could feel his paint stained T-shirt sticking to his back. His empty stomach growled. He turned his attention to the crab pot, pulled off his hat and wiped his brow with his forearm. He could smell his body in the rising heat. Agitated, he made a mental list. First the crab pots, then to Berlin to debrief Bandylegs at the barracks, and to Roxanna to check out the progress on the church. The Portuguese and Hispanic framers would be working on Saturday. The church was theirs. Our Lady of Perpetual Assistance would be the overflow church for the wealthy Bethany Beach summer crowd but also serve the mishmash of Central Americans who had bankrolled most of the cost with hard earned money.

He thanked his lucky stars that he had never worked in chicken. Everything else, but not that. He had an education, had seen as much of the world as he wanted and had come home to his Ma. There wasn't anybody else left.

"Hi. Are you going crabbing?"

He looked up at some kid stuff in designer shorts and an Abercrombie T-shirt. The dog was sniffing the bunker. The boy shifted his stance to block the sun and Booker stopped squinting.

"Yeah, looks that way."

"I know how to catch crabs. I've done it with chicken necks off the dock, crab pots and I worked a trotline too. You get the most with a trotline. Have you ever used one?"

"Well, you're real experienced, aren't you?" Know-it-all, he thought trying to remember his name.

"My granddaddy has a place on the water." He paused. "You're Mr. Booker. Do you remember me? I'm Sam." Again, he extended his pint-sized arm into the boat to shake hands. How 'bout that? Booker thought, ignoring him. So he wasn't putting on manners just for his mom's benefit that day on the back deck.

A dark shape outlined by the blinding sun approached. He wondered if he smelled worse than the bunker. He pulled off his cap and held it over his eyes to shield them.

"Hi. I hope Sam isn't bothering you." She took up position behind the kid, circling slender arms around his neck and locking her fingers under his chin.

"No. We were talking crabbing."

She put out her hand and he returned with his swollen one, smiling through the wince. Sweat was in his eyes and he couldn't see her face clearly. Like her son she stood back blocking the glare. He blinked a few times. Lots of hair surrounded creamy skin and large wide eyes. Red hair. This was the woman at Gallagher's the night of the drug bust. Like him, she hadn't put two and two together at first. He decided she didn't need to remember. He had worn dreadlocks and contacts that night. But she had no clue she had met him three months ago. Didn't all black men look the same to a white woman? Booker chortled quietly as he gazed at her. He had broken his number one rule that night warning her. It could have blown the whole bust.

"Claire, isn't it?" he asked.

"Yes, Claire Lamar and Sam. Are you Odessa's gardener?"

He exploded laughing. She looked a little surprised. Was he so grungy that he looked like a landscaper? Then it occurred to him that she probably didn't have brothers who ran the lawnmower. Still, it was stuffy of her. He looked at his torn shorts. What else could she think? He probably smelled like a pig farmer to a prissy white girl.

"I guess I'm not making the best presentation, am I?" he said. She looked a little alarmed.

"Oh, no—I mean yes. I didn't mean to imply—I'm sorry."

He jumped out of the boat and stepped nearer since it obviously didn't make a difference. "I'm not offended. I clean up well. Sam was saying you all come from a crabbing family."

"Oh, that's right. You're Booker, Odessa's son. Yes, we were on the Chesapeake but it's the same everywhere, right?"

"It's not the deadliest catch here in the bay. It's so shallow at low tide and during a full moon that you can run aground if you aren't watching your GPS." They chatted about her move, the house and the blue herons. Booker was never one to pass up an opportunity to talk up a hottie.

"Maybe tomorrow morning if you skip church we could go out and check the pots? I need a second body on the boat. You can only put out two per person and Ma will be singing in the choir tomorrow."

"Oh no, we don't want to impose," she said.

He shook his head. "Come on. It'll be fun."

She agreed and pointed to his cap. "You're a Terps fan. Did you go to Maryland?"

She was digging, interested. He smiled inwardly. "It seems a long time ago. I played football for them."

Sam interrupted, "You did? You know Torey Smith or Jared Gaither? They play for the Ravens now but they used to play for Maryland."

The kid was amazing. Booker couldn't guess how old he was but he seemed awfully young to know all these details. "No, they were after me. I played with Jermaine Lewis though....Ravens Superbowl legend. He was their—"

"Wide receiver," finished Sam. Booker felt his jaw drop and just as quickly shut his trap.

Claire smiled at his amazement but touched Sam on the shoulder and reminded him not to interrupt when others were speaking. To Booker she added, "He spent some Sundays watching football with my Dad. That male bonding thing, you know."

He didn't know. Kids were threatening, an annoying responsibility. He saw a kid and immediately thought 'child support.' Half his friends moaned about it over their beer. Booker was always bewildered at the number of his own relationships that had fizzled out when the woman, no matter how in love they claimed they were, realized he wasn't going to make babies. He always had a condom ready even if they said they had an IUD, or were on the pill, or whatever birth control method of the month they swore by. He always made sure.

He gave her his most engaging smile, the one that always worked, and they all agreed that they would meet the next morning at eight. Claire and her kid drifted away, waving at him as he powered up his boat. He opened up the 250 Honda engine and soared out on the calm water. This moment deserved some music and he hit the button on the dashboard, settling on Herbie Hancock, *When Loves Come to Town*.

The next morning Claire and Sam made their way through the high grass over to Booker's dock. As sunny as Saturday had been, Sunday was stony gray although a light breeze flickered with their hair. No blue peeked through the high clouds, and the water reflected the heaven's deep expanse in steel blue waves leaving Claire feeling small and insignificant. Rain was predicted later in the day.

Claire was uncomfortable, wondering if she was not just wasting time but questioning if she should be spending it with her landlord's son. She had boxes to unpack and Sam had homework to do. She zipped up her waterproof shirt as if it were lightweight armor. Two weeks had passed and the magnitude of the move had left her feeling doubtful about her job, the house, the people on the coast. Besides, she couldn't stop thinking about Booker's split knuckles as a sign that he was a hothead. She was plagued with questions and wondered why, at his age, did he live with his mother, if he was divorced, and why he worked so many jobs. Did he have a debt he was paying off? What kind of debt? To whom? She told herself it wasn't any of her business.

Sam must have sensed her uneasiness and slipped his small hand into hers. She looked down at him with a reassuring smile. He hopped a little in response. As they reached the dock, Booker raised up from the back of his boat and shouted to them. Big broad smile and that Terps hat. He didn't take it off this time.

"Hey, you made it. Crabs love a morning like this, and I bet we have a full load in those pots."

Crabs like every morning that's hot, she thought, but her mood brightened. She needed to be less rigid and repeated her new mantra that happiness was a decision she could make every morning. The glossiness of the move had worn off and made it a battle to get to this point everyday. Maybe, they would have a great time pulling up the crab pots. Maybe this guy Booker would be a new friend. He was educated, not pretentious and seemed genuine despite his knuckles. Maybe she would really enjoy the boat ride.

It was a small Grady-White center console fishing boat. She and Sam had made a deal to look sharp. Make a good impression as experienced first and second mates. She nodded to Sam who unhooked the ropes and threw them in to Claire, hopping in and donning the kid-sized life vest. It was brand new. A thoughtful man; he follows the rules on the water, she thought. She ringed the ropes in a circle fore and aft and helped to push off before settling in to the backseat. She watched Booker to see if he wanted anything else. Quick and easy. Sailing *The Dash* on the Tred Avon required way more patience and skill. But this was fast, faster than Uncle Alistair's yacht.

He wore a faded coral V-neck T-shirt and printed Hawaiian shorts covered in tropical Bird of Paradise. Too preppy for crabbing attire. The T-shirt stretched tight across his chest and arms. There was something familiar about him. Stop checking him out, she thought and looked out over the water.

Booker kicked the engine, and in a matter of minutes they were out on the bay cruising around the marshes to hook the crab pots. He pulled in nose first and jumped off the bow into the grasses, gripping the front rope. "Hold on. I got to check something."

The waves gently pushed the tail of the boat around, and Claire wondered if he wanted her to pull in the pots. They were lined up on the starboard side about twenty feet apart. She couldn't see what absorbed Booker's attention. Sam shrugged his shoulders and hooked the rope of the nearest pot. The boat drifted so Claire leaned in and together they pulled it up, but it was heavy. If they reached a tipping point, she thought it might pull them in with it. The heave-to, and the shake-shake to dump the catch was always difficult. The cage was bubbling with crabs, maybe twenty-five. A little thrill shivered down her spine. She had never seen so many so late in the season.

Sam was shouting in his excitement and she raised a single finger to her lips. On the count of three they leaned and yanked it onboard. Resting the muddy pot against her chest, she shook it over the bucket, and the crabs began to tumble in. Pinchers held and crabs dangled as she gave it one more herculean effort. Sam took the tongs and tapped their blue claws ineffectively.

The black mud from the shallow waters streaked down her legs and the floor of Booker's boat like an oil spill. If he had helped she could have dipped the cage a few times to get rid of the mud. Where *was* he? What could he be doing mucking around in the grasses? Suddenly she felt strong hands on her waist from behind.

"Here, let me shake it. You'll hurt your back."

No kidding. He smelled good, like….freshly baked cake. Her shoulders relaxed.

His brown hands were so warm and sure. She wanted to fall backward into him, to be enveloped by those arms, to turn and bury her face in his chest and have those hands stroke her hair. Jesus, she thought, I have the makings of a stalker.

And where would that lead? There was no conquest here. What was she doing making things up? They were just crabbing, for God's sake. She didn't even know him.

She knew Sam never missed a beat, watching her, watching the crabs, studying this man whose arms were wrapped around his mother. Still, Booker's nearness made her giddy. Sorting through the crabs looking for females, Sam glanced at her expecting some help and she wanted to respond. He flipped one over pointing to the carapace that looked like the Capitol dome.

That was their rule. They never ate a female. Her Dad's words came back to her, "If you eat a female, you're forfeiting next year's catch."

Suddenly Sam shouted. An undersized crab had jumped the bucket and was pinching the toe of his sneakers.

"Mommy, pull him off."

Her yearning faded. It wasn't the right time for her skin to electrify under any man's grasp, let alone a stranger. Booker took the errant crab by the back fin and yanked it from Sam's shoe, tossing it into the water. Claire grinned. He crabbed by the same rules. Claire grabbed some more bunker and stocked the cage. "All right to throw it in here?"

Booker looked up surprised. "Sure. You handled the bunker?"

"Crabbing isn't for the fainthearted, right?" But she spoke too soon. Tossing the cage overboard, she caught her ring finger on a torn wire and sliced it. Blood flowed like a spring, and alarmed she remembered the warnings of the lab tech; cuts need compression, big wounds mean the hospital. She tried to hide her finger but Booker watched.

"Hold on. Let me get the first aid kit."

"It's nothing, really," she said.

"Like hell. You're bleeding like a stuck pig." He squirted Bactine over her finger and pressed it with a towel. "Keep the pressure on while I get some tape." Carefully he pulled some sterile gauze from a wrapper and folded it on the cut, taping it with florescent green Duck Tape. "Hope you don't mind. I don't have any white adhesive."

She studied her finger and held it up saying, "Well, if we tape the others I'm a tree frog."

Booker laughed. "I'll get the rest of the pots," he said.

The next one was completely empty of crabs, the bunker eaten. He restocked the bait. No crabs in the last cage either. Booker shrugged his shoulders and asked Sam for the haul numbers. Only eleven males scrambled about in the bucket. Booker wiped his hands on a clean dishtowel and gave Claire another to wipe herself down. He reached in his pocket, palming a blue SD card that looked like the one she used in her digital camera. Pulling a small laptop from a Ziploc bag, he plugged it in.

The electronic light flared on the screen and drew Claire and Sam like moths. In the dark of night, a camouflaged viper duckboat, maybe fifteen feet long, moved around the marsh grass island, a spotlight on the bow. The boater pulled the crab pots, emptied the contents into his boat and moved to the next pot. As Claire watched over Booker's shoulder, she heard a small grunt of satisfaction as his finger shot to the boat's hull and the Delaware registration sticker. It was too small to read.

"You video'd a man stealing your crabs?" asked Sam.

"Uhhuh. Look here, Sam," Booker pointed to the Yamaha engine painted in camouflage to match the boat.

"I got an idea who it is. Now all I need to do is enlarge the frame with the ID sticker to prove it. I set up a moving wildlife camera a few days ago."

"No lie?" Sam's voice trilled with excitement. Claire could only imagine what was going on in that head: visions of late night captures, armed crab police, red-handed watermen. But then, she didn't know if Booker's approach would be much different. He was single and older than she. No responsibilities. Lived with mom. Split knuckles. He could be a big baby with a penchant for fights. Skeptical, she waited to hear what he would say.

"I'll probably report the number to DNREC and let them handle it."

Maybe he was more mature than he looked. She glanced at her muddy legs. She certainly wasn't appealing at the moment. She needed to stop judging him as if he were a potential love interest.

"Would you two like a tour of the bay?" he asked.

"Sure. Do you have a bucket so I can wash up?" she asked.

He put the laptop away and took a plastic pail from storage. When he dragged out the freshwater sprayer, Claire took it from his hands and let hers linger on his for the slightest second.

———

Swain's Lock

Carlos' expectations grew. Everyone had a skill that turned into a product. Esteban was a master at armaments, Mauricio pickpocketed the rich tourists with a light touch, and Luis could extort drug money from rival cliques without a protest. Each had killed out of necessity or revenge. In celebration, Hector played the interested uncle, hosting them for dinners at his house, his extended family.

"We have a problem," he said to Under as he grabbed a beer from the cooler and turned the burgers on the backyard grill. He carefully gave a hot dog to his four year old son and Under waited. Hector ruffled the boy's hair and said, "Go sit down at the table before you drop it." To Under he said, "Carlos has a task for you. You will erase one of our own."

Under listened to the plan and when Hector was finished, he nodded and walked through the sliding glass door to the kitchen. The women bustled about making cabbage salad and corncakes. Under smelled fried plantains, one of his favorites, but his mouth didn't water. Lolita's eyes danced when she saw him. She was spooning whipped frosting on the tres leches cake.

"José," she said, for she never called him Under. "You must have some. I made it especially for you."

He smiled and took a paper plate from the table. She cut a generous slice and added another spoonful of topping. "Sit with me," she said and moved away from the other women.

Under sprawled on Hector's easy chair, his appetite gone. She waddled over to a plastic chair. Her hips had grown big in balance to the child she carried. She grinned at him and laughed saying it was time for another fishing trip.

"Lolita, maybe you should think about going back to your parents," he said. "Your father must be crazy with worry by now."

"What are you saying José? He treated me badly and I am to go home with a big belly and prove him right? He would beat me. I will not be beaten again," she said, her face contorted in a frown.

The women in the kitchen laughed loudly and Under leaned closer. "Then we should go together," he said on impulse. He didn't want to do this. He did not want another man's child or even to care for Lolita. He just wanted the ball to stop rolling down the hill. "You move *a tumba abierta*," he said, "at breakneck speed."

"Que? A baby takes her time. There is nothing fast about this." She patted her belly. "Things will get better, José. I will make things better for us. You will see. You are not like the rest."

He was suddenly angry. "I am like them. You think you know so much." Impulsively, he kissed her cheek. "You are mistaken. You will never get out if you don't go now."

"Be happy, my friend," she answered and took his uneaten cake. She gobbled it down and rose, unsteady, to go back to the kitchen. "Gabriela, my cake is better than your stupid flan." She laughed at her joke and waved to Under to go back outside with the men.

It was a short drive down to the lock. Rock embankments shouldered either side of the rustic narrow road to the parking area of the C & O Canal. Hector got out and opened the trunk for their fishing gear. It was early evening and the sun crept through the dense tree cover in stabs of light. Esteban, Lolita and Under walked a good ways up the towpath, stopping at their sweet fishing hole near a footbridge. Lolita was excited and skipped clumsily, speaking rapidly in Spanish about the catfish.

She was proud of her pregnancy. She was an informant. She was a threat to the clique. Under plied her with beer once they cast their lines and the three companions fell quiet listening to the birds and the plop of insects on the green canal water. It wasn't long before Lolita had to pee. She was five months along and had lost her balance, so Under followed her across the towpath and grabbed her hand to pull her up into the woods. As always, she said, "Come with me and watch out." He stood a few feet away. She bent and pulled down her pants, her back to him. Under reached around her bent shoulder and plunged the knife in her chest and Lolita twisted to look him in the face, horrified. Then she understood. "José," she whispered, "you were my friend."

He stabbed her with the long dagger two more times as she gasped and fell to the soft forest floor without any struggle. Esteban appeared and knelt next to her, pinching her nose with one hand and covering her eyes with the other. He looked up at Under who held the dripping knife, staring down at her bloated body. "Carlos will be pleased." Under panted heavily, his heart beating in his ears.

They dug a shallow grave in the soft earth and covered her with dirt and leaves then walked back to their fishing gear. Gathering up their rods, they laughed and joked for the benefit of a couple who passed by on bikes, their dog trailing behind on a long leash. It veered toward the forest, catching the scent of blood but the man yanked and the dog fell into its trot behind the rolling wheel. Once he was sure no one was near, Under threw the knife and Lolita's rod into the deep water under the footbridge.

In ten minutes they reached the car and stowed their gear, only two instead of three. Hector asked, "Que?"

"It's done," said Under as he climbed in the front seat next to Hector. His hand shook a little on the door handle as he pulled it shut. He looked up the towpath, so still and quiet. The green water reflected the tree canopy. A little corner where God used to be, he thought. I will never come back here. He glanced at Hector and nodded.

"Do not cry for her," said Hector. "Bitch a *chivato*, a stool. You have earned a tear."

———

CHAPTER 2

Baring Her Soul

Odessa Solomon stood at the sink, one hand on the edge and the other on her hip, her eyes following her son as he cut a slice of yellow cake. "What you want with that white woman, anyhow?" Her voice was piercing. He fingered the chocolate icing off the edge of the knife and licked it down, reminding his mother of his eight-year-old self. He hurried over to the table, his back to his mom.

"What do you mean?" Casual, not taking the bait, he sat facing the view of the bay. Steady whitecaps were blowing east to west. High winds, maybe 25 miles an hour, he thought. He forked a bite into his mouth, the crumbs settling in his chin whiskers. The weather was supposed to take a turn for the worse and the Weather Channel was on TV. His Ma had turned the sound down when he came in the kitchen. An alert bannered across the bottom of the screen.

Not looking over at her, he feigned obliviousness. She turned on the faucet and slammed the baking pans, the bowl, and the beaters into the sink.

"Ma, leave it. I'll clean up." She called it his 'nocturnal' baking and told him that if he couldn't get a good night's sleep then guilt was gnawing at his soul. He ignored his Ma, slept in shifts, and enjoyed his cake.

"You heard me. You spent Sunday morning with that woman and that kid. Nothing wrong with her, but she's not our type."

His Ma had played uneducated farmer when she had Claire and Sam over for lunch, and he had caught her. He decided to boil right down to it. "What you mean is, she's not black." It was a challenge and he would pay for it. She was primed this morning. He got up to close the blinds, dimming the sunlight.

His mom said in a calculating voice, "Partly. She's not like us. She's been spoiled."

"Ma, I've told you to stay out of my business. You're just making yourself unhappy, and we aren't having this conversation." He sat, patting his thighs, ready to enjoy his cake.

"Well, we keep having it 'cause you aren't listening to me. When are you going to date a nice black girl?" Odessa's tone changed to bargaining, just short of pleading. "Lenora's daughter was in church the other day. She comes from a good family. Why can't you ask her out?"

"Here we go." Booker leaned back in the chair, looking upward as if entreating God. His thumb had found a familiar nick in the table edge and he rubbed it.

"Now, you just listen here a minute," she said. "That white woman is educated and I like you dating smart girls, but she's got some different ways about her."

This was a new tactic. Bringing race and brains into the mix. The older his mom got the sneakier she became. God, marriage and babies; that was all he ever heard. Booker glanced from his mother's face to the fluorescent light above her head. It flickered and began humming. Time to change the ballast. Better yet, maybe he would put in some recessed lights.

His mom cleared her throat. "You know she asked me if there was someone to mow the lawn for her. We're not her house blacks. She can mow her own lawn."

That brought his gaze level with hers.

"Now, what black woman do you know mows her lawn when there's a man around?" He nodded at her, hoping she would nod back. "Miss Landlord, that's a reasonable request."

His mom stared back, entrenched, jaw set. "I mowed the lawn over there when you were too little."

He tried to reason. "She came from the city and doesn't own a mower. Did she ask us to do it for free or was she going to pay?"

"Don't know. Didn't ask her. Thought it was awful presumptuous."

"Maybe it is but you can stop looking at me like I just grew another head," he said, scarfing up the rest of his cake. He decided to hurry this discussion along. The air conditioning was going full blast, and the slate floor was cool under his feet yet sweat coursed down the middle of his back. "This is just a tenant issue. The house is run down and needs to be fixed."

"Fixed? Just a month ago you gave me grief about fixing it up, don't you remember? And if she's just a tenant, does that mean you should be taking them out on your boat to go crabbing? You tell me, what's that all about?" Now she was spying on his doings. Booker shot up in anger.

"Will you stop? They were out by the dock and we got to chatting. I was being neighborly, that's all." He slammed his plate down next to the smeared knife on the counter. "They come from a boating family and know how to crab."

"Sunday morning. You should've been in church with me. The Lord knows what you doing."

Booker brushed his hand over his face as he passed by the refrigerator with its calendar from the Baptist church. Blonde, blue-eyed Jesus surrounded by little black kids. It annoyed the hell out of him. He pulled it down, knowing she would put it up once he was gone. "Oh for Christ's sake. Now, I'm a heathen. Can you stop?" Leaning over the counter toward his mom, the calendar between them, he spoke low and firm. "And, no, I'm not going to date Lenora Dixon's daughter. I don't care how tight you are with her mother. She's got two babies."

Vexed, Odessa leaned in toward Booker, her brown eyes like daggers. "You don't need to take the Lord's name in vain. Monique's working on an associate's degree. She's smart." The silence grew between them. Then, she said, surveying the counter for invisible crumbs, "I know you don't want to be saddled with nobody else's offspring."

"You're damn right." He slapped his hand on the calendar. This wasn't so much about the white woman next door. It was about grandchildren and the fact that there weren't any in the Solomon family. Momentary guilt surfaced. He scanned the deep wrinkles of her face. She had no daughters and complained that he was never home. New prescription bottles sat on the windowsill. He wondered what they were for but was too annoyed and too afraid to ask. He'd get talked into going to church.

"I want you to find a nice girl from Sussex. I was good enough for your Daddy and we made a good life together. We never had problems in this family until Olivia got in with that Baltimore crowd."

Booker folded like the bimini on his old boat. Olivia. The loss of his sister never waned. He circled the counter and put his arms around his Ma. She was a bundle of softness nestling in the crook of his shoulder, smelling like Nilla Wafers.

"Ma, Olivia made bad choices. She's dead. I'm alive. Stop living in the past."

"Honey, you all I got left." He waited for the rest. "People come here from the big cities and they bring their problems with them. That woman's here for a reason."

"I know, Ma. I'm almost forty years old, and you still treat me like I'm your little boy. I know how to handle people from the city." He had heard the same complaints from other long-time Sussex County residents both black and white: newcomers, immigrants, children leaving for the city, home invasions, being alone and afraid. But this was his mom. He held her out with both hands, looking into her eyes, looking for his strong-willed Ma. "I'm nobody's chump. I'm not a white woman's stud and I'm certainly not a mamma's boy, so you need to back off, hear?"

Odessa straightened. She pushed aside her Mason jar with the weedy white lace flowers to rearrange peaches in a bowl. She was inspecting for soft spots as if nothing was wrong. "All right. It's your life. But if you're living in my house, I got some say in how things run around here. You need to clean up your baking 'fore I get up in the morning." Then she blurted one last jab. "And if you're going to mow the lawn for that woman, you need to get paid."

"Right. Between bartending and building a church for the Guatemalans, I'll make sure I run by your rules, Ma." He never mentioned arresting drug runners on the shore. That only made her more anxiety-ridden. Booker started for the kitchen door adjusting his shoulder holster. Turning back, he made his last, ineffective bid to be house boss. "Check the weather today and see where that storm's going in Virginia. I'll call you later." He paused for emphasis, a smile playing around his mouth. "And don't' expect me to go to church with you." He grinned at her softening face. "Love you, Ma."

———

Point Park

Mrs. Tafano held her reading glasses up in one hand and Claire's after-school care agreement in the other. "John and Armando are old enough to meet Sam's bus. Where at? The traffic light? Damn, even the public school bus comes in the community. Must think they'll catch something," she said.

"I can ask them to drive in," said Claire

"Only to the four-way stop at the rental office. A big bus can't turn around on these streets. It's really not a problem. Gives the older boys something to do after school. But listen, if it's raining, he's still walking. I'm not packing the little ones up in the car to drive a half mile to get your son."

Claire wondered if that meant in a downpour. She had a vision of all three boys soaking wet when they got to the house. I'll get Sam a golf umbrella, she thought. Then reality struck. I can't micromanage this even if I want to. Nobody else is around to watch Sam after school.

Odessa had referred Mrs. Trixie Tafano, so on the third Saturday of her new life, Claire sat on this woman's broken-down couch in her paneled living room. Ambient light came from a clunky plasma TV airing another *Goosebumps* episode. A preschooler rolled around on the worn carpet. Claire thought she might find a Carlotta, or better yet a Franny, closer to Sam's school.

"Let's go in the kitchen where I can see this paperwork. John, you take Sam and go watch the little ones outside. Christopher's picked up a tire iron. Get it away from him before he hurts somebody."

Mrs. Tafano lived in a double-wide halfway down Salient Point, the adjacent road in the trailer park that connected with the Solomon's property. The rest of the streets were named after waterfowl and Claire wondered why this one was different but reasoned it was the only one that didn't dead end at the water. She had driven over on the gravel path, and now her Mini Cooper sat out front squeezed into a jumble of second hand bikes, toys and a rusted minivan. Odessa's Baptist Church had sponsored the family for years and although the place might look like an unmade bed, Mrs. Tafano was widely thought to be a good foster mother.

Sam's private school, fifteen miles across the state line in Maryland, didn't have an after-school program. Pembroke's office was an hour away in Georgetown, Delaware. Claire knew she wouldn't be able to meet the bus on time. Her schedule was flexible, but there would be days she would run late, especially when Pembroke was in court.

She followed Mrs. Tafano into the kitchen where she cleared the table, sweeping everything in one motion with her arm. A bottle of ketchup, crusted around the cap, teetered on the edge, and she tossed it onto some dishtowels on the counter.

"Little people have big ears, you know."

"Sure. No sense discussing it with the kids," said Claire.

"Exactly. Sam can stay late any day you need, even for dinner. We eat good around here. He likes Italian?" Fresh garlic filled a wire basket hung above the table. Sunlight streamed in through the sliding glass doors that looked out on a patch of grass and a muddy canal. Not much yard to play in, thought Claire. Stay focused, she thought. Food, the woman was talking about food.

"He loves Italian. That's very kind of you. I'm sure I wouldn't need him to stay that often, but what a relief to know he has a place to eat dinner and get his homework done."

"On homework," Mrs. Tafano said, her black eyebrows raised. "There's not going to be a lot of quiet time around here, so if he stays late, he's probably not gonna get much done."

"Okay. I can deal," said Claire. "What about pay?"

"I charge minimum wage and two bucks more an hour after five o'clock. Depends on how late he's here. If he stays overnight, it goes to a flat fee of thirty-five after 9 p.m."

"Oh, I won't ever need him to spend the night."

"I'm just telling you." She waved the contract in the air, winding up. "You got a separate paragraph for activities here. I don't do organized activities. They're boys. They make their own fun. They can fish in the canal, but they can't go in the water. I keep 'em outta trouble and feed 'em, patch 'em up when they got a booboo, and hold 'em when they cry." She pushed her glasses up her nose. "I don't make 'em pray, recite the Constitution or wash the toilet, except when they miss. I break up fights when it looks like somebody's gonna get hurt. I make 'em apologize when they're wrong. I might have to smack 'em if they think they're bigger than their britches. Just telling you.

"Next, you got security down here. We live in a trailer park, girl. There's two registered pedophiles in here. Look 'em up online. My kids know those two houses. They know to stay away. I got their mug shots and made each kid memorize their faces. Sam will too. You gonna have to trust me to handle this my way. And I'm not saying that's the only problem we got in this community. There's a house full of some harmless

Hispanic yard workers, a few drunks and addicts, but my kids come from homes where they seen that anyway. That's why they're in foster care. I tell 'em if they're gonna get high, I'm not their mom.

"The retirees around here got one foot in the grave, but they got eyes, believe me. Nothing happens they don't see it. My boys are good kids. A little rough around the edges for Sam but they won't hurt him any. Might be good for both of them. Learn something about the other side of life."

Claire stared at Mrs. Trixie Tafano not knowing where to start. 'You gonna have to trust me' struck a chord and she thought this big-bosomed woman with the black hair and garlic breath knew what she was talking about. Food, pay, security, discipline and cross-cultural ties had been covered in three minutes. Government could learn something from this lady.

"I have one question," said Claire "Where is Mr. Tafano?"

Mrs. Tafano nodded. "Dead as a doornail for twenty years and good riddance. I got a boyfriend, but I only let him spend the night on Saturday. So, if you got a problem with a Dago grandmother having premarital sex, don't let Sam spend the night on the weekends."

They got in the car and backed out when John, who looked to be about twelve, came running around the side of the trailer. The three younger ones followed. They waved goodbye to Sam.

Claire watched in the rearview mirror as Sam waved out the window. Four little hoodlums, Claire thought. "Is this good, Sam? Are you going to be okay with Mrs. Tafano?"

"Yeah, sure. The guys want to take me fishing in the canal. Awesome, huh?"

Rosa Robles

"Claire, I'm giving you a client." Pembroke stood in front of her desk. His pink shirt was rumpled at the waistband and the button was missing just above his trousers. He really needed a wife to dress him. He was a smart man, possibly even brilliant, but he always looked like he'd prefer to be in his pajamas. Flat feet, heavy jowls and florid cheeks hid a magnanimous soul. She looked at his mustachioed face and grinned. "Finally, you trust me."

"You wearing purple yet on the weekends? You're not in my inner circle till you wear purple."

"I'll reconsider, Howard. Redheads look great in purple."

"Here's her contact info. She's Salvadoran. Go practice your Spanglish." Pembroke was fluent and had no patience for her high school Spanish. She felt herself flush. He laughed.

Lately, she felt more like one of the interns at Wilcox and Stein than an experienced attorney. After graduation, she had passed the District bar exam, the Maryland bar and had reciprocity with other states that didn't extend to Delaware. Her impulsiveness had gotten the best of her and when she discovered she had to work five months for Pembroke before she could take the Delaware bar, she felt plain stupid. In her spare time, she would have to bone up on corporate law, a heavy focus as some 70 percent of corporations listed on the New York Stock Exchange were headquartered in Wilmington, Delaware. If she passed, it would be February before she could actually represent someone in court. Pembroke didn't seem to be worried probably because the first pay raise was delayed. There had to be another way to make money. She wasn't above driving for Uber, but her car was too small. And besides, she would only work on weekends when Sam was with his father. At least she wasn't putting her paycheck in the gas tank.

Within her first week of work, Claire learned Pembroke was in-house counsel for DelAire, a large chicken packinghouse. The company was dwarfed by Perdue Farms but wasn't as small as the family-owned Atkins-Hoyle. To get up to speed, after she put Sam to bed, she read Pembroke's closed cases. She discovered he had defended DelAire against a state lawsuit over pollution of a local river (won), represented them in contract disputes with local chicken farmers (lost), and most recently was trying to obtain legal status for reliable workers who had immigration problems. DelAire apparently valued their employees.

"What's Ms. Robles' problem?"

Pembroke was shuffling toward her door and he turned back. "She says she has temporary H2B worker status but a customs official typed her name incorrectly. I'm sure there's more. Always is."

With the federal push to deport illegals with one felony, Pembroke's work was ballooning. He called the immigrants the bottom of the food chain—not bottom feeders, but those getting eaten.

Over the next few days Claire had multiple visits with Ms. Robles in the HR office at the processing plant. She didn't ask about her work at first, wanting to stick to the immigration issue. She spoke broken English but they fell into an easy communication. Rosa was grateful, almost subservient, her head bowed and smiling big only when Claire asked about her family.

"I have baby girl at home. She two."

"Are you her sole support?"

"You mean my money? She have only me. My husband, he die."

"Oh, I'm so sorry."

After her interview with Rosa, Claire was given a tour of the plant. Levi, a line supervisor whose name was embroidered on his shirt, handed her a clean uniform and paper slippers to cover her shoes before she entered the loading dock. A sour stench hit her, and surreptitiously she raised a hand to her nose. She followed him to a darkened room, the only light coming from an open bay that led to the trucking station.

Four swarthy men dressed in smeared white aprons, rubber gloves, hairnets and facemasks unloaded the fluttering, clucking chickens. They placed the cages one by one in an electrified bath that numbed the birds. The workers grabbed their legs and hung them on conveyor hooks upside down. The belt whirred into the next room as their heads jerked this way and that, their red eyes flat but fearful.

Claire followed Levi across the gangway, and when she caught a glimpse ahead, the hair on her arms stood on end. An overhead wire shocked the wet chickens again, killing most. Feathers floated. The assembly line rattled and shook. Up ahead, she saw necks sliced by an automatic blade. Blood puddled on the floor. Some were missed but once another cutter sliced off their legs, they fell into the hands of a checker who finished the job by hand. The smell of offal gagged her, and seeing her revulsion, Levi offered her a sample tube of Vicks VapoRub, yelling over the din, "Here, put some of this under your nose. I shoulda given it to you earlier. Sorry, I forget sometimes. I can't smell it anymore."

Claire stared at him wordlessly.

He yelled, "The men in here are rotated every sixty days so they don't become traumatized."

Sixty-one, she thought, and you become a screaming idiot? She followed him into a large room with at least a hundred workers, mostly women, dressed in the same white gowns and blue plastic gloves. This was where Rosa worked most often. Above, a sign in English and Spanish read, "Democracies depend on the political participation of its citizens, but not in the workplace."

Lines and lines of translucent chicken hung together tightly on hooks, blood still dripping from headless carcasses. Gas flames singed off the remaining feathers. A claw-like hand eviscerated them, splattering blood and guts into a trough. Odors of peppermint mixed with Clorox and ammonia bombarded her nostrils and a sourness that she could only think was the smell of death. Clanking metal armatures sped around at shoulder height while the women wielded knives slicing off breasts, thighs, drumsticks and wings.

Claire gawked and asked, "How fast? How many chickens are they processing?"

"Thirty-five to forty a minute. 2400 an hour. Upper management always pushes for more. I'm against it. Makes my job harder," said Levi. "When someone needs to use the restroom, the line super has to find a replacement so the speed don't slow down. I've had workers pee themselves for fear they'll lose their job. It's tough work."

A kind man, thought Claire. "Did you come up through the ranks?" she asked.

"Uh-huh. They used to move us white folk up before the native speakers. But my Spanish isn't that good.

"It's as good as mine," she answered.

Levi smiled. "We need more native speakers these days. That's why they're looking to promote Ms. Robles. She's been here seven years."

But there was the problem of her H2B status, thought Claire. If Levi knew, would he be less sympathetic? Later, back at Pembroke's office, Claire called Sister Aida Guttierez, Rosa's mentor from the social services agency, La Casa. Together, they pieced together the story from Rosa's immigration folder.

Her papers indicated she was from the lowlands of El Salvador and had immigrated after a major earthquake demolished her village. She had a son whom she left behind with her parents in San Salvador, the capitol city. Her husband, John Granger, an American teacher, accompanied her. The next page in the file was his death certificate.

"By all rights, she's a U.S. citizen through marriage," said Claire.

"They never filed for her naturalization during their marriage. She never demonstrated intent to live here," responded Sister.

"But they had a child. He should have U.S. citizenship through his father."

"No birth certificate. Read on. It gets worse."

Claire fumbled with restaurant pay stubs for Rosa Robles dated 1999 that showed taxes withheld. Next, was a letter from the Spanish Community Center in Gaithersburg, Maryland, stating *Rita* Robles qualified for Temporary Protected Status or TPS. She could become an unskilled laborer in a 'high need industry.' She would not be granted permanent residency but could earn a living.

A few days later, Sister Aida said, alone and nearly penniless, Rosa was on her way to Delaware carrying her first United States TPS document that identified her as Rita Robles. In her hurry, she never noticed or questioned the community organizer about the mistake.

DelAire had kept detailed records, and by switching jobs internally, Rosa had escaped the ruinous carpal tunnel syndrome many of the female line workers suffered. Breast cutter to drumstick cutter to fat scraper to chiller hanger to cone loader to bagger and packer. But recent TPS documents were missing from the folder. One thing had changed. Claire could see by her work evaluations that she was valued.

Claire closed the folder and looked at Sister. "She got lazy about her paperwork, didn't she?" Eighteen months of TPS status had been filed only three times, a different CASA mentor's name on the each document.

"Everyone has a weakness. The system is harsh and unforgiving." Claire nodded when the woman asked if she knew that Telemundo was warning of changes because of something reporters were calling the Great Recession. "Americano suicides," she said, "are on the rise, and it will come back to haunt us Latinos. We will be blamed for the loss of their jobs. Americans say they want work, but they really don't want chicken work."

Sister said Rosa had sent money home regularly to her mother. But in 2006, her mother wrote to say that Rosa's son had been barred from the American School for incomplete tuition. Days later, he had been taken from the streets of San Salvador, the grandmother suspected by the cartel.

Rosa was bereft with grief. Even with her money orders there had not been enough to support his schooling and now her son was gone.

Worried that her immigration status would trip a deportation, Rosa hired Pembroke with the support of La Casa. She wanted to file TPS papers with her corrected name. Simple enough, thought Claire. But hadn't Pembroke said, "There's probably something else?" Claire made a note to interview Rosa again.

Claire thanked Sister Gutierrez and promised that she would stay in touch. A few days later she was sitting in her office when she received a call from Levi that Rosa had been detained at work. "Detained?" she asked.

"Yes, arrested. Immigration and Customs Enforcement was here. She's up for deportation," came the answer.

ICE agents had raided the poultry plant on the morning shift and rounded up 300 individuals. Guatamalans, Salvadorans, Mexicans, Vietnamese, Phillipinos and eight African Americans had been rounded up and separated by country, profiling the Hispanics in each room.

Levi said the assembly line was stopped, the water guns abandoned. He heard something he thought he would never hear inside the twenty-four hour line rooms: silence. DelAire management was incensed.

"Management handed over papers on everyone," said Levi. "ICE moved 43 workers into the lunchroom."

"And Rosa with them?" she asked.

"Yep. They bussed them to the detention center at the jail on Route 113. You'll get a call from management, but I wanted you to know. I like Rosa."

"Thanks, Levi. I'll head there in a minute." She called the jail. "Trust me," she said to Rosa. Why, she reasoned, after all this, would Rosa place any value in what she had to say? Or what the ICE agent said? Or the DelAire employment office? Pembroke was nowhere to be found. Claire called Sister Aida for advice but she wasn't in her office.

Sitting in the quiet of Pembroke's office, Claire thought everyone means well. Slowly she became aware of an old analogue wall clock that ticked loudly, interrupting her reasoning. If I halt the deportation, get Rosa out of detention and clear up the illegal alien status, there is still the problem of the incorrect document name. Claire was frustrated but not hopeless. Her memory of Rosa's story haunted her like a prayer.

This was a real person, a mother, and not some ephemeral hot-button issue in Congress. She pulled her hair up, winding a rubber band around it. Her hands shook slightly as she checked the address for the detention center. Claire's tiny office seemed too small to contain her. She slammed her desk drawer shut, grabbed her purse and ran out the door. She bolted down the steps and found herself opposite the bank. Money for bail—just an initial outlay. She couldn't afford much but five hundred might do, and she was sure Pembroke would pay her back.

She paused to cross the street near The Circle and in that moment came face to face with a historic marker, a remnant of Sussex County's penal code, called Red Hannah. Odessa had told her about the whipping post, nicknamed by Sussex County blacks, who wrapped their arms around her to receive their lashes. As children, Booker's great grandparents had stood in a crowd of 2,000 onlookers and watched a flogging. To Claire, the stump looked like a miniature black granite Washington Monument. Entranced by the sign embedded in the grass, she read that it was last used in 1952 to tie a poor black man convicted of wife beating. She shook her head. Red Hannah had remained legal for another twenty years. Claire circled the stone and wondered what possessed people to persist in using such methods of punishment, a remnant of the Middle Ages.

It seemed that the world lined up on offense or defense. Everywhere, people wanted to fight a battle, confuse the enemy with lies, or compromise their principles. Since her father's death, she sensed that her family and friends were not the same people she thought they had been all her life. The only sure comfort was a home to run to but she didn't even have that anymore. Her home was Sam.

As she stared at Red Hannah, she wondered if it wasn't always like this. Wasn't cruel and unusual a song for the ages? Even if near poverty was self-inflicted, her choice was clear. She reached in her purse and pulled out her checkbook. The balance read $400.00 and she wasn't sure that was accurate. Her lousy accounting habits. Damn Vance, she thought. She was sick and tired of being tied to the house in Chevy Chase and needed to call her attorney about the partition lawsuit or mediation or something. In the meantime, she thought, can I quash my pride and ask Dean for money from the trust?

By three o'clock, Claire arrived at the detention center. Surrounded by twelve-foot fencing topped with concertina wire, the complex was a gray wash of cement box structures with narrow windows. Each looked to be about three stories high with sodium-powered spotlights posted at every corner. Cameras followed her stride from the asphalt parking lot to the cement sidewalk to the bricked steps and the blank metal door. She smoothed her suit jacket, wiping her palms down her pant legs. Then, pressing the intercom button, she identified herself and her purpose. A faceless female voice told her to wait. She rolled her head around on her neck trying to loosen up her shoulder muscles.

The door opened and an armed officer in blues led her along a polished hallway to a receiving room. He seated her at a table in a folding aluminum chair and told her that she could see the ICE officer in charge while she waited for Rosa. It was her chance to gather information. Hundreds, perhaps close to a thousand illegal immigrants lived in Sussex. Why had they picked on DelAire today and what made gentle Rosa a target? It couldn't be the misspelling of her name.

He arrived in tactical pants and a black polo with a shoulder badge identifying him as FBI. Investigative Special Agent Brent Fowler introduced himself, shaking Claire's hand vigorously, his face lit by an easy smile. He carried a single heavy manila file and laid it across the table between them. Claire followed it, glancing at the flat-black, snub-nosed gun holstered at his hip. She thought that Rosa's imprisonment was bigger than her client who had never been arrested, didn't drink or carouse and didn't drive. That file couldn't possibly be hers. She raised her chin in a flashy smile, exuding confidence

"Ms. Lamar, you have been retained to represent Ms. Robles?"

"That's correct. To correct a misspelling of her name on her original papers."

"Really? What is your understanding of Ms. Robles' legal status?"

"Perhaps you can tell me first why she is being detained, why she was removed from her jobsite at a significant loss of pay and embarrassment in front of her employers who have given her positive evaluations for the past seven, I repeat, *seven* years?" She smiled and stared at him with cold eyes.

"I can give you that information. Her status is illegal. She hasn't filed for TPS or H2B status in almost three years. And her original TPS status reflects a name of Rita Santiago Robles."

"Oh, uh-huh. Let's get real. Rosa is one of eleven million illegal immigrants in this country. We are arresting hardworking immigrants over misspelled names now?"

He pushed the file forward and opened it to a picture of a Hispanic youth.

"Who is this?" she asked.

"This is her son, Ms. Lamar. José Robles, in this country we think for the past four years and recently seen in Sussex County. He is wanted for robbery, murder and terroristic acts. He's an MS13 gang member."

She paused, not flustered, just curious. Not something Rosa had shared.

"Well you can hold Ms. Robles for her elapsed status, but it looks to me like you want something else?"

"We want to question her about her son."

"Okay, if she cooperates I will insist that you correct her status. And you may question her only in my presence."

"She is illegal and has no rights, Ms. Lamar." The agent nodded. "But I'll see what I can do."

On the last day of September in early morning, Claire scooted along Zion Church Road in the Mini Cooper. Freshly manured fields pumped their ripe odor through the vents of the little car. Better than bus exhaust, she thought. The fog had not lifted and visibility was poor. Her wipers flashed back and forth sifting through the mist. Shifting the car, watching for deer and peering through the fog didn't keep her from probing her conscience.

Rosa. Claire wanted to see her again. The interview had produced nothing for the FBI agent. Rosa was noncommittal and resolute. She knew nothing about her grown son and appeared shocked at the information in the folder. Agent Fowler admitted that he had no evidence to incriminate Rosa, but the fact that her records had lapsed was enough to detain her. Claire knew that ICE couldn't hold her for long over some vague insinuation that her gang-related son might be in the area. Mrs. Hutchinson, the DelAire Human Resources representative took a stand with Agent Fowler about Rosa's employment, making a call that they wanted to promote her to line supervisor.

As Claire passed the little hamlet of Roxanna, the fog lifted and sat suspended above the pastures and fields. Even though her car sat low to the ground, a band of white mist prevented her from seeing a doe that appeared in the right front fog lights. She jammed on the brakes. The Mini reared slightly and Claire overcorrected sliding across the lane. The animal hesitated for a brief second and ran across the road chased by a buck that Claire barely missed. No oncoming cars. Her heart raced in her chest and she broke out in a clammy sweat.

Claire passed through the little town of Hudson near the chicken-processing plant where abandoned factory cottages sat in a line of overgrown weeds. Rosa said she lived close to DelAire and Claire decided that on her way home, she would visit her at the detention center.

The morning sped by and before lunch Claire squeezed in a phone call to Agent Fowler. Trying to crack his frosty exterior, she was warm and friendly, only to find that Rosa had been released. Claire called her at home suggesting that she stop by, but Rosa became evasive saying she had to prepare for work the next day. Disappointed, Claire told her she would visit the processing plant before the morning shift began.

At three that afternoon, Claire threw Rosa's file into her briefcase. The humidity of summer had evaporated and with the windows down and the sunroof open, she let her hair fly in the wind, feeling free. As she crossed the railroad tracks by the Mexican restaurant, Claire could see the gray barrack-style building sitting incongruently between two large ramshackle Victorians. A cluster of lean, bare-chested young men huddled under the hood of a car. Their jeans clung low on their hips, their boxers bunched above heavy leather belts. The balconies of the apartments were filled with toys and strung with clotheslines. Claire detected the unmistakable smell of cumin wafting on a light breeze. Laughter erupted from one balcony and children's voices squealed in answer.

Apartment 203-B. Upstairs, back left. She knocked softly on the dented steel door. She heard voices inside, a baby crying. Then nothing. She knocked again, louder. The door opened partway. Rosa's round face peeked at Claire with worry. Her eyes grew wider and she smiled.

Relieved, Claire berated herself for thinking Rosa wouldn't want to see her. Poor woman, she was scared of everything. Of being hauled back to detention, or being deported. And who would take care of her daughter? Who was the father anyway? Claire wondered how much of a support system Rosa had.

"Rosa, how are you? I hope you'll forgive me for not calling. I have a letter for you, from Immigration."

"Yes, yes. Okay. You come in, Miss."

Claire stood inside the door on the worn beige carpet. The room was sparsely furnished and the only indication that a baby might live there was an old playpen in the corner filled with stuffed animals. Claire heard a radio in another room playing jiggly Spanish music. Rosa offered her an iced tea.

"I spoke with the immigration officer this morning. We've applied for EB3 status to get your green card. It's a long shot, but it's worth trying."

Rosa stopped dead in her tracks holding two plastic cups in her hand. "Oh, Miss, thank you for getting me out. I not break any laws but they not listen to me, you know?"

"This isn't cleared up yet. DelAire committed in writing saying that your job is permanent, but this name change has to be fixed. Do you have any documents, like utility bills with your legal name, Rosa Robles, on them? I need three printed with that name."

Rosa set the iced tea down on the coffee table. "Sure, sure, I find in a minute. I go to my bedroom and look." She scurried down the hallway.

Claire drank her tea and walked toward the balcony. The view from the back of the apartment was peaceful and Claire stepped outside. A small mowed area abutted an overgrown woods. On closer look, she saw an abandoned car covered in vines, rusting in the sun. Claire turned to go inside when a glint of silver caught her eye. Standing in the corner of the balcony was a machete. It was huge, maybe a three-foot blade, thick at the end, slightly curved, with a wooden handle. What on earth, she thought? Maybe someone was going to use it to clear the woods. Was there a husband, a boyfriend? Or was it her son's? She heard whispering, growing louder and insistent, coming from the bedroom. The baby started to cry. Claire hurried back over to the couch and sat down.

Rosa shut the bedroom door and returned all smiles with the baby in her arms. The child fussed, pink cheeked, as if she had woken from a nap. On seeing Claire, she ducked her dark curls into her mother's neck, stuck a thumb in her mouth and watched her warily.

"She's beautiful, Rosa," Claire said. "Aren't you lucky to have such a sweetheart? You must be very proud." It was obvious that the sun rose and set with this round-eyed child with her café au lait skin and petulant mouth. Rosa beamed.

Claire thanked Rosa for the letters, saved in the original envelopes, and told her that she would copy and return them right away.

"I have my paperwork. I keep file."

Claire complemented her and encouraged her to call with any questions. Then she asked, "Rosa, have you had any contact with your son?"

Rosa blinked once, twice. Quietly she bowed her head and said, "No, Miss, I not matter to him."

Claire tried again, thinking she didn't understand the question. She changed her tone, becoming stern. "Rosa, you cannot have contact with him. Immigration is searching for him as a criminal suspect. You can't jeopardize your status claim."

"I understand, Miss. He not come here."

Getting into her car with Rosa's three utility envelopes in hand, it occurred to Claire that young Robles might have found a safe house with his mother. She worried that Agent Fowler would be right behind her.

———•———

CHAPTER 3

Will the Real Booker Solomon Please Stand Up?

*T*he barn door swung shut, leaving Claire in relative blackness, a thin line trailing her heels. She cleared her throat and waited for her eyes to focus. Coming straight from the office in a suit she fanned the air to keep the dust from settling on her jacket. "Booker?"

Claire hoped she was not overstepping her boundaries by walking into the Solomon's barn unannounced. The light from the window drew her in.

In the dimness, she scanned the rest of the barn. A long center aisle was lined with empty stalls on either side. A bricked floor led to rear double doors. Not your normal barn, she thought. Her steps echoed in the stillness. No bales of hay, no pitchforks, no animals. At one time, she thought, the barn must have been a thriving enterprise.

She raised her eyes upward to the post and beam construction, built in a sunrise pattern forty feet above. Barn swallows huddled silently on one beam, their heads craned studying the intruder. A light gleamed beneath a door.

She pushed it open calling to Booker. The room was empty but filled with the smell of burnt coffee. A picture window looked out upon the gravel drive between the house and barn. Inside, soft gray walls absorbed the light from a swing arm lamp above an aluminum drafting table. On the walls were a series of old wooden measures, a right angle, scale, three sided rules, triangles, circles, ellipses and templates hung in ascending sizes, like artwork. A converted tack room, she thought. On a shelf sat the scalded coffeepot, its clock reading 2:10 and the red light gleaming. She punched off the warmer.

On the far wall another door was secured with a padlock A custom cabinet held drawing tubes and dog-eared blueprints. She nosed around reading the labels on the shallow-drawer steel file. *Our Lady of Perpetual Assistance, Possum Point Theatre, Civic Center,* and the rest below were unmarked. He's been busy, she thought. Above, a green light caught her eye from a small music audio board that read *Low End Theory..A Tribe Called Quest.* Booker was a man of classic hip-hop. On the drafting table were CAD drawings of a church with a tall steeple.

She heard the sound of tires on gravel and saw a heavy black sport utility with tinted windows sweep into the yard. She leaned up against the file drawers, deflated. Crap, she thought, I'm uninvited, poking around his office. What is the matter with me?

Booker climbed out, a dark blue ball cap pulled low over his forehead, his whole body wired in concentration as if he were a boxer getting pumped for a fight. Excited, she ran out to the stable.

He pulled a small bag from the front seat as she called to him. Startled, he stepped behind the truck for a moment, and then her voice registered.

"Booker, it's me, Claire. How are you?"

He fumbled and laid something she couldn't see on the car seat. He walked around the SUV holding a gym bag over his shoulder. "Hey, Claire. What you doing here?" He said, not waiting for an answer. "I got away from the job site for a second and thought I'd come home to eat. What can I do for you?"

His voice, so much baritone, kept her fluttering. His presence was large, not dwarfed by the immensity of the barn. He moved toward her in great strides, meeting her on the concrete pad in front of the office door. His ruggedness smelled of salt water and wind making her palms wet like a teenager's. He grabbed the doorknob to the office and held it open saying, "Come on in. You want a beer?"

He unlocked the padlocked interior door. Claire followed into a small apartment and ran her eyes over the outlines, savoring the mood. A stained concrete floor with a heavy leather couch sat in front of a slate fireplace. A small galley kitchen with gleaming metal counters was starkly clean. She realized this was his cave. She hadn't meant to get into his personal space.

He was standing in the light before the open refrigerator door holding out a Dogfish Head beer. Drinking this early? She couldn't play ingénue when she clearly had been snooping. Besides, she didn't have to pick up Sam until four.

Booker grabbed a bag of Doritos and split it open. She moved to the other side of the kitchen bar where the whole room opened up further, revealing a large bed made with military corners. Two heavily shaded windows blocked out the sun. He must have sensed that she was uncomfortable because he hit a switch and the shades rose. She found herself in the middle of the room absorbing the uncomplicated muscular surroundings of a single man. He spoke again, "So what brings you over? Something broken at the farmhouse?"

"No, I mean, yes. Lots needs to be fixed. That's not why—I really came over to talk to someone. Odessa isn't home," she ended lamely. She was giving him the impression she was looking for his mom when she really wanted to see him. I'm such a coward, she thought, and stepped back, folding her arms.

"Mom has choir practice on Thursdays. She goes over early to work with the organist. You missed her." He sounded diffident.

She started over, putting her hands on the counter. "It doesn't matter. I'm glad to see you."

His brown eyes softened and his face split with that flamboyant smile and sparkling white, white teeth. He grabbed her hand and pulled her to one of the high barstools. She followed, clambering up opposite him and leaned on the counter for balance. She felt awkward and overdressed in heels and a suit. Her feet dangled precariously until she found a rail. He opened a deli bag bulging with a stuffed turkey sandwich.

"Haven't had time for lunch. You want half? It's got Thousand Island dressing on it."

She grabbed a chip and shook her head, wobbling on her perch. "No, you go ahead. I'll watch you eat. I'm trying to drop a couple of pounds anyway."

"Woman," he looked at her frankly, "you don't need to take none of that good stuff off. You're just right the way you are."

Someone else had called her 'woman.' It wasn't at Wilcox and Stein. "Well, thanks but you know dieting's an American pastime."

"So is drinking beer and shooting guns."

She laughed. He asked about Sam. She yammered about his school in Maryland and how he was struggling to meet kids who lived in Delaware. She realized she was talking about children to a man who didn't have any. "Sam has soccer practice today after school and then he's going over to a friend's house. I think it's a horse farm," she said.

"Yeah, there are some wealthy horse farmers in the area although not as many as when I was growing up." He was quiet a moment. "I boarded race horses here after my dad died but it got old and I decided to join the Army." She looked at him sideways, fingering the edge of the Dorito bag. Of course, that's why he was so organized.

"Did you serve in Afghanistan?"

"No, I'm old. I was in Somalia. Ranger. I wouldn't want to do the stints these kids are doing now."

"I know, but Somalia wasn't any party. Still a hellhole." So he was older than he looked, she thought calculating. He must be near forty.

He changed the subject. "We have a nor'easter coming in tonight. Heavy rains and flooding. The water will come right up the porch at high tide tomorrow. Don't let it freak you out."

"I heard on the car radio on the way home. My cell reception and internet are really spotty at the house. I only get one bar."

"Everybody gets bad reception on Route 54 between here and Harpoon Hannah's. Dead spots. When the storm blows in, we could lose TV."

"Lights too?"

"Might. Tell you what, call me when you get home with Sam and I'll come over with some camp lights."

"Thanks Booker," Claire said. She didn't want to impose but he seemed so willing and capable. "Anything else I should do?"

"Have some towels at the ready for leaks. Fill some water jugs and the bathtub."

He made it sound like a picnic. The local news station was warning people in low-lying coastal areas to evacuate, but she had nowhere else to go.

"I was wondering... do you know a lot of Hispanic people in the area?"

He raised his eyebrows. "Some. I have great subcontractors. Foundations, steel stud, carpentry. Why?"

"I have a client who's Hispanic and she was detained for close to a week."

"That's unusual. The police don't bother them if they're working, not anymore, even if they don't have a driver's license."

"What do you mean, 'not anymore?'"

Booker leaned against the wall. "There was a time when the first wave of immigrants came, that folks were annoyed by them congregating in town. Public drinking and driving, pissing on the sidewalk, that kind of thing. But then they filled the chicken processing jobs, became hotel maids and landscapers. People realized they just wanted work. They get some respect now," Booker sighed, "or maybe it's tolerance. Is that what you're asking?"

"My boss is all tied up in a big case and I have a bunch of questions. Like are they involved in a lot of crime?""

"If they're dealing, they'll get deported fast," he said, staring at her closely as he laid his fist on the counter.

"I got that, but is there a gang presence on the shore?"

"Gangs follow drugs. We have a drug problem." He pursed his lips. "My workers are clean though."

"I wasn't implying anything about your people. I guess I'm wondering if the police are overly aggressive," asked Claire.

He rolled his eyes at her. "Look, if you're asking me, a black man, about the judicial process out here in white man country, you're opening a hornet's nest."

He became business-like, wrapping up his trash. "Get back to the farmhouse and batten down the hatches. Bring the aluminum furniture inside. Tie down the back screen door, or it'll blow off. I have twine in the barn. And make sure the windows are locked." He walked over to the door. "Call me when you get back, and I'll come over and help you tape them. We can talk more then. I have to get to the jobsite and make sure the guys have finished buttoning up." He opened the door.

She cursed herself for being too nosy, digging too much. She needed to lighten up. She should call Pembroke over the weekend and ask him. Booker might have the real lowdown, but she wasn't implying he would be experienced with the wrong side of the law.

"Okay," she said. "Come eat dinner with us. I'm not a great cook like your mom, but she gave me a recipe for her smothered chicken. You don't mind being my guinea pig?"

His eyes lit up. "Oh, man. That's the best. Sure, I'll stay for dinner. I'm on the schedule to bartend tonight, but with this weather, they're probably going to close."

Claire followed him through the barn, stopping to take some twine. Their hands touched and this time he paused, holding the moment. He felt it, too. She studied his long fingers and clear, rounded nails, not the hands of a laborer. He didn't do the construction himself. Maybe his split knuckles the day they crabbed were from gardening.

She felt her cheeks warm and kept her head down so as not to embarrass herself. He walked around the SUV giving her a quick "See you later." She noted the size of the truck's side mirrors and thought he must need them for trailering his boat. As she walked the length of the vehicle, she realized all the windows were blackened including the front passenger side. Maybe Delaware allowed tinted front windows. Damn thing looked like a Secret Service SUV.

The nor'easter strengthened along the coastline as Claire and Sam trundled their way along the country roads to the farmhouse. She had phoned the family Sam was going to visit. The mother sounded relieved that Claire was cancelling. Sam was disappointed when she showed up at the soccer field but the rain had started spitting and soon the coach called the game.

Exhausted from excitement, he was fighting sleep in the backseat of the Mini. The rain started in earnest. She took the back roads from the school passing a large chicken truck that spewed water over the windshield. Buffets of wind and rain reminded her of summer storms on the Tred Avon River. Claire clung to the steering wheel with both hands feeling every pothole.

She wanted to see Booker again and hoped he didn't cancel. That lanky stance and swaggering walk. She imagined the feel of his arms wrapped around her as he took the crab pot. After drunken groping at Friday night happy hours in D.C., she hadn't let another man near her for a long time. Warm anticipation filled her as she turned onto Lighthouse Road.

This cooking business wasn't as hard as she thought it would be. She had carefully followed the steps of Odessa's recipe. She would turn the oven back on and boil some packaged rice. She had splurged on blueberry goat cheese for an appetizer and out of habit looked for her favorite wine, an expensive Saxon Brown Semillon. She settled for a jug of Pinot Grigio, rationalizing that it was like getting three for the price of one. She bought Booker an IPA sixpack.

Almost home, she breathed a sigh of relief as she pulled into the trailer park. The shortcut off Route 54 was paved the entire way to the edge of the farmhouse property unlike the dirt road between the Solomon home and the front door of the old farmhouse. Row after row of low slung single and doublewide trailers were lit from within, cars lined up in front of each residence in a herringbone pattern at the street's edge. Zipped up tight. Through the windows, Claire could see elderly faces gathered around tables. They hadn't evacuated. She crossed onto the Solomon property close to the kitchen door, landing the front right tire in a sandy pothole. Sam was strapped into the backseat and two paper bags with beer and wine rested against him. Another band of heavy rain engulfed the Mini, and she wished she had bought a tank instead.

Torrents washed over the windshield, blanking out anything but a vague outline of the steps. *I guess we're going to get soaked*, she thought. She paused and looked in the rearview mirror at sleeping Sam. Strands of string cheese lay uneaten in his hands. What had Odessa called him, *sugar melt?* Her boy was pure sugar.

Claire jumped at a sharp rap on her window. Booker's hooded face appeared beside her. He was in an enormous poncho, holding part of it over her door. She struggled out under its cover and pushed the seat forward to grab Sam. He woke abruptly and fumbled for his seatbelt. Crawling out, he held the string cheese, a grin on his sleepy-eyed face.

"Booker! You're coming for dinner? Awesome."

"Look, help your mom and pass the other grocery bags out, will you?"

Inside the kitchen, Claire and Sam began stripping off their rain gear, and Booker went back outside to get the three LED camping lamps. He set them on the kitchen table and promptly lit one.

"Pretty sure we're going to lose power?" asked Claire.

"Can I light the other two?" asked Sam.

"Let's wait and see if we need them, okay? No sense in wasting the batteries." Booker answered.

Claire hung their wet raincoats on the back of the kitchen door and placed a towel underneath to absorb the drips. Compass nosed their ankles until Claire pointed to his mat in the corner and told him to go lay down. He wasn't done gathering scents and blew her off turning to Booker's boots. Claire was impressed when Booker firmly cupped the dog's chin in his hand and looked into his chocolate brown eyes.

"Compass, down." The dog turned immediately to his corner and curled up to watch the proceedings.

Sam laughed saying, "Watch this Booker. Compass, mom wants you to turn on the lights."

The dog's ears perked up as he looked directly at Sam.

Claire repeated, "Lights, Compass."

The dog bounded across the room to the doorjamb, stood on his hind legs and pressed his front paws toward the switch plate, flicking on the overhead light in the kitchen.

They all burst out laughing and Compass bronco'd like a mechanical bull in a bar.

"You're such a clown. Come here," said Sam and he reached out to scratch the dog's cheeks in utter devotion.

Sam and Booker set the table. Claire turned the oven on and made the salad. Before long, they began to hear the drip, drip, drip of rainwater inside the house. Booker tilted his head and suggested they take a tour. Claire grabbed the pile of towels and an empty pot.

She stopped at the front door where rain was seeping in and tucked the towels across the sill. Sam followed Booker up the rickety staircase. The wind roared about the house and caused the lights to flicker.

"We need a bucket up here. Leak in your bedroom," hollered Booker. Sam shot down the stairs, Compass on his heels.

"Look in the laundry room, Sam."

Claire turned back to the windows on either side of the front door, stuffing tea towels into the wedges of their gnarled and splintered sills. She stared through the panes at the night's blackness. Her mirrored face warmed with a slow smile as she saw Booker's reflection next to hers.

"Sounds like the devil trying to get in." His arm circled her waist.

"Too much sweetness in one house," she answered.

Sam's voice broke the moment. "I'm hungry, you guys. Come on, let's eat."

"Oh my God, the chicken!" yelled Claire.

The casserole looked a bit wrinkled. They congratulated themselves on warding off Mother Nature when the lights flickered and went out, pitching them into near darkness. Palming his way to the camp light, Booker turned up the glow. With a disappointed sigh, Claire placed the chicken on the trivets and lit a candle for the table. She watched Booker wander to the kitchen door. He waved her over, putting his arm around her shoulders as they watched the screens on the porch rippling loose in a wild dance. Compass sat in his dark corner and began a plaintive warble, "ahhhrrooo," as if calling the rest of his pack. A low rumbly laugh came from Booker and he said, "I like the song of your tribe, Compass."

There was little to clean up after the storm. Floodwaters never came into the house, only to the porch door as Booker had predicted. The bay water receded and returned with each successive high tide, depositing trash and reed grass at the doorstep as it wore away the marsh reminding her that what was given could be taken away.

Booker located the source of the leaks and sent two of his men to repair the loose shingles after they finished work on the church. They replaced the porch screens, filled the driveway potholes and a fresh coat of paint was planned to cover the interior water damage.

Claire grew more attached to Booker, enjoying his easy manner. He made time for them, stopping in to fix a leaky faucet or playing a quick game of cards with Sam. They fished for minnows off his pier, and late at night when he wasn't bartending he sat on the porch with her after Sam went to bed. They talked about nothing and about everything. She shared her most embarrassing moment as a child (wetting her pants on her first communion), and he confessed he loved listening to Cher sing "Gypsies, Tramps and Thieves." Her heart melted. She told him her name came with obligations and not knowing what she meant, he asked if she had any idea what it was like to be saddled with the name of a civil rights icon who famously said, 'it's at the bottom of life that we must begin, not at the top.' "So much for a man's dreams," said Booker. "At that rate I could be dead before I get to where some folks start." Claire wondered if the comment was directed at her but didn't ask.

The day the men finished the work on the farmhouse roof, Booker spoke of their dedication, but she was bothered that they lived on the edge of subsistence, some hounded by compulsions. Claire didn't like their torn clothes, cigarettes and cervezas, their rapid conversations and raucous laughter. She only caught bits and pieces of their meaning and some of it was lewd. She didn't care if he thought her a prude so she set rules that his workers could only smoke outside and there was no drinking on the job. To Booker, she was clear. "This is my home with my son and I will not have drunks or addicts working here." He blinked in surprise but said only that they were good men. He didn't work with criminals.

Sam went to bed by eight and rose early with his mom to greet the sunrise. As she made breakfast, he played games on her laptop. Their evenings were filled with Indian summer sun and mild breezes. Claire settled into her job and Sam into his school.

Mrs. Hutchinson, worried about Rosa, called her at work on the first of October to say that another worker had reported a bad man living at Rosa's. Claire fretted knowing it must be her son, the gang member, but decided that Rosa had to make her choices and deal with the consequences. Instead, Claire learned to cook under Odessa's direction. Some nights, Booker taught Sam some pasteurized rap from the '90s.

Trapped in Muddy Waters

Booker chugged a beer as he chafed to throttle up coming out of The Ditch by Catch 54. He glanced at his watch again. 9:30. He needed to get home. The congested waterway by Harpoon Hannah's was restrictive, six miles per hour. The water police sometimes hung out behind the bridge and when he saw a brace of ducks paddling nearby he slowed to a crawl.

His Grady White wove through the channel markers and into the mild chop of the bay. The wind beat at his clothes and held the ever so slight chill of autumn.

Booker downed the last drop of beer and threw it into his gear. He'd come up empty on his fishing trip. He had watched the sunrise by the Route 50 bridge in Ocean City, a swath of pink and purple and he thought red sky at night, sailor's delight; red sky in the morning, sailor's warning. He was sure more rain was on the horizon.

But he wanted one last moment out on the water. His odd work hours, shifting gears between office, investigations and the construction site kept him from any self-reflection. If he wasn't busy, he ate too much, got sloppy and started thinking about his life, what was missing, what could've been. The pull of a woman confused him.

Claire. He was getting sucked in. That messy burnt red hair, the way she looked at him over her shoulder, her dapple-colored eyes challenging him for more. More of him. More of them.

This was the crux of his problem: having to conform to a woman's grand designs instead of following his own. Booker had always prided himself on dealing in realities, knowing his true north at all times. There were unintended consequences to commitment. Demands surfaced like 'where were you?' and statements like 'I need you,' but most of all, 'you'd make such a good daddy.'

He was breaking his one rule of engagement: catch and release. For him, pursuing women was much like onshore fishing. He wasn't a deep water man. He liked angling in the familiar man-made channels away from the dangerous shoals. Claire was definitely very deep water.

His attraction to her had stirred the pot with his mom. Odessa was annoyed with him and he couldn't figure why. His mother might not be enamored of his seeing a white woman, but that wasn't her real objection. There was something else. She never said exactly, and her evasiveness drove him to work more hours. Now it was driving him to Claire.

He cocked his head, hearing a soft blues refrain he had recorded for the boat.

Booker turned up the sound and sang the lyrics, "*Going down in Louisiana,*"....Muddy Waters.

His baritone reached the dogs on the far shore and they began howling in answer. The bay grew quiet except for the wind rustling the reeds in the marshes. He let his boat drift aimlessly, resisting time.

She had him on speed dial, asking his opinions, plying him with comical gossip about Washington headliners and then nestling quietly in his arms with a glass of wine. She asked to go fishing with him, one of his few solitary pastimes. On the other hand, she never asked for money, never asked him to watch Sam and, most importantly, never bossed him around.

He had always followed the minimum size limits for fish... and for women—they had never been more than five years his junior. Now that he was older, the women his age came with baggage like debt and children. Claire was much younger than his experience but Sam, even if he was likeable, was still a kid. Why did Claire leave a well-paid job in the city to take one beneath her? She was running from money problems or maybe something worse.

He was thinking rationally for the first time in weeks, as the sun beat down on his head. The sky was cloudless with no hint of the impending rain to come, and he realized that he'd lost his dispassionate outlook on women. Or at least this woman.

It was time to go back to his normal routine at the local fishing holes, the regular pickups at the bars where he worked as undercover. She had never said anything about meeting him at Gallagher's the night of the drug bust. His cover was that good or her memory was that bad. If it was meant to be, things with Claire would play out. She obviously had her secrets and he had his. Their lack of honesty clouded his perspective like muddied bay water.

It was just before ten and his mom would be at the Baptist service, singing *Jesus Has Come For Me* or *Beulah Land* or something else she belted out all day long. He was relieved and looking forward to extending his solitary morning into a solitary afternoon after he inspected the church site.

Booker tied up at his dock and glanced over at the farmhouse. Everything looks quiet over there, he thought. He grabbed the bait cooler and strode up the path to the back deck. A shower and a second breakfast and he would get this woman nonsense out of his head. The leaves rustled in a soft fall wind, crackling under foot. He heard the sliding glass doors open and looked up. His mother's voice was strident.

"Booker, where've you been? I got to get to church." She stepped out on the deck, dressed in her Sunday finest, a blue hat, and matching pocketbook. He squinted in the sunlight.

"Well, go, Ma. I'm not holding you up," he said. *Christ*. Was she waiting for him to go with her? A small shadow moved behind her and stepped out onto the deck. It was Sam, who grinned as if he had a date with Santa Claus. The kid was in jeans and a T-shirt. She wasn't taking him to church dressed like that.

"Ma. What you talking about? I'll take Sam home. You go on ahead."

"Claire has to work. Mrs. Tafano took all her kids to Philly yesterday. You got to watch Sam for us." Odessa delivered this news with a broad smile.

'For us?' Since when were Claire and his mom a team? She seemed to be chortling at him. He burped slightly from the chugged beer and tried to mask his reaction. Booker didn't want Sam to feel unwanted. The kid had enough to deal with. An egotist for a father, a new home, a new school and Tafano's street kids to compete with every day. But this was the last thing *he* needed right now.

He had promised himself he would drift away from Claire, but he never wanted to cross his Ma on a church day. No telling what she would pray for. Booker climbed the stairs up to the deck and thought he needed to choose his words carefully.

"Ma, you coulda called me. I had my cell. I can't take care of Sam. I got to head over to the construction site." He sidled over to his mother, grabbed her elbow and tried to wedge himself between them.

"Hi, Sam. How you doing?"

"I'm great! I'll be good, Booker." Sam reached up for a fistbump.

"Yeah, my man. That's what I'm saying!" Then he turned and shuffled his mother in the other direction.

He whispered, "Ma, really? Come on. Take him with you." Odessa made a beeline for the stairs, waving back. "I'll be home around three and fix you all some dinner. Maybe Claire will be back by then, too. Nice pot roast in the crockpot for everybody. Have fun, now." Booker gritted his teeth and went inside. Sam followed.

He took a long look at the boy who stood with a faltering smile.

"Can we go get Compass at my house and put him in the back of the truck? Compass hasn't ever been in a truck before."

Observant kid. Again. Nothing escaped him, even how locals traveled around in trucks with their big dogs in the back. He thought of the first time he had seen Claire, Sam and Compass stuffed in the Mini Cooper. Little family, little car.

Booker's whole demeanor slumped in resignation. He would need to find an extra hardhat. "Have you eaten?" he asked before he noticed the sink full of pots and pans. Odessa had made a concerted effort to add to his breakfast mess and had left a note taped to the refrigerator door. BOOKER—WASH THE DISHES BEFORE I GET HOME. LOVE, MA. A heart was drawn below her signature.

Ten minutes later the kitchen was tidied. Compass, the building plans and two hardhats were loaded in the truck while Sam and Booker sat miles apart on the bench seat. As he turned onto Route 20, Booker realized that the seatbelt cut Sam under his chin almost strangling him. Was the child too timid to complain? Not my problem, thought Booker. Sam had the window wide open and the breeze whipped the hair on the top his head. He clutched a red and gold Iron Man action figure, pushing its legs back and forth against his jeans in time to the crackle of music on the radio.

They reached the church building site on Roxana Road, and as Sam looked up at the intricate three-story steel skeleton he uttered a single, "Wow." Then he asked, "Booker, are you the boss?"

"Yeah, that means everybody listens to me including you."

Sam nodded as he took in the crew of Hispanic workers who were perched on a multi-tiered scaffold like birds on a leafless tree, shooting in the steel track and studs that would support the walls. The air pulsed with the sound of framing shotguns and wisps of smoke trailed upward in the wind. Booker got out, tossed the hard hat to Sam and told him to stay close.

He strode off, looking back only once to see Sam, his head rolling around in the hardhat as if it were a gallon bucket, his eyes on the ground as he skipped to keep up with Booker's long stride. Loping up the slow grade into the church frame, Booker shouted "*Hola!*" to the squat foreman who went by one name: Rodrigo. At the sight of Booker, Rodrigo's leathered brown face lit up with a gap-toothed smile.

"Big boss!" he answered, both arms outstretched in welcome. He spoke broken English and Booker spoke broken Spanish. Their common language was the building plans.

Five minutes into the conversation, Compass started whining, then barked. The truck was parked in the shade near a flat loaded with recyclable building materials. Finally, he began howling a lonesome dirge which drew laughter from the workers still strung on their high wires.

Booker looked around for Sam and yelled too loudly at him for wandering off to watch the workers. Sam came running so fast that for a moment Booker feared the kid would face plant in the construction dirt. Alarmed, he hollered again to slow down. He didn't need a skinned up Sam to take home to his mother. He needed to find something to occupy the kid, even if it was momentary. He told Sam to walk Compass by the fence line, and then put him back in the truck with some water.

More than an hour later, Booker and Rodrigo rolled the architectural plans up and slipped them into their canisters. Booker slapped the stocky foreman on the back and gathered the tubes under his arm. Waving, he shouted, "Adios, *hasta luego*," He loved working with these guys. Hard workers. Good attitudes. Got the job done. Looking around at the workers and across the pebbled construction lot, he thought he was leaving something else undone. He hoofed it to the truck when it came to him. Compass wasn't in the truck bed and Sam was nowhere in sight.

Booker yelled for him and threw the building plans through the open truck window. He pushed his sunglasses up on his nose and scanned the lot. Worry crept into his thoughts but just as quickly anger overcame him. This was why he didn't want kids. You couldn't trust them. They weren't reliable.

Just like his sister, Olivia. He was always rescuing her, getting her out of some fix or another. The end of his first week of high school she disappeared from school.

Where the hell was Sam? Compass would come if he called. Wouldn't Sam? He ran his hand across his sweaty brow and realized he was breathing heavily.

He had hollered for Olivia too, years ago when he was a lowly high school freshman and she was a junior. That day's events had been resolved but only because Booker was so determined. He had found her in the company of some crackhead ghetto boys in Salisbury and that was when she began snorting her life away. Getting her out of there had been easy because in those days, dealers weren't so territorial and cautious. Or maybe it was because they had just started freebasing. The real problem had been getting her home without their parents' finding out. The moment marked the beginning of their split.

Now this was an eight-year-old, not his drug-addled sister. Booker slammed the truck door and walked near the construction flat loaded with debris. It had been disturbed. Disturbed? Hell, it was organized into broken chips of concrete, siding, pieces of aluminum roofing and smaller piles of cut steel studs, track and screws. Next to the flat was a piece of lightweight steel stud arranged in the grass with a flanged tip like an arrow. He leaned back on his heels. This was a game. A game of hide and seek! The kid was playing him like a mouse in a maze. Anger welled up in a rising tide. Muttering, he strode off in the direction of the arrow thinking when he caught up to Sam he would take him down a peg or two. It would make it easier to get Claire out of his head. She was just the renter after all. Why didn't the kid sit in the truck and wait for him?

Walking the fence line that separated the church property from an independent family farm cooled him off a little. Booker had seen how obedient Sam was to his mom. This behavior was probably the influence of the Tafano kids. He looked at his watch. It was close to two o'clock and time to get back. Claire might be waiting. What would she think if he lost her kid, or worse, what if the kid was hurt? He yelled again, "Samuel, Compass!"

Booker stopped when he saw a speck of gold and red sitting on the split rail. He reached for the Iron Man action figure whose articulated leg was crooked over the post. Booker put both hands on his hips and surveyed the scene. There was no sign of a struggle, no trampled grass, no blood. No need to get worked up. All the evidence pointed to Sam. Booker looked around and saw huge rolls of hay on one side of the fence and meadow before him. When he called Compass this time, there was an outburst of barking. He ran ahead to find the dog tied to an oak tree. He reared up on seeing Booker. "Down. Good dog. I bet you're thirsty." He looked down an embankment to the creek. There were no small footprints in the mud. "Where is that bad Sam?"

An acorn fell from the tree near Booker's knee, then another and another. Soon, it was raining acorns and Booker shielded his face as he looked up at Sam who was dissolving into laughter in the crook of a tall branch. "Get down here, right now. I told you to stay close to me."

"Booker, why're you mad? I was playing detective. I gave you clues," Sam said. Booker's anger evaporated and, surprised at himself, he felt like the child. He stared upward, confused by his own shame and relief. He chortled once, twice, held his arms up toward Sam and slapped his chest signaling him to jump down. Sam pushed off the branch and slipped into Booker's long arms. He held him tightly, "Sam, you didn't follow my directions. Did I say it was okay to play detective?"

"No. I'm sorry, Booker. But we had fun."

Booker set Sam on the ground and the boy raced toward the truck with Compass in hot pursuit. He shouted after him, "That's a matter of perspective," then under his breath, "you little shit." For a moment, Booker didn't know what to think, except that he was okay with being made the fool. He pondered when the kid had squirmed his way into his heart.

Booker ordered Sam to pick up debris in the construction yard since he was so good at organizing the recycled materials, he could put it all back where it belonged. Booker inspected the kid's job before he ordered him into the truck. Driving home, the two were quiet until Sam asked him if he had ever caught the man who stole his crab pots. Wanting to enjoy a quiet Sunday afternoon without any further conflict, he tried to deflect Sam's interest.

"No. DNREC never followed up on it as far as I know." He sucked on sunflower seeds and wondered why he hadn't heard back from Natural Resources. "I think the guy swiped a lot of them this summer."

"Well, you could get him Booker. Your mom told me you're a detective, right? I'm not supposed to tell my mom, though."

"Ma told you that, did she?" he answered doubtfully, spitting some husks out the window. He felt a rising anger, this time with his mother. "Why do you suppose Ma told you that?"

" 'Cause, I told her I was worried about Mom. She was in a bad explosion at her old job. She needs somebody to watch out for her."

So that explained the scars. Was this a loaded statement, the kind that kids say innocently and then make blanket assumptions about how life works? He didn't want to get involved. His Ma knew how to sabotage him, but she had always been discreet. Why tell Sam? "Different police officers work for different states and cities and even have different jobs. I work in Maryland so I'm not allowed to police the creek in Delaware."

They crossed the wide creek on Old Mill Bridge Road and Booker waved an arm out the window toward the silvery water. Two crusty-looking fishermen stood at the edge, their lines cast out, large plastic buckets at their feet.

Sam wasn't going to give up. His blue eyes pierced Booker's complacency. "But you know who stole your crab pots. Why don't you go talk to him and ask him to stop stealing?"

Why hadn't he? Clarence Hoffsnider was an old country derelict who had animals that Booker's father had treated. As a teenager, Booker had visited his farmette with his dad to treat a mare's infected hoof. What was the harm in driving to his house and having a talk with him? Booker pulled the truck over. The kid was right. He was so busy, so entrenched in his own work, that he had stopped extending himself with locals.

Booker made a quick phone call home and left a message saying that they had one more stop. He threw his cell phone on the seat and smiled at Sam who was singing along with the golden oldies station.

Booker made a U-turn and drove the north side of the creek that fed the bay. They passed new waterfront mansions, one massive Italianate with an electric iron gate and tiled roof. He tooled along the gravel road that quickly turned to dirt. The truck bounced through the ruts of a drive that hadn't been tended in years. Low scrub pine disappeared as the road widened toward a muddy boat ramp where a flat bottom fishing boat sat on a trailer.

"That's it, that's the boat in the video you took," said Sam.

"Yeah." The kid was getting overly excited. Sam saw this social call as detective work. Booker would have to set him straight.

A rusty mobile home with a corrugated tin roof edged the sandy driveway apron. Opposite was a one story barn with an attached shed and a run-down chicken coop. Free range hens and a rooster pecked the dirt. The smell of dead fish and seawater dissipated with each passing breeze. Booker hadn't remembered the place looking so neglected. Sam patted Booker's arm and pointed to an older man in jeans and suspenders, his bare chest sunken and wrinkled. He had exited the shed and was heading toward his garden, a hoe slung over his shoulder.

"You stay here, Sam. Don't get out of the truck. That's Hoffsnider. I'll have a friendly talk with him and we'll leave."

"Can I go look at the chickens?"

Booker eyed him. "Just the chickens, understand?"

As the truck door squeaked, the old man turned, frowning against the sun to see who was in his driveway. Booker shouted a greeting and waved as the man's face relaxed in a smile. He must have recognized the veterinarian's old Ford.

They shook hands and chatted, strolling over to see the pumpkin crop. Booker asked after Hoffsnider's wife, what was her name,.... "Miriam?" He was crestfallen to hear she had 'passed on' almost two years ago and Booker apologized for not knowing. He remembered the oatmeal cookies and lemonade she brought them that day in the barn with the mare.

With a perfunctory grunt the old man informed him that he wasn't entitled to any of her social security. The money had "gone to her shit-faced first husband. We were common law, you know."

Booker scrutinized the fungus-ridden pumpkins rotting on the ground. There wasn't much of a living to be made here. Hoffsnider's face was thin and his jeans hung on him. His rheumy eyes filled slightly and the old man made a visible effort to get a grip with a cough and a knotty hand passing over his face. The moment to say something about the crab pots and stolen crabs had passed. Embarrassed to be intruding on his private misery, Booker told him he needed to get home for Sunday dinner.

"Call if you need any help this winter." He patted Clarence's bony back and turned toward the truck.

He gaped as the door to the shed flew open and Sam darted across the dirt drive, feet flying and arms waving. A belligerent Rhode Island Red spread its wings and charged his victim. Chickens scurried out of the way as the rooster pecked at the boy's heels. Sam shrieked and sprinted toward the truck, latching onto the door handle. He yanked it open just as the rooster took flight at his back. The boy jumped in, slamming the door. The rooster calmly strutted back to his hens and his domain, the winner.

Booker strode toward the truck and rested his crossed arms on the window ledge. Sam's chest was heaving and his hands gripped the seat. Where to begin? He nodded at the child's fear. He couldn't follow a simple direction. A talk with Claire was in order. He couldn't go around flaunting orders even if it was for the sake of having fun. Maybe Claire should find a better babysitter than Tafano and her brood.

The kid looked at him warily. *Good. He knows he's in trouble this time.* Out of the corner of his eye Booker watched as Sam pushed something deep into his jeans pocket. He turned to include Hoffsnider. Clarence moved in closer to get a good look.

"Samuel, this is Mr. Hoffsnider. Say hello."

Sam did more than that. Suddenly his private school education and polished manners kicked in. He ducked his head and pushed the door of the truck open, hopping down into the dirt. With a broad smile he stretched his hand out. Amazed, Booker wondered where the panic had gone. Wide eyed, Hoffsnider's eyebrows receded up into his wiry gray hair. He shook hands with the kid.

"Hi, Mr. Hoffsnider. I didn't mean to upset your rooster. I was feeding the chickens some sunflower seeds, and I followed your rooster into the shed."

"You came out alive, I see. That old rooster's mean. Lucky for you he didn't peck your shins up when he got you inside." The old man chuckled.

"Oh no, I was careful. My granddaddy always said if you follow a rooster, be prepared for a fight."

Roosters. This city kid knew about roosters. Or maybe he was bullshitting them both. Then Sam reached deep in his pocket and pulled out Booker's cell phone. Feet planted in the ground, his hands on his hips, Booker's heart sunk as the kid continued.

"I hope you don't mind, Mr. Hoffsnider. I took a picture of him to show my mom." In the afternoon glare the cell photo was whited out so Sam moved back into the shade of the truck and both men followed like ants to a hill, their heads bent over the small screen. There in Sam's grubby little hand was a clear picture of Hoffsnider's Rhode Island Red perched on a stack of crab pots inside the coop. His neck feathers were spread, his wings slightly raised, master of his universe.

Sam continued, "He sure likes standing there on those crab pots." Clarence Hoffsnider was not living off a steady diet of chicken, at least not during crabbing season. Attached to each crab pot were buoys, some gallon bleach bottles, some detergent jugs, and some store-bought, tubular white buoys. Each was clearly labeled according to DNREC regulations with the owner's name. When Booker looked closely he could just make out what he thought was one of his crab pots.

Hoffsnider spluttered and grunted. Finally, he answered, "Yeah, he's what you call the king of the roost." He glanced sideways at Booker who quickly put the matter to rest by steering Sam into the truck.

"Clarence, I meant what I said about giving you a hand this winter. If you need anything, give me a call."

"I don't believe I'll be needing anything. I manage fine here by myself. But that's real good of you." His words were stilted and he threw his arm after them as if he could toss them away like a rotten pumpkin. They drove off and Booker shot a grim look in the dusty review mirror at the broken-down man at his broken-down palace, brought lower by hunger and in want of better company than a Rhode Island Red.

"Aren't you happy? We got him. We got more evidence. Now you can go to DNREC and get him arrested." Sam bounced on the seat next to him.

Booker drove into the afternoon sun, squinting and slapped the visor down. If only he could yell a few choice words and ride home in silence, hand the kid over to his mother and be done with the two of them.

He drove the truck along the rutted road, his thoughts a jumble. There was the day when his dad sat where he sat now, quietly explaining the rules of life. His dad, always too subservient in Booker's mind, smarter than his clients, was well liked by all. The glare on the dirty windshield made it hard to see and he flipped on the washer fluid. The window streaked worse except for a large clear patch under the rearview mirror.

"Samuel." Could he sound fatherly? Booker decided to begin at the beginning. "You didn't follow my directions. What did you see today?" He put up his hand between them to stop the kid before he could answer. This time he was going to be firmly in control of the conversation.

"First, you saw those guys over at the church working on a Sunday. And no doubt they're all a bunch of Catholics like you and your mom, and they would love to be inside that finished church singing in Spanish instead of crawling over a steel frame. "And then you met Mr. Hoffsnider who has a few chickens and some moldy pumpkins. But he was ready with a hoe to work his garden, on a Sunday, I might add.

"And then, while you're playing detective, I was busy fine-tuning a construction job, which happens to be my second job, which I'm doing on a Sunday when I'd rather be out fishing."

Sam started, "but—b—b—" Booker's hand went up again.

"And let's not forget the reason you're here today in the first place. Your mom had to go to work, on a Sunday, a day she would probably like to spend with you."

Booker kept his gaze on the road, but he could feel Sam's blue eyes burning a hole in the side of his cheek. He let the silence deepen in the truck and finally Sam spoke up.

"You're disappointed in me because I was ignoring everybody working. I was having an adventure."

He wondered how spoiled the boy was. He had never seen him do any chores except clear the table after dinner, which wasn't a great way to teach him to be a man. Did he have any responsibility for anything other than his schoolwork?

"Do you get it, Sam? Everyone's working, including your mom, to put food on the table and pay for a roof over their heads, yours being one of them?"

"Yeah." Sam slumped down, the seatbelt cutting into his neck as he looked down at his grimy jeans. "Everybody works. Shit. Everybody works all the time. Mom, Dad, even my Grandad. I didn't get to spend the summer with him before he died."

He was mildly surprised to hear the kid cuss. Sam never expressed disappointment. He was always upbeat, almost like it was—a job. The kid's sourness sat in the air between them.

As a boy, Booker had spent every waking minute he wasn't in school following his dad on vet jobs. Every job was an adventure, too. Now, when he looked back, he was sure it was always nothing but work for his dad. Listening to Sam, Booker realized what he had lost. What they had both lost.

"So you miss him, huh? He was retired and had plenty of time for you?"

"I went everywhere with Granddaddy in the summer when I wasn't at camp. He said work was a game to be won or lost, but he would never lose me." Sam's voice stitched up. Booker waited while he pulled himself together.

"We don't have to talk about it if you don't want to, Sam."

"It's okay. I don't ever talk about him to Mom because she always cries." Then he took a deep breath and confessed. "Grandad took good care of us. Better than my Dad." A few large tears spilled over, streaking his cheek.

"Sometimes, when you're older like that, you have more time to spend with your family," said Booker.

"He loved me a lot. Mom thinks he loved me more than her." Sam wiped his face, leaving it dirt-smudged. "He told me he was leaving everything to me. Now, Mom says she has to do this by herself."

"Do what?" Booker felt a passing guilt probing about Claire but ignored it.

"Make our own way. We have to live on our own just the two of us. She's going to raise me without any help from anybody," Sam said, parroting his mom's voice, wagging his head back and forth.

Booker grinned, thinking Sam looked a lot like the kid from the Little Rascals, his baseball cap on backwards, and a pout on his face. "Sam, that's the way most parents do it. On their own without any help."

"Never mind. I'm not supposed to talk about it." Sullen again, he picked up the Iron Man action figure off the seat and pulled on its head until he yanked it off.

"Talk about what?" Exasperated, Booker reached for the bag of sunflower seeds on the dash but they were gone. Rooster feed.

"I can't decide if this is better. Mom says it is, but I don't know."

"What's better?"

"Like I don't have a nanny, I have Mrs. Tafano. And I get bossed around by John. I still have soccer, though." This last seemed to calm the kid down a little, but then he burst out with "We never eat Chinese or Indian anymore."

"Chinese?" What was the kid so upset about? "That's easy to solve. We can eat Chinese this week, okay?" Booker didn't want to dismiss the kid outright, but he had to put it into perspective. "This isn't so bad here. We don't have Indian but you got boating and fishing. You have my mom. She's like a grandmother, isn't she?"

"Yeah, she's real nice but …. I miss my Granddad."

Disarmed and curious, Booker asked, "Sounds like you spent a lot of time with him. He took you along to work when you didn't have a baby-sitter?" He couldn't bring himself to say 'nanny.'

"I always got to leave early on weekends with my Granddad to go to Tred Avon."

"Special treatment. What did your mom and dad do? Come later?"

"Just mom. She'd come by car but Granddad and I flew."

"What? You flew? From D.C. to Easton? What did that take? Like a half hour?"

"Maybe. Granddaddy said it took longer to drive from his house to the airport than to fly from the airport to Easton."

Corporate plane or helicopter? And here he thought the man was a construction supervisor. And the house on Tred Avon probably wasn't a Chesapeake Bay crab shack either.

"Sam, what was your grandfather's name?"

"Abraham but everybody called him Ham."

"What's his last name?"

"Oh, McIntosh. Same as Mommy. Whoops, I'm not supposed to tell you that."

Oxford was right next to St. Michael's and it was full of high rollers and dinosaurs from the Bush administration like Rumsfeld and Cheney. Rumor had it that Michael Jackson owned a property there when he was alive. Bet he had a problem fitting in.

So Claire had something to hide. Poor little rich girl. Everything about her screamed 'devoted mother.' But why was she living on the lam if Sam was left with everything? No wonder she seemed so fragile in quiet moments.

Nothing made sense but at least he had a lead. He wouldn't give this woman up yet. Too much mystery. He pulled between the barn and his mom's house. Claire's Mini sat by the front door and he heard her voice from the porch.

"There are my guys." She pushed open the screened door and ran toward the truck. Compass huffed, his toenails clicking on the truckbed in excitement. Booker punched Sam's shoulder. She had called them 'my guys.'

"Don't worry. I won't let on I know."

Her voice cut through their buddy moment. "Samuel, we need to get home. You have homework. She shot of look of recrimination at Booker.

"I thought you all were going to stay for dinner. Ma made something."

"I explained to her that we couldn't. Thanks anyway." Claire bustled Sam and Compass out of the truck. Booker watched them take off down the dirt road in a cloud. He wasn't mistaken. That was a brush-off. What the hell?

—◆—

The Watchman

Claire met Vance at the Denton gas station, the halfway point between them to drop Sam off. Vance complained about having to drive and whispered that he could tie things up in court for years, "you crazy bitch." The whole process irritated her, and while she was cheerful and encouraging with Sam, now that he was out of the car, Claire succumbed to her worries. Turning onto Lighthouse Road brought unexpected tears. Was this the pull of home, of belonging in a place? She decided she was a bundle of hormones. The air in the car felt stale, so she opened her window and a sea gust dried her face.

As she turned into the trailer park, the growing darkness was dispelled by dimly lit streetlights. A spotlight shone on the activity sign at the entrance: *Pork & Sauerkraut Dinner/Bingo-Sat. 5:30.* She drove slowly down Salient Point to her farmhouse, careful to dodge the haphazard paths of resident rabbits. The bumpers of each gas-guzzling sedan were right at eye level of the Mini so she read the specialty license plates: the Masons, Elks, Rotary, Knights of Columbus, and the Veterans of Foreign Wars. Pride of belonging flaunted on their cars.

Booker was bartending in Ocean City. They hadn't talked all week, and the prospect of spending a weekend alone added to her agitation. She regretted driving off in a huff, but she was mad that Booker had taken Sam to the job site with all those workers around. And to make it worse, Sam was closemouthed about his day.

Compass spun in a circle as she entered the kitchen. She let him out, and he nosed his way through the screened door into the backyard. Claire flipped on the porch light to watch him, wrapping her sweater close in the light chill. He ran through the tall grass, his nose to the ground, captured by a scent. She called him, but he stopped and stood his ground looking away into the night. Clouds obscured the moon and the night sky. Claire called again and banged the screen door, a noise that meant she was coming to get him.

Compass trotted to the porch.

"What did you smell, boy?" He paused at the door and didn't go for a second sniff but nosed his bowl. Fed and watered, he curled up in his corner. She stood at the kitchen sink looking glumly at the day's dirty dishes. The window opened to the blank night and she felt hollow and directionless, her empty purse driving her down. Her loneliness was inescapable. She thought she needed to find some girlfriends and wondered what Odessa was doing.

She reached for the wine, slugging right from the bottle. Guiltily, she opened a metal cabinet door for a wine glass and saw the prescription bottle tucked into the side of the bottom shelf. Snatching it, she read Alprozam, her green triangles of generic relief. Three milligrams of cheap Xanax. In a second, she pulled off the top and scooped out two pills washing them down with the cabernet.

She awoke later on the living room couch, groggy and her face wet from drool. Incessant, loud, something frenetic in her peripheral vision, back and forth, back and forth. Trying to focus, she got to her feet but tripped over an end table. She knocked the lamp. "Oh, fuck!"

Compass' nose was in her face. He growled and whined.

"Okay. Okay." She pushed the lamp onto the table and made it to the hallway. Compass was desperate to go out. Claire rubbed her face hard and pulled her hair back. Sighing, she stumbled to the door. He charged into the night, barking in a frenzy.

At this rate he would wake Odessa and the entire trailer park. Claire glanced at her watch. Two-thirty in the morning. She stepped onto the cold cement of the porch shocking her bare feet. Darkness lay thickly over the water. She belted out, "Here, Compass. Here!" All was quiet. Then she heard a loud yelp followed by whining.

Shaking the cobwebs from her head, Claire ran to the kitchen and fumbled in the broom closet for the flashlight. She wrapped her fingers around its barrel and ran out into the wet grass. She screamed for her dog, waving the light back and forth on the silvery grass. Pulling up short, she heard him whimper. There, in the grass was a mound of fur, and in the light he scrabbled to his feet but fell again. The flashlight shone over his body and his eye turned up wildly at Claire. She saw the dark stain at his neck and shoulder. Blood.

"Oh, Compass, what happened?" The grass had an odor....gasoline? She realized they were not alone and stood over her dog and yelled into the darkness, "I have a gun, you son of a bitch." Kneeling down, she put her palm on Compass' heaving side while the other hovered atop the gash. It looked like a knife wound. With alarm, she heard a soft 'whoosh.'

A stream of fire on the dry grass moved toward them from the direction of the rickety dock. Beyond the flames, a tinny boat motor sprang to life, revving in the darkness. She realized someone was leaving in a big hurry.

Claire grabbed Compass around the hips and dragged him toward the house. He didn't struggle. My phone, she thought. There was no way to carry him. Her heart pounded in her throat, and she spoke to him hoarsely, "Compass, everything's going to be all right, baby." She laid the flashlight next to him and ran, slamming her shoulder on the porch doorframe. In the kitchen, she gathered towels in her bloody hands and rummaged in her purse for her cell. Compass' eye opened when she arrived, but he seemed sleepy and his panting was shallow. She pressed on the blood flow with a towel and called 911. Three rings and a calm voice answered. Words tumbled out as her mind raced.

"Are you hurt, Ma'am?"

"No, aren't you listening? My dog is. Someone tried to slash his throat. We're outside by the dock and there's a fire"

"Leave the dog, Ma'am. Stay on the line and go inside. Lock the door till the police arrive."

"Yeah, okay. I'm not doing that. Just get here, will you?"

"Ma'am, you need to make sure you're safe so you can take care of the dog."

"I don't care. Send someone over."

"Stay on the phone with me, Ma'am. The police are on their way."

Suddenly, lights from the road careened across the grass, glaring into the backyard. A figure, backlit in the truck headlights, hollered, "Claire, what happened?" Booker ran toward them. Her phone fell into the grass.

"Compass is hurt. He's bleeding. I, I, can you…."

"For God's sake, the dock's on fire. Get inside."

"No, I'm staying with Compass. Whoever did it took off."

"Get inside, now," he ordered. He scooped up the limp dog and she ran ahead opening doors. "Lock it," he shouted as he laid Compass on the table. He pulled the bloody towel off and looked at the pink flesh of the open wound. Blood seeped but didn't pulse. No artery cut. He checked the gums. Still pink.

"Press down here. I'm going to search the house." He pulled a gun from under his jacket and strode from room to room. Claire listened to his steps above, amazed at his timing and his gun.

"All's clear. How's he doing?"

"Oh, Booker, he can't die."

"He won't. I got this. The fire truck will get here soon. State police will be a while coming from Georgetown. Come here." He wrapped his arm around her and looked into her eyes. "You okay, Woman?"

She dissolved into his arms. "Sure, I can deal with the police. Can you take Compass to the vet? There's a 24-hour clinic in Rehoboth."

Lights and sirens neared and fire engines rolled into the drive. He picked up the dog and walked to the front door. "Don't need to. Got the best vet tech in the county at the house. Ma's seen it all." He smiled and leaned over to kiss her, Compass' body between them. "Tell me again you're okay. You can handle this?"

"I can. Go. You don't need to come back. Take care of Compass." She stepped on her toes and kissed him.

"He'll be fine with Ma," said Booker. "I want the fucknut who did this. I'm coming back."

Claire measured his anger, surprised at his intensity.

He was gone and suddenly she wasn't sure she could handle it. She was exhausted. The police would want information. Who she was. Where she was from. Somebody with a cause had done this, or somebody with a need, mired in retribution. Was it one of Booker's workers? But why hurt an innocent dog?

The fire smoldered and red lights cast an eerie glow over the backyard. It was past three in the morning when two officers arrived decked out in gray-blues and campaign hats. Delaware State Police. Keeping it simple, she invited them in only saying she was renting. One waited on the back porch ready to take a description while the other spoke to the firemen. She offered them coffee although she had none made. What had she done since Booker left? She knew she looked awful. A glimpse in the hall mirror revealed smudged makeup under her eyes, her hair a tangled mess, her sweater covered in Compass' blood. She pushed at her cuticles and scraped at the dried blood under her nails. What had he asked her?

"I'm sorry. I'm so tired. What did you say?"

Officer Hickman repeated, "Has anyone searched the house?"

"Yes, yes, of course." There was a knock at the door and Claire jumped up startled. She didn't miss the look of surprise on the officer's face. Who would be knocking at her door so late?

"Booker. Thank God. How is he? How does it look?"

"He'll be fine. Mom's cleaning him up. A lot of stitches...." He broke off looking over her head at Hickman.

"Booker Solomon. I'm the property owner. Live next door."

Booker had parked his truck with the headlights on the backyard. The officers walked with Booker, scanning the burnt grass and dock with their flashlights. The smell of gasoline hung in the air. Claire stood at the porch door in her bare feet trying to hear the conversation. They moved over to the smoldering dock and she saw Booker reach into his back pocket to hand them something from his wallet. They nodded in agreement and walked back slowly toward her. Whatever they were saying seemed very confidential and secure. She could go to sleep soon.

They convened in the kitchen. Someone from the fire investigation unit would come out the following day. It was time to leave, they said, time for her to get some rest. Then Hickman asked, "Ma'am, could I see your driver's license for my report?"

Her heart sunk as his eyes scanned the table and chairs, the kitchen counter, the open cabernet and bottle of pills next to it. He stood between her and the counter. Booker was talking to the other officer about Compass' wound.

"Oh, sure." She reached over to the kitchen chair for her purse. Out of the corner of her eye, she noticed Hickman put his hand on the counter casually knocking over the pill bottle. He picked it up, looking at it too closely. He set it down upright.

Claire pushed her sleeves above her elbows. "It's a Maryland license. I haven't been down to DMV to get a Delaware license yet."

"Yes ma'am, I understand. You have sixty days after you move permanently to get it switched." He wrote down her information. The kitchen grew silent, as she waited for closure.

"Thank you, Ms. McIntosh. Fire police investigators will be here this afternoon. Get some sleep." He nodded. "Mr. Solomon." Booker followed them to the cruiser. When he returned, he put his arms around her and bent his lips to her ear, whispering, "Let's get you to bed. You can explain who you really are, Ms. McIntosh, tomorrow."

Claire slept hard and didn't really register the presence of a warm body next to hers. Sometime before eight, the sound of snoring woke her. Sleep was gone in an instant. A heaviness kept her pinioned. His long arm lay across her hip as if he belonged there, like the first day they were on his boat and he had stood behind her to shake the crabs from the pot.

He had pulled the curtains but in the grainy light she could barely see the hump of his dark hand nestled in the white sheets. She touched it softly with her fingertips. It wasn't ridged and scarred like a workingman's hands. Was he really building a church? How could he do that and bartend too? And take care of his mother, his property and now her dog?

For the first time in nearly two years she was in bed with an attractive man and what was she doing? Thinking. She scanned his outline. His long lashes fanned his cheeks. He had been patient with her tonight, with her paralysis and her petulance.

She pushed at these thoughts, closed her eyes and yearned for sleep. She felt ragged and he felt warm. She had let herself be led up the rickety stairs, let him pull off her sweater, then her T-shirt and unbutton her jeans to tuck her in. He had tossed his pants and shirt across the floor and now cuddled her as if this happened every day. She could roll over and kiss him awake but sleep overtook her again.

Gray light outlined the white duvet and the footboard. On the wall he could make out the framed dimpled bottom of a woman. Nude art. Booker had never seen the likes of this in someone's home. The sheets felt smooth and tight as if he had just climbed into a freshly made bed. He glanced at Claire curled up next to him, the mass of unruly hair spread across the pillow.

He made his way to the hall bath and opening the medicine cabinet heard something clank. Twisted around the aluminum catch was an enormous gold pocket watch dangling from a chain. He captured it, fingering the engraved metal cover. When he pressed the stem, the case opened to reveal a delicate face with the words, *Tiffany & Co.* and *Patek Philippe*, below it. The inside cover had been engraved.

Abraham
For Our Country,
Your Father
1929

Booker put it back. Probably more significant than finding her method of birth control. As he scanned the shelves hoping for the flat plastic package, he wondered what would bring a woman of her background to a tumble-down farmhouse and a second-rate job working with immigrants. He had seen advertising for Patek Philippe: white fathers passing down their expensive watches to their white sons. It was possibly more expensive than a Rolex. Why on earth would she keep it in her medicine cabinet where any drug dealing thief would look first? At times she seemed brilliant and at other times just plain dumb.

Rolling around a swig of mouthwash, he stared at himself in the mirror. What was he doing with this woman? From the moment he met her in Gallagher's, he had been mesmerized by her weird eyes, auburn hair and creamy skin. He was sure she was living an off-script lifestyle, hiding something more than her lack of inheritance. But there were the curves, the softness bursting from her tiny frame.

He spit in the sink. They were friends until last weekend when she left in a huff and then there was silence. He had been agitated all week without her. She didn't want a baby daddy or a stepfather for Sam. She was on her own, fiercely private, and he found it enticing. And now he was in her bed, naked. Or would be in a second.

He folded himself quietly next to her and she turned toward him, her eyes barely open. He ran one hand up her thigh and over her breast where he paused and whispered, "All better?" She smiled softly, "Almost." She kissed him long and slow, her hunger increasing. He rested his hand on her waist and moved downward slowly to her silkiness. She slid toward him and his hand palmed the small of her back like the curve of a violin. He pulled her over, playing to her rhythm, plucking her strings until he could feel the moment ripe. He was careful not to smother her with his full weight. Her kisses grew more insistent, and he buried his other hand in the tangle of her hair, tugging a little, and looked closely into her eyes, questioning, searching. "Yes," she said and he took her at her word.

They awoke late to a thin drizzle and dank chill in the air that could only be repaired by hot coffee. Standing side by side at the kitchen sink they looked broodingly at the damage from the night before. Water lapped at the charred boards and the lone pilings stood in a row, blackened soldiers at attention. Booker could feel Claire's anxiety swirling so he whirled her around the kitchen in a mock waltz. Laughing and hungry, they stuck their heads in the fridge to forage. Booker made a ham and cheese omelet and Claire buttered the toast. She broached the subject first.

"Was it one of your sketchy workers angry with you? 'Cause if that's the case, I have to move out."

"Don't know, Woman. Could be one of your shady clients bringing trouble. And if that's the case, maybe I need a new renter." He raised his eyebrows.

Hmmm," she said tapping her finger to her lips. "I bet Odessa would rather keep me and get rid of you."

"Probably. But Sam would miss me." They were silent for a second. "So which is it, McIntosh or Lamar?"

"Both. Claire Lamar McIntosh," she answered.

"Which one is your ex?" he asked.

"Neither. Sam is Peyton, not me. I never took my ex's last name."

"Make it easy on me. You're too smart to rent as Lamar when McIntosh is your last name. I know you told old man Pembroke your name is McIntosh."

"I told you there's too much tied up in that name. That's all I can say about it. Enough with the questions." Claire got up from her chair and sat in his lap, her arms around his shoulders. "Should we go see Compass?"

Booker kissed her neck and she struggled to ask, "Isn't it your turn to explain?"

He laughed and fondled her. She pushed his hand back, playfully. She had been honest—to a degree. He needed to step up to the plate. His odd hours, his nightlife, his friendships with people she saw as beneath him....and now, the gun. She wanted to know before she would allow him to be alone with her son again. Sam had maintained his silence about his afternoon with Booker and it put her off. She didn't want to jump to conclusions but....

Booker held a blue and white braided rope in his hand. He flipped it back and forth like he was trying to make up his mind. It looked like gimp. She hadn't seen that flat plastic spaghetti in years and suddenly her mood shifted. She decided to take charge of the conversation, not wait for him to probe and she left to wonder their status. Wanting to shock him into honesty, letting her impulsiveness fly, she said, "I've let this go too far. I can't help thinking you're hiding something. Like being a drug dealer."

"Whoa! Drug dealer? Where'd that come from?" His exasperation shot through his arms as he grabbed her shoulders. "What you talking about? You know my Ma, and you think I'm a drug dealer? What the hell?" He nodded emphatically. "Woman, I just got finished saying you ain't no ditzy Martha Stewart!"

"What's that supposed to mean? Is that some sideways insult of white women?" Claire bristled.

"Hey, don't get uppity with me." He pushed her off his lap and got up for more coffee, his face contained. They had been sparing for fun but she was growing increasingly defensive and unsure.

"Uppity? You're the one who's shutting me out. What are you doing here—with me?" She asked and folded her arms across her chest. She hadn't realized before but...she wanted, she needed to know who they were, together. Was there even a 'together?'

"With you—and Sam, isn't it? You've always been wary of me being with your little prince, haven't you? That's what pissed you off Sunday."

He stared her down, frozen to the spot, waiting for the slightest tremor of weakness.

"And you aren't a forty-year-old little prince?" Despite herself, she backed up against the kitchen cabinet to gain some support, but never lowered her gaze. She couldn't stand that his mother, with her choir singing and church going ways, didn't have a clue as to the company he kept.

"Prince and a drug dealer?" He took a step toward her.

"I don't know who you are. We just had sex and I don't know who you are. This goes against everything...."

"Oh, I see. That's how it is. You white women—goes against this, goes against that. Like your standards are the only ones." He snorted derisively and waved his coffee mug in the air. "Can't risk more than a one-night stand with the black man. Well you love it enough while it's happening, don't you?"

Embarrassed, she felt a slow burn rising up her neck. She switched tacks. "That's not what I'm talking about. I want Sam to be safe, to be with safe people, and if he's with you wandering around God knows where, I don't know if that's happening."

Booker nodded patiently as if he were preparing for the next assault. "You know we met before you rented this place. You never figured that out."

"I never met you."

"Gallagher's. Sunset. I made you a redheaded slut."

She blinked and her jaw dropped ever so slightly. Britt drunk, the bartender's warning, the police in the parking lot—it all came back to her. "You called me Woman," She said. "You're the bartender. What happened to the dreadlocks?"

"It's a wig."

She mocked, "A wig? And you had green eyes! I said they were contacts! Why are you dressing up to be a bartender? Afraid women won't like the bald look?"

"The women love me any way they get it. In a bar, missy, people say things they would regret if they were sober."

"So you don't want the drunks around here recognizing you on the street?"

"Not too many black dudes on the coast, and you know we all look alike to you white folk."

She punched his shoulder. Hard as rock. "Stop. I never said that. I'd recognize you anywhere now that I've had a little." She kidded, attempting a smile but he wasn't letting up.

"See what I mean? So I was right." He pushed her hair away from her face and gazed into her eyes. "How'd you get that scar? It's kinda fresh, isn't it?"

Claire tossed her head away from his hand. He continued to fish but wasn't giving up his story either. Pretty lame excuse for wearing a disguise. "That's not how this is going to work. I'll tell you if you tell me. How did you know those guys were drug dealers? You knew before we sat down with them." She raised her chin, daring him to lie to her again.

Booker's eyes shifted. He smiled but hesitated. Something was up and she wasn't satisfied one iota when he said, "People tell me things behind the bar and I call it in. I play both sides. I'm not above informing the authorities."

She lowered her head and in a hoarse whisper condemned him. "And I suppose that's how you make your connections?"

Booker leaned casually against the kitchen sink. "Connections, huh? That's what you think? Well, counselor, I thought it would appear plain as the nose on your face. You and your bat-shit crazy girlfriends got off because of me." He leaned toward her. "That blonde was getting you into a pot of trouble. You haven't put it together that I'm undercover?"

"Undercover?" Claire blinked. She paused, gulped and her thoughts whirled with images. Booker's office wired with all the latest technology. That big, black SUV she had only seen once that he parked in the barn. The jeep and the truck sat outside. He had been so cautious that day when she surprised him. She thought it was because she was snooping around but he hadn't been angry. He had invited her into his apartment. Just like he had invited her for a walk when he was finished bartending. He was trying to protect her. She wasn't crazy, she was stupid, really stupid and... embarrassed.

"I didn't put that together. The church, a lame job like bartending, and your odd hours." She ended flatly, falling back into the chair across from him. Her hands were dead weights at her sides, pulled down by her own obtuseness. She squinted. "You said you could play it both ways. I thought you meant being on either side of the law, not undercover."

"Just like every honkey white woman with money. The black man shady. Gots to be a criminal." He raised both hands in the air, wiggling his fingers in mock fear and rolled his eyes.

She was stung to the core by his sarcasm and growing angrier. She wasn't some ignorant, white racist. How could he say such a thing? She caught her breath and scanned his face for the truth.

She saw him for the first time as an ordinary man, stunning in his virile power, but fallible. He filled the room with his presence, but was oh, so human. She was struck by their simple difference, that other world and his experiences that she couldn't know. He had grown up differently from her. She imagined the reactions of older white women and men, the glances of worry, maybe even fear that led to brief hellos and quietly locked doors.

Beyond that her imagination failed her, because it led to pat schooling and sensitivity training, black sitcoms and barroom jokes. She looked down at her hands folded on the table, holding onto an unseen intolerance that was centuries old, and knew she could be guilty of something so raw and so wrong. With all her education, all her worldly exposure, she had thought herself above those kinds of assumptions. She covered her face in her hands. Was she the one who was screwing up this conversation?

He had not been honest with her. He had never told her he worked undercover. Never uttered one word about police work. One word and it would have bridged the chasm that opened between them. She looked up and felt a wetness sting her lashes. He was being too hard on her.

"Don't put me in that category, Booker. It's not fair. You weren't honest, either, you know? I'm just a mom protecting her son. And Sam can't find another man to love and lose him again."

He waffled and said with disgust, "If you thought that, why didn't you ask me? You were snooping around my office and didn't find any bags of cocaine, no bricks of hundred dollar bills. You saw me drive in the barn in the SUV. Didn't you see the laptop mounted in it?"

Claire didn't respond at first trying to think this out. She hung her head, her hair covering her eyes. She had been so righteous, thinking she was protecting Sam. So full of her new role as provider and mother bear in a strange land. Wrapped up in her newfound independence, had she thought she was better than he, than everyone she met? Britt had called her a snob.

She hadn't thought herself better than Pembroke and his sloppy ways. Or better than Trixie, who remained staidly unimpressed with her city polish. Or better than Odessa and her fried okra. Out of habit, she had orchestrated her image for each of her new friends. These people, Odessa, and especially Booker, had included her in their family. He was so close but so far away. Had she lost him?

She shifted toward him. His hand moved next to hers and he dropped the blue and white rope down on the table between them.

"I have been laboring under an assumption—the worst kind of assumption. I am so sorry."

He was silent.

"There isn't any good excuse. It was stupid of me. I wish you had said something earlier. Undercover."

The wind picked up outside and the windows rattled. Claire nestled her small hand in his. He was warm and his fingers closed around hers. Still his brow furrowed, his nose pinched, and his brown eyes galled with anger.

He nodded slightly and said, "We better get your damn dog."

Something broke inside her at the thought of Compass bleeding and she wondered who had done it. "You know Booker, I'm a mom first and foremost. Sam led a very structured, careful life until we came here. I always keep tabs on who he associates with and when you came into our lives I was thrilled until I discovered you worked with people living on the edge: construction workers and barflies. And you want me to ignore that now because you're an undercover detective? It might reassure me but it doesn't change the fact that we don't know who did this. It's not me they were after. It's your property."

Finished with her little speech she searched for order in the mess around her. Claire stood to hang up their coats from the night before. The pocket of Booker's jacket pulled like it was filled with rocks. The gun, needed for his job. She dragged it, but he swept the coat from her arm and put it on the chair next to him. She paused, waiting for his next move.

He grabbed the blue and white cord and held it up for her to see. Entwined in his fingers hung a steel cross and a medal of the Virgin Mother, her hands open by her sides and the words, "Our Lady of Peace" inscribed above and "Pray for Us" below.

"Where did you get that, Booker?"

"Found it last night out in the yard. Is it yours or Sam's?"

She shook her head.

"Decided not to give it to our illustrious boys in blue. Thought I'd do my own research." His voice was even, if a little reserved. He was going to help. Maybe it wasn't over between them.

Saturday afternoon Claire and Booker took Compass to the Selbyville Animal Hospital where the vet remarked that the stitching looked professional. He warned that the dog would fuss with the wound with his back paw. Questions about how it happened, the odd looks from the office staff and the vet's curiosity brought back the defensiveness she felt after the terrorist attack. Booker glanced quizzically at her stumbling responses and, to her relief, took over the conversation. The vet remembered the Solomon name. Compass came home in an Elizabethan collar. Odessa offered to keep him while Claire was at work. Although Claire was reluctant to impose, Odessa pleaded to have an animal in her care again.

In the late afternoon on Columbus Day, Claire drove to pick up Sam in Denton. By the time they arrived home it was close to six and the sun was on its slow descent across the water. The sky swirled in a mix of lavenders and the torched grasses looked raw in the fading light. When Sam walked out back, he was full of questions. Claire and Booker had decided not to alarm him. They concocted a story about the old Evinrude engine leaking gas.

Claire waited until he was settled at the kitchen table amidst his workbooks and warned him to be very careful around the property. She told him to come home immediately if he saw any strangers. He nodded casually, avoiding his mother's gaze, and Claire realized at that moment that her little boy was growing up, not buying tall tales and adult lies. Was his world tilted toward his father now after his visit? She felt they were both a little more hardened, aware the world wasn't always theirs.

In the scheduled forty-five minutes of dedicated homework time, Claire interrupted Sam, asking about his weekend with his dad and the house. But she was disappointed when Sam answered in monosyllables, his head down, his fingers wrapped around his pencil. His hand didn't look so pudgy anymore and he held the pencil masterfully. He had been schooled by his father, she assumed, and she made a huge effort to quiet her anxiety and ask innocuous questions about his old playmates, the house and her garden. He finally looked up and asked her if he could please get his spelling done. Embarrassed, she apologized and looked around the kitchen for something to do. The dishes were done, the counter cleaned. Things were tidy, not in their normal disarray. A bearded blue heron squawked outside in the dark, adjusting to the charred dock posts that were his perch.

She was left with a vague worry that she didn't know everything about her Sam anymore. Letting go was not easy. She had always been the fixer, the peacemaker, the negotiator who knew the details, connecting the family dots. The bomb and her recuperation had only made her more determined to find her old self. She walked away from the table and Sam and looked at the empty dog bed.

A pile of clean clothes and sheets waited to be folded in the little laundry room next to the kitchen. She stacked the sheets to the side and held a pillowcase to her chest thinking of Booker's fingers entwined in hers. He had traced the scar beneath her hair and she hadn't told him of that day. He hadn't asked why or how. He hadn't even asked about her last name again. She took his lead, not wanting to ruin the rest of their weekend. But then there was Sam and his safety to consider. Undercover? It was a double-edged sword.

Claire took Sam's clothes from his overnight backpack and sorted them for the wash. After a few loads of reds bleeding into whites, embarrassed, she had asked Odessa what she was doing wrong. The old woman had a guidebook for everything. The only thing Odessa couldn't conquer was her son. She was annoyed when Booker baked in the middle of the night in her kitchen and she woke to find the dishes in the sink. She had complained about his nocturnal habits, his late-night arrivals from work that had added to Claire's doubts. But there was pride in her voice when she said, "He has a tough schedule to keep." She had never even hinted of his real job. The uneven flow of income had affected so many that Claire understood Odessa's comment to mean that he was building the church and bartending too.

She took the stack of folded laundry and peaked around the corner to the kitchen. "Doing your math? Need any help?" The warm light from the table enveloped Sam, curled on one knee with the other foot dangling and kicking the chair leg. "Nope, Mom, I got it." She walked down the darkened hall, the worn floorboards creaking with each step. Loaded down with clothes, she flicked on the staircase light and crept up to Sam's room in the back of the house. She pulled his shades and turned on his Winnie the Pooh lamp thinking it was past time for a new one with a soccer ball.

She carried the towels to their hall bath and hung them. Opening the medicine cabinet to grab a brush, she realized the watchcase was slightly open revealing the inscription. Booker must have found it. He hadn't said anything and perhaps that was a sign that he didn't care about who she was. It hung there as comfort, a reminder of family, its shine becoming almost invisible in her daily habits, open and close, open and close. But now she saw how easy it was for someone else to find. She unwound it, her fingers closing tightly around its coolness. She put it in her pocket and brushed out her hair.

She flipped on the light by her bedroom door and crossed to the painted blanket chest. Its musty interior was scented by a lavender-filled ceramic pig. A painted primitive rooster graced the lid, his tail plumes still a bright blue. Odessa had told Claire she could use it in good health.

That week the police combed the backyard for clues. There was nothing, only a partial footprint and the religious medal that only she and Booker knew about. He had texted her to say he had done some research and he wanted to ask her about it. He told her to keep the doors locked, her car parked prominently in the driveway and the lights on all night on the back porch. It only made her more scared. But the neighborhood was quiet and so eventually were her nerves.

———

Promises

"Carlos wants to see you," said Hector. He stood, a hulking outline filling the door.

Under bowed his head. He had been waiting and was glad the summons happened so quickly after he returned from the Eastern Shore. Fears built in his head, squawking at him like that heron in the grasses by the woman's dock. Some ancient message telling him to flee. And yet some small part of him was grateful. Whatever Carlos would do to him would be a sign to others that he could handle a job of immense importance. He only had to reassure Carlos that he could finish it.

Hector's Honda smelled like bleach and pine. It was his wife's car. The backseat was loaded with buckets and bottles, rags and mopheads. Under enjoyed her cheerful smiles and their noisy children. What did the Americans say, "Happy-go-lucky?" It was the way he remembered his mother. If he could finish the job, he would be rewarded and he would make a life for his mother and his baby half sister.

They arrived at the warehouse in the dark and Hector sounded the horn. The garage door opened and they pulled inside. Under took a deep breath and limped to the office past Esteban who was assembling an AK-47 from a parts kit.

"Buena noches, my friend," said Carlos with exaggerated deference as he waved him into the room. This is good, thought Under. If he is to get rid of me, he would make me stand in the corner and wait. He is in the mood for a spectacle.

Under sat in the vinyl-covered chair in front of Carlos' desk. The office was spare. No rug, no computer, no bookcases—just chairs and a metal desk. Easy to wipe clean in an emergency. A cobwebbed palm sat in one corner and a plate glass window looked out on the empty warehouse where Hector and the others congregated. The shade was up in preparation for a show. Under's fear rose from his gut as a hard ball of burning saliva. He swallowed. Many times before he had watched from the other side of the window but he was too valuable to be killed, wasn't he?

"You did not get rid of the dog."

"El Cortador, no," he said sorrowfully. "It lives." Better not explain. He had reached to slice its throat but heard the woman shout, and his stroke of the machete was too low. The dog was maned and ruffed like a lion. It was too big to dispose of quickly.

Secretly, he thought later, he lacked the will. When his fingers touched its fur, the dog had quieted and leaned toward him ready to be petted, almost a sacrificial offering. The animal had thought his hand was the touch of love. He wondered later what it was like, to have a dog that trusted you. This was the life of the woman and her child.

"The plan was to take the child by boat," said Carlos. "But now you have raised suspicions. The Solomon man and his police cohorts are alerted."

"The dog will not be a problem. She keeps it inside while it heals. Americans treat their animals like babies."

He grunted and said, "The mother and her friend will be watchful. You have made a grave error."

"The detective is very busy. He has spent the night with the woman only once. He will not be around overnight when the son is there," said Under. On the other side of the window, members of the clique were silent. Under drew his eyebrows together and spoke with confidence. "The child walks from his babysitter's everyday unless it rains. The mother is lazy. She doesn't walk with him like the mothers of our children." His fingernails dug nervously at a hole in the vinyl armrest. It was a small lie about the mother, he thought. Carlos followed the movement of his hand, and Under tapped his fingers instead.

The child's mother was watchful but distracted. She worked, talked on her phone and read papers when she was with her son. Still, he would not take the child in front of her. He would wait until she was occupied.

"There's not enough time for you to take him on this walk home," said Carlos. "No matter how lazy she is, she will miss him and call the police. You must take him from his bed at night when she is asleep."

"I could break an upper window while they are away and wait for them inside."

Anger flashed across Carlos' face flushing to his ears. "And be discovered? Fool. This is why I shouldn't invest in you half-breeds. You cannot think for yourselves."

"I'll take him while the mother sleeps. I can drug her."

"You have made this more difficult by your failure. Hector will take over." Deadly concern spread across Carlos' face as he moved to stand in front of Under.

"One more chance," pleaded Under. "I prove that I can do this. I have been inside the house. There is always an open wine bottle on the counter and she drinks alone at night. I can add something to it."

Carlos stepped back and seemed to mull this over. Then he said, "You will meet the contact in Ocean City, near the inlet and leave from there.

We will meet you later. If you make a mistake and the authorities appear, we will not intervene."

"I'll have the child. How will I know where to go?"

"Hector will call you. After, throw the phone in the water and make haste."

"And the contact?"

"The child will tell you."

It was a mystery. Under looked down at his hands knowing it would be unwise to challenge Carlos. His boss would not give him the contact and that made taking the child more risky. He would have to make friends with him. They had met once, twice. Maybe the boy was not afraid of him because they both had blue eyes. His growing tattoos could be hidden, even the teardrop at the corner of his eye could be covered. He would make the boy rely on him as he relied on Hector.

Under glanced through the window. Hector watched from the other side, his arms crossed and legs akimbo. The man's eyes widened, a grimace of satisfaction on his face. Under swiveled toward Carlos too late and caught the glint of silver. With an adept flick of his wrist, the man sliced off the top of Under's ear. He yelped like a dog and grabbed his head as the blood gushed through his fingers.

El Cortador laughed and held up a trophy flap of skin and white cartilage. "You will be successful or you will lose more the next time, my friend."

CHAPTER 4

Sam's Birthday

*I*t was midafternoon, two weeks into pumpkin season, and Claire had a reprieve from the Friday night slog to drop Sam at the gas station. Vance had emailed saying he was busy with a campaign fundraiser in Bethesda, Maryland and would meet them Saturday afternoon. To her consternation, Sam was spending Sunday, his birthday, with his father. Not to be outdone, she invited his two friends from school, the Tafano family, Odessa and Booker for a birthday party on Friday night.

She set out from work with a list of errands: balloons, the Dollar Store and Good Earth Market for their specialty breads. Booker would make the cake. In D.C., she would have hired a party planner but there was no money now. She had researched an after hours event at the local Energy Gym but it was a serious workout place for adults who sweated 24/7 on key passes. No, an old fashioned birthday was in order. A happy thought occurred to her that for once there were no other parents to impress. Just Sam and his new buds.

Claire flurried up and down the aisles at the grocery store and hustled to the car where she stuffed the last item in the Mini. Everyone was due to arrive at 4:30, and she pressed herself to have it all set up on time. She stood at the kitchen counter emptying the plastic bags, running through the list of games, the food and the favor bags. Once she took stock, she realized she had forgotten the ice cream. She heard a tap at the kitchen door. When it squeaked open, she welcomed two smiling faces, Odessa's and Booker's. They were laden with packages wrapped in blue paper, a yellow cake with chocolate icing and a carton of vanilla ice cream, Sam's favorite just like his grandfather. She shouted in relief.

Everyone bustled around the kitchen, sidestepping Compass who seemed befuddled in his white plastic cone of shame. His skin was shaved bare in an eight-inch railroad track of stiches across his neck. Claire grabbed a dog treat. "Compass, over here. Lay down, that's a good boy." Two weeks after the attack he was healing nicely but waddled around bumping into everything.

Booker laughed, "No peripheral vision. Compass, the bumper car." The three of them got to work.

Claire organized the party bags at the table, Odessa finished up the spicy Sloppy Joe's on the stove, and Booker set up the party games. Musical Chairs and Pin the Tail were in the front room and Bobbing for Apples on the back porch that was festooned with orange and black streamers. Once finished, they admired their handiwork. Using leftover porch paint, Booker painted a "Happy Birthday Sam" sign and clothes pinned each sheet of paper to the clothesline. Claire grabbed his hand whispering that she would thank him later. He smiled and pinched her butt when Odessa wasn't looking.

A few days after their argument, Claire had visited Odessa late in the afternoon with some homemade pumpkin bread—her first—with the hope that she would run into Booker. Sam had been pestering her to have them over. She suspected his kid radar was blasting that there was something wrong. On the back deck –she going—Booker coming, they stopped for a moment, speechless, their contact still electric. They stumbled about each other and he took charge of the situation, putting his hands on her shoulders, drawing her near. "We can dance later. What are you doing?"

"Going to pick up Sam."

"I think you should join me for a beer. Bring Sam and the dog." She nodded and he kissed her.

They arrived to find a cookout and the great Solomon hospitality. The smell of a charcoal fire made her mouth water. In a hot second, while Sam and Odessa were gathering dishes inside, Booker apologized to Claire for holding back about himself.

"I should have trusted you," he said and held her close, resting his chin on her head. She raised her eyes and was met with a hungry kiss. Her heart split in two. They pulled apart quickly when they heard the sliding glass doors. Sam watched them intently the rest of the night.

That was a week ago and now Claire tied the last ribbon on a party bag and looked about the kitchen satisfied. The doorbell rang and the Tafanos swept into the farmhouse with Sam in tow, carrying a present wrapped in newspaper. Sam's school friends arrived, and the seven kids ate, their grins spread in tomato sauce mustaches. Potato chips and Cheetos littered the floor and Compass stayed under the table, vacuuming the crumbs, trying to avoid the sneakered feet.

Flustered but laughing, Claire moved them to the front parlor to play Musical Chairs while Booker stopped and started the Shrek version of 'Halleluiah.' Her cell phone rang before she got back to the kitchen. It was Uncle Alistair calling to wish Sam a happy birthday. He was going to be in Ocean City for Corvette weekend and promised to take them for Sunday brunch. Claire explained that Sam would be at his father's. "Then I'll take you, Claire," he said. Happily, she jotted a reminder on a piece of paper. She hadn't seen her uncle in ages.

Trixie bellowed at Johnny, the oldest, who had tried to win the last chair by pushing Sam off. Johnny grumbled under his breath until Sam squirted him with a water-filled balloon. Booker and Trixie quickly scooted the bigger boys out on the porch for a balloon fight and the littlest ones played Pin the Tail inside with Claire and Odessa. As the sun fell low in the sky, Claire decided it was time to open the presents at the kitchen table.

She was proud of Sam who showed practiced enthusiasm for two more action figures. He had just told his mom that week that he was too old for silly dolls and it was time to donate them to needy kids. With seamless appreciation, he opened a stomp rocket and a new soccer ball, which she was sure more than made up for the action figures. He glanced at Booker and tore at the paper of his present. The boys, jostling about like piggies in a pen, struggled to look at the erector set, loudly exclaiming their approval. Sam stood and pushed his way over to kiss Odessa's cheek and shake Booker's hand. When he opened the night vision goggles from his mom, he jumped from his chair and hugged her close. She leaned over slightly, careful not to be too demonstrative in front of his guy friends.

Later, in the twilight, the boys burst through the porch door to lay waste to the new toys, leaving only the erector set inside. It wasn't long before Sam returned to the porch with the night vision goggles complaining that they were too big for his head. Claire fussed with it until Booker removed his Terps cap and fitted it on Sam's head backward, strapping the goggle headset over the cap. Sam was off, running to the door but Claire shouted for him to say thank you. He turned and blinded them all with the LED light. Holding her arm up to her eyes, she ordered, "Out!"

The adults settled in the porch chairs to watch the kids swarm over the yard, and Claire remembered past Fourth of July parties at Tred Avon.

Children playing with sparklers, their sunburned bodies, the smell of the crabs and the summer sunset over the water. It was the last time she had felt secure in the affection of neighbors. It was the last time she had seen her dad alive at his summer best. Her eyes filled up and she abruptly went inside the house.

She returned from the kitchen with a bottle of wine to refill everyone's glasses and found Trixie and Odessa seated, chatting amicably and Booker at the screen door peering through the dense blackness of a starless sky. Kid voices echoed against the water. All they could see was a bead of white light bouncing from Sam's head. Booker put an arm around her shoulders holding her close, and Claire realized then that he was quietly announcing to his Ma and Trixie that they were a pair. Claire rested in the nook of his body, happy and safe.

———

The Knife

Claire let Compass in to eat and he thumped to his bed, a wet mass of reddish-blonde fur, snoring within seconds. Rain had fallen for days, and both she and Sam tried to find respite from their cabin fever. Their voices, the dog's breathing, and the close squawk of seagulls on the chimney lulled them into a quiet peacefulness. It was past bedtime and Sam leaned languidly against her breast as she closed his math notebook and reluctantly pushed him upright. She grabbed his latest Harry Potter book and he followed her up the stairs, dragging behind.

Claire looked around exasperated at the mess in Sam's room. She had learned to keep house, Sam had not. He sat on the edge of his bed watching her movements, nearly catatonic. The room was close, humid from the warm fall rain. She stopped at the window to open it and noticed a patchwork of silver filigree hanging in the outside corner. The bedroom lamp reflected against the web's concentric lace. A large spider sat in its midst.

"Sam, come look at this. He's built this web since last night."

"I know I already saw him. What kind of spider is he?"

Claire studied the web. "Just a harmless barn spider. Isn't he magnificent?"

"No."

"He won't hurt you."

"I don't care. I don't want him coming in my room in the middle of the night. Just leave the window shut, okay?"

"Okay. I'll open the other one."

"No, Mom, I don't want a window open."

"Jeez, Sam. It's hot in here. I'll open one until I come up for bed and then I'll close it after you're asleep."

"Mom, I'm not hot."

She paused inspecting this new Sam. He was irritated, his small face tightened, and he tugged at a corner of his sheet. She wouldn't press him for what was wrong. "Okay, hop in bed and we'll read a little."

"I don't want to read tonight. Can you leave my dresser light on instead of the hall light?"

"Sure. It won't keep you awake?" He pushed into bed and turning away on his side, he scrunched his pillow up under his head. Claire leaned over to kiss his hot, sweaty cheek and noticed a black handle sticking up between the mattress and the headboard. She pulled it out, holding it in disbelief—a large, jagged tactical knife.

"Sam, where did you get this?" Her voice was too loud, she knew, but she couldn't help herself.

"I...I need it Mom...for protection. You know, in—in case...."

Now she was yelling. "No, I don't know. Please explain."

"I just want to make sure that if someone comes in my room at night that, that—I can—I can take care of myself."

"So you got a war knife? Samuel, this is not some kitchen knife. Where did you get it?"

"John gave it to me. He got it off the internet in case someone attacked us in our sleep."

This was not a reasonable explanation. They were just boys pretending to be soldiers. All this reporting on war in the Middle East was having an effect. Still, she was frustrated that he didn't trust her. She thought Little John was nothing but a thug in the making. In a panic, it occurred to Claire that Sam might take the knife to school to show off. Quickly, she calmed herself thinking she didn't need to make a bigger deal than it already was. Of course he was feeling threatened on the second floor of the farmhouse after Compass was attacked and the pier set afire. There was no keeping secrets from this kid. She worried that too much had happened over the last six months, too much for even an adult to cope with.

"Samuel, who would come in your room at night? They would have to get past my room. I wouldn't let anyone come in your room."

"Right, Mom. And you have a knife in your mattress? Or maybe a gun?" He had turned over, sitting up in bed, his blue eyes lit from the bedside light. Silence fell between them. "Trixie has a gun and Little John knows where it is. It's not loaded but I've seen it. He says it's for bad people."

She dropped onto his bed staring at the knife in her hand. "What bad people?"

"Trixie says you're naïve and you don't think bad about anyone. She says working on immigration is dumb 'cause they're just taking jobs away from people like her. Little John says we're spoiled and don't know how to take care of ourselves. He says everybody over there thinks you have something to hide, like you robbed a bank or something and that's why we moved here." He fell quiet. Then, "Why *did* we move here anyway?"

"I thought it would be a good thing to raise you around real people who work hard everyday for their money. People who love their families and are loyal to them."

"Mom, I had that. You and Dad weren't in the same house but he was close by. I made friends at my school. We don't ever go to Tred Avon."

He bunched the comforter up. "I want to pretend Granddaddy's still alive." Sam began to cry and threw himself face down on his bed.

Claire leaned over to rub his back but he pulled away. Stricken, she laid her hands in her lap and looked down at her upturned palms. What had she done? She thought he was happy. Was she a naïve city girl, lost in a world her nine-year-old son had a better handle on than she? Booker had never said she needed to be cautious about the trailer park residents. She had met many of them and they were sweet, private people. They weren't the problem.

Alcohol was everywhere at the beach. Bars and restaurants lined the ocean highway. Trixie had said the heroin situation was bad. It was laced with (Claire reached back, trying to remember)...fentanyl that made it particularly addictive and deadly. But she reasoned that there were drugs everywhere. Congress, the schools, never mind everyone's private stash of pot… and the world still carried on.

Sam had grown up with security systems, grown up watching parents, grandparents and Tosh employees punch numbers in keypads to gain access. There were bodyguards at company events and cameras everywhere; his fingerprints, DNA, and pictures of his moles and scars were on file. It was their way of life, until now.

She studied him, her innocent boy, now more composed but his face smeared wet. Leaning on one arm, he watched her quietly and waited, looking much older than his years. This had transpired under her nose. Her obtuseness about Booker. Oblivious. Rosa and her son. Foolish. And now Sam. She bordered on stupidity and could not, would not, blame her brain injury. She needed to take responsibility. It was time to research. Time to anticipate and plan.

"You think you're the man of the house. Listen to me very carefully. You are not old enough or strong enough to fight off an intruder. I'm going to talk to Booker tomorrow. I'll talk to Trixie and find out about this gun." Claire set her jaw and felt the muscles working tightly in her cheek. If there was a gun in Trixie's house she was going to find out where and how it was stored. Fucking guns. It had better be locked up, or she would move Sam to another after-school care location. She hadn't even thought to ask Trixie a gun question when she interviewed her.

She needed more money, a security system on this house. First, she would call her attorney. Still, no date for mediation had been set, only a challenge from Vance for custody claiming she was unfit. He implied she was damaged goods, unable or unwilling to provide properly for their son. Claire was ready to ask Ross what she could have from the trust. It was for Sam, not for her. She blubbered a little as she walked down the steps with the knife in her hand.

———

Lost in the Laundry

As they stood at the sink that Thursday night washing the dishes by hand, Booker asked if she had checked to make sure nothing had been taken inside the house. Sheepishly, she told him that the only thing missing was her great great grandfather's pocket watch. The Patek Philipe. She had moved it from the medicine chest and misplaced it. "It will turn up," she said, thinking she was getting more like her father hiding things.

Rain was coming down for the fourth day in a row—a deluge, so heavy that even Compass didn't want to go out. Claire picked up another plate to dry and looked out the blackened kitchen window, seeing only their faces mirrored in the light over the sink. She studied Booker, his dark eyes, straight nose and pinched nostrils. He had developed a little pouch of worry skin between his brows that she hadn't noticed before.

Sam was doing his homework at the kitchen table behind them, but Claire thought he must have grown restless with his math, because his workbook dropped from the table. He crawled on the floor picking up this, playing with that and petting the dog who was sleeping when Claire said, "C'mon, Mister Sam. Let's get back to it. You want some help?"

Annoyed at being caught, he said, "Nope, Mom."

Claire smiled, conscious that he never called her Mommy anymore. He wanted a haircut because John made fun of his red curls. He wanted some new T-shirts, the kind that John wore painted with motorcycles and skulls. Claire rolled her eyes inwardly, then chided herself for judging.

This was what she had wanted. She wanted Sam to be exposed to people from all walks of life, to not be some hothouse kid. He had to handle tough kids and stick up for himself. What was missing was that he didn't look the part. He needed some after-school clothes to fit in with Trixie's kids. Besides, she was tired of washing his school uniform khakis almost every night.

She needed to have confidence in his ability to take care of himself. A trip to Walmart for the wannabe biker look might be fun. Just the two of them looking for after- school and weekend clothes that would stay at the farmhouse, never to be worn to his father's. Vance would go ballistic.

She picked up the last few plates on the table and turned back to the counter. Vance was getting more and more rigid and uncooperative. Emails demanded she move closer, give him more visitation time and that Sam spend all of his Christmas break in D.C. Claire had responded, "Sell the house and I'll be more cooperative." He shot back, "I will keep the house and Sam will return to me."

Booker wiped his hands on the towel and punched Sam's shoulder lightly. "You want some help?"

Sam brightened and said, "Sure."

Booker propped his chin in his hand as he pointed to Sam's work-book. His frame bent over her son's head, his burly arm around the boy's shoulders. It gave her momentary comfort. He was such a positive influence on Sam. Vance never sat down with his son to do homework.

Nor had he sold the house. With his Senate campaign, his ego had grown, increasing his desire for fame and power. Sam was *her* child to raise not some political commodity or a stage puppet. His father would see him every other weekend and that was all. And she would stop perseverating on Vance.

With the lilt of Sam's questions and Booker's rumbling responses in the background, she washed the last plate and put it on the rack to dry. Later, homework done, she put Sam to bed tucking him in and planting a kiss on his forehead.

He tickled her fingers, "Mom, we should talk."

Claire sat on the edge of his Iron Man comforter, thinking he wanted to say something about Booker, but he clammed up and said, "It's okay. Tomorrow."

She turned on his table lamp but paused at the door. "Are you sure?"

"I'm sure. This weekend, okay?" he asked.

"Okay," she said as she blew him another kiss that he caught mid-air. She pulled his door halfway shut and left the light on at the foot of the stairs. The kitchen glistened and Booker was pulling on his coat. Disappointed, she asked, "You can't stay?"

"Working an investigation on Route 13. Lock up tight. I might not be over till Saturday." Then he was gone into the pouring rain.

She left work at three the next day. Finally, the rain lightened to a drizzle. The streets were sloppy with pools of water edging the open roadside storm drains. She drove slowly, holding tightly to the steering wheel. She and Sam had errands to do and she wanted to be home before sunset.

An hour later, she picked Sam up at Trixie's. Turning down an invite to dinner she drove south to the O.C. Barbershop. Scissors and a razor made quick work of Sam's curls. The little boy look disappeared. Claire plucked a lock from the floor to save. Shorn of his bronzed ringlets, Sam hopped into the car and flipped down the mirror, rubbing his hands over the stubble. Claire glanced at his angular face and smiled forlornly. There was no baby left in her boy now.

Fueled with independence, Sam was wired for the trip to Walmart even ignoring the smell of Fisher's Popcorn at the state line. Go, Mom, go! The clouds lifted to patches of blue. The trip over the Indian River Inlet Bridge was near euphoric. Purple rain clouds loomed overhead, but a slim crack of yellow and orange peaked through in the westward sky. Sam chattered away, pointing to the shore on the right, saying look at the waves—they were big and powerful—look at the seagulls, look at the surfers, look, look, look. Claire was so happy in the moment that she forgot all about the arson, all about Vance, all about Sam's fear, and basked in thoughts of Booker.

By the time they reached the sea of blacktop outside Walmart, Sam was prattling away about Little John. There was nothing 'little' about him. He stood a good five inches taller than Sam but was only three years older. Big, clumsy and jealous, Little John was in the habit of making fun of the kids who mostly ignored him until he picked a new target. Sam had been his latest: his hair, his clothes, his choice of sports.

"Why do you think he teases so much?" asked Claire.

"John doesn't know who his real dad is and his mom's in jail," explained Sam with the extra year of assurance that being nine provided. "He doesn't care though. That's what Trixie says."

Inside the store, Sam thumbed slowly through the T-shirt rounder in the boy's section, studying each one as if wearing it would be a window into his soul. Something was on his mind and squinting in anxiety, he said, "John says I'm no better than any of Trixie's kids because I don't have a dad, or grandparents or anybody but you." Sam swung from the rounder between the hangers until Claire frowned and shook her head at him. "Little John thinks nobody needs parents, because 'they're slippier than snot' and you can't count on them."

Claire felt her eyes well up and Sam turned around to inspect the T-shirts, not wanting to see his mom cry. She blinked furiously and pulled one from the rack. A Star Wars storm trooper held a weapon across his white breastplate. Claire read aloud, "I Had Friends on That Deathstar."

Sam said, "Get that one." He picked out a Maryland Terps ballcap like Booker's. A few minutes later they were on the way to the car. The heavens were still thick with clouds. She hoped there would be a sunset.

The rain had stopped and the air was salty. They were both hungry and decided to wait in the drive-thru at McDonald's before heading home, something she swore she would never do. Sam took a bite of his chicken nuggets and asked his mom if she was afraid where they were living.

She paused, a little surprised, thinking she needed to answer carefully. "You mean because of the fire?"

"Mom, get real. Look what happened to Compass. And the people around there."

The smell of grease filled the car. She cracked her window. "What people?"

"You know, like in the trailer park."

"You aren't talking about Trixie and the kids?"

"Of course not," he said, sounding frustrated. He turned his ballcap backwards. "People on different streets."

She dipped her fingers in the french fries and held them up in the space between them. "Has someone said something to you?"

"Mom, Don't get all spastic. There're some people who look weird. Little John says they're drug addicts."

"They might be, Sam. You need to stay away from people like that, right? We talked about that." She stuffed the fries in her mouth and downshifted at the red light.

"I know," he said with impatience. "There's this one guy. He keeps looking at me. John says it's because of my red hair."

Claire asked with studied calm, "Does he talk to you boys?"

"Yeah, he said 'Hola'."

"That's all? Sounds pretty harmless. Don't ride your bikes down that street if it bothers you." She might drive by and take a look herself. Wonder what Trixie would say? Sam's red hair caused a lot of second looks. Glances—not practiced gazes. The zoo, she thought. Something happened at the zoo that worried her but at the moment she couldn't remember.

"You guys stay in a pack, right?" The sign for Fenwick Island was ahead on the median. She slowed to 35 watching for the town cop.

"Mom," he cleared his throat and said, "Um, I took something of yours to show Little John." There was a longer pause that seemed fraught with tension. "Grandad's watch."

"Sam, you mean you—"

"I—I just wanted to prove to him that I have a family. You know that we have a family." She looked at him. His bristly head was down, his eyes avoiding hers.

Claire was relieved. Riddle solved! Her boy was trying to stick up for himself the only way he knew how—with possessions and words, engraved words on a watch. Her father had given it to her and Sam had taken it from her. Funny, the power one little object could have on so many people.

"Do you have it, Sam, or does Little John?"

"I didn't *give* it to him. I just wanted to *show* it to him."

"Has he seen it? What did he say?"

"I haven't had a chance to show it to him yet. Can I?"

If she asked for it back, she would ruin Sam's bid for status with Little John. If she let him flash it around with the Tafano kids, he might lose it or one of the other kids could take it. The watch could be gone forever. Was it the sum total of her family history?

What else did she need? She had Sam. Claire relaxed and reached into her heart. "Sam, the watch is a thing. Things are unimportant compared to people. But it is my reminder of Grandad. Don't take it to school and give it back Monday after you show it to him—all in one piece, okay? And you get to do the dishes for a week for taking something without asking."

"Awww, Mom," he said, but she could see he was content with this deal.

They pulled into the rutted driveway to see Booker's jeep coming down the drive from his house. She glanced at her wrist. Six o'clock. The farmhouse looked so warm and softened in the early evening light. She didn't care about the peeling paint and the lopsided rain gutter. Booker was making the effort to come see them despite his schedule.

As she held the kitchen door for Sam to come in and Compass to go out, she examined his school uniform. Dirty, greenish-brown knees on the khakis. Didn't that school have inside recess in the rain?

"Go change, Sam. Bring me the uniform for the wash."

"Can I put on my Deathstar T-shirt?" he asked.

She nodded and heard his feet pound up the steps. The kitchen door slammed behind her, and she smiled at Booker who listened briefly for those footsteps above. In two steps he had her against the wall kissing her, his hand pushing up her jacket and shirt.

She laughed and pushed back at him still locked in the kiss.

"Stop. Stop. He's coming back." She won and he leaned one arm against the wall above her head staring into her eyes.

"I have some news, but we can talk in the laundry room," he said. "I can't go to work without having some," he said. His other hand swept around to handle her ass and she pushed him away just as Sam rounded the corner, looking at them suspiciously through his night vision goggles. He was in jeans and his new T-shirt. The goggle headpiece was strapped across the top of his ball cap just like Booker had shown him the night of his birthday party.

Sam gave her his dirty uniform. "Can I go out mom? Just for a minute….please?" His plea was so desperate. Days of rain had kept him from playing with his new presents except the erector set. She glanced at her watch. Compass was out back. Nearing twilight, he could play for a half hour at least.

"Okay, put your coat on and stay where I can see you from the window. And say hello to Booker, for goodness sake," she said. So excited, he only heard the "Okay," and was gone. The door slammed shut behind him.

"Better for us, Red. Let's go do a load," said Booker, nodding.

She grinned but shoved him back, and he followed her into the laundry room. She didn't flip the light switch but peered out the window and spotted Sam's shadow in the dim light, the white beam of his night vision goggles bouncing along as he ran. He stopped here and there to inspect the grasses.

"Look," she said to Booker. He put his head next to hers and slipped her coat from her shoulders.

He whispered in her ear, "I think he's occupied for a few minutes."

She turned around and kissed him but then wheeled her way to the washer, quickly shoving the clothes and the soap in and slammed the lid shut. She turned around and began unbuttoning her blouse.

"Is this what you were looking for?" she asked. Moments later her heels, dress slacks and panties were on the floor and he had lifted her onto the washer. It banged away, lurching from side to side in a rhythm that matched theirs. Every once in while she glanced out the window, and Sam's figure began to blend into the darkness until she could only see his white light, his secret weapon, that shot far and near.

They were frantic in their lovemaking, sloppy and brutal, yearning for each other's bodies as the rain of the past week, their obligations, and distance had separated them. They ended, kissing, nuzzling and lifting their heads at the same time to another noise that broke through their consciousness.

Cell phones trilled in tandem. Hers was "Irish Beat," a modern call to war, something a contemporary Braveheart would play going into battle and Booker's was James Brown's "I Feel Good." By the time the second ring played they were fumbling with their clothes.

He loped into the kitchen. She zipped and buttoned, tucked in half a shirttail while her divorce attorney told her to sit down because he had something to tell her. She leaned against the kitchen doorjamb, listening.

"Vance requested another continuance to delay the hearing on the partition lawsuit. This time, he used his Senate campaign schedule as an excuse. I'm sorry, Claire. The judge bought it."

Distracted, Claire glanced at Booker. He slid into his coat, his phone to his ear. He was leaving, damn it. She wanted to say good-bye.

"This is the part that's important. Are you listening, Claire?" her attorney asked.

I've heard this before, she thought. But it was unusual for him to call so late on a Friday night. "Yes. What's up?" she asked impatiently.

"In researching, we found a home equity line of credit filed against the deed. The property can't be sold until the line of credit is paid. Claire, he's taking money out of the house."

"Wait, wait," she yelled into the phone grabbing the kitchen chair and sitting down. "He can't do that without my signature."

Forged signatures, he said. "I reported it to the Maryland attorney general. I'm sorry if you didn't want that but it's a lack of ethics. I'm required. That's some real balls running for office and stealing money from his ex-wife. This is a criminal case."

A criminal case against Vance? The Maryland attorney general. Son of a bitch. That could take forever. She and Sam would be dragged into the fray. What had happened to her husband? She didn't know who he was anymore. "Can't I just get my money through the partition before you do that?"

"That's what I'm saying. There may not be any money left. That's why it needs to become a criminal case. I'm not asking you, Claire. The man is running for office and the people need to be protected from someone like this."

She thought, and I'm one of them, right? Silence. She looked up at Booker and his eyes met hers across the room. He was standing by the door. She could see he wanted to talk. He tapped his watch.

She glanced out the kitchen window quickly and saw Sam's light beaming away in the darkness. The sun had set, but she could tell he was standing by the old dock. She thought she heard Compass barking.

"Claire, this is serious stuff. He's stealing from you, living in your house and playing the great politician," said her attorney.

"I know. I know. I just can't believe he'd sink this low." She got up and walked over to the door. Booker was waving good-bye. He paused, looking at her with concern and pecked her on the lips. Then he was gone.

The attorney apologized for the bad news and hung up. She pulled her hair up and knotted it on her head. Once the attorney general was involved, Vance's bid for the Senate would be over. The media would get a hold of it, and he would be dinner table fodder for weeks.

She couldn't imagine why he would be so bone-headed, but looking back on the way he ingratiated himself with her father she thought maybe she was the one who had been bone-headed and that he had been a chimera from the beginning. He might be Sam's father, but what kind of father could he be after losing his license to practice law, maybe even going to jail? She didn't want Sam to be around him ever again.

The lawyer would request a stay on the partition while the criminal case got resolved. Nine months, she thought. Vance had friends in local government and business, people with money who would help him out. It wouldn't be over quickly. The press would find her. Her gentle life at the beach, Sam's easy existence, his fun, would be gone. His friends' parents would find out and drop them socially. A circus. She couldn't stand it and was so agitated that she tossed her cell phone toward the table.

Claire sat for a moment, hurting, confused and angry. She picked up a school bulletin from the table. There was a pizza drive that ended the following week. Sam was supposed to be selling them but everyone knew the parents did the work. She put it down and stabbed it hard with a knife. Surprised at her own anger, she looked underneath and rubbed her fingers over the pierced Formica. It was Odessa's table. Jeez, her split-second anger! And what was all that noise?

Compass was growing hoarse barking. He had come to the back porch door and was scratching furiously. She sighed and dragged herself out the kitchen door to let him in. It was time to call Sam for a bath. She glanced at her watch: seven-forty. For God's sake, the evening was getting away from them. Friday night. It was dark out and he was lost in play. She pushed the creaky screened door open.

"Sam, time to come in," she called.

Nothing.

"Samuel." She stared into the darkness looking right at the light from his night vision goggles. Of course he could hear her. Was he ignoring her? God damn it. She didn't need a disobedient kid right now. She looked up at the sky and clouds hid the stars. The night was pitch black.

"Samuel," she yelled again. Nothing. The light didn't move, not an inch. What in God's name? She bolted through the door, running, a growing panic powering her legs. The grass was wet on her bare feet. Cold hit her face and wrapped around her thin silk blouse. She hardly noticed. She was breathing fast as she slid to a stop in the muddy, burned grasses. The moon was covered in passing clouds, and its silver light momentarily outlined the stump of a half-burned and blackened post on the old dock. Sam's goggles and hat were hung on it. From a distance, the small post had looked like it was Sam. Sam at the water's edge, Sam investigating some creature, some web, some nonsense. It was Sam. She had taken her eyes off him.

"Sam?" she said quietly looking down at the goggles in her hand. Where was he? She scanned the darkness. No sound, no answer. She screamed his name over and over while Compass stood at her side, looking up at her. She screamed and dropped to her knees in the mud, crying, knowing he was gone.

Compass pushed against her cheek with his wet nose and she got up, slid and fell to her knee but recovered and ran for the door. She searched for her phone finally locating it on the floor under the kitchen cabinet and dialed 911. The call dropped. She ran to the front door and dialed again and it went through.

"911. What is the nature of your emergency?"

"My name is Claire McIntosh and my son has been taken. Samuel McIntosh Peyton. He is nine years old. He has been taken from my backyard just now. I know this because someone has been stalking our property. He has blue eyes and dark red hair and…." with that she began to sob.

———

CHAPTER 5

Booker Investigates

*W*hen Booker left the farmhouse, he returned to his home to put on street clothes. Tattooed, urban with a splash of whiskey on his clothes, he was ready for nighttime deals in the heroin market. He wasn't bartending in Ocean City but heading to the Canton Inn, a stripper bar, for a talk with some Chino heavyweights. He was on the phone with his partner when the call came in from Claire and went to voicemail. Running late after their dalliance in the laundry room, Booker quickly donned his dreads, green contacts and applied the tattoo on his neck that the Canton clientele knew him by.

Claire called again and he listened, a sinking feeling in the pit of his stomach. Booker closed his eyes sucking in air as he ruminated over what action to take. He reacted on instinct, telling her he would be there in just a minute. After he hung up, he realized it wasn't where he was needed most. He called his partner, listened to his horseshit and told him to handle it himself. Then he called his Ma who was at the church bustling around at their monthly Friday night Simple Supper. Odessa said she would drop everything and go to Claire. Better choice.

He vacillated momentarily looking at his watch for the first time that evening: 7:50. Water or land? Statistically, he knew the first few minutes and hours after a kidnapping brought the greatest success. He grabbed his boat keys from the bulletin board, strapped on his shoulder harness, holstered his Beretta under his jacket and sped down the gravel walkway to the boat, skittering pebbles as he went.

His heart pounded in his chest and blood beat in his ears. It was cold outside, not freezing, but his fingers were numb as he slipped the ropes off the dock cleats and pushed off. His thoughts were locked on Sam. He felt compelled, almost nauseous. But he knew Sam was his boy now. Sam on the dock that first day boldly introducing himself to a black man who tended crab traps. The boy in designer sweats whom he held at arm's length because he was coddled, or a brainiac, or too lily white. Whatever. He had been wrong. Sam was scrappy, pure and innocent. Sam was *him*, catching crabs with his dad, riding in the vet truck, working on math problems after dinner. And Sam was everything Claire had.

And everything Booker had. If he lost Sam, he feared he would lose Claire. Mother and child. He throttled up into the middle of the creek and cut the engine. Silence. He listened for anything. A hoot owl, ducks quacking, and the distant squawk of a blue heron. It was so deadly quiet he heard plops on dimpled water. Fish fed nearby. But there were no other sounds from either shore. Thoughts that he hadn't done enough gnawed at him.

He shouldn't have cornered Claire in the laundry room and distracted her. He should have kept an eye on Sam. He should have called him inside before he left. Fuck. He was always in such a goddamned hurry to get to work, the next job, to check the next item on the list. Why couldn't he ever set his priorities straight?

After the arson, he suspected they were a target, but he reasoned nothing would happen again so soon—certainly not with their cars in the driveway, the house lights on and early in the evening. He had wanted to warn her but truly thought that the threat came from her job. He reached in his jacket pocket and looked at the holy medal. Mother of God. 'Pray for Us.' He had an idea of who it was. How had this gang found where she lived? She had rented through a private property owner, wasn't using her last name and couldn't represent anyone in the Delaware courts for another three months. There was only one person: Vance.

Booker checked his watch: 8:47. He flicked on the spotlights and circled the bay, scanning both shores in sweeping motions. Nothing. He was missing something. No use to waste time. He needed to hit the trailer park.

After Claire called 911, Odessa bustled in and took charge. At the sight of the old woman's bespectacled face at the front door, Claire fell into her arms. She composed herself and asked Odessa if she would help her make a list of who to call. At Odessa's urging, she wrote the first name, Vance, and realized she couldn't call him. She wouldn't call him. She was filled with hate. It was him, of course. He was the one behind this. It was time to call Dean at Tosh Enterprises.

She had to hand this over. It was beyond her now. At 10 p.m., Booker still had not arrived. She was growing more confused as people in uniforms filled the farmhouse. The man in charge was State Police Detective Charles Lowery who made quick work of calling in the FBI. Then that familiar agent whom she had met at the prison, Brent Fowler, approached with her cell phone. She couldn't remember giving it to him. She read a text saying," Arrived at O.C. airport. Tosh." An hour later, her father's retinue entered the door with solemn looks and quiet voices as if they were attending a funeral. She introduced Dean, the lawyer, Ross, the accountant, Leslie VanAnden, the great communicator and even Mercer, the security chief who clustered in the front hall as relief washed over her. They didn't interrupt the interview with the detective but Claire knew they were listening to every word. So comforting to have them there. Back in the fold. They would know what to do.

Lowery had appointed four other detectives to search the area outside. They returned saying that numerous footprints were around the dock area but none led to the driveway. The ground was soft. They called in boats from DNREC. Claire said she only heard one car on the driveway and that was Booker leaving. But that was before she ran out to find Sam's night vision goggles on the dock post.

"Night vision goggles?"

"A toy. A twenty dollar online toy he got for his birthday. But they have an LED light. I could see it from inside."

"So the light was moving around and then it stood still?" Lowery made notes on his pad.

"Yes. But I was on the phone with my attorney," she said.

"What window where you watching Sam from?" he asked.

"The laundry room and then the kitchen. But the light was fixed when I was in the kitchen." Was everyone looking at her too closely? Even Odessa?

"When did the attorney call?" he asked.

"I was in the laundry room." She looked at her cell. The attorney's call read 7:11. It was dark outside by then. She estimated how long Sam had been romping in the yard and when she first saw his light linger by the dock. Twenty minutes until Booker left. Twenty minutes and her little boy had disappeared. Twenty minutes that she didn't have her eyes on him. No noise, no screams, nothing but his night vision goggles and ball cap. And Compass barking.

Voices droned inside the farmhouse like talk radio. She was glued to the couch, growing weaker by the minute, all of her years of practiced composure in a crisis evaporating. She heard herself sighing and whimpering and was powerless to stop. She looked at her hands, blue with cold and shaking. Her fingers nervously worked the hem of her shirt. Where was Booker? He would know what to say. He should give his professional opinion. The questions went on endlessly.

An afghan was caped loosely around her shoulders. She sat, her bare feet under her. With a start of surprise she wished for a hot shower. She wasn't completely numb although her own voice sounded alien to her. Disconnected. She looked down at her feet that were still muddy from the...she couldn't finish the thought, not even in her mind.

Booker pushed the Grady White across the still water, its engine humming low, leaving a V of white froth in its wake. He was intent, almost hyperfocused. His movements, machine-like. He saw the farmhouse alight with activity. He needed to get inside his house before the uniforms discovered him. Staties. They would call in the FBI to establish if Sam was kidnapped or a runaway.

He needed to get a grip on himself. He was far too involved and letting his emotions cloud his thinking. He was satisfied that if a detective talked to Claire for a few seconds, the troopers would make quick work of the investigation. He had seen her in action after the fire. She knew how to hold it together, how to plow through in an emergency.

They would come outside soon and secure the crime scene. His presence would slow things down. They knew he informed for Maryland State Police but they didn't know he was undercover, and his appearance would derail the line of questioning. Besides, Claire would rely on him too much, stifling the information dump to the investigators. He ran across his graveled driveway and pulled open the door to his dad's old vet truck.

On the seat of the old pickup were printouts of the people that he knew were court adjudicated in Point Park. Still dressed as Booker, the bartender, he would find out what they knew of Sam. When he questioned a suspect, fear and submission were his friends.

9:46. The pedophile. White, close to middle age. Definitely intimidated. Dead end.

10:11. The drug house. Three white males, two white females well past fifty. Aging hippies. Pot, maybe some other recreationals. Friendly but dispassionate, empty. No leads.

10:42. Six Hispanic males. Landscape workers. He showed them the holy medals. Soberly, they had nodded in unison, their slick, black hair bobbing like bowling balls when one pointed out, "You know that gang colors. MS-13." He did know from working undercover in Highlandtown, Baltimore where the cops closed a Mexican restaurant after a bloodletting on its doorstep.

The Hispanics in Sussex were cautious, respectful. They sent their earnings home, but obeyed the local laws. Booker sat on an old webbed lawn chair in the landscapers' tidy yard. The overnight guest they housed two weeks earlier was gone, had disappeared and none of them knew where. It was plain they didn't like him, thought him a threat to their safety and had pushed him out of the house. But they gave Booker a description. He took out a pad and pencil.

Height: 5' 6-8. Hair: light brown, wavy, parted in the middle, over his ears to the chin. Eyes: blue? Distinctive marks: teardrop tattoo at the corner of his left eye. Answered to the name Under. Booker asked them to spell it. U-n-d-e-r. He studied his scribble. Maybe 25 years old, he wore jeans, black sneakers and a black hoodie. Just like everyone else on the beach in October.

Then he trucked over to Trixie's. The beating heart of the community, she and her kids knew everything. Leaving his dreadlocks and green contacts in the truck, he bolted up her steps. He was relieved when she met him at the door. Standing on the stoop in her flimsy nightgown, the outline of her breasts tugged at the material. Trixie, sexy as always. Her black hair was up, and she wiped her hand over her face and down her neck as if she was having a hot flash.

"What's goin' on over there, Booker?" She nodded to the action across at the farmhouse. The investigation was in full swing. DNREC boats had arrived at the burned-out dock, and high-powered LED lights were positioned around the yellow tape that cordoned off the quarter-acre backyard. A couple of camera flashes punctuated the night. Forensics. He glanced at his watch: 11:32. He turned back to Trixie.

"Let's go inside," he said as he walked past her into the house. The living room was dark except for the big screen flashing late night stand-up comedy. The sound was off. He could still smell the garlic from dinner. A florescent light shone in the kitchen.

"Are you going to tell me, or do you want to stay and watch the kids while I go over there?" She spoke in a stage whisper and stood just inside the door, blocking it with a hand on her hip. He didn't want to annoy her. He needed her help.

"Sam's gone. He's been taken. Can you tell me anything?"

The blood drained from her face.

"Maybe about the landscapers?" he asked.

He could see she was ticking off something in her mind. When Trixie was lost in thought, whether over her hand in a card game or trying to remember how much wine she had put in the sauce, her eyebrows shot up and together. She looked like a lioness on alert.

"John said one of them had been talking to them recently. He seemed to want to get Sam in a conversation but Sam wouldn't bite."

"Okay. I have a description. Let's see if it matches Johnny Boy's. Can you wake him up?"

"Yeah, sure." She bustled along the creaky hallway and returned with the kid, looking rumpled and sleepy and more than a little grumpy. She pushed him toward Booker.

"Wake up there. I'll go get you a Coke." She shook him gently. "Booker has some questions for you." She shoved him unceremoniously onto the couch and disappeared down the hall.

It was Booker's turn. He didn't have a lot of confidence in his ability to draw the kid out. John was usually surly and had attitude. Booker was sure it was some latent tough guy racism brewing that Trixie had always kept a lid on. Well, now the kid needed to get over himself. He started off with his reasonable voice.

"This is an emergency. You can help. Your buddy Sam is gone. We think kidnapped."

"No shit?"

"Yes shit. You've been around Sam a lot. Trixie says you know about something going on at the Hispanic's house."

"Nothin' goin' on. We rode our bikes around there couple of times when Trixie had the little ones. That's all." The kid sounded overly defensive.

"I'm not here to get you in trouble with Trixie." He could hear Trixie's heavy steps in the hall. Crap, the woman walked on her heels. No wonder the kids knew when she was coming. "Just tell me."

John started again. "There's this new guy. I never seen him before a couple a weeks ago. He don't look like a Spic."

Trixie bore down on him like a Mack truck. "What'd I tell you about talking like that?"

"Well, you say it."

Booker intervened. "Trix. It's okay." He looked at John, "Drink some Coke. He's an American?"

John eyed Booker with suspicion. "Naw, I mean he don't look like the rest of 'em. His hair's light and his eyes aren't black. He had a dot or something by his eye." John pointed to the corner of his own and waited to see if the adults were satisfied but they stood there looming over him.

Booker decided to kneel on one knee in front of the kid and offer up some information to see if any would come back in trade. "Light hair? Did you notice anything else? What was he wearing?"

"I don't know. Both times he had on jeans and a sweatshirt." He paused and seemed to wake up a little because he sat up straighter. "He said somethin' to Sam the second time we was over there. I couldn't hear 'cause we was going so fast on our bikes, but the dude had something in his hand on a blue and white rope." He slumped back into the couch and yawned. "I couldn't really tell. Looked like that shit the girls at school make keychains from."

"Like this," Booker asked and pulled the Virgin medal from his pocket.

He bent over Booker's hand. "Yeah. Just like that. You know who it is?"

"Not yet, but I'm going find out. You can go back to bed."

"You gonna find Little Spam?"

Trixie snorted. "You heard the man. Back to bed." She slapped his arm, saying, "Good job. We'll find him. We got a handle on this, right Booker?"

Booker wasn't so sure. But if this was how you put a kid's worries to rest, he'd follow her lead. He put his hand on John's shoulder and the kid didn't pull away. Progress.

"There will be a police investigator here tomorrow morning. Tell him everything you told me. No need to mention that I was here." Booker smiled. "That's our business." And he left for the farmhouse. 12:12 a.m.

Claire saw Mercer in the kitchen talking to the FBI agent. Ross and Dean were drinking coffee in the hallway. Leslie, perfect and unwrinkled in a black suit, stood at the kitchen sink. She was busy phoning everyone including Vance. He apparently wasn't answering his cell; typical, especially on a Friday night. Despite a request by Detective Lowery to cease and desist from alerting the world about Sam's disappearance until the father had been notified, she continued calling members of the board of Tosh Enterprises.

Detective Lowery pulled a kitchen chair into the living room and sat directly opposite Claire, a pencil tucked behind his ear and a pad of paper on his knee. An older man with a bulbous nose, red cheeks and friendly blue eyes, he had not inspired much confidence in her, but now he tried to put her at ease chatting about her move to Sussex County. Despite the late hour, he was dressed in a dark green suit and green tie painted with a white marlin.

She couldn't take her eyes off the fish. There was a stain on the tie and the more she looked the more she wanted to rip it from around his neck. He seemed too unprofessional, a sport fisherman with a beer belly and stained tie asking her personal questions. Why wasn't he directing the officers standing around?

She sucked in air needing to clear her head. Lowery's casual demeanor, his quiet tone, and pursed lips lifted to a brief smile that helped her focus. She answered his questions, haltingly at first. She started with Vance—his forgery of her name on the loan and his recent pressure to gain custody of Sam. She discussed her job unemotionally, how she was trying to help Rosa and Pembroke. She even remembered to give him the lock of Sam's hair from her purse. She racked her brain for anything—anything that might be important. Then she mentioned the Hispanic man who had said hello to Sam in Point Park.

Agent Brent Fowler appeared in the doorway to listen. Two other detectives, also in suits, now milled about in the front hall and living room. She couldn't remember their names, but they must have expected that because they put their business cards down on the coffee table. One had a computer notebook and the other was on his cell speaking very softly. She wanted to shout at them to do something. After about an hour, Lowery nodded silently to one of his subordinates who made a single phone call. More FBI agents arrived with an entourage. They moved to the dining room with some black suitcases.

A little after midnight, Booker came through the front door dressed in baggy khakis and a black hoodie she had never seen before. The sight of him brought instant relief and she exhaled, realizing for the first time how tensely she was coiled. She wanted to throw herself into his arms but she stopped short and instead stood up stiffly, surprised at his appearance. She sized him up and down. He had gone to work instead of coming to her.

She wanted to ask him. Surely Sam was hiding from them somewhere. He wasn't kidnapped. He was at Trixie's. Had they checked Trixie's? She thought that this was some extended, awful dream that she couldn't wake from. She couldn't take her eyes off Booker, but he seemed like a stranger.

A heavy silver chain hung from his front belt to his back pocket. Another looped around his neck. He smelled of booze, and she could see a tattoo of some kind below his ear. His jeans were tucked into unlaced black Timberlands. She had never seen this side of him. She was embarrassed and confused and couldn't look at him.

Just when she needed his quiet support, just when she and Lowery had reached some plane of understanding, Booker stole everyone's attention with his hiphop rapper getup. She felt like she was floating, disembodied from the whole scene, standing in a corner away from everyone.

Claire watched as all four detectives smirked and traded glances. How could they not? He strode into the house without knocking. His presence overpowered the other men. At a distance, she heard voices and recognized Odessa's. She introduced him as the son of the property owner. Claire watched as Booker shook hands with Lowery and gave him a business card. The detective's silent hesitation made her suspect that he didn't believe what was on the card. She could only imagine: Booker Solomon, Undercover.

Really? She thought she was too tired to laugh at herself when a hysterical giggle escaped her lips. Lowery glanced and asked if she was all right. "Certainly," she uttered in disbelief. "I wasn't expecting…." She waved her arm in Booker's direction. His brow furrowed and he stood his distance. Realization sliced through her fog like a sharp knife. There was no sense in giving them irrelevant information about the black landlord and the white tenant.

"Detective Solomon, you have input from the arson and the dog." asked Lowery. It was more a statement than a question. "It's probably related."

"I think you'd better check another report in D.C. as well. Claire, have you told them about the bombing?" Booker asked.

She shook her head. Her thoughts about the past ten months were disjointed. Could she remember? The big events, her father's death, the reading of the will, quitting her job stuck with her. Then she and Sam had moved. But she struggled to recall other details, especially about the bombing at Wilcox and Stein.

How much had she told the detective? Vance, her dad, her job and the move, certainly. But not her money troubles. Even she thought the drama too much to be believed.

Claire looked intently at Lowery and leaned in saying with as much emphasis as she could muster, "It was the office building on K Street last January. The one that was bombed by the abortion hater. The bomb blew up my car. There was nothing left of it," she said as she waved her hand nonchalantly in the air. She didn't care if she sounded flippant. She was sick to death of the questions. They needed to stick to Sam. "Never mind I almost died. But Homeland Security and the FBI exonerated me. It was parked in the wrong place at the wrong time."

"I saw that on the evening news. We aren't completely out of the loop here in slower, lower Delaware." Lowery chuckled at his own joke and then said straight-faced, "Ms. McIntosh, forgive me for pointing this out, but that's an awful lot of bad luck for one person in a very short period of time."

"Yes it is." All this talk, talk, talk isn't leading anywhere, she thought. "What are you doing about Sam? Why are we just sitting here?" Her voice trembled as she thought about Sam playing soccer, dancing in her bedroom, and rolling with Compass on the floor.

Lowery looked at her with understanding eyes. An FBI agent and Mercer stood in the hallway listening. They stared at her, looking very sympathetic but doing nothing. She glanced at the clock on side table. 12:17 a.m.

"Claire, may I call you Claire?" Lowery asked. At the sound of her name she came back to the present. She didn't care what he called her. It wasn't a tea party for God's sake. She stood unsteadily. The blanket fell from her shoulders.

"You can call me anything you damn well like. You rolled in here with your equipment and your people. Everyone's milling around whispering. You aren't telling me anything. He's my son. You need to take some action, here, now." She screamed at them, "Do something. Now, not tomorrow. Before my baby is gone forever."

Odessa threw her arms around her and sat her down on the couch. "They're trying, Claire," she said.

VanAnden arrived with a scotch. She pulled a prescription bottle from her suit pocket. "Claire, here take these. It'll help you sleep."

Dean asked, "Perhaps, Officer Lowery, you could let Claire get some rest?"

"Mr. Campbell, isn't it? I have one more question," said Lowery.

Claire nodded, exasperated but controlled. Her own outburst had scared her. She never yelled at people. Her mother yelled at people. Louisa yelled at people. Words from her dad came barreling back at her: once you start yelling, no one listens except the news media.

She apologized. She fussed at the hem of her shirt but she didn't swallow the pills. "I need to be awake, Leslie," she said pushing them away. She caught Booker watching the Tosh handlers at work. She had seen that look on his face after the fire. He was evaluating. She didn't care if she appeared pampered. He disappeared down the hallway.

Lowery smiled in approval at her refusal to take the sedative. He began, "I guess if Homeland Security says something, it must be true. But, if you were to speculate, who do you think would plant a bomb at your work?" Her old fears surfaced. Please God, please don't let there be a connection. Please keep Sam safe. She had to believe what Homeland Security told her.

"You're asking me if I have any enemies. I don't know. That happened before my dad died, before the estate was settled. Besides, what would that have to with Sam getting snatched in another state ten months later?" Vance. It was Vance. She couldn't say it. She couldn't accuse him aloud—not yet.

"Well, that's what we need to find out." He stood up and thanked her. "Now, I have some things I want to show you," he said.

He asked for the TV remote. She blinked, trying to focus on the screen as Lowery pointed to words that crept across the bottom of the TV. "Child Amber Alert: Samuel Peyton, 9 years old. Caucasian, Red hair, Blue eyes. Near Fenwick Island, DE. Look across State Lines. Call 911." He added that it was being broadcast 'Peninsula wide.'

Lowery called one of his detectives over to show her a series of text messages and emails alerts. A roadblock had been set up in each direction on Lighthouse Road despite the fact that they didn't have a description of a getaway car.

Then he escorted her to the kitchen to look out back. A small army of investigators had cordoned off the area in yellow tape. The entire yard was lit as men and women in uniform combed the grass, sweeping small areas as they walked in a line with flashlights. Cameras flashed by the dock, and a generator hummed somewhere in the background. "We've been knocking on doors in the trailer park," he said.

She pushed past him and made her way to the porch. The cold air cleared her head and a light wind blew her hair about her face. She re-knotted it impatiently and breathed in gulps. Grasping the wood frame of the screen door, she could make out two boats in the bay. Equipped with high power lights, they seemed to be crisscrossing the water, lighting up the edges of each sawgrass island.

She felt a blanket, heavy and warm, envelope her and she succumbed, leaning back. Dean led her inside and passed her on to VanAnden who gave her the sleeping pill and scotch. Odessa led her upstairs to bed. Each step was a mountain to climb.

They stopped on the landing when they heard Lowery talking to Booker and both bent down over the railing to listen. The front hall light was off and there was a glow from the living room. Odessa tugged on Claire's arm as a warning. Claire could see the distrust in her eyes.

When Booker had knocked an icy blonde, wearing an expensive suit and pointy heels, opened the door. She radiated understated elegance. He wondered who she was and looked around for his Ma. With a raised brow, the woman said she was VanAnden from Tosh Enterprises and asked if she could help. A cluster of middle-aged suits, with the same suspicious gaze, stood between him and the living room. Tosh. McIntosh. It came to him. So these were *The* Tosh, mega-builders of the nation's capital. He'd seen their signs on monstrous construction sites all over the metropolitan area. Thank God he had removed the dreads but cursed that he hadn't gone home to change and wash away the smell of the whiskey. Way to make a good first impression, he thought.

The reception from the Delaware Staties was friendly if dismissive. After the fire on the property they knew only that he was Booker Solomon, sometime informant and bartender. He thought there was a good chance his cover was in jeopardy, two years of planned concealment gone in a matter of minutes. The only way to retain it would be to walk away from Sam, from Claire and drive to the Canton Inn for his night-time rendezvous. He couldn't do it.

Booker migrated to the dining room where an FBI tech was setting up a rudimentary metal box that looked like something out of a Marvel Comic. Stingray was written in script across it in red letters. Claire's laptop and landline were lined up next to it. It was a pen/trap for phone tapping. Were they covering her cell too? He had to ask.

"You guys already got the warrant for that?"

A man who had undercover written all over him was talking to one of the Tosh suits and turned to stare at Booker. The man's delayed smile was clinical. He dismissed the corporation rep with a nod, and the suit drifted to the living room.

"We don't need one," he said to Booker. "This is simple traffic analysis. We can't pick up the content of the conversation, only the location of the caller. Ms. McIntosh has given us permission. Who are you, may I ask?"

"I'm the landlord. That's all."

"Yes, I thought so, Detective Solomon. I'm Special Agent Fowler, FBI."

Well, that's it for my cover, thought Booker. They knew but he wasn't sure who 'they' encompassed. Agencies share information when it's relevant, he thought, or when their egos aren't going to get bruised. And in a kidnapping.

"You're undercover for State of Maryland. I've been working on something related to the case, as have you."

"Whoa, I haven't been working on this case," said Booker.

"No, I don't mean the child's disappearance. You've been working on the increase in the heroin trade through Maryland and making some headway on the gang that's behind it."

He didn't have to maintain the ruse any longer. The FBI was here, but what did they have to do wi—he blinked and leaned toward the agent. Nose to nose. "We're working on the same thing?"

"MS13, Detective Solomon. Yes. They have a toehold on Delmarva and are moving large amounts of drugs away from the I-95 corridor."

Booker nodded, waiting for more.

"The heroin market is increasing, as you know," said Agent Fowler. "We suspect an MS13 suspect in the child's disappearance."

The agent was composed. Booker felt disheveled and blindsided that he was never made aware the FBI was involved. What the fuck? Why hadn't Bandylegs briefed them? He hadn't thought it out. Who else would coordinate behind the scenes? There were three states on the Delmarva Peninsula.

"DEA is in on this too?" he asked standing back on his heels.

Fowler reached for a manila folder on the table and opened it. He passed it to Booker. "This is the suspect, also a rising member of the clique." He pointed to the picture and said, "Ms. McIntosh is representing his mother, Rosa Robles, on immigration issues."

There he was—a grainy black and white of a short Hispanic guy taking a package on a street corner. Then a color one, clearer than the first, a three-quarter view of his face over someone's shoulder but unmistakable sandy brown hair and blue eyes. Lastly, there was a shot of the same man, years younger in a lineup, without a shirt and his slender chest was tattooed in medieval script, "Mara Salvatrucha 13," along with the Devil's House, a closed fist, pointer and pinky up, long nails like claws rising from his navel. Booker grunted. He was the trailer park visitor and the owner of the medal. Booker decided not to say anything yet.

"Looks like you guys got this under control," he said and smiled at the agent.

He wanted to see how the investigation shook out. Booker strolled into the living room looking for Claire. She was a shell, white and trembling off and on, surrounded by police and Tosh people. He wanted to put his arms around her, carry her to bed and hold her. But a man in a worn green suit called him. Booker knew the drill. This was lead State Detective Lowery, who was all questions.

"Detective Solomon," Lowery nodded. "I understand you were here earlier in the evening before the boy disappeared. Did you see a boat, maybe running lights out on the water? Hear a boat engine?"

"No, sorry." It wasn't a lie.

Lowery pressed. "Did the dog bark or get excited tonight? Can you hear him from your home?"

"No. My house is past the woods too far to see what's going on here."

Lowery stuck a pencil behind his ear. "Did you see any cars on the access road to Point Park?

Booker looked at Claire who wouldn't raise her eyes to him. "When I came over to speak to Ms. McIntosh earlier the washing machine was clanking away. Sam had gone to play outside, and no one was around as far as I could see.

"What'd you want to talk to Ms. McIntosh about?" asked Lowery.

Nosy, thought Booker, but a good detective. Not very subtle. "A rent adjustment." Claire sat, her head down. Was she embarrassed or angry with him? He was sure she was desperate, but the only sign was her fingers toying with a thread she had pulled from her shirttail.

Lowery turned to Claire to ask why the dog didn't bark if someone was threatening Sam.

"He was barking," she said. Her voice was low but steady. "I didn't hear him. I was on the phone with my divorce attorney."

"I don't have a dog myself," said Lowery.

Booker had been holding his breath and let it out softly. My Claire, he thought, still composed, meeting the demands of others. It would've been crushing for her to explain the laundry room scene and might even create an aura of suspicion about them both. Claire caught his eye momentarily. She was drained and wary, maybe even mistrustful.

Hell, Booker knew everyone was a suspect until they weren't. It was 2:10 a.m when his Ma appeared from the kitchen. Her eyes were full of warning directed at him and she urged Claire to go to bed, saying there wasn't anything more she could do by staying up. The blonde woman from Tosh came in with pills and a drink for Claire and a round of coffee for everyone else. Steaming hot and black, it was the jolt he needed. Steering Claire to the steps, his Ma passed him and whispered, "Those Tosh folk came in on a helicopter." She nodded to him once as if telling him, 'Be careful what you say.'

The two suits from the family business were broaching a topic with another Statie that Booker didn't fully understand. He cocked his ear to listen. Commercial real estate investments had plummeted in value. Campbell, the soft looking intellectual in wire rims said, "We have investors who are bailing on current projects."

So what else is new, thought Booker? Same story everywhere from what he could figure, but these folks were still wearing expensive clothes. Take a look around when the sun rises, he thought, and maybe you'll see what a recession does to the little people. He was annoyed, but he reminded himself that Claire was a Tosh. Then a uniformed statie burst in the front door.

"Some black dude was ahead of us, Detective. He stopped at two of the houses we identified. The ped and the druggies. Both looked clean but they had time since…" He trailed off when he saw Booker standing in the corner by the couch and rephrased his comments, "an African American male questioned residents in both homes." All eyes settled on Booker.

Lowery's neck grew red and he yelled, "What the hell are you doing, Solomon? You're out of area. This is Delaware territory."

Here we go, thought Booker. All the white men ready to string up the derelict black guy. Agent Fowler wandered in to see what the ruckus was but faded into the dining room, apparently uninterested.

Booker faced Lowery. "I know the people in Point Park," he said calmly. "You know timing is everything in a kidnapping."

"Stay out of it," said Lowery. "I'll let you know when we need Maryland to do our work. Got it?"

Campbell spoke up. Now that Claire had gone to bed, everybody was posturing. Lowery turned on him aggressively asking, "What do you want now?"

"Gentlemen, there is a complication, and possibly a motive. I hear everyone speculating about this Hispanic man, but you need some background. When Claire's office was bombed in January it was determined by the Washington FBI office that an abortion terrorist was the perpetrator. Personally, we always thought the bomber was a pawn, but the bureau couldn't find other leads."

Booker remembered the news feed. The office building blown out like the buildings in Mogadishu. Dead and wounded. And Claire had a scar on her forehead to show for it.

Campbell was speaking. "Mr. McIntosh took out a kidnap and ransom insurance policy on immediate family members five years ago. It provided multimillion dollar payouts in case anyone was kidnapped anywhere in the world." His pea-eyed gaze took in the surprise on every face. "Not a small amount."

"What do you mean?'" asked Lowery.

"I believe it's authorized up to twenty million per person."

Stunned silence spread throughout the room. Lowery didn't miss a beat. "Who knows about these policies?" he asked.

Campbell leaned against the wall. "No one—only Mr. McIntosh who passed away in July and the four Tosh representatives who are standing before you. It will not pay out to a family member who kidnaps a relative."

"Well, that puts you on a list, doesn't it?" said Lowery throwing his hands in the air.

Booker pieced this new information together. He had to admit old man McIntosh was a master of control, even from beyond the grave. No wonder Claire was a detail-oriented person.

"Detective Solomon, what has Claire said? Is it Vance Peyton who wants his kid back, because I have to tell you, we don't have a ransom demand and it's been five hours."

"The father is running for the Senate in Maryland. Why would he risk it?"

Lowery chewed on that for a second, then answered, "What better way to get the sympathy vote? He can always have his kid turn up later after he's in office."

"I suppose. Claire's talked about him a little. I never got the impression that he would go that far. Besides, you don't want to *wait* for Sam to turn up."

Claire and Odessa hunched in the darkness of the upstairs landing. That's my man, thought Claire. Booker would prod them for the information she had missed. Odessa patted her arm resting on the bannister.

"Mr. Campbell, Dean isn't it? Who stands to gain from this besides the father?" asked Lowery.

"Forgive me, Detective Lowery." Claire watched Dean move out of the shadows. He stood in the doorway to the living room, situated his wire rims on the end of his nose and sniffled. Booker and Lowery were around the corner by the couch and she couldn't see them.

"We came because we have some information you may need. We have given the DNA sample to the FBI agent and also the pictures of Sam's identifying marks. The mole under his left ear and a half-moon scar on his knee. We don't want to interrupt the proceedings, but you need to know what Mr. Mercer has to say."

Lowery's voice rose. Claire looked at Odessa. Odessa frowned back, questioning, and Claire nodded toward the conversation with her forefinger up to her lips. The corporate team had always been there for the family. Twenty years later and they had only gotten better in a crisis. They were paid to fix things.

Lowery was impatient. "What? There are plenty of people standing around here waiting to take information, man. Go ahead. Don't hold back."

Claire had not seen much of Mercer since they arrived. Menacing Mercer. He moved into view, next to Dean. In the light, she could see him pull papers from his breast pocket. His voice was confidential and low.

"I have all the identifying information on the boy. Hopefully we won't have to use it. I also know that her father, Ham McIntosh, was worried about Claire's safety."

"*Her* safety," Lowery said with puzzlement in his voice. "Come in here, where I can hear you."

"Yes, we have done our own investigation based on requests from her father. He had grown suspicious of her ex-husband."

Claire couldn't catch the rest. She looked blankly at Odessa and clutched at her elbow pulling her into her bedroom. What had they not told her? No one would keep information from her—not about Sam. "You have to go downstairs and listen," she whispered. "See what he has to say. Booker would tell me but we haven't had a chance to talk."

Odessa nodded. She pushed her glasses. "Why would your father keep something like that from you? He should've told you if he was worried."

"In a perfect world…" She felt drowsy, unable to reason, and the conversation downstairs was likely to continue well past dawn. She wanted to know what her dad knew. After a little nap she could take charge. She looked down at her muddied feet. A shower would clear her head. In the meantime, she could count on Odessa. "He was dying of cancer. He didn't keep secrets without a reason. But toward the end he couldn't talk." She jiggled Odessa's elbow. "Please, just go listen, before we miss too much."

She had to figure out a way to talk to Booker if the corporate team wouldn't come clean with her. All of the leadership was here except Uncle Alistair. Uncle Alistair. She had forgotten. He was going to be in town for the Corvette Club weekend. Sunday brunch. Had Leslie reached him? He would be beside himself. She wondered who had her phone but as she turned to her bed, she fell onto it heavily. Sleep overtook her.

Booker looked at his watch: 3:10 a.m. The focus was off him. His Ma had appeared at the foot of the staircase, wide awake. She whispered to him, "Go on home and do what you got to do, Booker."

Alone at his kitchen table, the overhead light blazing and a bowl of homemade chili from the church supper steaming in front of him, he wrote down the suspects and went back to number them.

2.) Under MS13
1.) Vance Peyton
3.) Tosh suits
5.) investors
4.) other family members
6.) Rosa Robles

CHAPTER 6

Finding Sam

hree hours later, a morning mist settled over the stubbled cornfields. Booker drove like a madman down Double Bridges Road.
The sun was rising in the eastern sky already blindingly bright. The
days of heavy rain had washed the earth and cleaned the air.

Booker's mind was clear. This was his last stop. His elbow lay propped
on his open window, his hand tucked under his nose as he ran it back and
forth over his mustache. He hit the accelerator. The truck lurched ahead
over the little wooden bridge, the headlights dispelling the mist that en-
croached from the water below. Thank God for the old V8. Automatically,
he glanced in his mirror. The boys in blue were still at the house. So was
the FBI. He still didn't want to be caught doing investigative work on the
wrong side of the state line.

For the second time in three weeks, he wound his way down the road
that paralleled Dirickson Creek. The old man might know secrets and
provide insight. Where the macadam ended on Hoffsnider's property, his
tires hit gravel, spitting it everywhere. Hopefully, he had seen something
after prowling the bay before dawn for late-season crab traps.

The place looked deserted. No chickens pecking the dirt. Hoffsnider's
old Buick station wagon was gone. No lights on in the trailer. And the
flat-bottomed johnboat was pulled up on the ramp, the boat trailer gone.
Did he sell it without the boat? Poor old guy needed money that bad. The
only thing of value were his chickens and they were simple enough to get
rid of. Lots of chicken farms around.

Booker threw the truck into park and got out, jogging over to the
boat. The rain should have filled it like a small swimming pool, but it was

empty, the plug perfectly sealed. Only a wet few rags sat in the bottom of it. He jumped in and climbed over the seats to the old Johnson motor. Bending over it, he pumped the bulb that primed the motor. It was hard, not like one that had been sitting for weeks. He raised up to look over the stern which sat in a foot of water. Whoever brought it in was in a hurry-didn't even take the time to raise the prop out of the water.

He moved quickly and silently toward the trailer, his hand up under his jacket. Placing each foot gingerly, he crouched under the frosted windows. He placed one hand on the doorknob to turn it, surprised when it opened easily to the paneled living room. He breathed softly in anticipation, gun raised. Two steps up, both arms pointing the gun first one way, then the other, he slid against the wall and scanned the space. No one.

The room was filled with old furniture, a sunken couch of indeterminate color, a recliner and various end tables cluttered with newspapers, fishing lures and faded blue maps of the inland bays. The sun cut across the room from the opposing windows, which didn't so much afford a view as cast a glow in the dingy interior. Light caught the whorls of dust stirred by the open door, speckles floating in the yellow air.

Booker put his gun arm to his side and sidled down the hall to the kitchen, opening bedroom doors along the way. Each one was tinier than the next. Newspapers pasted to the windows kept out the light. The rooms were empty save for an old mattress in one, covered in a moldy sheet printed with seahorses and clamshells. He walked in and pushed open the closet door. A worn pair of bib overalls hung from a hook and below was a pair of stained work boots, the toes stretched and curved upward. Hoffsnider had taken his clothes. Perhaps he had moved back in with his daughter in Baltimore.

He turned to go. A crumpled pile of navy and orange material lay in the corner. Booker toed it recognizing the Northface insignia. His heart surged: Sam's rain jacket. It was the one he had put on as he ran from the kitchen the night before. Booker needed to move fast. They could still be on the property, could be watching him now as he stumbled around. Automatically, he crouched lower, heading quickly to the kitchen.

A card table took up most of the space. Old wooden cabinets in various stages of disrepair lined two walls. The sink overflowed with dirty dishes and pans.

At the edge of the sink was a rectangular box imprinted with the picture of a woman with long brown hair. Revlon hair color. Booker peered into the sink splattered dark brown. Someone dyed Sam's head to cover up the blaze of red. He turned to go but first scanned the mess on the table. Something small glistened in the morning light. He picked it up and rolled the small metal stem and curved gold loop that surrounded it. The pocket watch—the one Claire was afraid she had lost. The one he had seen hanging in the bathroom from the mirror on their first morning.

Sam might still be alive. He closed his hand around the gold stem and pocketed it. Sam had left him a clue just like Iron Man on the fence.

He walked the pumpkin patch and searched the shed and the chicken coop. Nothing but crab traps and moldy feed. Lowery needed this information. There was enough evidence here. Forensics would find fingerprints and Sam's hair. Once in the truck, he called 911. "Yah, that Amber Alert. I seen a guy holding a kid with red hair." He gave Hoffsnider's address and hung up before they could ask more.

When Claire woke before dawn, she was groggy, cotton-mouthed and achy. The house was quiet except for a mourning dove that cooed outside her window. Struggling from the sheets, she thumped stiff-legged over to the window and looked down where halogen pole lights still shone on the grass and water.

In the pinkish glow of sunrise, she saw fewer people in the yard, and boats still patrolled the shallow waters. The scene had changed. Like gondoliers, each boat had a line of occupants on either side who poled their way across the murky waters. They were searching for Sam's body. She fell to the floor with a thud. "Please, dear God. I'll do anything, just, please, let them find Sam alive."

Claire showered, holding her head under the spray, hoping to wash away all the brittleness and grief. She shut her eyes against the glare from the white tiles and tried to center herself against a rising dizziness. Stepping out, she clutched the edge of the sink and wiped the steam off the mirror in a widening circle, glimpsing her drawn face, her eyelids red-rimmed and puffy. She held cold compresses to them and tried not to think. She almost wished for the time when her brain had shut down on its own. But now, her entire being was irritated and worn.

She dressed, and out of habit, started to make her bed. As she swept her hand across the crumpled sheets, dried flakes of mud stuck to her still damp palm. Angrily, she stripped the bed, gathered up her muddy clothes and hugged the laundry like a pillow as she walked to the landing. She paused. People were talking downstairs softly. Odessa stood at the door to Sam's room in a headscarf and her wrinkled clothes from the night before. Claire smiled.

"You didn't have to stay."

"I wanted to. We'll talk and then I'll go home to get a bath and bring back some food. How're you feeling?" She wrapped a slender arm around Claire.

"Bone tired. I guess I fell asleep before you came back upstairs last night."

"Across the bed in your clothes. I pulled your jeans off and tucked you in." She looked at the bundle in Claire's arms. "I'll wash them for you."

"No, no. It gives me something to do. You should go back to bed." Odessa had to be running on fumes. Claire kissed her cheek and hugged her.

As they descended, Claire peeked in the living room. Coffee mugs and napkins littered every surface. The vestiges of a sad little party. No one had lingered. Odessa tugged her elbow and pointed to the dining room.

An agent sat at the oak table, his shape outlined in the morning sun that streamed in the window. The blue and yellow flowered curtains that hung behind him looked strangely incongruous against his robotic movements. He was manning what she assumed was the phone tap. Her laptop was open, and the black landline that hardly ever rang sat alongside it. A checklist on the table had items crossed off. A manual of some kind with the FBI logo lay next to him. She wanted to believe they had made some progress overnight.

Another agent, seeing her enter the room, strode over with her cell phone. Claire tried to smile over the laundry in her arms. A tall woman, whom she had not met, blocked the doorway to the kitchen and the coffee. She was talking to a uniformed trooper. Claire's presence broke up their conversation.

The agent, all business, shoved her phone at her and said, "Good morning, Ms. McIntosh. You have multiple text and phone messages. I'd advise you to respond only to the closest family and friends and ignore the rest for the time being."

When had she given them her cell? She realized this was how they got the job done. She didn't respond and looked down at her phone blankly. She didn't feel like reaching out to the world.... She couldn't. What would she say? Perhaps it was her silence or the fact that she must be looking perplexed, because the Amazon blocking the coffeepot swooped over in two long steps.

"Ms. McIntosh, how do you do?" she asked, proffering a hand with long, cool fingers. "I'm Special Agent Angela Myers. I'm your communications liaison. I'll work with you to make decisions about how to disseminate information. Answering questions that come up from outside sources can be a full-time job in and of itself."

She looked up at the woman. Angela was six feet if she was an inch and had light brown hair pulled back in a severe knot. High cheekbones, a small nose and gentle eyes were emphasized by a web of laugh wrinkles that fanned either side of her face. It gave her the appearance of a grinning chimpanzee.

"Thank you, but I have someone who is handling contacts. Ms. VanAnden with Tosh has always taken care of communications and the press."

"And quite competently, I'm sure. However, this is a different situation. We need to work with Ms. VanAnden to trace all incoming calls, texts and emails." Then softly, "It has been eleven and a half hours."

"Yes, of course."

Eleven and a half. Not ten. Not twelve. Eleven and a half. Claire wondered what the average time was for the ransom demand. They knew, but she wasn't going to ask. They were waiting for it, the ransom call that would mean he was alive.

She and Odessa pushed past her to the laundry room. Claire pulled Sam's school uniform slacks from the washer and put them lovingly in the dryer. Quietly, she filled the washer and turned the chipped silver dial. Odessa took some old sneakers from the shelf and put them in the dryer to drown out their conversation. They could barely hear each other over the clanging and bumping. It seemed like an eon in another universe, but the night before she and Booker were here, the two of them, together. The noise, the heat....Claire couldn't make eye contact with Odessa.

"What did you find out?" she whispered.

Odessa clutched Claire's arm. "The security man, Mercy, said there was a ransom policy, maybe worth millions." No one was supposed to know except the folks from her dad's company. "Because," she whispered heatedly, "if people find out about millions in ransom, I guess you'd be a target for kidnapping. Talk about the tail wagging the dog."

She said the FBI suggested it could be a conspiracy. That a Hispanic gang was behind it. "They're ruining our country," Odessa said. She immediately saw the effect her words had on Claire and retreated. She hugged Claire and said, "If we could all be innocent children, we would stay precious in His sight." Claire smiled weakly. The walls were close, Odessa's face so near. She meant God's sight? Claire straightened her shoulders. Was God blind? What had she ever asked for? Where was her almighty God? Why didn't He take me? Punish me, not Sam. What justice is there in taking a little boy? Claire nodded automatically to Odessa as if in agreement. There was no use in challenging her. She was too old to change.

Odessa had talked to Booker "...without them hearing and he said the FBI was right as rain. They know what the guy looks like. Got a picture of him." Claire absorbed this information slowly. Her mind latched on to a splinter of hope. She thought about Rosa's son and the picture Agent Fowler had shown her at the detention center. It couldn't be. If they knew the man's identity, everyone would be on the lookout. It would be on the news feed, go out to the world. They only had to get a description of the car. Claire hugged Odessa, saying "thank you" over and over.

"He said for me to tell you that he was hoping something would break today. And that he loves you."

He loved her. Had he ever said it before? A strangled mew erupted in her throat and died there. She needed him, his gravelly whispers in her ear, his heavy arms wrapped around her. She felt her shoulders slump.

A ransom policy. Claire folded herself over the dryer and laid her head on her crossed arms, defeated. The tears had been wrung out of her. Odessa rubbed her back and talked away about the Good Lord watching over Sam and her. Her sincerity lay like a warm blanket while the dryer pounded beneath her.

Her father wasn't wrong to buy ransom and kidnap insurance. His action reflected how vulnerable the family had become as their bank accounts grew. He had fostered a belief that they were strong, when in reality they could only survive by feeding off of each other. And feeding off her father's money. Ransom love.

She clung to Odessa's last words. Booker loved her. He loved her despite the fact that she had no money. He loved her despite her dirty pedigree as a K Street lobbyist, despite her forgetfulness and despite the fact she was a lousy cook. He loved her. Just the way she was. Me, Claire.

"I know who they're talking about. He's the son of a client and half American. We just can't prove it. And he probably *is* a bad guy. But there's no way that he could've found out that Sam is worth a lot of money—not without inside information."

She stood ready to face the strangers in her house. She smoothed her shirttail over her hips. She could smell the coffee calling her. They walked into the kitchen and were met by a wiggling Compass and a furious discussion between Lowery and Brent Fowler. Claire patted Compass and took off his white plastic cone. Both men looked a little grizzled despite the fact that Fowler had on a freshly laundered button-down and Lowery had brushed his white cloud of hair back into place.

The State Police were responding to a tip. They had a description of a child's jacket that had been found at an abandoned trailer on the other side of the bay. They were combing the property for more evidence, but a picture of the jacket was on Lowery's phone. He held it for Claire to see.

"We're having it brought over here. This is the first strong lead we have. There was also evidence that someone used dark brown hair dye in the sink."

Relief. Blinding relief. Tears began to stream. He was alive. This meant her baby was alive. Wait. A worry surfaced that she had suppressed. A detail she ignored in an effort to have some control. She leaned against the cabinets. Someone was moving toward her: Lowery. He reached. She straightened. "Was there any evidence that he was hurt?"

"If you mean was there blood anywhere, no." Lowery didn't elaborate. She pressed. "Was there a struggle?"

"It's too early to tell. We'll run forensics on the jacket and other surfaces." He pulled out a kitchen chair. She flopped down. Sam's green backpack lay flat on the table. Lowery and Fowler needed to tell her everything. It was time for the whole story. Odessa guarded the kitchen door and gave her an encouraging nod as if to say, 'Come on girl, you can do this.'

"I understand that Mercer said there is a ransom policy."

Lowery responded. "It may give us insight into why Sam was kidnapped, but it doesn't tell us who has him or where he is. There's nothing like searching for hard evidence. That's what we have here at this trailer. We may find more."

Her hands sat lifeless on the table. Compass pushed up against her legs and laid his warm head on her lap. Unconsciously, she stroked him. "Well, you know a lot about this Under guy—that's the one you suspect, Rosa's son—but—if it is him, someone would've had to divulge to him that there's a ransom policy." Her voice sounded flat. She laid a hand on the backpack, pulled it closer and ran the zipper back and forth.

"What do you know about José Robles?"

"Sam said something last night when we were shopping about a Hispanic man in the trailer park. He sounded fearful, and I didn't read him correctly. I thought he was being bullied by an older kid."

Fowler interrupted. "Doesn't matter. You knew he was a person of interest to us. We didn't need to lead you in that direction because we were already there in the investigation."

Had they been looking for José Robles all this time? She thought about the day she had visited the prison on Route 113. Fowler wasn't forthcoming then. But she was a threat, an attorney, representing her client whom they had jailed on a flimsy excuse. Now she was a victim, a desperate mother, and he still withheld information from her. She couldn't trust him then and she couldn't trust him now.

Fowler continued. "So perhaps you could tell me if there is anyone in the family who might have caught wind of the policy and who stands to gain from it."

"I don't know. Did anyone from Tosh bring a copy?"

"No. I was hoping you knew more about it. It appears that after everything was signed and notarized on the policy, it disappeared. Did your father mention where he might have put it?"

"He didn't tell me he had the policy drawn up, for God's sake. Everything important was always kept in the safe at Tosh headquarters." She slapped her palms on the table and glanced from Lowery to Fowler and back again. "You mean to tell me Ross and Dean can't find it?"

Was this a smokescreen to see if they could draw more information from her? To see if she was guilty, if she had arranged her own son's kidnapping because she was so desperate for money? She took a deep breath and turned to look for Dean. He must be in the living room watching television. She could hear it droning away. Where was VanAnden? She felt like a stranger in her own home.

"Ms. McIntosh," Fowler put a hand over hers drawing her eyes to him. She could feel her bones, small and birdlike beneath his grip. She wanted Bookers's encircling arms, or Odessa's palm patting her back, or Dean's hold on her shoulders but not Fowler's touch. If he meant to comfort her, he only increased her anxiety.

"Your Tosh execs have not given us the documents. However, they say the ransom policy exists. If the policy was drawn up while you were

still married... well, we have contacted Mr. Peyton. He will be interviewed this afternoon in Maryland. He has a campaign obligation this
morning but has agreed to the meeting. Could he be wrapped up in
this?"

So they did suspect Vance. In the clear light of day, she no longer felt
sure of Vance's guilt. How could a father do such a thing?

She didn't answer right away and gave an imperceptible nod to Odessa
who let Compass outside. Odessa watched him through the kitchen window, but Claire knew she was listening to every word. She glanced at the
coffeepot, almost empty. She would have to make a new pot but couldn't
bring herself to get up.

She reached inside Sam's backpack and pulled out his fourth grade
reader. The book was emblazoned with the word "Impressions," and a
green dragonfly hovered over a purple lotus blossom. She wiped her hand
across the glossy cover as if she could feel Sam's hand through the pages.
He was such a good reader and writer. She was so proud of his spelling
grades on Friday tests. Did he get an A yesterday? She had sat here at the
kitchen table Thursday night, quizzing him aloud. Claire reached for his
spiral notebook and looked around her, lost in her own home. Lowery
and Fowler were staring at her, waiting for a response.

"What do you want me to say? If you're trying to accuse Vance or
me, it's obvious that I'm right here and Sam's not." She flipped open Sam's
notebook. "You'll have to do better. I just don't know anymore." There,
she finally got out her challenge. Both men remained impassive.

She heard a voice behind her. "And if Ham McIntosh was gone, and
both Claire and Sam, or either one of them separately, were kidnapped, then
Tosh Enterprises would benefit from the policy," said Ross. "I know that
when I discussed the terms with Claire's father, he would not allow a family member to benefit individually." Claire bent her head around Lowery
and saw Ross standing in the kitchen doorway. He rarely commented on
proceedings in groups. He looked as if he hadn't lain down all the night but
his suit was crisp, every graying hair was in place, and his gray eyes, framed
in dark lashes and brows, seemed like cool pools of water rimmed in deep
circles. Ross, who had been her father's financial right hand, always had the
preservation and growth of Tosh foremost in his mind.

"How is that, Mr. Ross?" asked Fowler.

Before he could answer, a muffled crash came from the living room.
With the same urgency as a dog whose tail was stepped on, Leslie
VanAnden cried, "Oh, my God. How could they do such a thing?"

Lowery nodded to Fowler as if saying, I'll handle this one, and sauntered down the narrow hallway. Claire could hear Dean's voice, low and astonished and his soft drone drew Ross away from them as well. She raised her eyebrows at Fowler as if to remind him that the world wasn't lying at his feet. Then, still clutching Sam's notebook, Claire followed Ross.

There on the screen was a breaking news story from the parking lot of an upscale Chevy Chase hotel. People were scattered, huddled in groups. The lights from emergency vehicles bounced off the television camera lens. The TV news showed every detail of the scene in cinematic truth as the image panned a large podium cluttered with overturned folding chairs, as if a small tornado had struck. Blood was spattered across the podium. A wave of nausea rose inside her, and she grabbed the back of the armchair for support.

"We are on the scene at Chevy Chase Commons in lower Montgomery County where a few minutes ago dignitaries were taking their places for a campaign event when shots rang out. We have confirmed reports of one dead and two others wounded. Vance Peyton, the Republican candidate for the Senate in Maryland, was pronounced dead at the scene. His assailant is still at large."

Her existence faded, her heartbeat slowed. Voices grew distant and there was ringing in her ears. The TV narrowed to pinpoints of light. Her bones could hardly hold her upright. She swayed briefly and slumped to the floor.

When she woke, she was lying on the couch and Odessa's concerned frown hovered. Someone was plying her with water and holding her head. Her hair fell into the glass and she tried to flip it away. The blinds were down, the shadow of slats cast against the wall like the light from a confessional window. Dean's face replaced Odessa's. His normally florid cheeks were gone, his face ashen.

"Claire, can you hear me?" he asked.

"I'm good. Sorry."

"I'm feeling a little out of my element too. But we have great support here, with the FBI and Lowery."

"I feel so guilty. I thought it was Vance," she confessed.

"Everyone was entertaining that thought after the business with the home equity loan. We didn't say anything to you. I guess this takes him out of the equation." Dean grabbed a chair and pulled it to the couch while Claire sat and sipped at the water. From the dining room, she could hear multiple conversations at once. A flurry of information was coming in.

Odessa picked up a few coffee mugs and ambled toward the kitchen. "You okay for a minute? I'm going to stir up some food. You need to eat."

Claire smiled wanly and Odessa left.

"I just saw Vance at a cocktail….," Dean said as he pulled off his glasses to polish them with a handkerchief. He kept talking but she drifted away. He mumbled and she caught, "…never get elected. Thought he'd make a sea change in Maryland. Should've carpetbagged Richmond where they'd appreciate his politics."

"He sent me flowers and a card when I was in the hospital. He wanted to come but Dad had put him on the No Visit list. There was a poem in the card, by A.E. Stallings."

Dean smirked knowingly. "He was regretting the divorce?"

"Maybe. It was her poem, 'Failure.' The last line is about unconditional love."

Dean smiled broadly and put his hands up behind his head, tipping his chair back. "You don't realize what you lost until it's gone."

"I don't know. He and Rebekah were making a go of it," she said. "Sam said Vance was scared for me, that I wouldn't be myself after the bombing."

"But then he wanted to use it against you. Well, it appears that you are doing just fine."

Odessa tottered into the living room carrying a platter of sandwiches. "I just don't know about you white folks sometimes. Nothing but peanut butter and jelly in that kitchen. And no white bread. Whoever heard of PB&J on artisan bread?" She grinned and threw a paper napkin on Claire's lap, sat next to her and passed out the sandwiches.

"I asked that Leslie woman to bring us in some milk. We need to talk."

All ears, she had been in the kitchen listening to conversations in the dining room including the phone calls. Fowler had gotten Chief Manger from Montgomery County on the phone. Vance's death had all the markings of an assassination. She grabbed Claire's hand and tapped it up and down on the cushion as she spoke. "They're saying you got to stay inside the house. No going out until this is over. But the Chief of Police said reporters were speculating up there in Washington. They think there's a ransom insurance policy."

"Why didn't we expect that: media speculation." Dean's chair dropped forward, hard. "Must be a slow day for the news. So everybody knows Claire's at risk."

"Well from what they were saying, she's been a target for a long time," said Odessa.

Claire followed Odessa around in a haze. It was long after noon when they took seats across from each other at the kitchen table, each eating a bagel. The wrinkles on Odessa's face seemed deeper somehow. She wished the old woman would lie down for a nap but there was no pushing her. Rock solid.

She knew Odessa preferred a good biscuit, but at present the toasted sesame slice with a slathering of butter and raspberry jam seemed to suffice. Shocking in its sweetness, Claire gobbled it greedily licking her fingertips.

Odessa poured orange juice from a pitcher. Claire wondered why the carton wasn't good enough but then smiled seeing the Mason jar filled with chrysanthemums. Odessa had set a family table, cheerful and ordinary, and put a casserole in the oven that smelled like turkey.

Booker's voice rose above the conversation in the dining room. Arriving a few minutes before, he stared straight across the room at Claire, his dark brown eyes searching. Holding her breath, she waited for him to say something, anything. She longed to talk to him, alone.

She wanted to know if he felt as guilty as she did for their encounter, twenty minutes of neglecting to watch Sam. His face was unreadable. When he nodded to her, he mouthed something that she didn't understand. Claire reasoned that he wouldn't willingly expose their relationship as more than friendship. But she found herself caving to fear. Did his distance mean he was withdrawing from her?

He had been chewed up and spit out by Lowery for crossing state lines—dismissed as irrelevant, meddling in their investigation. His cover was completely blown among these men and lastly, but not insignificantly, he was the only black man working as a detective. He wouldn't be able to work undercover on the Peninsula again.

Claire opened Sam's notebook and flipped through six spelling tests, one for every week in fourth grade. Six weeks was all the time it took to know Booker and fall in love. All Sam's grades, 100s.

She could hear Lowery giving Booker the rundown on the morning events. The jacket, the shooting. A shout from the agent manning the StingRay caused everyone to move like chess pieces. Lowery grabbed headphones. A heavily accented Hispanic female, distinctively high-pitched and nasal, stated that they had Sam and that he was in good health.

They had killed Vance and weren't afraid to kill again. The ransom was $20 million. She would call back with instructions. The line went dead.

Claire stood in the entrance to the dining room. She didn't want to distract them. It was hard to breathe but she promised herself she would not faint again.

The agent was able to triangulate off three pings from the K2 Tower three-tenths of a mile west of Stephen Decatur High School, the Miemms tower and the Ocean City fire tower. The location was general and the woman wasn't identified, but they knew she was near the Ocean City Inlet calling from a burner, a disposable cell phone. Heads shook in disappointment and Fowler said, "Stay on it. We're getting close." Claire exhaled.

The analyst said that after the second call, he hoped to track the identity of the kidnapper, if the gang had not switched to a different burner. Still, this one piece of information produced immediate action. The analyst called the Maryland State Police to increase the search area into old Ocean City, twelve miles from the farmhouse in Fenwick Island.

The kitchen smelled like stale coffee and dead air. The day was unseasonably warm and Odessa opened a window. Claire looked around for Compass. She wandered into the dining room and then the living room, calling for him quietly. At some point, all talk in the house stopped, and they understood that another calamity had occurred.

"I'll look for him," said Odessa as she headed to the back porch calling for the dog. "Compass, here Compass. You get here right now."

Claire heard her voice growing more distant. She sat on the living room couch, the spiral notebook digging at her side. She laid it on her sunken belly, staring up at the ceiling. Plaster cracks and a water stain in the corner—nothing was perfect. Maybe the ceiling would cave in on her right here as she lay on the couch and she would worry no more. Her life was slipping away from her.

She opened the spiral notebook and Sam's tidy printing jumped out. It was an immediate connection, as if he lay next to her, his head on her chest, both reading a bedtime story. She paged through the spelling, the reading vocabulary and found a section marked 'Journal.' She read the first entry, written after their arrival in Fenwick.

Sept. 4, '08. We are here at our new house. Mom is happy. I'm happy. Compass is waaay happy. We met a man named Booker. He has a boat and he took us crabbing. We didn't get many but I got to use his laptop. He has a video of a man's boat. He was stealing crab pots in the dark. Booker is going to catch him.

Sept. 9, '08. I like Trixie. She takes care of me after school. She has lots of kids. Four. They are called Fawster kids. That means they don't have moms or dads. John is the oldest. We ride our bikes around the park. I live next to a trailer park.

Sept. 11, '08. John and I took Compass on the sawgrass island at the end of his street. John pushed me and I got real muddy. Compass needed a bath. Mom and Trixie were mad. We didn't tell them but we saw plants growing in pots in the tall grass. Mom's still mad about my school uniform.

Sept. 16, '08. I went to visit my dad this weekend. We went out to dinner with Rebekah and Uncle Alistair. I miss everybody at home. I like the beach. I like riding my bike when I want. I like going out on the boat with Booker. I like his mom. She's a really good cook. I miss my Dad and my Uncle. I wish I could have both. But most of all I wish I had Granddaddy.

A tiny yip of astonishment escaped her lips. She looked around to see if anyone was watching her. Why on earth would Vance be seeing Uncle Alistair? They were never close.

Sept. 18, '08. John called me a scaredy cat. I'm not scared. There are some people in the trailer park who look different. One guy walks funny and his eyes are far apart. An old man has a chin that touches the tip of his nose. Like he doesn't have a mouth. Mom says not to make fun but that's what John does. He calls them reetards. John has a pocketknife. I'm going to get one. Some people sit on their porch all day long smoking. John says they are hippies. He says they smoke pot.

Sept. 23, '08. Booker is a detective. I asked him if he has a gun. He said it was not for me to see. He said kids don't need guns because adults keep us safe. He said I have a good mom. He told me not to worry and if I did to tell him. He would take care of it.

The living room wasn't private enough. She was afraid that someone would come in and see her face and ask her what was wrong. The invasion of her space, the people milling about—it was relentless. Just one moment of privacy in Sam's world was all she needed. It wasn't that she wanted to hide his words but…yes, that was exactly it. She wanted to hide the journal from their peering eyes. It was hers to read—not theirs.

She stumbled up the stairs to her room. She dragged a wooden chair over to the window and looked out on the bay. The water was flat, seamlessly unbroken and silver from the glistening sunlight. Another nor'easter was coming. The DNREC boats were gone but the yellow tape stretched around the yard. Two state police cars blocked her driveway. Beyond them was a cluster of media vans, satellite dishes mounted on top. The troopers were engaged in deep conversation with reporters. No one in, no one out. She turned back to the journal.

> Sept. 25, '08. I'm going to see my dad this weekend. He doesn't have much time to spend with me. Sometimes Rebekah yells at me. They said I could have a friend over from my old school. I hope so, because I get bored.

Oh, Sam, she thought. I knew you didn't want to go. She twirled a strand of hair and her knee jiggled up and down.

> Sept. 30, '08. I had fun with Dad. And Uncle Alistair. We went to Tred Avon on Saturday. No one else was there. I'm not going to tell Mom because she might be jealous. Sometimes she worries. We went out on Uncle Alistair's big boat. It's really fast. It has two inboard motors not like Booker's. I haven't been on it in a long time. They promised the next time we can take Granddaddy's sailboat. Me and Granddaddy and mom used to go sailing on *The Dash* in the summertime. I can't wait. And my birthday is coming.

"Claire." It was Booker's voice behind her. She turned, and there he was with his finger to his lips smiling at her, his bulk filling the doorway. She hadn't heard him come up the stairs. She dropped the notebook and rushed to him. His head bent and he smothered her with kisses. His warmth, his skin so smooth and chocolate against her whiteness. He mumbled but no words were distinguishable. Finally.

She reached up and put her hands on either side of his face, pulling him to her and drinking him in till her hands rested upon his chest. She pleaded softly, "Why, why? I should have kept my eye on him. We shouldn't have done what we did."

"Shhhh, Woman," he whispered back. "We're close. We'll find him. I gave them the description of the car. The farmer's old Oldsmobile station wagon that was stolen off his property is down at the Inlet."

"What? Sam's at the Inlet? We have to go. You can take me. I want to be there when they find him. He must be so scared."

"No, no. Look, they only found the car and they're running forensics. The Corvette Club competition is going on and the place is a zoo. They're searching every car, stopping everyone that remotely fits the description. Troopers and FBI are all over the place. Besides, Claire, you can't leave the property. The news media are sitting at the entrance to my driveway on Route 20 and on the connector to Point Park."

The Inlet. Corvettes. Brunch. She was supposed to meet Uncle Alistair for brunch on Sunday morning. He was coming up for the Corvette show. Was that today? He trailered that car, his baby, wherever he went. He would never deign to ride with the men he hired to tow it. He flew to competitions and used them as an excuse for an extended boating, golfing or whoring vacation.

"I have something you have to see. Come here." She pulled Booker toward the window, picking up Sam's notebook and opened it. She pushed him into the rickety chair and stood over his shoulder, leaning against him.

"Look what Sam was writing. He never told me he had a journal. The kids must get time to write in school but it's not graded. And he says he was with Uncle Alistair and Vance the last two times at Tred Avon, not in Washington. That house is closed up. No one lives there anymore." Her hands fluttered over the pages, trying to extract all the information. Booker pulled her down on his lap to keep her still. When her phone binged, she stood to read the text. It was Alistair. "No police. I'll pay him off @ T. Avon. Meet there. Hand him back to you. Call Mercer."

"Oh my God. Alistair has him. He's taking him to Tred Avon." Her thumbs hovered ready to text back.

Booker grabbed her phone in one swift movement. "Don't do that. Not yet."

Claire froze.

What was she doing wrong? This was her uncle. What could possibly be wrong with responding?

Booker studied the phone and said, "They'll get a ping off his text. Won't be much, but they might get a general location." He looked at her, calculating. "He's paying off the kidnapper? You believe that? How can he come up with 20 million in three hours on a Saturday? Or did he pay off José and the rest of the clique are still waiting for the 20 million? Too many questions."

She didn't care about the questions. She wanted to do something. She felt like she would explode if she spent one more minute cooped up. "Booker, we have to go. I won't tell them downstairs. I trust my Uncle. He may be a dilettante, but he loves Sam and me."

"Claire, don't be blind. Love ain't a reason to ignore the whole story." He stood by the window, his shadow cast long across the floor. Of course, he was right. He was always so measured, so careful. He was the only person she could trust totally.

"Here's the plan. I'm going back to the barracks and get another vehicle. I'll be back before nightfall. You go downstairs now, and when they ask about the text—because they will—tell them it was from your uncle who came into town for Sunday brunch with you. Tell them about his Corvette. That's the truth. He decided to leave because of this hullabaloo. They won't tell you the location of the ping, but they'll know the cell phone is registered to him. Feign a vague interest in where he is and come up with a reason he would be in that area. Visiting a girlfriend, whatever."

"We're going aren't we? To Tred Avon?"

"Yes, of course, after dark. Lowery and Fowler aren't going to let you out of the house. Make it as close to seven o'clock as you can. Say you need to crash early and go to bed. They'll all be in the kitchen or dining room. I'll get Ma to distract them, and you slip out the front door. Come up the path. It's close to a full moon so wear black and tuck in your hair. Stay at the edge of the woods, and I'll be waiting on the other side."

She nodded. Hung on every word. They were going to get Sam. What if there were more than José? Was he holding Sam and Uncle Alistair at gunpoint? What car were they in? She didn't care all of a sudden. The questions lost their urgency and she trusted Booker's plan.

"I need to be prepared. We may need to call for backup, depending on the situation. But the whole tri-state area is on alert and they'll respond. Goddamned congressional candidate is dead. I'm wondering why your Uncle is involved."

"Does it matter? He has Sam," said Claire. "How are we going to do this? When we get there, I mean, if they have guns and are holding Sam hostage?"

"Trust me, Claire. Trust me."

She did.

The wind whistled. All manner of things blew into the yard from the waiting media trucks and Point Park. Newspapers, plastic water bottles, and milk cartons all skittered about on her sandy driveway, eventually finding a home in the bushes. Someone's recycle bin must have turned over, she thought, looking out the kitchen window. Claire's eyes were glued to the weatherman on TV who predicted a cold front arriving from Canada overnight. Heavy winds and driving rain.

Odessa was gone, still looking for Compass, Claire assumed. VanAnden, Ross and Dean had gone back to their hotel for a nap, and now she felt so alone. Mercer had posted watch in the dining room. The digital clock on the television clicked at a turtle crawl till finally at five the Tosh team arrived with more food and large amounts of alcohol as if they were preparing for a Scottish wake. At six, she told the hangers-on in the kitchen that she was exhausted. Leslie asked if she wanted a wine to take up with her and she waited for her to pour a glass. They had brought several bottles of her favorite, Pere et Fils Chardonnay.

Dressed in black, she padded her ankle and taped Sam's mattress knife to it. Then, she tied her hair up and stared at herself in the mirror. Her face was bloodless, her heart a stone. She was past being hurt or a victim, being helpless or numb. Claire stood at the top of the steps, waiting. She wasn't certain exactly what she waited for, but she would know when it was time to escape. She shifted her weight from one foot to another on the landing waiting for a sign. Then she heard the kitchen door open and Odessa's voice.

"Look who I found moseying around the church kitchen. Come on. Get your furry butt in here, Compass."

Claire heard a chorus of clapping and congratulations and she pictured them moving into the kitchen to see Compass. She started down and paused at the foot of the stairs. Two strides and she would be gone. Would they hear the door creak?

"He's not looking any worse for wear but sure could use a bath. Must a rolled in something in the woods before he got over to the church. Stinkin' mess, that dog. Where's Claire?"

VanAnden said, "She went up to bed for a nap. Let's not wake her up. Poor thing hasn't gotten much sleep. She'll be so glad Compass is back. Has he eaten at the church already?" Her voice was light and everyone laughed.

"I expect he has, but I'll get him some more dinner to make sure and take him up to my house for a bath. Then I'm going to lay down for a while. Let me put some of these pots and pans away and tidy up around here." Odessa was the center of attention and began banging away in the kitchen. Claire ran for it.

Clouds obscured the moon. She trotted toward the stand of beech trees. The wind whistled through the leaves and they crackled, hiding the sound of her footsteps. The tree trunks stood close like an army at attention, shoulder-to-shoulder. The path narrowed, and she could barely detect the lighter shade of dark ahead.

Woodland sounds, the scurry of a rodent, the tweet of a bird, followed her up the hill. She broke into a jog and as she neared the clearing a smoking SUV headlight shimmered in the night.

She ran to the passenger side and yanked open the door to see Booker, smiling, dressed completely in black, a rifle poking up between the seats. The overhead light was off and his face was chiseled, illuminated by the under dash glow.

"You ready? Get in my chariot."

"Are you serious?" she asked. Booker had on a bulletproof vest and handed her one as she climbed in. She took it and held it in her lap as she buckled up.

"No, put it on now," he said.

She followed his direction, noticing grimly that a gun similar to Vance's Glock was mounted under the steering wheel. She returned his smile tentatively, ducking her head into the vest and tightening the straps under her arms. Encased, she fastened her seat belt.

"Let's go," she said.

"Have you shot a gun before?" He held out the glistening black metal in his caramel palm. Booker picked her hand up and tucked her fingers around the grip. It fit nicely.

She nodded. "Target practice. I can aim."

"Aim is good. Hitting is better. Tuck it into your waistband in the back. Keep your hands free. When we get there, watch for my signals. Step where I step and follow me closely. You good?"

"Yes."

Booker drove the country roads while Claire drew a map of the compound. She explained every entrance, security barrier and road access. "Booker," she said, "there is only one road into Oxford and one road out. Morris Street to the Oxford Road."

"It's okay. By that time we'll have back up.""

They arrived in town to howling winds and spitting rain that whipped the shadowy tendrils of a great willow tree across the beam of headlights as if to yank them from the safety of their seatbelts. A fox darted across the road, and Claire pressed her feet against the floorboards, sucking air as Booker hit the brakes. A bad omen.

He pulled the lumbering Suburban over before the service driveway into Tred Avon House. They leaned back in their seats, silent for a moment, staring ahead. The wipers continued their squeal and whine over the glass. He turned them off.

"Claire, listen to me." His words came from far away, but she was lost to him, already envisioning her boy in her arms. Booker grabbed her forearm and squeezed. She snapped to and looked at him.

"This is no time to third degree your uncle. Don't try to find out why this happened."

"Okay. Got it."

"We're just getting in and getting out with Sam."

"I know. Save it for later." She saw him: Sam's face, his blue eyes, a dusting of freckles. She heard his magpie chatter. Thoughts that had lacerated her for twenty-four hours swamped her mind again. She saw him crumpled on the ground, and when she turned him over, he was a rag doll, his eyes huge, looking at her with blame. She didn't want to ask Booker but had to, "What if he's hurt?"

He paused. "He won't be. He's worth too much."

"What if they drugged him?"

"We carry him out. We can sit here and speculate all night. Show me the map." He guided her hand onto his solid thigh and leaned in close. She listened as he intoned his instructions.

"Stay clear of my aim. Keep your head down. Stay in the shadows. Once we have Sam, grab him and run. Don't look back for me or anyone else. When you've got him in the truck, drive as fast as you can out of here."

"Wait. What about you?"

"I'll be right behind you. Ain't nobody gonna have a field day with me."

Her hand shook as she handed him a battered envelope on which she had drawn the layout of the property and surrounding roads. Booker took it from her, clicking on a small Maglite and running his eyes over the diagram quickly.

"Should we call Lowery?" she asked.

"He knows we're gone," said Booker. "Maryland State will be all over us shortly."

"It's the timing. We have to get Sam while Uncle Alistair has control of the situation."

"I know," he said.

She stared at the glow from the Robert Morris Inn in the distance. The town was so quiet. She heard crickets and a hoot owl some distance away. Claire put her fingers on the door latch.

"I'm going to case the grounds," said Booker. "Where does your uncle hang out?"

"Wherever there's a bar." She poked at the map. "In the kitchen, the conservatory, and in the cabin, here. If he drove in, he'll be in the kitchen. Let me come with you."

"Nope. You stay here. I'll come back before I go in." He pointed to the smaller square on the map. "What's this?"

"The garage. And that's the breezeway that connects it to the house. I know where everything is. It'll be faster."

"Is there security on the breezeway?"

"It's all secure. The cabin is closest to the dock and it's self-sufficient with a kitchen and bath. It has a well-stocked bar which is really appealing to Uncle Alistair."

"Let's hope he's not wasted. What else is there?"

"Dad's carving bench. Lots of carved wildfowl. And a root cellar below."

"What's in the conservatory?" he asked.

"Probably dead plants and gas heaters."

Booker backed the SUV partway up the service driveway watching his mirrors. He paused to look through the trees for cars at the front entrance.

Empty. Parking at the edge of the pea gravel path by the breezeway, he cut the engine.

"The path leads to the carriage house and beyond it to the log cabin," Claire whispered. "If we follow the path around, it'll open up to the backyard. A pier juts out into the river."

"Could they be on a boat?"

"Not Dad's sailboat. Uncle Alistair's boat might be at the pier."

"Does Alistair have keys to everything?"

"No keys, just codes.. The carriage house, the cabin, the breezeway, even doors here and at corporate. He thinks he's head of security for the company and can disable remotely. It's all on a system and he knows the codes."

"Do you?"

"I think I remember them."

"Cameras?"

"Sure, recording. But I bet no one is actively watching the house anymore."

"Don't bet. Not all of Tosh is sitting in your living room. At this point the whole fucking world knows about Sam. We got to stay a step ahead if we're gonna find him before they descend on us." He paused, reconsidering. "You can come with me but only if you stay back."

Booker nodded to her, grabbed his AR15, and they both climbed out of the vehicle. She could feel the cold metal of the handgun pressing against the small of her back.

Booker stepped nimbly up the path, the semi-automatic slung comfortably over his shoulder and Claire followed as his shadow. They hunched down as they trotted along the side of the breezeway, their feet barely crunching in the packed oyster shells. Booker raised the penlight to peer in the windows of the carriage house. He saw her father's Jaguar XK120 roadster, its cover pulled rakishly back to reveal the muscular curves of the bonnet and fenders as if someone was showing it off. He wondered if a theft was in progress.

High winds scudded clouds across the sky in the light from the moon. Flecks of rain splattered as Booker and Claire rounded the corner of the cabin. He stopped in front of her, pointing at Alistair's yacht sitting at the pier. Like a sharp-nosed predator, its hull was silhouetted black against the bluish night sky. The navigation lights had not been turned off. Someone was in a hurry. In the distance, the channel buoy in the river blinked red and green, signaling shallow waters. Booker raised two fingers and pointed again. She nodded to the pier that was littered with clothes and a cooler.

Two gentle rectangles of light shone on the grass from the log cabin. She hung back against Booker's arm, looking across the lawn where the main house stood with its yawning windows. So ghostly and empty, it appeared to be more a museum than her childhood home. The clouds separated briefly and the moon cast its light against the white walls. Stately and imperious. The shiny black foliage of her father's rose bushes outlined the deck, a few late season white blossoms caught the light. Spats of wind-driven rain hit her face and hair. The blossoms would be gone soon.

Booker handed her a cell phone. "Text him that you're here." Turning, he slid up to the ledge and peeked inside. He rolled his hand toward her as if directing traffic. Holding her breath, she approached, leaning against the log wall.

Inside, she watched Alistair at the pool table, practicing a bank shot with the cue ball when he jumped, excited, his cell phone in his hand. Searching the room for Sam, Claire thought it unchanged. The sight of her father's empty chair in front of his carving bench raised the hair on the nape of her neck. She could see his last project, a sleeping black-faced swan, her neck thrown over her back, her beak nestled under her wing in innocent repose.

Scanning the room, she recognized Robles from his FBI pictures. He was sitting on the couch opposite Alistair. She gasped as she realized the pile of clothes next to him was Sam who rose leadenly as if awakened from a deep sleep. A small chirp escaped her lips, and she slapped her hand across her mouth.

Booker's held her back against his chest, his hand atop hers. He spoke softly. "Wait. Sam looks fine."

She nodded, unwilling to take her eyes off of her son for fear he would evaporate. Alistair was talking to Robles. They seemed so casual. Her eyes raked the floor, the surface of the couches and tables. No guns, no machete. Wasn't Robles known for carrying a machete? Alistair's white hair was blown into a wild mess. Sam's burr head wobbled and his eyes hung huge and dark in his pallid face. He sat up a little off-balance and she saw he still wore his Death Star T-shirt. An involuntary shudder took her.

Something was amiss here. Robles' appearance fit the police pictures. His light brown hair rippled to his shoulders. The table lamp shone on his cheekbones and brows that protruded like crested buttes, his eyes, deep-set beetles sandwiched between. His ear appeared deformed. She could make out the teardrop at the corner of his eye. One kill. He should have been terrifying but his manner was soft. He sat with one hand supporting Sam, smiling at him gently, unmoved by Alistair's excitement. Where was the malevolent force of this supposed gang member? Agitated, Claire pulled against Booker's arm, wanting to scream, "Sam, run," when she stepped on something hard and twisted her ankle. She stooped to pick up a tent peg.

A two-foot commercial spike had worked its way out of the soft ground around the rose bushes. It was left over from the days of outdoor summer parties before her dad and Louisa had moved their social life to Washington. The recent rains had washed the heavy iron peg to the surface.

The phone pinged. They both looked down to read Alistair's response. "Come to the cabin."

Booker pulled her back into the shadows around the corner. Sideways rain pelted them as they stood under the roof's overhang. She heard a low roll of distant thunder across the bay.

"This doesn't look right," she whispered heatedly.

"Like they're dressed to go boating but telling the world it's a kidnapping." Booker's face hovered above her, his eyes riveted to hers. "Your trust in your uncle is misplaced. He's in on this."

She felt her shoulders give. He was right. She threw the tent peg into the yard.

"What do we do now?" she asked.

"I'm calling our detective. He can't be far behind us anyhow. Then we go in."

She waited as he finished the call. It seemed simple enough. She climbed the four brick steps to the cabin door that sat slightly open, waiting for them. She remembered Booker's words. This was no time to discover why. She pushed the door.

"Claire," Alistair looked at her expectantly, so welcoming.

"Mommy, you're here! I knew you'd come." Sam ran to her and crumpled in her arms. Claire knelt by her father's carving bench, suffocating her son with kisses, feeling Booker's solid presence behind her.

"You must be Alistair. I'm Booker Solomon." She glanced up, brushing her wet cheek against the stubble of Sam's hair, just as Booker stepped around them and moved forward, holding up the AR15 which he pointed directly at Robles. Or was it Alistair?

"Hey, no need for guns. You can just put that down now, my man," said Alistair.

"Yeah, sure. Both of you. Sit down over there," he said, waving the rifle toward the couch. She watched Robles move to sit opposite them.

His eyes were blue and as he turned his head she saw that the top of his left ear had been lobbed off.

"Claire, who is this man? He doesn't understand," said Alistair. "He needs to stay out of this, and it'll work out how we want."

Claire bolted up, anger pulsing in her chest and she pushed Sam behind her. "And how's that Uncle? How is it that we want this to work out? There's no "we" about this."

"All right, Red. Of course you're upset. Let me explain. Then we'll have a drink and go home in a few hours." Alistair's florid face hovered above hers as he waved an amber drink in the air. "Where there's muck there's money. We just have to wait for the Powers That Be to come through."

"The insurance company? You won't get any money. You know the policies are written so that no family member gets a payout."

"No, no. It won't look like a family member. No one will know it's me…or you." He stepped back and his smile grew with his self-satisfaction. "Now that you're here, I can cut you in, Claire. You need the money."

She snorted. "The world needs money. Everyone is in the same boat. What makes you special?"

"Coming from you, that's a joke, isn't it?" His eyebrows drew together. "You lost your house and your job. Ham isn't here to put you before me Princess. I just have some simple gambling debts. "

Claire charged in her uncle's direction and pushed him. "Gambling debts? You stole Sam over gambling debts?" Booker grabbed her arm, pulling her away. She strained against his grip, yelling at Alistair, "What are you thinking? You've lost it, you stupid, stupid old man. There's an Amber Alert." She jabbed her finger at Robles. "Even if this man is actually able to get the money, what makes you think you'll see any of it?"

"He's working for me," said Alistair.

"That guarantees his loyalty?"

"Yes, it does. He wants a green card. He wants to work in our country, my dear. I have connections, which is more than you can say at this point. You're a disgrace to the family."

Booker rolled his eyes. "Fuck this shit." He strode in front of Claire and Sam, the rifle pointed at Alistair who retreated to the couch. Robles inched away from Alistair.

Booker spoke. The force of his words broke through her anger. "Let's wrap this up. Claire, you and Sam need to get out of here. Go, now." He tossed the keys toward her. They fell at her feet as she heard the heavy wooden door squeak behind them. Rain swooped into the room.

"Mi amigos," came a desultory voice from the darkness. Claire and Booker turned to see a black haired stranger, his face tanned against a rain-splattered white dress shirt. He entered the cabin followed by three thuggish Hispanics. He was unarmed, carrying only a leather jacket over his arm. Booker pointed the rifle. The man was unmoved, casually glancing his way before he threw his coat over the back of the carving chair.

"It is warm in here, no?" One look, full of disdain, dismissed Booker immediately. "Mr. Solomon, you are one against many. I am so sorry." The men fanned out into the room, circling the couches, each carrying semiautomatic rifles with silencers.

"Kalishnakovs," muttered Booker.

"Yes, yes," the man said, tilting his head from side to side as if he were listening to music. "We should make introductions. My name is Carlos and these gentlemen here are Hector, Esteban, and Mauricio." The master of ceremonies, he pointed to each. Claire recognized the long fingered tattoo on Esteban's face. He was the man from the zoo encounter. She watched in revulsion as Carlos sat in her father's throne. He swiveled in the chair and gazed at the liquor cabinet with the crystal Waterford goblets and tumblers, sparkling in the light. His hand waved to the liquor. "Hector. What a lovely bar! Fix me a drink."

Hector nodded and shouldered his rifle. The other two remained focused on the gathering, their guns raised.

Claire shuffled backward toward Booker whipping her head about, trying to take it all in when she heard a loud click, click. Carlos was staring at Sam with a salacious smile, a switchblade flipping open and closed in his hand. As he wheeled the chair closer she could see a crossed blade tattoo visible above his collar. Repulsed, she wrapped her arms around Sam and walked him backward toward Booker. Carlos nodded to her. He turned to the assemblage.

"Under, I see you have been successful," he said as he glanced at Robles and then at Alistair. He grunted twice. "I hope the boat trip from Ocean City was not too stressful. Myself, I love to boat at night but not in the open ocean. I much prefer the bay. Safer."

The room was silent. Claire held on to Sam, feeling his heart beating like a bird's under his rib cage. It's steady thump, thump, thump wiped the sludgy tension from her thoughts. She waited and so did Booker.

"Ms. McIntosh," Carlos said turning his doleful eyes on her. "I am sorry for the loss of your ex-husband. But it was the right thing to do. You have sole possession of that lovely mansion in Chevy Chase, and the populace can breathe easy that another corrupt politician is out of the running."

"Mommy?" Sam's plaintive voice drew her to him. She felt his questioning eyes upon her.

"Oh, oh, sorry," said Carlos with exaggerated concern. He clicked the switchblade shut. "The young master didn't know, did he? I beg your pardon." He looked at Sam, his eyes filled with sorrow. "What a terrible way to find out your father is dead."

"Mo—m?"

"Shhh, Sam." She kissed her son, wiped his face, took a deep breath and held him close. "I can guess who you are. And what you want." This was the malevolent force. She needed to address him, reckon with him. This man had orchestrated every moment from behind the scenes since the beginning, maybe since the explosion at work.

"Once you have the kidnapping money, you will let us go?"

"Yes, yes. We do not indiscriminately murder people of your stature, my dear. Under, did you gas the yacht as I instructed?"

"El Cortador, both tanks are full." It was the first time Claire had heard Robles speak. His voice was high pitched almost like a girl. She looked at him closely. Surprisingly he had only a slight accent and his demeanor was submissive. They called him Under. And his boss, The Cutter?

"Good." Hector brought Carlos a drink that looked like a setting sun. Their boss tucked the switchblade in his pocket and leaned back in her father's chair, enjoying himself and his surroundings.

Claire glanced at Alistair whose face was ashen. Booker stood back, his head down, watching out of the corner of his eye. Claire had spotted this stance earlier in her living room with Lowery.

"Allow me to explain what will happen here. Mr. McIntosh, may I call you Alistair? So unusual. I'm sure it must be a family name, no?"

Alistair nodded silently.

"We are getting back on your yacht. You will give me the codes for the corporate office. I have associates waiting to gain access."

Leaning down, Carlos looked at his black trousers closely. He wet his index finger and thumb, pinching away an invisible smudge on the crease of his pants, making them wait for his next thought.

"I also have two men over in the main house who will, how do you say, raise hell." The last two words were uttered with emphasis and a direct stare at Claire. "Since I am sure the authorities are coming, it will provide a distraction." He passed his eyes over each of them. He spoke ponderously, with a look of mild annoyance as if they were children who had disobeyed their father. "Mr. McIntosh, Miss McIntosh, and the young master, will come with me. Mr. Solomon, you will stay here. Mauricio and Under, please take care of the detective and meet us later in Norfolk at the Naval Museum." He waved a manicured hand in the direction of his nearest servant. "Hector, the uniform."

Hector laid his rifle down and threw a backpack on the gaming table. He unzipped it and pulled out a wrinkled Navy utility uniform. A small bottle rolled across the felt. Claire recognized the label. Revlon foundation. "Under, please cover your marks and cut your hair before you leave. It would not do to have you recognized." A full smile played about his lips. His work was almost completed.

Claire looked at Booker who shook his head imperceptibly. What did he mean 'take care' of him? They wouldn't kill him. She inched closer to Booker thinking proximity would keep them safe. Hector deftly handed Booker's rifle to Under. Feeling cored out, she realized now she was the only one armed. She had the tactical knife at her ankle and a pistol at her back. A cold sweat gripped her and she pushed her hair behind her ear. Would they search her? Esteban waved her to the door. Her thoughts were crystal clear.

"Wait. Booker has to come with us. He can negotiate the deal."

Carlos was unmoved. "Mr. Solomon has many talents, but we don't need a hostage negotiator among our ranks. He will stay here."

Hector pushed her with his gun. Booker nodded, trying to reassure her and mouthed, Go. She moved slowly, never taking her hands off Sam who walked in the protection of her arm. She couldn't leave Booker. Desperately, she reached for him and Hector shoved her harder.

"Take me instead," said Booker. "I'm worth something. The State will bargain for me."

Carlos arched an eyebrow. "Aaah. How ludicrous. You are in love with the white woman." He laughed then, a trilling sound that set Claire's teeth on edge. "Under and Mauricio, need I warn you? He is trained. It must appear to be an accident."

Claire yelled, "You'll get life in prison." Carlos laughed again, louder. Hector pushed the rifle against her back. "Nooo…Booker, please." Grabbing her free arm Hector shoved her, then Sam, through the open door. Alistair followed.

Outside, rain drenched their faces and they hung close to the cabin walls. Claire turned for one last glimpse of Booker, but her view was blocked by Carlos, who held his leather jacket over his head.

On the opposite edge of the lawn, Claire heard a shout and two men burst through the French doors of Louisa's glass conservatory, racing over the deck. They shouted, "*Vamanos!*" She froze midstep, her gaze drawn by roiling flames that had erupted near the ceiling inside. The blackness of the night formed a backdrop to the orange mushrooms stoked by blue gas from the radiant heaters. The flames flared and lit the whole room. The palm trees crinkled in the heat, and the fireball expanded in size, filling the conservatory.

Everyone stood transfixed for an indelible instant until suddenly the reflective glass, in an optical illusion, seemed to pulse outward, and the thick panels exploded in one heavy *boom*. It echoed like a jet breaking the sound barrier, the metal stanchions nakedly reaching up into the night sky, the rib cage of some prehistoric dinosaur. Huge panes of glass splintered, caught the light, spun in the heavy winds and finally dove spearlike into the grass.

Sam shrieked in fear, and with a sense of dread, Claire felt him break free of her grasp. "Sam, no. Wait!"

He charged away toward the pier, but turned his face once toward his mother, searching. She ran to him and watched, horrified, as he tripped and fell. Claire reached, rolling him toward the roses as she threw herself protectively over him. Thorns raked their faces, but their bodies landed with a thud in soft earth.

Claire raised her head and watched as Hector ran toward his compadres seemingly in slow motion unable to avoid a spinning shard of glass. It pierced his foot and he howled in pain.

"Sam, run." She heard a slight whimper of doubt, and he raised up on one knee nodding as he saw the pistol in her hand. She rolled onto her back and took careful aim. Only ten feet from her, Hector leaned on one foot as he yanked the glass spear from the other, leaning on his rifle for balance.

Her hand shook and she steadied it, both arms extended. He must have smelled her fear for he raised his eyes to hers, contorted in rage. She pulled the trigger and hit him squarely in the face. A red circle appeared on his cheek, dark as pigeon's blood, and he dropped heavily near her feet.

Claire heard another shout and following it with the outstretched gun, she saw a dark figure moving quickly in her direction. Esteban readied the Kalishnikov, pointing at her but Claire shot again, this time without as much accuracy, sending a bullet into his thigh. He staggered and screamed as his trigger finger reacted, sending a spray of bullets through the air.

The tension in her arms drained and she dropped the pistol into the grass. Reflexively, she yelled again, "Sam, run!"

The boy scrambled to his feet and reached to grab something from the lawn. Claire saw Alistair, hunched in the dark, running toward the pier. The two men who had set the fire stopped in front of Carlos who yelled for one of them to go after Claire and Sam. The other shouldered a long slender gun with a bulbous tip.

Sam swayed by his mother. "Mom, get up." Their eyes met and he pulled at her. "Hurry."

Claire gasped for air as she felt about in the wet grass for the Beretta. The fire lit up the yard. She had lost her momentum. Carlos would close in and she prayed he wouldn't fire at them. She hadn't seen a gun, only his knife. They weren't worth anything dead.

From the door of the log cabin Booker charged at the other man standing with Carlos, pushing him down. Carlos side-stepped them, watching as they tumbled over each other. They landed their fists with sickening thuds. Desperate, she dragged herself up and sprinted toward Carlos, throwing her weight into his knees. They fell, her head and arms entangled in his legs. She scrabbled to her feet.

He rolled away, the switchblade open in his hand, and rested on one knee, ready to pounce. She raised her foot, kicking. He grabbed Claire's ankle, upending her into the soaked grass. Booker broke free and dove at Carlos, knocking him flat again. The thug recovered, and aiming his handgun to protect his boss, tried to separate Booker from the rest. He gave up and instead pummeled him across the head and back with his rifle. Booker staggered but didn't go down. He drove his fist into the man's gut sending him into the grass and beat his face.

Behind her, Sam appeared, his arms high in the air. He held the tent stake above his head, and Claire could see his face was filled with grit. "You killed my Dad," he raged and drove the stake at Carlos who turned, deflecting Sam's strike with his forearm. The stake flew in the air landing at Claire's feet. Grimly, she crawled toward Carlos and reached for the tactical knife at her ankle, plunging it into his shoulder. He grunted like a pig and said, "Aaahh, you will die now, my dear," but he paused, his fingers around the hilt and deftly pulled it out. He rolled on the grass in pain. Frozen, Sam stood above his mom, his eyes wild and watery in the burning light.

Just feet from the cabin stairs, Claire heard a single muffled gunshot from inside the cabin. She crawled on all fours as Sam tugged at her coat. Booker ran for the door, his arm outstretched, summoning them. He said nothing, a semiautomatic in his other hand, as he calculated everyone's position and fired at the men to hold them off.

He shouted, "Move," and she drew herself up, yanking Sam past Booker and through the door. Booker slammed it shut, throwing the deadbolt. He pushed them to the floor just as the front windows shattered in a hail of bullets that passed over their heads. Under answered the fire from inside, aiming Booker's AR15 back and forth out the windows. Mauricio's body lay slumped near the couch, a spreading flower of blood on his chest.

Claire panted, flattened on the rug and looked at Booker in disbelief. Under was with them!

"I'll hold them off. Get out of here," yelled Under as he fired again.

Booker crawled across the floor toward the cabin's kitchen door as slivers of wood and glass sprayed through the room. Boxes of carving supplies and stacks of balsa wood duck forms blocked the door. They all might be dead before he cleared the way.

Claire called to him, "Wait."

Hunched over, she ran to the carving bench and pushed the chair away. Reaching beneath the worn prayer rug, she caught the ring and heaved the trapdoor up with both hands, a soft groan escaping her lips. Cool air rose onto her hot face. Feeling for the edge of the opening, she flipped a switch, and a dim glow from a single bare bulb was cast onto the floor of the root cellar.

"Here, Booker, quick." She watched as Booker pushed boxes away from the back door, as if it were their escape path. She couldn't argue with him, but it seemed he was wasting time. She was losing energy. She pleaded, "This way!" Bending over, he crossed the room in six long strides, gathered up Sam and held the trap door open for her. "Get over here, now," he said.

"Take Sam down," she shouted over the din of gunfire. She glanced one last time at Under who aimed at nothing and everything outside. Inextricably drawn, she stumbled over to him.

Kneeling by the window frame, he nodded once in her direction, his face grim. "Thank you," Claire mouthed over the piercing holler of gunfire. Her ears sang and she could barely think what to do next but wanted him to know. Under looked at her, his face a mix of sorrow and determination. She crawled closer to hear him. He said, his eyes questioning, "Go to your son. I have sinned enough."

An earsplitting shrillness broke through the hail of bullets and as it grew louder, sailing above them, Claire and Under moved toward each other, perhaps looking for safety. Gazing up at the noise Claire gaped in disbelief. Under grabbed her and threw her to the floor behind the couch. He landed on top of her just as a rocket burst through the roof cascading debris and fire about the cabin. Rafters fell. Hearing a beam crack above their heads, Under rolled them away as it fell across the couch, barely suspended above them. Claire watched as the gaming cabinet teetered and crashed over the trap door. She screamed.

Carlos' men kicked in the cabin door and burst into the rapidly growing fire. They shouted at Under who leveled the gun at them, firing his last shots. He blasted one and turned the butt of the gun on the other's head before the man could take aim. Claire ran toward her father's chair when Carlos appeared at the door, searching the room, an eyebrow raised in anger or pain, she couldn't tell. "I'm right here," she yelled and grabbed the only weapon she could find: a burning timber. She swung it back and forth in front of her nemesis and seeing wariness in his eyes, her strength grew.

"You royal bitch," he said, "I should have killed you when we arrived."

Remembering, she said, "Someone else called me a bitch in a fire not long ago and he's dead. Now it's your turn."

"I do not need you. You were worthless to your father and you are nothing but shit stuck to my heel," answered Carlos.

Claire jabbed the flame at him. He stepped back. "*I'm* worthless?" she said. "You destroy lives. Not mine. We are ending this here and now."

Carlos taunted her with his blade. The other arm hung useless. Claire watched as Under moved toward his weak side.

"Under," shouted Carlos, "Take that from her. You will be my lieutenant. We will have our revenge." Then fear broke through his veneer. "You will die if you don't help me, Under. They will find you and slit your throat."

A man renewed, Under chortled and moved in closer. Carlos glanced his way and Claire took her chance. She swiped his face with the flaming board. Red embers blinded him and crumbled onto his shirt as his greased hair caught fire. A wrenching scream split the night air. He tried to smother the flames with his hands, slapping at his head. Under slammed him against the doorframe, and they fell into the night. Claire stumbled after them still holding the burning wood.

She heard sirens and through the fog spotlights lit the grass. Uniformed men raced toward her, shouting, their guns raised.

"Where is your son, Ms. McIntosh? Have you seen Detective Solomon?"

Four officers grabbed Carlos and Under, sliding plastic handcuffs on them behind their backs. "Take this one," an officer said dragging Carlos away. Looking at Under, another said, "You are José Robles? We have been looking for you." He jerked him from Claire and she heard someone begin, "Buddy, you got no rights under our laws."

She shouted, "Wait. He saved my life."

———

The Making of a Superhero

Intermittent gunfire spat overhead and Booker knew that Under was holding his own but Claire had not made it down the ladder. He held Sam as he heard the pop and searing scream in the distance that grew closer. He remembered the sound from Somalia: a rocket launcher. It exploded through the roof and the floor above him shook, dust sifting through the boards onto his head. He turned off the light so as not to draw attention and pitched the root cellar into darkness. He set Sam down, and the boy whimpered. Booker reached for him, rocking him back and forth, cupping his head against his chest.

The cool hard-packed earth chilled his legs from toes to thighs. The space was barely five feet high. Whitewashed stone walls lined with rudimentary shelves were hung heavy with cobwebs. He shot the Maglite pen at the opposite wall and saw a short paneled door behind the shelving two feet above the floor. The gunfire dissipated above.

"We're all right, Sam," whispered Booker and he flashed the narrow beam over his hand. He crooked a finger at Sam and shot the light over the half-door.

The boy's whisper sounded strangled in the darkness. "It's a tunnel. It leads to the grave house."

Booker cocked his head. He heard the crackling of fire and thought the dry old cabin would burn quickly. He prayed silently that Claire was safe. She was strong. He would find her and bring Sam to her. Suddenly, there was a huge crash overhead. Booker reached up, pushing at the trap door. It wouldn't budge an inch. He could feel the heat and knew his options were narrowing. He decided that first he and Sam would have to live. They could wait for rescue and be burned to death or try the tunnel.

He held the light between his teeth and ducked beneath the low ceiling to the other wall, leading Sam along by the hand. Gingerly, he tugged at the shelving, moving it a fraction. He pulled harder and it spun outward, creaking softly.

They had no way to exit above. Booker ran his hand over the edge of the half-door, finding a latch and it opened. Moldy air rushed in. Shining the light, he peered into its depths, wiping cobwebs away. Muffled voices grew louder and he heard the clump and scurry of footsteps overhead. He turned his head and in the small beam of light he could see a quarter of Sam's face, glazed with fear.

He lifted the boy into the tunnel. Then he launched himself through the opening and pulled the door shut. "We're in. You okay?" Sitting curled inside their haven, he turned the light on Sam. His eyes were a bit swollen and glittered expectantly.

CHAPTER 7

The Weight of Family

Booker expected the cabin would collapse into the cellar. He directed the white light into the tunnel's depths, ending in blackness. It was narrow, but a reasonable height. Maybe four feet from where they were, the tunnel appeared to be supported by wooden timbers and lined with new scrap wood. Someone had kept it up. He wondered how old it was. He shined the light on Sam's face. The boy laid his head on Booker's arm. He was quiet.

"Sam, why does it go to the gravesite?"

"For slaves to escape."

"What? About 150 years old, then. It's probably collapsed down the way," said Booker.

"I don't think so. Granddaddy wanted to make it a part of an Underground Railroad tour."

"No shit? If it worked for all those other dudes, it can work for us. How long is it?"

"I don't know. It ends at the grave house and from there, mom says they went up the Choptank River to Philly. How far is that?"

He didn't get it. "Not the Railroad. How long is the tunnel?"

"Oh, not far. We walked there from the house in ten minutes but the cabin is closer."

"Yeah? Well, we got to get moving." The boy looked at him questioning, his face ghostly in the light.

"I'm going first and we'll make a train. You come after me."

"Booker, I'm scared," Sam whispered.

"Me too. But we'll be fine the two of us together."

It would be slow going. His knees slid across the damp earth leaving a groove for his toes to track.

Booker counted each time he moved his palms against the dirt, crawling on all fours. After forty feet, he raised the pen light down the passage-way—a tangle of tree roots were ahead and more blackness. Thick wet air filled his nostrils, and he wondered if water had breached the tunnel.

"Sam, is the gravesite in the woods or out in the open by the river?"

"In the woods. It's not very far from the water. We went there last winter. Lots of trees."

"Pines?" Booker knew the oaks and poplars would be inland.

"Nope. Deciduous."

Smartass kid. "That's good. The pines are by the river." He tucked the light between his shoulder and jaw shining it down on Sam.

The boy asked, "Booker, is mom gonna be okay?"

He took a lesson from Trixie talking to Little John. It seemed like days since he'd had that conversation. "Sure. Your mom is a force all her own. We just got to get outta here." He thought the earth in this part of the tunnel would be hard-packed, not as sandy. So far the tunnel walls were solid. They had a chance.

But within minutes, Booker made contact with tree roots and couldn't make himself small enough to slide past them. He turned the light. He could push some up, but one large root grew out from the tunnel ceiling into the dirt floor.

"For God's sake," he said quietly. He couldn't even lie down on his side and squeeze through. Had they gotten this far to face defeat?

"What is it?" asked Sam trying to see around him.

"Tree roots."

"I have a knife, Booker. I took it from the galley on the boat." Damn, Booker thought, resourceful family.

The boy carefully unwrapped a dishtowel tucked into his shirt. In the narrow beam of the Maglite, Booker could make out a saw-toothed butcher knife. Inwardly, he held a glimmer of hope. He wanted to pass it on.

"We're gonna make it, Samuel. Not to worry."

"I'm Tosh, you're a detective. Let's put our minds to it." Sam rested his chin on Booker's knee.

Booker took the knife and turned on the tree root with a vengeance. He made short work of it and they crawled slowly, the dampness increasing. In another twenty feet Booker faced a rustic wooden barrier. This was the end. A solid wood door, apparently recently installed and painted white, it fit the opening from the other side of the tunnel braces. He exhaled slowly. The light was growing weak.

"Booker, point it over here."

He followed Sam's outstretched arm to the right. There, just past his foot was a connecting tunnel. The walls were unsupported, and it was barely big enough for a child.

"Sam, I can't get through."

"I know—I can."

Booker gave Sam the light, weak as it was. They couldn't go back the way they had come, and it would take hours they didn't have to kick or saw out the wooden barrier.

Sam bent on hands and knees and crawled on top of Booker, and as he slid to the tunnel floor, Booker hugged him close.

"Look Little Man, you got the keys to the kingdom."

"So do you," said Sam.

"Go quietly until you know it's safe." He felt Sam's small hand pat his chest, reassuring. "Here's the knife," Booker said. "Hold it flat on the ground so you don't cut yourself."

"I know. I practiced with one at night before I went to sleep."

"Once you see an opening and its safe holler to me so I know how far you've gone," said Booker.

"Yep." Sam pressed his hands against Booker's broad chest. "You gonna be okay?"

"Sure. Just gonna lie here and take a nap." Booker slapped Sam's butt lightly and watched as the dim light wavered, disappearing down the sandy tunnel. Worried, he yelled out to him, and instantly Sam yelled back.

All of a sudden Sam's voice rose louder. "Booker. There's a whole bunch of branches with thorns on them."

Booker's heart sank. The kid wouldn't be strong enough to cut through them. This was the end. He'd have to start kicking on the wooden barrier.

"Sam, come on back. We'll figure something else out,"

"Wait. I can see light. I can see some stars through the branches," yelled Sam.

Booker raised his head and leaned it back against the tunnel wall. Was there a chance? "Can you see anything else?"

With that, Sam bellowed, "Ahhh. Ahhh!" and fell silent.

"Sam, Sam, what is it?" Booker listened as his heart thumped in panic. He tried to crawl after him. There was nothing.

Edgy and tearful, Claire watched as the fire hoses drenched the flames rocking the cabin. The walls had caved in one by one and only the support beams stood. Behind her, the fire in the conservatory glowed as embers. Thank God someone had found the gas shutoff. A wet acrid smell filled the air and Claire coughed slightly as she said, "You've got to get them out of there."

"We can't go in until we determine if the floor is stable. Is there another way?" said the Oxford fire chief.

"The mausoleum. There's a tunnel from there back to the root cellar."

A young officer approached and uncertain, he mumbled, "Excuse me, sir. I-I'm sorry to interrupt but that gang guy is mouthing off about getting them out. He says there's an entrance in the woods over there." He pointed just beyond the rock wall that bordered the main house. "He says he's been in the mausoleum tunnel and it's blocked but he thinks if we had shovels, maybe a pickax, we could get in over there."

"Well, what are you waiting for, man? We've got shovels and a pickax on the trucks," replied the fire chief.

In ten minutes a fireman heaved the pickax over his head and landed it in around the grate tangled with vines. Claire and Under watched as shovels dove into the sandy dirt. For a moment she couldn't see and angled this way and that over their yellow slickers hoping the opening wouldn't cave in. She bent, peering through the forest of their legs as firemen shoved boards into the sides of the hole and sandwiched another across the top. Claire hung back thinking if Sam and Booker were nestled in the tunnel near the cabin it could be hours before they reached them. And then she heard a scream. A little boy's scream and she burst through their midst.

"Sam, Sam. Is that you? I'm here," she yelled. "Oh, Sam, we can get you out. Is Booker there? It's all going to be okay."

Two weeks had passed when Claire and Booker got a call from Detective Lowery saying that they could comb the wreckage of the cabin for personal belongings.

Sitting at the farmhouse breakfast table Sam looked at them expectantly. "I want to go," he said.

Claire and Booker's eyes met in a steady gaze. She nodded imperceptibly. Closure, she thought. Sam needed closure. So did they.

An hour and a half later they arrived to pick through the charred skeleton of the cabin for the first time. The yellow police tape had been removed in anticipation of a cleanup crew scheduled the following day. The morning was cool, the sun hadn't warmed the air yet but it was high in the fall sky. The trees had turned brown waiting for their winter sleep. Claire thought it was the kind of day that beckoned families outside.

Compass bounded about the yard barking at ducks and chasing scents. The fire chief had certified the floor was stable and Claire poked around looking for family mementos. Ham's beloved collection of hand carved wildfowl had burned. The framework of the bar and gaming cabinet lay like jigsaw pieces waiting to be fitted together across the blackened floor. The pine boards were intact, but the fire had burned through near the trapdoor, fueled by air from below. Yellow tape still cordoned off the entrance to the root cellar. Bright silver caught Sam's eye and he picked up the holy medal attached to melted blue and white gimp. He held it up and said, "This is Under's, Mom. We should give it to him." Then he paused and asked slowly, "What's going to happen to him?"

"He's in jail for now, Sam. He's giving the police information about those bad men."

"He was nice to me. Nicer than Uncle Alistair."

"I know. But we won't ever have to see Uncle Alistair again. He's gone for good."

Sam kicked a piece of charred wood that crumbled into little white pieces. Claire looked out over the Tred Avon River where mallard ducks winged in close formation across the blue water, squawking, heading for new territory. Her uncle's yacht bobbed gently in the tide, empty and shuttered. "Your Granddaddy said a long time ago that people are never who you think they are," said Claire.

Sam prodded the debris with his sneaker. He was thinner and didn't chatter nonsensically anymore. In the time since they were rescued, he had not returned to school and Claire and Booker had cut back on work. Our Lady of Perpetual Assistance was completely roughed out and Bandylegs told Booker to take a break. One morning there was a rap on the farmhouse door and Booker went to answer it. Special Agent Fowler entered, humble and pensive. He stood in the front hall and Booker did not invite him further. Claire nodded from the kitchen, a dish towel in her hands. Fowler explained that the FBI had an opening on the Peninsula for someone with extensive experience dealing with gangs and drugs. He asked Booker to apply. Booker chortled in that deep baritone and told him he would consider it. There were no promises made on either side.

Pembroke told Claire to study up on the football season so they could lay bets once she returned. She laughed weakly and told him she would need a handicap. Bruises still covered her arms and legs from the blood thinner and she was thankful for the cool weather sweaters and slacks that covered her physical memory of that night. When she undressed at night, Booker traced them with his long fingers and kissed her marks tenderly. Her concentration was poor again and she had trouble following the plot of Sam's Saturday cartoons. She took comfort that every morning their little family discussed their plans for the day at breakfast. At night they talked about their dreams as they tucked Sam into bed. In between, they hung close to each other boating, fishing and reading aloud from Harry Potter.

"Mom," said Sam as he puttered through the fallen gaming cabinet and reached down with a shout. He pulled a small lockbox from the wreckage. Picking his way over to his her, he turned it upside down, wonderment filling his wide eyes. The key was still taped to the bottom.

"What is it?" asked Booker.

"Just some of my dad's junk," said Claire. She brushed off the brick doorstep of the ruined cabin and sat. Booker plopped next to her, his legs outstretched.

"Mom, don't you remember?" asked Sam. "Granddaddy said it was for the safe, for you and me, if we needed something."

"Sam, your Grandfather hid his Navy medals and baseball cards. None of it was ever worth anything."

"Let's see," said Sam, his face drawn in an elfish grin.

Claire turned the key and opened the lid, finding two colonial clay pipes and a coin engraved with a kneeling slave, his bound hands raised in supplication.

"Let me see that," said Booker, and he flipped the coin over in his hand. "Well, if it isn't Rodney King still trying to get along with everybody."

Claire rolled with laughter and Sam shot Booker a quizzical frown.

"Nevermind. I'll explain it to you someday," said Booker.

"Mom, look." Sam pulled a folded piece of paper from the box. "It's the combination to the safe. Remember?"

Claire struggled to think, but her mind was blank.

Sam searched around the remnants of the gaming shelves, its blackened boards and cabinet doors, when he yelled again and dragged a fire safe from the pile. "I found it. Here it is!" He ran to Booker and set it in his lap.

Claire dusted the face of the combination lock and Sam handed her the paper.

"Read it to me," said Booker. Claire called out the numbers and he turned the dial this way and that. Inside was a sheath of documents. Claire pulled the heavy papers from their folder and opened them, revealing the kidnapping insurance policy. She laughed and passed it to Booker. "And here's the cause of all our problems," she said.

"Feel like burning it?" he asked.

"Yeah, but I've had enough fire to last a lifetime."

Next was a set of stock documents. Worthless, she thought. What was Dad thinking? The stock market was still in an inexorable slide, halving investments, leaving people destitute.

"This is silly. It's just stocks," she said.

Booker looked over her shoulder reading the print. "Woman, that's not just stocks. It's copper futures."

"Copper?" She paused not understanding. "It's not worthless like everything else?"

"Hell, no. Trust me. Thieves are stripping copper from abandoned homes to recycle. They strip HVAC units in commercial buildings and even farm irrigators. It's a real problem for investigators. No, what you have there is a miracle."

Claire laughed and kissed Booker. "Well, you can have it. We're fine just the way we are, aren't we Sam?"

"Yep. I don't want anything to change."

"We can have it together," said Booker. "How about we put a copper ring on it?" he asked twining her fingers into his. He kissed her again and Sam uttered an "Ewww," loudly as he tossed the coin in the air.

"So that's the Tred Avon," said Booker nodding to the river. Claire leaned into his warm body and they looked across to the choppy gray waters to the Chesapeake Bay. The sky was creamy blue, the air fresh and the future seemed wide open. A blue heron squawked as Compass came close. It stretched its wings, beat them and rose slowly in the air—an arrow across the water.

"What does it mean, Tred Avon?" he asked.

Claire looked at him, loving his curiosity. Loving everything about him. "The first colonists came up the Chesapeake looking for a safe haven. This was the third harbor they found, and the safest waters."

"I like fishing safe waters," he said.

A distant thwap, thwap, thwap stole their attention skyward and they watched as a black dot grew in size from the westward shore approaching

Tred Avon House. They watched curious, wondering where the helicopter was headed and sat immobilized as it slowed above them. As it grew near they could see a media station logo emblazoned behind the open side door. A long nosed camera was pointed sweeping the property and paused, directed at them, at their little family.

Discussion Guide

1. Claire is emotionally unattached to her colleagues at "Wilcox and Stein, Lobbyists" who appear to her as a "little United Nations" in pursuit of money and stature. Discuss the ways that their pursuit of money as the Holy Grail has stifled the lives of these young professionals and their bosses. What's different about Claire?

2. Tosh Enterprises had built an empire on the shoulders of others over the generations. Discuss how the control that Ham McIntosh wielded affects his wives and Claire.

3. Ham McIntosh slips a gun into his pocket to enjoy an ice cream a few steps from his office with Claire. Discuss the motivations and skill at gun ownership by Ham, Booker and Trixie.

4. Claire exhibits impulsiveness in her decision-making and has a brain injury that she tries to keep secret. How does this affect her?

5. Booker is compulsive about work. Why has he not settled down as his mother wants?

6. Prejudice and misconceptions about people and cultures abound in Claire and Booker's perspectives. Discuss how Booker carefully presents himself at work and to Claire. What mistakes does Claire make with him and the Hispanic workers?

7. "Cookey," the chef cookie jar that Claire discovers on the Gleason's kitchen table is emblematic of the disguises people wear in the story. Discuss Claire's interview with Pembroke, Odessa's first meeting with Claire, Trixie's daycare speech and Booker's interview of Little John and Trixie after the kidnapping.

8. Under searches for family and becomes embroiled in MS 13 in order to survive. Discuss how immigration laws, gang life and his own desperate needs trap this young man. He murders one of his own friends for the gang. In the end, does he earn redemption?

9. Discuss the barriers Rosa has faced since she crossed the border into the United States. Is she, and others like her, necessary to U. S. chicken production? What other industries in the United States are dependent on foreign workers?

10. The need for family is an eternal quest. Discuss what Claire wanted for Sam and how she gave up everything she knew to pursue a different life. Was she a fool? Does she earn the ending or is it a gift from beyond the grave?

11. What was Claire's relationship with religion and God? Ham's? Booker's? Odessa's? Under's? What is the significance of the funeral scene at the National Cathedral where Claire studies the statue of a young St. Peter?

12. Discuss the difference between opportunity and entitlement for Claire, Naomi, Sam, Booker and the residents of the coastal area. What sacrifices do they make to live the life they seek?

13. Sam has suffered multiple losses in his short life. How did he change and grow up? What do you predict for his future?

14. When did you know who was ultimately behind the kidnapping? Do you know of other famous cases where a person used their family members to keep them from self-destruction?

15. This novel is written in three parts, with chapters trilogies bookended by Under's story until the advent of Booker. Claire is saved in the beginning by three small "miracles." The family home is on the Tred Avon River, a name that is a colonial bastardization of the words "Third Haven." This is a reference to the third harbor that became the safest place to build their settlement in Oxford, Maryland on the Chesapeake Bay. Lastly, in Judaic and Christian traditions, the Tree of Life and redemption can be found in the third level of heaven. Discuss the paths of Third Haven's three mothers, how they intersect and create conflict for each. What goals do Claire, Odessa and Rosa share for their children and do they reach them?

16. Booker tells Sam that he has the keys to the kingdom. Does the "kingdom" present itself to Booker and does he want it? What do you see in the future for Claire and Booker?

Made in the USA
Middletown, DE
28 March 2017